DESTROYER
OF EARTH

A *JUST CAUSE UNIVERSE* NOVEL

IAN THOMAS HEALY

Local Hero Press Edition

Destroyer of Earth
Published by Local Hero Press, LLC
http://localheropress.com

1st Printing
Local Hero Press: trade paperback, February 2, 2021
Printed in the United States of America

ISBN-13: 9781971445205

Cover art by Nathaniel Dickson
Book design by Local Hero Press, LLC

Books by Local Hero Press

The *Just Cause Universe*

Just Cause
The Archmage
Day of the Destroyer
Deep Six
Jackrabbit
Champion
Castles
The Lion and the Five Deadly
Serpents
Tusks
The Neighborhood Watch
Jackrabbit: Big In Japan
Arena
Hero Academy
The Path
Cinco de Mayo
Search and Rescue
Rooftops
Plague
Soldiers of Fortune
Just Cause Universe Compendium
Destroyer of Earth
Flint and Steel
The Club
Jackrabbit: Rinse and Repeat
Posse
Extinction Event
Rain Must Fall

Pariah of Verigo

Pariah's Moon
Pariah's War

Three Flavors of Tacos

The Guitarist
Making the Cut
The Scene Stealers

Collections

Airship Lies
High Contrast
The Good Fight
The Good Fight 3: Sidekicks
The Good Fight 4: Homefront
The Good Fight 5: The Golden Age
Muddy Creek Tales
Caped

Other Novels

Assassin
Blood on the Ice
Funeral Games
Hope and Undead Elvis
Horde
The Murder Squad (2026)
Roast Wyvern (and Other Recipes)
Starf*cker
Strings
The Oilman's Daughter
Troubleshooters

Nonfiction

Action! Writing Better Action
Using Cinematic Techniques

Author Notes

That's how I began Chapter Eight of the first Just Cause novel. It's not the first time readers meet Harlan Washington, for he turns up in Chapter Two of the book. I hope I'm not spoiling anything by telling you he beats up on Mustang Sally and a team called the Lucky Seven with the help of his battlesuit. That quote at the beginning of Chapter Eight is really the first time I started to think about exploring Harlan Washington's backstory, and over the next twenty books, his own arc has been every bit as complex as Mustang Sally's. In many ways, the series is as much about him as it is about her, and about their complicated relationship.

From his humble origins in Day of the Destroyer to his devastating assault on Just Cause in 1985 that killed Sally's father to her facing him in the climax of *Just Cause*, Harlan Washington has been the greatest villain my superheroes have faced. That wasn't enough for me. The problem with supervillains is that they don't really work in real life, and it's important to me to add that feeling of reality to my (admittedly not-very-real) superhero stories. It's all well and good for a villain to claim he wants to rule the world, but does anyone *really* want to do that? You'd spend all your time doing paperwork. That's no fun.

Every villain is the hero of his own story, and the best villains believe this fervently. Over the years, I really dug into this philosophy and how it applied to Harlan. I gave him reasons for all of his actions—even those that were brutal and terrible. Somewhere along the way, I realized he'd become one of my favorite characters to write, and that required him to grow and change. Harlan's about a decade older than me, and as I grow closer to his age, I'm understanding him more and more. Maybe that means I'm a sociopath as well—but I sure hope not!

As all heroes eventually fall from grace, so do all villains eventually find redemption. Harlan's redemption came in *Arena*, but his story clearly wasn't done. What happens to someone who's lived a life full of anger and hate, when they no longer have that reason to be angry and hateful? That became the seed for the plot of *Destroyer of Earth*. I hope you enjoy reading it as much as I did writing it.

* * *

As always, I'm grateful to those individuals who helped bring this book to completion. Uncounted thanks are due to Ira, who is not only a terrific editor and beta reader, but has developed the kind of encyclopedic knowledge of the JCU that makes him a walking talking wiki. I'm grateful to long-time friend and fan Allison, who I can always trust to find the right nits to pick. Likewise, my friend AJ has been a wonderful sounding board. Few things are more entertaining than telling him "I wrote something really cool last night *and you have to wait to read it.*" Nathaniel brought out another outstanding cover and really captured the essence of the motley crew of aliens.

Finally, I thank you, the fans. Without you, I'd be shouting these stories into an uncaring void, instead of sitting around a cheerful fire recounting tales to my friends.

Ian Thomas Healy
January, 2021

CHAPTER ONE

Location Unknown

Harlan opened his eyes. He was adrift in space, twisting and turning slowly, barely able to move with his suit power levels down to bare minimums. The vastness of the cosmos stretched before him in all directions, with no nearby stars, planets, or moons anywhere he could see. He was alone in the silence, surrounded by the beauty of the Universe.

Well, if he had to die, there were worse places to do so. He configured a portion of his remaining power to keep him in suspended animation. It would last a specified amount of time, and then he would simply die, lost and alone. The rest of his power went toward a beacon. It would be dim compared to the brightness of the firmament, quiet compared to the background hiss of trillions of stars, but it would at least serve as a tombstone, a marker to show that in the end, he had mattered.

He shivered as the armor plunged his body temperature and his last thought before his eyes froze over was of Penny.

* * *

Harlan's consciousness swam through murky darkness and his first thought was that he should be dead. Perhaps he was, he thought wryly, for he had no prior experience with dying. But his skeptic's mind told him otherwise, and he gradually became aware of an environment providing warmth and breathable air. The

1

typical response for a person awakening in an unknown environment would have been to open one's eyes and sit up in surprise.

Harlan was hardly typical.

He took stock of what he could detect without sight. The air was warmer than he would have expected, and was dry as an American Southwestern desert. It carried a peculiar mélange of scents he didn't recognize and had neither the experience nor the vocabulary to describe. No light filtered through his eyelids. Gravity held him upon a hard, concave surface. He was not wearing his armor; only the simple bodysuit he wore beneath it. That much was to be expected, as his power level had reached critical levels. Critical levels weren't quite the same as total failure, though, and he mentally requested a status update from the cyberassistant node ensconced at the base of his skull.

No response.

No voice in his inner ear, no scrolling data in the corner of his vision. At that sobering bit of information, he did open his eyes and sit up.

A shadow with giant glittering eyes reared up in the near darkness. Harlan reacted in what was for him a predictable way. He raised a hand to fire an energy blast at the thing. Instead of his nanotech creating a nearly instantaneous weapon barrel and spitting forth a destructive particle beam, dust swirled around him. Even in the dim lighting, he saw more dust falling away from his arm. Thousands of dead nanites leached from his pores. He frowned. Even without power, his nanotech should have simply gone inert. Why was it leaving his body altogether? More dust shifted around him and sloughed away from his skin, making him look like he'd fallen into a vat of photocopier toner. He looked around the room. It was roughly cubical, with a high ceiling and tall doors—much taller than the creature in the room with him, which appeared to be roughly the size and shape of a four-foot-tall bear.

The creature chattered and squalled like a giant rodent, making clicking sounds he assumed were its teeth. Clearly, he'd been rescued, although nothing indicated that he was safe.

Without nanotech, his options were limited. He wasn't a great hand-to-hand fighter. He wasn't even a good one. He was . . . old. Other strategies were in order, and he cleared his throat.

His beastly companion stopped making noise instantly. Was it a dumb animal, or an intelligent being? It certainly wasn't a Hind. He'd spent enough time among the centaurian predators to recognize them. Perhaps one of the races they'd conquered, then? He recalled seeing information about it in their systems when he'd hacked them, but without his cyberassistant, he could neither access nor review that data.

"Hello," he said. "My name is Harlan Washington. Can you understand me?"

The creature made no immediate noise, nor any immediately threatening moves, but it did reach a thick, furred appendage out to touch a control panel. So, not a pet or guard animal, then. It chattered and clicked its teeth, and received a growling response from an unseen speaker. Whoever was in charge now knew Harlan was awake. The creature waiting in the room with him made no other sounds or movements, so Harlan took the opportunity to glean more information about his surroundings. He couldn't tell if he was in a cell or a medical bay or something else. The walls clearly contained both electronic and mechanical devices and there were cabinets or drawers with recognizable handles. The platform upon which he'd been placed was slightly concave, which meant he was resting in a sooty puddle of dead nanites. An arrhythmic, nearly subsonic thrum permeated the room, just enough to make Harlan feel like it would probably give him a headache. He wondered if it was an engine, and if so, why was it so irregular in its pulsations?

The door slid open and a dinosaur walked into the room.

Of course, it wasn't an actual dinosaur, but it had a narrow head atop a long neck, a long tail to balance itself out, and walked on two slender, muscular legs with clever four-digited hands at the end of its arms. It was clearly reptilian from what Harlan could see. It didn't appear to wear any clothing beyond a harness to which devices and tools were attached. Its scaly skin had an oily sheen even in the dim lighting. Its eyes were protected by a bony ridge extending to a point at the back of its head. It spoke with a hissing buzz and the bear-thing responded in its chittering tongue. They seemed to understand each other despite clearly speaking different languages. The Hind had translation technology. Perhaps these races did as well. That could make communication with them much simpler if their device could learn from Harlan.

The dinosaur—he wasn't going to think of it as anything else until he learned differently—stepped close to him and hissed some more. Harlan made himself sit still. His death had been all but guaranteed, but somehow they had found and rescued him. As much as he tended to dislike people, he recognized he was alive at their sufferance, and could stand to show a little gratitude.

"I don't understand you," he said. Try as he might, he couldn't remember any of the Hind language his cyberassistant had downloaded when he'd hacked into their systems.

The dinosaur stepped back quickly and lowered its head until it was at the same height as Harlan's. Its gaze met his and he stared back, unblinking. He imagined what he saw in its eyes was intelligence and curiosity. Perhaps he was anthropomorphizing, but surely he was as much a curiosity to it as it was to him. It spoke again, and he saw a lengthy, forked tongue vibrating between the sharp teeth of a carnivore.

Despite its hunched posture, Harlan could tell it was probably eight or nine feet tall when standing erect. It was slender, built for running instead of fighting, although the wicked claws on its toes gave indication to how it probably hunted.

With another garbled hiss, the dinosaur spoke to its companion. As Harlan's eyes adjusted to the dim lighting, he had a better sense of the smaller creature. With buck teeth, jowls, and a broad nose, he immediately thought of a guinea pig. How an animal clearly not an apex predator had evolved to sapience was unclear, but the evidence stood before him. In spite of his avowed dislike of people, he was curious about these beings. The aliens presented a new mystery, with new technology to learn and exploit.

And if there was one thing Harlan was good at, it was exploiting technology.

A clomping in the corridor beyond made him turn away from the rodent and dinosaur, wondering what new creature would arrive to investigate their human guest—or captive, he supposed, not wanting to leap to conclusions. The vehicle that entered the room was so far from anything he might have imagined that he could only stare in wonder.

It walked in on four jointed legs, operated by hydraulics so simple Harlan could have improved them in his sleep. The legs supported a transparent tank of material that wasn't quite plastic, wasn't quite glass. In Harlan's estimation, it was probably a natural secretion, perhaps created by the creature inside the water contained within the tank.

It was a squid. Or at least, it had ten tentacles and an arrow-shaped body. A hole at the top of the arrow flexed regularly, drawing in the fluid and expelling it. Two of the squid's tentacles wrapped around a pair of levers built into the base. Harlan almost laughed. A sapient squid? The Universe was turning into a stranger place than even he could imagine.

The walking squid bottle approached the table upon which Harlan sat. He remained still, deciding this was not a threatening act. He couldn't do much in his current state anyway. Instead he waited and observed, learning what he could about the aliens and his surroundings as the squid stopped adjacent to him. It slid open a port in the top of the tank and slowly but deliberately extended one tentacle toward Harlan, stopping short of physical contact. It held the tentacle where he could see it and waited, perhaps to see if he would touch it. Unlike earthly squid and octopi, the alien's tentacles didn't have suckers on its underside. Instead, it had a series of overlapping muscle bands with serrated tips of harder material like fingernails.

Aware that all eyes in the room were watching him, Harlan slowly raised one hand toward the tentacle, stopping before he touched it. He spread his fingers to see what the squid might do. It flattened its tentacle, spreading out the muscle bands until the end of the tentacle was broad and flat like a paddle. It twisted the tentacle so the serrated side faced up. It was showing him its palm and that it was empty.

"Okay, I guess we're doing this," he said, and touched his fingers against the tentacle.

The squid's skin was warm, suggesting either it was warm-blooded or retained heat from the tank. The texture reminded Harlan of the skin on the roof of his mouth. What he thought had been fingernail equivalents were instead toughened skin, like calluses. The squid gently curled its tentacle pad around Harlan's fingers, and in turn, he closed his thumb atop the tentacle in the most unlikely handshake in human history.

Greetings, sea-brother tool-user. This is safe water.

The strange voice echoed inside Harlan's head and he jerked back in surprise. It wasn't his first experience with telepathy, but coming from an alien was startling.

Understand this sea-brother tool-user?

The second telepathic contact came without physical touch. The damn squid was in his head! Harlan bristled at the intrusion of his privacy, followed almost immediately by realization and wonder. The squid—an alien being evolved on a completely different world from Harlan—had managed to speak to him and he had understood. It had called him *sea-brother tool-user*. The first certainly felt like a peaceful overture and the second an understanding that Harlan was an evolved creature, not a dumb animal. How should he respond? He was no telepath, and hadn't the slightest idea how to send a thought message. Well, the squid had made itself understood, so perhaps that understanding worked both ways. "Yes, I understand you," Harlan said aloud.

The dinosaur murmured something to the gopher and somehow, even though Harlan clearly heard breathy hisses and guttural moans, he understood it. "It speaks."

"Do you understand us as well?" The gopher gestured toward itself and the dinosaur. Both were staring intently at Harlan.

Somehow, the squid must have used its telepathy to give them all understanding of each others' languages. It was different than the Hind-based translation technology. This was a linguistic triumph. None of them had to speak in alien tongues to be understood. In the space of a few seconds, Harlan realized he had suddenly become quadrolingual. "I do," Harlan said, speaking slowly even though he suspected he wouldn't need to. "Who are you, and where am I?"

"I am Skarst, first officer of this vessel," the dinosaur said, and then indicated the rodent to its left. "This is Tchkit, a medical doctor." Finally, it swept one of its forearms toward the squid in the tank. "This Prodoni has a name that cannot be pronounced by those who breathe air. We call it Bubble. You are aboard our ship, the *Yamar*."

Harlan nodded, then considered the gesture might be unrecognizable to the others. The way he understood the dinosaur's language was stiff and formal. He wondered if that was the way the creature spoke or awkwardness in understanding the language. "My name is Harlan. I'm . . . grateful you rescued me. How did you find me?"

"It was not our intent. An unknown event pulled the *Yamar* from the skiplane and damaged our engine. The captain is attempting to repair it. Our sensors detected you adrift and you were brought aboard."

"You are fortunate," Doctor Tchkit chittered. For the first time, Harlan realized the doctor had a device mounted upon its nose that incongruously resembled a set of *pince-nez* glasses. Flickers of what Harlan presumed was data flickered across the lenses, which sat low enough on the creature's face to provide information without interfering with the field of view. Harlan had accomplished the same thing with his nanotech, except the information was displayed around the edges of his eyes. "Your life support was failing and your vacuum suit dissolved around you. If I were not experienced with the physiology of other races besides my own, you might not have survived."

"The event that interfered with your . . . skiplane. What was it?" Harlan had a great many other questions. He knew he would eventually get his answers, but as a guest—or perhaps prisoner—it would be best for him to try to be tactful. No point in annoying his rescuers until they decided they'd be better off if he was breathing vacuum.

"It was some sort of subspace energy surge," Skarst said. "It burned out several components of the skip drive. What do you know about it?"

Skarst wasn't one to be tactful or polite. Harlan appreciated the directness. He didn't like playing games either. "I may have caused it. My homeworld was under attack by . . ." He paused. Should he mention the Hind? Did these new species know of the centaurian aggressors who'd attacked New York? What if they were allies? That would make Harlan complicit in what could conceivably be a war crime. No, better he kept that off the table for the moment. ". . . an expeditionary force. I used antimatter technology to destroy the attackers and it seems the resultant energies catapulted me through subspace." He would have shrugged if the gesture would have meant anything to the other sapients in the chamber. "I don't know where I am. I don't know if I'm even in the same time. I could have been catapulted anywhere, at potentially any time." He spread his hands wide. "I . . . apologize for any harm I may have caused."

Apologizing for himself was something new, something he wouldn't have done as a younger man. He had always stood by his decisions, right or wrong. Perhaps getting older was making him weaker. Or perhaps his recent experiences with Mustang Sally and Penny Lane had made him soft.

"Is that possible?" Tchkit asked Skarst.

The dinosaur looked at the gopher. "I do not know. Krastins may know."

"You should ask him when his tail is no longer wrapped around the engines." Tchkit made an untranslatable sound that Harlan interpreted as laughter.

Skarst returned its attention to Harlan. "We will speak to Krastins later. In the meantime, do you require anything? Tchkit has investigated your physiology and determined our atmosphere is compatible with your biology. We do not know if our food will be edible, dangerous, or merely unpleasant to you. Do you consume liquid water?"

"I do, and I am thirsty," Harlan said. "I can digest a variety of raw or prepared nutrients." His stomach rumbled. "And I'm game to try whatever you have."

"Doctor Tchkit and Bubble will monitor you," Skarst said, then turned to the gopher. "Take the visitor to the galley. I will go speak to Krastins." Skarst disappeared through the door.

Tchkit waved to the door. "Come, Harlan. I will take you to get water and possible nourishment."

Harlan slipped off the table, testing the strength of his legs. The gravity seemed weaker than Earth's, though higher than that of the Moon. He wondered how these aliens created their artificial gravity. He had so many technical questions that he didn't know where to begin. A cloud of dead nanites swirled around him as he moved. He suspected he was leaving stains everywhere he moved, but it was still dark enough inside the *Yamar* that he couldn't tell. Perhaps the other species saw in different wavelengths than he did?

"I'm finding it difficult to see. I'm used to much brighter light. Do you have a portable light source I could borrow?"

Tchkit rummaged through a supply closet packed full of so much intriguing equipment it made Harlan's fingers itch. The gopher returned with a device resembling an Earthly flashlight so much it was disappointing. "This switch activates the beam, and this dial adjusts brightness along the spectrum."

Harlan played with the controls until he had a beam of yellow light clearly showing the floor. "This will work for me. Do your species see longer wavelengths?"

Tchkit blew air into its cheeks for a moment, distorting its face like a squirrel with a mouthful of nuts. Harlan decided that was a shrug. "My species is called the Jemmar. Singular Jemra. We are an underground species and see heat more easily than light. The Prodoni are oceanic and likewise see better in low light conditions."

"How about Skarst?"

"Skarst is an Aski Shantar. Her home planet orbits a small red star. The *Yamar* is lit to our comfort level."

"Skarst is female. I am male. Are you and Bubble from binary-sex species as well?" Harlan asked.

"I am male, and yes, Jemmar are primarily dimorphic. Prodoni are a tri-sex species. They do not have analogues to male or female, and their species require genetic material from all three sexes to reproduce."

Tchkit led Harlan through the corridors of the *Yamar*. He couldn't get much of a sense of the vessel's size. The interior corridor was tall and broad, either to accommodate larger species or cargo or equipment. "What type of vessel is the *Yamar*? Military? Exploratory?" Harlan knew he was peppering Tchkit with questions, but it was rare for him to find himself in an entirely unfamiliar situation, and the breadth of the unknown made him feel thirty years younger.

Tchkit didn't answer immediately. Was it an error in translation or was the furry alien coming up with a suitable lie? "The *Yamar* is a cargo ship," Tchkit said at last. "Here we are."

The galley was recognizable as such, with counter spaces and containers labeled in unreadable alien text. Tall cabinets built into the bulkhead might have been pantries, refrigerators, or freezers. Harlan spotted something he thought might have been a water dispenser and felt vindicated when Tchkit went to it and paused, staring back at Harlan. "How do you consume water and food?"

Harlan almost laughed. It was such a basic question that he wouldn't have thought to ask. He explained how humans ingested their nutrients, and that led into a frank discussion on elimination processes. Tchkit was a doctor, and curious about such things, and sooner or later Harlan would have to address that metabolic function and didn't want to inadvertently offend.

He was given water in a shallow bowl and drank it gratefully, not realizing how thirsty he was until given the opportunity to slake it. The water had a flat, reconstituted taste, like what was available in his secret Moonbase. It reminded him of home and made his surroundings less alien.

The food was more challenging. He was omnivorous and not picky; he often forgot to eat when immersed in a project and ate whatever was available and convenient. Food held little joy for him beyond fuel to keep his body going. When nanites had infused his body, they took power using miniaturized atomic reactions. They could absorb material from the surrounding environment and convert it into nutrient chains to feed Harlan's cells. Sometimes he didn't have to eat for days at a time.

Doctor Tchkit put a selection of foods on a table before Harlan, his glasses sparkling with data. The table had chairs, but they were designed for creatures with tails who were either much taller or much shorter than Harlan, so he stood.

"I don't think these will be poisonous to you based upon what of your physiology I've scanned," the Jemra motioned to the foods. "These are basic ingredients, unprepared. They may be . . . unappetizing, and for that I apologize. Perhaps if some of them are not too awful, you can help us determine what will improve them. Aski Shantar are carnivorous. Jemmar like myself are herbivores and insectivores. Prodoni subsist upon other forms of sea life."

Harlan selected a small cube that was unquestionably raw meat. "Humans can eat raw meat, but we often cook it and season it to improve the taste and kill dangerous bacteria."

"I assure you, this meat is free from bacteria." Although the psychic translation was largely emotionless, Harlan thought he detected a slight peevishness in the tone.

Harlan popped the piece into his mouth and rolled it around before chewing. It had a distinctive gamy flavor, verging on unpleasant, like lamb that was nearly spoiled. The texture was striated and juicy, like beef. He swallowed and grimaced at the aftertaste. "Yummy. I think it would be better cooked over open flame with the addition of salt and other spices."

Doctor Tchkit made notes on a tablet computer.

The first meat cube was the best of the trio the doctor offered. The second had such a strong flavor that

Harlan nearly spat it out. He was no chef and couldn't think of any way to improve upon it. The final piece was more like meat-flavored mush than anything else. The texture was so awful he gagged upon it. "That one is no good."

Tchkit chittered a giggle. "Skarst agrees with you, but Krastins is particular about it."

The Prodoni seafood was quite a bit better, one reminding Harlan of tuna and another of scallops, but the last he tried had such a metallic taste that he did have to spit it out. "I cannot eat that one at all."

Tchkit swept it into a hole in the center of the table. "No concern. This is all experimentation. I have to say, I'm enjoying the experience of meeting a brand new species."

"How many—no, let's continue this first. I am hungry and it's going to be important to know what I can eat since I don't know how long I will be here."

He found several edible items among the Jemmar food, from vegetables with flavors and textures that he felt he could tolerate, to a grainy cake-like item that was sour to the taste but felt substantial. The insects offered were so similar looking to grasshoppers he nearly balked, but their shells crumbled under his teeth and their gooey insides were almost sweet, making it seem like he was eating a cookie. He smiled. Bugs for dessert.

Skarst—or an Aski Shantar he assumed was Skarst —joined him in the galley. She had another Aski Shantar with her whose scales were smeared with a glowing greasy substance. The new Aski Shantar took a cloth from one of the cabinets and began wiping the substance away.

"Harlan, this is Krastins, captain of the *Yamar*."

"Captain—" Harlan began, but the new Aski Shantar interrupted him.

"I ought to space you right now, alien."

CHAPTER TWO

Harlan didn't respond to the provocation, but only because he knew he had nothing to protect himself. His armor was in ruins, a pile of dust in a storeroom. He was unarmed, undefended, fragile. He hated that feeling of being weak. It reminded him of the time Just Cause had peeled him out of his first battlesuit, all those years ago, and destroyed it out of pure spite. Oh, he'd gotten his revenge upon them later, but he'd sworn never again to let himself be that weak.

And now here he was, with nothing but his words when his entire life had been spoken through deeds of violence.

"Captain, I'm sorry for the damage to your ship. I had no idea it would happen."

"How could you not know?" Krastins hissed, leaning down to glare into Harlan's face. Seen up close, the Aski Shantar looked even stranger. His head was narrow, like a greyhound's, and his teeth weren't just pointed, but forked. Harlan guessed the lizard couldn't have bitten off his head—at least not literally—but could leave his face a ruin.

Still, he wasn't going to let the Aski Shantar's attack go without a response. "Because, Captain . . . shit happens."

A surprised burble came from Bubble's tank, followed by laughter from Doctor Tchkit as the psychic translation imparted itself into his mind.

Skarst sat on the deck with a sudden whump, her tongue flickering out of her mouth up and down like a ribbon in the breeze.

"Why . . . why would you say that? Of course it does. It is a natural . . ." Krastins stopped as Doctor Tchkit reached a furry paw out to pat his side.

"Shit happens," Tchkit repeated. "That . . ." He chittered again. "That is wonderful. Next time a job goes awry, and I have to heal your wounds, I will tell you shit happens."

Skarst's tongue flickered even faster.

Krastins snarled at Harlan and Harlan tensed, expecting an attack. He had no weapon to defend himself but the tray upon which Tchkit had set the various sample foods for him to try. He closed his fingers around the edge, not liking his odds against the tall lizard with the razor-sharp teeth lining his jaws. Then the Aski Shantar whirled on his heel and stalked away, tail lashing like an angry cat's.

"I think he likes you," Tchkit chittered.

Harlan snorted. The psionic translation was growing less stilted and formal. He assumed that meant his mind was beginning to understand not just the words but the underlying meanings and idioms. "I'd space me, too," he said. "Space travel is dangerous enough without unexpected visitors."

Skarst coiled her tail underneath her like a cushion and sat back upon it with her knees raised and her feet resting upon the floor. She cleaned her eyes with her tongue. "Krastins will get over it. I'll see to that. Once we get the skipdrive repaired and can make planetfall, I'll try to set you off in the right direction to find your home."

"You've probably never heard of my homeworld. We're not spacefarers."

"You seem well-versed in the notion," Dr Tchkit said. "And you were in a pressurized suit when we found you. Well, *barely* pressurized."

"I'm the exception to the rule." Harlan wondered if he was about to make a serious mistake, but it was the best chance he saw to find his way back to Earth. *Did* he want to return to Earth? His homeworld was an unpleasant place for him, full of unfortunate memories. When he'd relocated to the Moon, he'd done so without looking back. Something still dragged at him, tugging him back toward that small blue island in the deep black ocean. Something . . . or perhaps some *one*. Dammit, why was he obsessing over her, anyway?

"You've spent time in space, then?" Skarst asked. "You're an astronaut? Engineer?"

"Yes, on both accounts. And a warrior. I fought to defend the Earth from invaders. Destroying them is how I came to be here."

"You've mentioned these invaders twice," Doctor Tchkit said. "But you haven't described them nor have you given us any additional information." He paused. "Are they us? I mean, do they resemble any of our species? To my knowledge, none of our species have attacked other sapients, but that doesn't mean it couldn't have been a fringe group, or will happen sometime in the future. You did say you'd been transported through space and possibly through time as well. You don't know if you are in your past, your future, or your present."

"No, it wasn't any of you. It was a species who called themselves the Hind." Harlan watched the others to see if the name triggered any kind of reaction.

He wasn't disappointed.

Skarst looked sharply at Doctor Tchkit, whose cheeks puffed out, perhaps an expression of surprise. Bubble thrashed back and forth in its tank, suddenly agitated.

"I take it you know them."

"We do know the Hind," Skarst said. "We are at war with them."

The chill of a familiar enemy made its way down Harlan's back. "Tell me more."

"We don't know where they came from. They use a different technology for faster-than-light travel than we do. They just appear in a system and launch their attacks."

Harlan nodded. "That was how they attacked us. They sent five ships loaded with troops and threatened to destroy one of our largest cities."

Skarst's nose wrinkled in a snarl. "Five. That's less than even a standard attack squadron for them. And you defeated them?"

"I think so. I'm assuming the antimatter bombs were effective in either destroying or removing them from our star system as they did to me."

"Perhaps it is because they thought you a primitive species," Doctor Tchkit said. "They have tended towards overconfidence when dealing with low-tech species. We have been fortunate that we were sufficiently advanced to repel their initial assault."

Harlan shook his head. He was a genius, and even he could only barely begin to comprehend the logistics, the strategy, the sheer *expense* of waging an interstellar war. "Tell me what—"

Before he could finish his question, yellow lights began flashing in the corners of the room and a wail like a grinder peeling paint off steel filled the air.

Skarst leaped to her feet and raced from the room, her tail slapping against the hatch frame on her way through. Bubble clanked after her, the mobile tank moving with an unexpectedly rapid gait.

"What is it?" Harlan didn't doubt it was an emergency alert from the suddenness of its appearance and Skarst's reaction.

"Shit is happening," Dr Tchkit said. "You had better come with me, Harlan. I will be needed on the bridge and it will be the safest place aboard the *Yamar*."

Harlan followed the Jemra from the galley down a short corridor that ascended against the *Yamar*'s internal gravity. They passed through a heavy hatch in a bulkhead and wound up in a roughly rectangular room with a ceiling that would have been cramped for an Aski Shantar standing at full height but didn't come close to Harlan's head. It was wide enough for three duty stations side by side, each with their own odd-looking seat or harness and banks of controls within easy reach. Perhaps five meters from port to starboard bulkhead and equally as deep front to aft, a meter-high pane of clear material wrapping around the bridge above the control panels gave Harlan an unobstructed view of the stars beyond.

Skarst was seated in the center in the middle, her hands wrapped around recognizable control yokes. Bubble's tank was clamped against the aft bulkhead, its legs withdrawn and a thick cable plugged into a stained port that looked like it had been jury-rigged into place with sloppy welds and exposed wiring around it. Harlan nearly *tsk*ed at the unprofessional workmanship, but it was not the time or place.

Doctor Tchkit motioned Harlan toward a seat to Skarst's left. It was clearly built for Aski Shantar physiology, with a bifurcated back to allow for a tail and a ring-shaped seat that frankly reminded Harlan of a toilet. "Sit. I will do my best to strap you in securely, Harlan."

Harlan made himself as comfortable as possible as the Jemra fussed with adjusting restraints around him. The air of the bridge had a peculiar funk about it that hadn't been noticcable elsewhere in the ship. It might have been stress hormones or sweat, although Harlan couldn't see how either the Aski Shantar or Jemra was built for sweating. "How big is the *Yamar*?" Harlan asked. "How many more crew beyond those I've met?"

Tchkit finished tightening the straps around Harlan and flung himself into the seat opposite Skarst. "This is all of us. The *Yamar* is not a large vessel."

"And they shouldn't have found us," Skarst added as she wiped a panel of controls with her palm, activating numerous lights and indicators.

"Who are *they*?"

A voice crackled over hidden cabin speakers. "*Yamar*, this is the ASN *Iskafari*. Shut down your engines and prepare to be boarded."

"Molting bastards," Skarst hissed. "Krastins, I need skipdrive right away or we're a footnote."

"Stall them," Krastins called back over the cabin speakers. "I've only got one tail."

"Are they pirates?" Harlan asked.

"Worse," Skarst said. "It's the Navy."

It didn't take Harlan long to put two and two together from Skarst's angry outburst about the boarding threat. "You're smugglers."

"We are . . . independent traders," Doctor Tchkit began.

". . . Who smuggle," Skarst finished. "Krastins?"

"I'm working on it."

Harlan leaned back to look past Skarst at Doctor Tchkit. "How bad is it if they board us?"

Tchkit's fur rippled from the top of his head down his sides and back. A Jemmar shrug, perhaps, different than the air-puffed cheeks? "They probably won't space us. Probably. I hear they need conscripts for the war and laborers for the camps. How's your racial capacity for working until you drop?"

Harlan frowned. Suddenly he was feeling himself in far more familiar territory. After he'd escaped juvenile hall at fourteen, he'd spent several years in Philadelphia, working his way up the chain of gangs until he was running a narcotics distribution network with a large side of violence. He'd had more run-ins with the law than he could remember.

And he could remember quite a bit.

"Let me go help the Captain," Harlan urged. "I'm an engineer. I understand technology."

"No," Skarst said. "We don't know enough about you." She pulled an auxiliary console down from overhead and began operating controls on it with one hand while keeping her other busy upon the primary controls. She seemed to be dividing her attention equally between both. Her level of focus and concentration impressed Harlan. Her work seemed equivalent to typing different information one-handed on two different keyboards at the same time. Harlan couldn't have done it and said as much to Doctor Tchkit.

"It's a peculiarity of Aski Shantar evolution," the doctor said. "They have two brains, one at each end of the spinal column. It allows them to concentrate fully on two tasks independently." He paused, perhaps wistful. "I wish I could do that."

"*Yamar*, this is the ASN *Iskafari*. We will not repeat ourselves a third time. Shut down your engines and prepare to be boarded or we will open fire." The distorted voice blared through the ship's speakers, making Skarst hiss in frustration.

"Krastins, it's now or never," she said, her eyes fixed upon her controls.

"I know," retorted the ship's captain from the engine room.

"If they board us, we'll be eating space before supper," Doctor Tchkit added.

"I *know!*" Krastins shouted.

A previously darkened panel flickered to life, limned first in yellow light, then red.

Skarst crowed in wordless triumph, snapped a round switch ninety degrees to the left, and the world turned inside out—or at least, Harlan's stomach felt like that's what happened.

The skipdrive seemed to live up to its name. Harlan felt like he was riding a flat stone flung across water, except the ship bounced in and out of an alternate dimension. Outside the *Yamar*, the cosmos flickered like a poorly-synchronized film, stars appearing to double and flex back and forth. To distract himself from the discomfort, he theorized how it might work differently than the hyperspace that the Hind seemed to use.

Krastins burst onto the bridge from engineering, his scales marred by grease and burns. He moved to where Harlan was sitting and stopped, clearly not expecting the human to be occupying what was probably his seat. Harlan reached for his straps. "I'll move."

"No, Harlan," Doctor Tchkit said. "We don't have anywhere else to put you."

Krastins yanked a mechanical fold-down seat from the bulkhead and threw himself into it, tail between his legs in the gap. The tip twitched like an angry cat's. As he tightened his straps with one hand, he pulled a display panel on an armature toward him and angled it so he could see what was happening. Harlan craned his head over to see if he could learn anything.

"Are they in pursuit?" the captain asked.

"Of course," Skarst grumbled. "We're keeping apace for now, but it won't be long until they catch up to us. That cruiser has long legs."

"And sharp fangs," added Krastins. "We need to lose them before they get our range."

"Working on it," Skarst said.

"What the hell kind of contraband are you carrying?" Harlan asked Doctor Tchkit. "Weapons? Narcotics? Something else?"

"Something else," the doctor said. "It's an Osi Fain egg."

"What's that, some kind of rare delicacy?"

"Living starship," Skarst said as she lashed fingers across the controls. "Captain, I've got a system with a skiplane terminus at extreme sensor range."

Krastins worked his own controls. "I see it. No data from the beacon. Is it a dead node?"

Skarst slapped her tail against the deck. "It can't be a dead node or we wouldn't read the terminus at all. I'm trying to get any kind of navigational fix but it's completely dead out there."

"Can't be completely dead," Krastins retorted. "The Navy found us."

"Did they?" Harlan asked suddenly. "Or could they have fallen victim to the same energy surge that brought me here and damaged the *Yamar*?"

"That could be," Krastins said. "But the only way they would have wound up near us would be if they were already in the same skiplane."

"If they were, maybe they were already tracking you," Harlan said.

Skarst stamped a foot on the deck, her claws making a clicking sound against the metal. "Damn it. We were set up. Somebody talked."

"It doesn't have to be that," Doctor Tchkit began.

"No, but it's the most likely outcome, thanks to one of those stillborn bastards on Sto Shantu. We were probably heading into an ambush," Krastins said. "Maybe your appearance was more lucky for us than we knew."

"Maybe the way I interfered with your skiplane interfered with theirs too. Are you . . . already wanted for something else?" Harlan asked.

"Oh, we're dangerous criminals, we are," Doctor Tchkit said. "With a storied past to share among the roots—"

"Stow it, Doctor," Krastins said. "Skarst?"

Skarst's display screen changed from yellow to red. "Systems have rebooted. We can jump, but I wouldn't push it past that system out there."

Krastins drew patterns on two different screens, swaying his head back and forth as he considered information from each. "Do it. If we burn out the drive, at least we have a head start. Maybe there's somewhere in that system we can hunker down for repairs."

Harlan leaned back to speak to Doctor Tchkit so he wouldn't distract the Aski Shantar, even though he was learning they were quite capable of focusing on two things at once. "Doc, what's the difference between a skip and a jump? Distance?"

The Jemra blew air into his cheeks. "I'm a doctor, not an engineer."

Harlan nearly laughed. "Well, that's one thing they got right," he murmured. "A layman's knowledge, then."

Doctor Tchkit held up a hand and counted off on his digits in a very human gesture. "There are three aspects of superluminal drive. Skipdrive involves brief transitions into a different dimension, which is the pulsating sensation you feel. It allows us to travel within star systems at speeds approaching lightspeed but never exceeding it." He closed down a finger. "Skiplanes are natural interdimensional connections between stars. When a ship triggers its skipdrive within the skiplane nexus, it is catapulted along the skiplane to emerge at the far end."

"Like a wormhole," Harlan suggested.

Doctor Tchkit blew out his cheeks. "I don't recognize the term as you have used it. Maybe it's specific to your species and has no translation into Jemmar. Worms are pests."

"So a jump is . . . something else?" Harlan asked.

"A jump is when you overcharge your skipdrive in an attempt to cover a significant distance without using a skiplane to do so," Skarst said without looking back. "It's dangerous and causes extensive—and expensive— damage to propulsion systems. It's an emergency act." She raised a control panel back to the ceiling and glanced at Krastins. "And it's ready."

Something Harlan identified as a new alarm began a rhythmic hooting that made him feel like his ears were being driven deep into his skull. *Yamar* shuddered and a section of controls went dark.

"*Iskafari* is firing on us!" Krastins shouted over the din. "Do it now!"

Skarst lashed out a thumb and stabbed it so hard against a shielded control that she shattered the cover and cracked the button.

The Universe turned upside down and inside out at the same time. Harlan felt like he was being drawn through a hole far too small for him. Pain wracked his body from head to toe. His organs flip-flopped within his abdomen and his brain spun around in his skull. He retched, helpless, and struggled to retain control of his body.

At least he wasn't the only one suffering. Skarst and Krastins both thrashed about, clawing at their heads and tails, while Doctor Tchkit made untranslatable sounds. In its tank, Bubble's skin rippled and shuffled through a kaleidoscope of colors.

All the lights on the bridge flickered and went out, leaving the bridge bathed in white light reflecting from a ringed gas giant off to the port side. It traversed across the windows as the *Yamar* drifted, powerless.

CHAPTER
THREE

Krastins was already out of his temporary seat and racing back down toward the engine room before Harlan's head stopped spinning.

"Doctor, go after him," Skarst ordered. "I'm reading elevated radiation levels and an increasing static charge in the engine room. The drive is leaking."

"I'll dose him," the Doctor said, and scurried after the Aski Shantar.

"What can I do to help?" Harlan asked. He wasn't an altruist by nature, but even a selfish bastard could understand the implications of a starship with a failing engine.

"Bubble, Harlan needs orthography. Can you help him out with that?" Skarst popped open a wall panel and slid a rack of components out, examining each.

The Prodoni slid open the top of its tank and extended a tentacle toward Harlan. Harlan didn't hesitate and reached out to clasp the end of it. Orthography meant written language, and if he could read, he could learn without having to wait for Doctor Tchkit's admittedly poor explanations.

Greetings, sea-brother tool-user, came the telepathic contact. Information flowed into Harlan's brain. Symbols and written language data dumped into Harlan's language centers like someone had turned on a fire hose. His head grew hot like he had a fever. Like he was burning out a hard drive. His stomach lurched and his tongue stuck to the roof of his mouth, paralyzed. The Prodoni broke contact and Harlan fell back against his seat, eyes watering, struggling to draw breath.

Skarst slid the panel back into the wall and spun around to pull a different one free, using the tip of her tail to dog shut the one she'd closed. "Do you see the display to the left of my station, to your right?"

Harlan drew a shaking, ragged breath. "Y-yes." He was suffering the mental equivalent of trying to run across an icy lake surface. "I . . ." He realized he could understand what he saw. He was looking at the Aski Shantar written language, which read right to left and utilized a complex script of pictogram characters representing entire words instead of phonetic sounds. "I can read it."

"Good. Do you know how to operate a display?"

"Is it operated by touch?"

"Yes."

"I can figure it out. What do you need me to do?"

Skarst slammed the panel back into the wall a little harder than necessary. "None of these are bad. I've got one more to check but it's the junction in the corridor. Listen for me and report on what I ask."

Harlan nodded, then said "Yes," realizing translation didn't extend to physiological responses.

Skarst left the bridge, leaving Harlan alone but for the Prodoni, who offered no judgment or communication of its own. Unsupervised, in a room full of advanced technology . . . he might as well have been a sugar addict turned lose in a candy factory.

Harlan explored the *Yamar*'s systems through the display Skarst had indicated. It was organized in a way he considered both intuitive and intelligent, and found navigating the file system so easy he soon became thoroughly absorbed in the layout. He called up the ship's navigation systems and was dismayed to learn they were offline. He began rerouting paths, enjoying the old-school methods of making physical changes to a system instead of doing so with the aid of his nanotechnology. His parahuman ability to control electrical and mechanical systems helped, but in the end, it was more about his intuition and dawning comprehension of the *Yamar*'s technology.

Primary power on the bridge flickered to life momentarily then went dark again. Harlan glanced up, irritated with the interruption.

"Anything?" Skarst called from down the corridor.

"Only for a moment," Harlan said. "I believe I have determined where we are."

"What, already?"

"A system called Tokras." Harlan paused. "It is listed as *proscribed* but I haven't been able to figure out why yet."

Skarst appeared in the bridge hatch. "That's because it's unstable." She leaned over to pull additional information onto the display Harlan hadn't discovered yet. "Tokras is prone to high-level, irregular flares. Dangerous radiation levels for unprotected life forms. Vessels with less than military-grade shielding will suffer system failures. There's no good reason to be in this system."

"So we find the skiplane and leave."

"Easier said than done. This system doesn't have a beacon for the skiplane node. It wouldn't do any good. The first flare that hit it would shred the circuits, even with shielding. Nodes are too close to stars."

"How did explorers first find skiplane nodes then? Surely beacons are a more recent development."

"That is a long story for another time," Skarst said. Harlan figured when they had some downtime, he might dig into whatever passed for Wikipedia and do some research.

Krastins returned to the bridge, more smudges marring his scales. Doctor Tchkit was right behind him, fur matted with sweat or some other kind of fluid. "We're going to have to set down somewhere," the Captain said without preamble. "The drive is shot. Next time we try to skip, I wouldn't give us odds not to explode. We can maybe limp along with half a tail for another day but then we're adrift for good. Are there any facilities in this system at all?"

"Unlikely," Skarst said. "Too much risk with the flare star."

"Doesn't change the fact that we need raw materials to fabricate repair parts. Find a safe port."

Harlan looked up from the display he'd been examining. "Here," he said, and used what knowledge he'd learned to send the data from the smaller display to the main screen. "This moon is tidally locked to its parent planet. It's close enough to the parent that the gas giant's magnetic field will help protect it from flares, and if we land on the side facing away from the star, the mass of the moon will protect us from radiation and particles."

Skarst thumped her tail on the deck. "That is brilliant."

Nictating membranes sliced across Krastins' eyes in what Harlan interpreted as a gesture of surprise. "Who *are* you?"

"I told you, I'm an engineer."

* * *

Harlan was elbows-deep into the open panels in the bulkheads. The *Yamar* used some sort of solid-state electronic chips instead of wires and circuits. The chips sat in racks like server farms. Although the technology was unfamiliar, he was learning his way around it quickly thanks to his parahuman power of technopathy, or what most people colloquially termed *super-engineering*. He was working on rerouting what little power the ship's propulsion systems could spare into the sensor platform while Skarst struggled to reconfigure the ship's detectors to recognize the raw, unenhanced quantum state of a skiplane node. Krastins, having been thoroughly dosed against radiation by the doctor, returned to the engine room to try to coax a little more power out of the damaged skipdrive. If he'd had the right to do so, Harlan would have made a joke about reversing the polarity, but even at the best of times, he'd been terrible at telling jokes, and he doubted his humor would transcend species barriers anyway.

Doctor Tchkit had gone to check on their cargo. Harlan wished he could have gone too. He was curious about a native spacefaring species. How did they travel? Could they exceed light speed? Did they have natural weapons? He was less curious about them from a biological standpoint than he was intrigued by the idea of manipulating his own body in such a way as to obtain the same abilities. He imagined what it would be like to fly among the stars, unfettered by natural law.

The ship's intercom crackled with interference from the damaged drive. Krastins said, "You'll get maybe twelve minutes of thrust before the drive fails completely. If *Yamar* isn't on the ground by then, it'll be a crash."

"It may be a crash anyway," Skarst snarled. "I've only got fifteen percent navigational control." Harlan tweaked a circuit board. "Make that twenty-eight percent. I like this alien, Krastins. Can we keep him?"

"Another mouth to feed," Doctor Tchkit said, returning to the cabin. "The egg is still intact, probably a good forty or forty-eight days from hatching."

"If we can't get the *Yamar* raised, we may end up waiting until the baby is big enough and fly it out of here ourselves," Skarst said. "How long does that take?"

Doctor Tchkit chittered a laugh. "Longer than we would have supplies to stay alive. I suggest you get us down in one piece." He strapped into his seat.

An unpleasant idea came to Harlan, one that had been rolling around in the back of his mind since he first learned of the *Yamar*'s cargo. "Hey, this living starship egg. Is it sapient?"

"Yes," Doctor Tchkit said.

"Possibly," Skarst countered. "There's not a scientific consensus as far as I know. They're smart, but they're smart the way pets or beasts of burden are. They're a protected species, which is why they have to be smuggled, but they're also rich peoples' toys, which is why there's a market."

"Because if you all are trafficking in slaves, I've got a real problem with that. Bad history on my own world."

Doctor Tchkit blew out his cheeks. "It's not a great job, and we wouldn't have taken it if the Captain wasn't in dire straits. He owes a lot of credits for losing a prior cargo."

"Which wasn't lost," Skarst said. "I maintain it was stolen. Probably by the same people who hired us for it in the first place."

"No honor among thieves," Harlan muttered. "But this Osi critter . . . What's going to happen to it?"

"Right now, it's going down with the rest of us," the Jemra said.

"I mean ultimately."

"Like I told you, it's a rich person's toy. It will be penned up where some rich snow eater can show it off to other rich snow eaters and they can all ooh and aah about it until they get bored and set it free." Skarst grumbled.

"Or kill it for fun," Doctor Tchkit added. "Rich people are a peculiar substrate of society."

"On my world, too," Harlan said.

Skarst canted her narrow head toward the intercom pickup. "Captain, Harlan got some sensors back online. Tokras Prime is giving off some ugly levels of radiation. We could be only minutes away from a flare. We've got to land now."

"Do it," Krastins said.

Skarst rotated the *Yamar* on its vertical axis, pointed it toward a brilliant gas giant in the near distance, and opened the engines to full.

* * *

Harlan had landed his personal shuttlecraft upon Earth's airless moon, and upon the Earth itself. Landing on the moon of the unnamed gas giant in the Tokras system was unlike either.

Although Skarst was occupied keeping the *Yamar* on a relatively safe descent, she still took the time to interpret the data to Harlan as he manually recalibrated the sensors when the automatic systems failed. "The graph on the left shows saturation of dangerous radiation and particles. Dangerous to most spacefaring species, anyway. Prodoni are resistant to particles but more vulnerable to energy. What is your species called, Harlan?"

"Human," he said in an absent-minded way as he tried to use his newfound written language expertise to understand the shorthand information presented on the display. "We are vulnerable to radiation in all forms. Our homeworld has a strong natural magnetic field that protects us from it, so we never evolved defenses."

The numbers on the graph blurred and a moment later, the *Yamar*'s systems failed as a powerful energy blast washed across it at the speed of light. "Snow!" Skarst spat the word with all the venom of an epithet and banged a fist off the console. "Caught a glancing blow. The moon took the brunt of it. We're not completely iced, but it's getting colder by the second."

Harlan was already out of his seat and slid a panel free from the bulkhead. "These components are done. This is navigation and sensors, isn't it?"

"Yes," Skarst said. "I've got less than twelve percent directional control remaining."

Harlan slid the ruined components back into the wall. He felt blind without the constant flow of information from his nanotech. "Switch life support power into thrusters. We're already in the moon's gravitational pull. It's not a question of landing, it's a question of how hard we hit."

"Captain, get back up here. We're going to need to seal off all sections to save air," Skarst called into the intercom.

The doctor clenched his fingers around the edges of his seat arms. "What about the cargo?"

"We keep it for now. Vacuum won't harm an Osi Fain. They evolved in it."

Tchkit's eye fell on Bubble the same time Harlan saw it. The Prodoni's tank illumination had failed and the creature within drifted listlessly, tentacles dangling, while its skin was darkening to a mottled brown visible even in the dim bridge.

31

"Bubble!" The doctor pulled a device from a pouch.

Harlan thought about assisting the doctor, who had been nothing but polite and helpful since he'd first awakened, but knew he would only be in the way. He knew nothing about Prodoni physiology beyond the tidbits he'd been told earlier. They were sensitive to radiation energy, and the flare that had taken out the *Yamar*'s systems might have been lethal to the telepathic squid.

"Do you have a vacuum suit that will fit me?" Harlan asked. "I'm not going to be able to recreate mine."

"Third panel to your left has emergency envelopes," Skarst said as she fought the controls. "There's not a spare in this ship that will match your physiological configuration." She glanced back at Doctor Tchkit and Bubble. "Doctor?"

"Unresponsive. There's nothing I can do." Doctor Tchkit stomped a foot on the deck. "Maybe if I had a full medical suite and enough raw Prodoni protoplasm."

"Get into your suit. We're going to come down hard." Skarst pulled a package from beneath her seat and, using her feet and tail, began opening it.

Krastins stepped onto the bridge and closed the hatch behind him. "How long until we're down?"

"Four and a half minutes," Skarst replied, making Harlan wonder how Aski Shantar calculated time and how his psychic translation converted it to durations he understood.

"Hey," he said, as a new thought occurred to him. "When Bubble dies, will we lose our ability to understand each other?"

"Not as far as I understand the process," Doctor Tchkit said. "It's a—"

"Later, Doctor," Krastins said. "Get into your suit." He reached past Skarst to handle the controls while she pulled her own suit over her head and sealed it.

A minute later, Harlan had shoved himself into a plasticine artificial womb that felt entirely too flimsy to protect him from explosive decompression and a spaceship crash landing. If he was the sort to utter timely, pithy comments, he would have made some sort of dark-humored joke about it, but after five decades of humorless existence, he saw no reason to act any differently than normal.

Krastins used auxiliary straps to bind Harlan's emergency envelope to the bulkhead, then strapped himself to his seat. "Bottle up the remaining atmosphere, then blow all hatches and locks," the Captain ordered.

Harlan's envelope inflated as the pressure on the bridge dropped to zero. The noises of the bridge vanished, only carrying through his feet in contact with the deck. Would the *Yamar* break apart upon impact with the nameless moon? Or would it retain enough power to suffuse itself with whatever energies kept its gravity functioning and kept its crew from being compressed into jelly with acceleration?

A light flared into existence on the display Harlan had been monitoring. He pointed at it, not knowing what it indicated except that it was important. "What's that?"

Krastins reached for the controls. The Aski Shantar's voice came over a speaker in the envelope. "A ping. Somebody's registered us."

"That's good, right?" Doctor Tchkit said.

"If we survive the landing, we may not be stranded." Krastins' hands raced over the display, which kept flickering as if it was suffering interrupted power. Harlan itched to get to work on fixing it. He could see how to do it in his mind as clear as day.

"What if it's the Navy?" Skarst asked. "Should we jettison the cargo?"

"No," Krastins said. "They already know we have it from their previous sensor records. If we jettison it, we're compounding the crime."

"You said this is a proscribed system," Harlan said. "Anyone who is here probably shouldn't be here."

His statement took a moment to sink in before Krastins lunged for the console.

"What are you doing?" Skarst shouted. "They could be pirates, or slavers, or worse!"

Her warning was to no effect, for Krastins transmitted the distress call. "We'll deal with the snowmelt as it flows. Get us down in one piece."

"Power's down to six percent and falling. Below three and the inertial dampeners will fail," Skarst said.

"How strong are the inertial dampeners? Do they protect from massive acceleration completely?" Harlan asked as ideas flowed into him.

"Essentially, yes. Why?" Krastins asked.

"Or massive *deceleration*," Harlan said. "Kill the drive completely and shunt all power into the inertial dampeners."

"Will that work?" Skarst asked. "The theory is sound. What if the dampener is the first thing destroyed in the crash?"

"Then we'll all be dead anyway," Krastins retorted. "Do it. This ship will never fly again, but we may walk away from it."

Skarst adjusted some controls and the thrum of the thrusters stopped transmitting through Harlan's feet.

He watched as the altitude gauge showed the rate of their descent, and it was far faster than he would have liked. The moon had no atmosphere to slow the *Yamar's* plummet, and thus gave Harlan a clear view of its surface. The sensors were no longer functioning, so he couldn't even tell whether the material of the generally smooth surface was fluid, ice, or rock. He hoped he was right about the inertial dampening system. He'd only been aboard the ship for a few hours and the surviving crew had placed their faith in his theory. He felt like he *should* be correct. The system was technological, and technology spoke to him in a language that transcended even its alien origins.

Collision alarms shrieked into the vacuum, inaudible except for what was carried through their feet on the deck. Skarst shut them off to conserve even the little bit of energy required to light the lights. The altimeter gauge dropped from three digits to two, then to one far too quickly.

Jagged peaks of dark stone rose around them, cutting like teeth into the brilliant face of the gas giant's clouds. Harlan held his breath, even though he knew it wouldn't help in the least.

The *Yamar* struck the surface of the moon and simply *stopped*.

CHAPTER FOUR

Harlan understood the physics of inertia, but it was still terribly unsettling to know that the *Yamar* had come to a complete halt instead of pancaking itself into dust with the impact.

The collision wasn't bloodless. The inertial dampening field protected the bridge first and foremost, followed by the power systems and the inertial dampener itself. Much of the rest of the ship suffered varying levels of structural damage depending upon distance from the generator. The most distant parts did indeed shatter into shreds of metal and plastic. The only indication of damage on the bridge was the cracks threading through the windows. Harlan couldn't move as the field suffused him. Nobody spoke as the field lessened, returning weight to them all.

The ship shuddered as inertia returned suddenly to several sections, smashing them belatedly. Harlan wondered if the same thing would happen to the bridge occupants, but instead their mass increase was safe and gradual.

"Everybody still alive?" Skarst asked, her voice coming across the speaker in Harlan's emergency envelope.

"Affirmative," Krastins said.

"Yes," Doctor Tchkit added. "Except for poor Bubble."

"I'm sorry they didn't make it," Harlan said, and was surprised to realize he really was sorry. Bubble had given him the greatest gift in the universe—the gift of language. "They say any landing you can walk away from is successful."

Doctor Tchkit chittered in laughter. "Your species has wonderful metaphors."

Harlan snorted. "You haven't heard anything yet. Wait until I get really angry."

"We'll probably find out what that's like soon enough," Skarst said. "I'm not looking forward to carrying you around like a hatchling, and I'm sure you're going to absolutely hate it."

Harlan looked down at his feet, first thinking there was nothing wrong with them before realizing he wouldn't be able to walk while inside the envelope. "I really need a suit of my own."

"We'll pick one up at the market," Tchkit said. "Along with some sweet cakes and herbivorous nutrient."

"Bread and milk," Harlan muttered.

"What?" Skarst asked.

"Something Humans say they have to get when they go to the store," Harlan said. "It's just a phrase."

Krastins strapped a harness around his throat, waist, and base of his tail. It held a recognizable pack and several unrecognizable implements, although Harlan was certain one was a sidearm. "Doctor, what about the egg? We can't bring it with us. It's too large and easily identifiable. Could it hatch while we're gone?"

Doctor Tchkit snorted through his helmet. "Even if the egg isn't damaged, Osi Fain can't hatch in a gravity well. It will need sunlight and available asteroids for its mineral nutrient requirements. They're silicon-based life forms. It'll go dormant."

"Then we can come back for it later," Krastins said. "But I won't leave without checking it first."

"Optimist," Skarst grumbled.

"I heard that."

"You were meant to."

Harlan wondered if they were a mated pair, or if that was even a thing among the Aski Shantar. They certainly argued like it.

Skarst ran a strap through integral loops on the emergency envelope and swung Harlan up onto her back like so much luggage. Her tail curled up to add support. He wondered how strong their tails were, but the unnamed moon had even lower gravity than Earth's moon, so he suspected fatigue wouldn't come into play.

The three aliens made their way through increasingly damaged portions of the ship until they reached a cargo bay. The bulkheads had buckled and Harlan saw the light of the gas giant streaming in through a large split in the hull. The bay contained what looked at first like a dark, mottled asteroid the size of a beach ball. Its rough surface was lined by thousands of low peaks, like someone had taken a sea urchin and snipped off all its spines close to the body. The short spikes were marred by dust and tiny pieces of debris. Even in the light gravity, they stuck firmly to the surface, suggesting either magnetism or static electricity.

In Harlan's mind, the egg was almost perfect for a creature adapted to grow and evolve in the vacuum of space. The dark eggshell would absorb ambient energy more effectively than something white and reflective. The spines pulled in particles, which were probably used as part of the growing creature's metabolic process. He suspected they were extremely hardy and long-lived creatures. No wonder they were in demand and tightly controlled.

Doctor Tchkit adjusted his glasses and examined the shell's surface. "Looks like the baby is unharmed. No indication of cracks in the shell." He patted it. "It takes more than a crash landing to disturb an Osi Fain."

Krastins looked up and down the egg. "We need to get it out of here."

"No, you should hide it," Harlan said.

The aliens looked at him.

"It's contraband, and someone is on their way here. We don't know who's coming. Secure the egg and we can come back for it later once we know it's safe to do so. If it's as valuable as you say, carrying it out in the open is a good way to get us all killed."

"He's right," Skarst said. "We're not going to do the egg any good if we die here from exposure to a cracked power core or run out of air. Or get detained by overzealous local law enforcement for crashing a ship in their territory."

Krastins and Skarst did their best in the low gravity to move debris around the egg without making it look like they were hiding something. In Harlan's opinion, their attempts were adequate at best. An inspired searcher would find it in a minute of looking.

"Do you have a beacon or something to guide whomever pinged us?" Harlan asked.

"Yes," Skarst said.

"Hopefully they won't be overly suspicious sorts," Doctor Tchkit said.

"Optimists are the worst," Skarst said.

* * *

The four travelers picked their way clear of the wrecked ship. Being carried on Skarst's back meant Harlan had more opportunity to look around than to watch where he placed his feet. He couldn't get a clear idea of the original shape of the *Yamar*, although in its undamaged form it must have been bigger than the biggest jumbo jet, albeit with a less streamlined profile. It had struck the moon's surface hard enough to form a shallow crater, sobering when he considered he'd been inside it for the impact.

The remains of the *Yamar*'s aft section glowed with heat and leaking radiation from the damaged power core. Krastins said they'd been lucky not to have the core explode with the collision, for it would have incinerated them all. Skarst said that quick death might have been preferable to a slow death by strangulation and dehydration on the airless moon. The two fell to arguing again and Harlan tuned them out.

The gas giant overhead dominated the sky from horizon to horizon with only a slender arc of black showing the edge. The cloud bands were heavy on the orange and purple, bathing the moon's landscape in a reddish glow. Storms the size of continents swirled in slow silence while lightning bolts flickered in their depths.

Unlike Earth's moon, this nameless moon had a much less severe and rocky surface. Much of it looked like the smooth pahoehoe lava flows from terrestrial volcanoes. Harlan was no geologist and didn't know whether that meant the moon was volcanically active or had been dormant for millions of years.

The small party moved across a plain of long-solidified lava flows, picking the smoothest path they could find. Doctor Tchkit checked his devices regularly and announced how soon they would be a safe distance from the *Yamar*'s ruptured core. Their travel shouldn't have been tiring in the low gravity, but Krastins needed to rest more and more frequently. Skarst no longer needled at him and Harlan noticed Doctor Tchkit spending a lot of time surreptitiously scanning Krastins and puffing his cheeks at the results.

The third time Tchkit checked Krastins as they passed through a valley between lava flows, Harlan decided enough was enough. "How sick is he?"

"What?" Tchkit turned to look at the human through his transparent suit helmet.

"Krastins. He's sick. I can see it just looking at him. Is it radiation or toxicity or something else?" True to Harlan's words, the Aski Shantar did not look healthy. His scales were showing an unusual mottling instead of the shine he'd seen on Skarst's hide. His eyes had a filmy coating upon them and his tail dragged along the ground when he walked.

"Radiation," Doctor Tchkit said softly, even though his suit microphone clearly transmitted it to all four.

"I thought you treated him for that on the ship," Harlan said.

"I did. I was . . . too late. It is easier to prevent radiation from getting hold than it is to remove the effects after it has done its damage."

"Send out your beacon," Harlan said. "Maybe whoever is here has a medical facility."

"It won't help." Krastins didn't seem to have enough energy to hold his head upright and his neck stretched

41

forward until it was nearly parallel with the ground. "When the drive first failed . . . I was exposed . . . to the core. The doctor's treatment . . . only postponed this." Krastins made an untranslatable noise. "Shit happens."

"Can't you do anything for him?" Harlan didn't have any emotional investment in the Aski Shantar's survival, but his knowledge and skills would die with him, and those might be necessary to Harlan's own survival.

"I cannot," said the Doctor.

"Activate your beacon," Harlan urged Skarst again. "We may need him."

Skarst touched a unit strapped to her chest. "It is done."

Krastins stumbled and Doctor Tchkit hurried to steady him. The Aski Shantar swayed in the low gravity. "I do not . . . I cannot stand."

Tchkit and Skarst helped Krastins lower himself into a resting position, laying on his belly with his tail curled around toward his head. The Aski Shantar twitched and amber fluid the color of honey spilled from his mouth.

"Why is this happening so quickly?" Harlan asked. "He seemed fine only a few minutes ago."

"The radiation treatment I gave him earlier has worn off," said Tchkit. "It was the only thing staving off his metabolic failure. Aski Shantar are most vulnerable to radiation in their respiratory systems. His body is not processing air properly any longer."

"Can you give him anything?" Harlan asked. "Anything to help him survive until help arrives?"

"Not without a pressurized facility and access to a drug synthesizer—*wait, no!*"

Skarst pushed aside the frantic Jemra, pulled Krastins' pistol from his belt, and shot him twice, once in the head, and once through the base of his tail.

Harlan couldn't fault Skarst for her quick actions. Krastins was going to die, and painfully. Shooting him solved the problem of waiting for the end. He would have done the same if he'd had access to a weapon. Yes, it was coldly logical, which was the way Harlan preferred to approach his solutions, but it was also humane.

Doctor Tchkit took it much harder. "Why would you do that?" the Jemra screeched.

"He was going to die," Skarst said. "I wasn't going to watch him suffer."

"She's right," Harlan said. "You already said you couldn't do anything to help him, Doctor. Killing him was . . . a kindness." The word felt odd in his mouth; he couldn't recall if he'd ever expressed the concept before. Clearly, the events leading to his expulsion from the Solar System had changed him.

"But . . . But . . ."

Skarst laid her hand upon the Jemra's head, much as if patting a dog. It made sense to Harlan, since Aski Shantar didn't really have shoulders. "Tchkit, he would have done the same for any of us."

"I hope he didn't have any important passcodes or knowledge we're going to need," Harlan said. "Your mind-reader is already dead."

"How far are we from the wreck?" Skarst asked Doctor Tchkit.

The Jemra checked his gear. "Far enough, I guess. Now we wait for rescue?"

A rectangular shadow crossed the gas giant's face and grew steadily larger, ringed by what had to be running lights. Harlan said, "I don't think we're going to have to wait long."

The approaching vessel was blocky, with several protuberances above and below its main hull. Harlan couldn't make out any distinct details about the vessel since it was back-lit by the gas giant and the moon's surface didn't reflect enough light back against it. "Can you tell anything about it from what you can see?" Harlan asked the others. "Who they might be?"

"It looks like an Aski Shantari vessel," Skarst said. "It's not shaped for atmospheric flight. I can't tell the size for certain, but I think it is probably half again as big as the *Yamar*. That means a larger crew. Or many automatics." She turned herself so she could watch the approaching ship as well.

"Automatics?" Harlan asked. "Like androids? Autonomous robots?"

"Nothing autonomous. We use dumb robots only. Equipping an autonomous device with complex cognitive properties has led to numerous incidents on every world upon which they have been developed. We have sophisticated information systems that provide us with complete, current data, but decision-making is necessarily left up to us organic beings."

"I suppose it doesn't hurt having two brains," Harlan said.

"You say that," Doctor Tchkit said, "but you should hear Aski Shantar arguing with themselves."

"I see you haven't lost your sense of humor," Skarst said. "Are we all better now?"

The Jemra puffed out his cheeks. "Death is an inevitable part of life. You're an apex predator while I'm evolved from prey. We grieve over the dead, but we can't dwell on it. That's the quickest way to get eaten next."

Harlan considered the alien logic and how it tracked with differences in evolution.

The vessel slowed to a near stop as it approached the wrecked *Yamar*, playing spotlights across the debris field from above. Harlan still couldn't see anything beyond the most basic details and he swore if he ever got access to a lab, the first thing he would build would be some light-enhancement goggles.

Skarst touched a button on a device from her harness and set it on the ground. A brilliant light flashed repeatedly atop the device. Harlan heard a repetitive crackle in his radio speaker as the device's energy bled into audio frequencies. The vessel closed in on their position, lights swinging around until they illuminated the three refugees and Krastins' corpse.

"They're going to know you shot him," Doctor Tchkit said quietly.

"He was dying. It was a kindness."

The ship slowed until it was nearly hovering over them. To Harlan, it felt like an office building was floating over his head. It was unnerving.

Landing gear unfolded from the ship's ventral hull, extending and twisting open like monstrous steel flowers. Lights bathed the landscape around the crash survivors as the ship dropped. Unlike human-designed vessels, there was no fury of flame and smoke and rocket exhaust. The ship must have used some form of repulsor to control its descent, even in the moon's low gravity. The landing proceeded in silence, although a low subsonic thrum carried through the ground as the repulsor emitters drew closer to the surface.

The ship settled to the ground, landing struts absorbing the vessel's inertia as it came to a rest. A ramp from the underside opened like a mouth, discharging six aliens in heavy-duty armored vacuum suits. Given the opaque helmets, Harlan couldn't identify their species, although he suspected five of them were Aski Shantar from their general shape and flexible tail sections. The sixth was a tailless humanoid figure, shorter than the Aski Shantar but much broader and more massive. It walked on stumpy, bowed legs and had arms that hung low like a gorilla's.

All the new arrivals were armed with rifles and pistols. If weapon size was any indicator of strength, the sixth alien's rifle was probably the equivalent of a bazooka.

Skarst raised her hands, as did Doctor Tchkit. Apparently the gesture of surrender transcended species barriers. Knowing he had no choice, trapped in the survival bubble as he was, Harlan raised his own as well.

* * *

"So . . . here we are," said the Aski Shantar with scars across his facial scales and across a pale, sightless eye. He wore a sleeveless vest over his torso, thick with what might have been armor plating, and a pair of pistols strapped to the sides of his belly. "A couple of smugglers, and I don't even know what to call this thing." He gestured with his head toward Harlan the way a human might have waved. "Is it a pet of some kind? A trained animal?"

"Something like that," Skarst said. "And it's mine."

"Not anymore," said their host.

Skarst, Doctor Tchkit, and Harlan were brought aboard the as-yet-unnamed vessel by the armed party, divested of their weapons, gear, and vacuum suits. Tchkit's and Skarst's wrists were bound by simple cords resembling zip ties, and likewise, Skarst's tail was folded up across her back and secured by another cord. Their captors had argued about what to do with Harlan and how to bind him, and in the end, they'd bound his wrists in front of him, which was much better than if they were behind his back.

The vessel's interior was even darker than the *Yamar* had been, and Harlan struggled to see anything. It was like an apartment with the lights off but moonlight coming through the windows. From what he could see, the vessel was in poor repair, with open panels exposing the ship's guts. Wiring dangled from overhead sockets or was looped around and tied. Aftermarket components and devices were haphazardly attached to bulkheads, with improvised connections to the ship's systems.

Harlan guessed it was an old ship that had seen a tremendous amount of use. Instead of scrapping it, its owners continued to upgrade it. As someone who had once innovated from piles of junk, Harlan understood that desire.

"Why do you say we're smugglers?" Doctor Tchkit asked.

"Are you denying it? Nobody would come to this system who wasn't sprinting from the Navy, and we pinged your vessel as a freighter. What were you carrying?"

"Combat stimulants," Skarst said. "But when the Navy tagged us, we dumped it. It's probably fallen into a gravity well by now."

"So they shot you down out of spite."

"Wouldn't you?" Skarst challenged.

"I might have, if given the opportunity. After all . . ." The Aski Shantar made a rapid stuttering tongue-click laugh. "We are the only law out here in Tokras."

"Why are you here?" Skarst asked, narrowing her gaze.

"It is . . . complicated. You will find out soon enough. Presuming, of course, I don't have you killed. Right now, that seems like a reasonably attractive option. After all, if I'm the law, I have clear evidence you've broken it. Your murdered companion. Do you deny you shot him?" He paused. "No, of course you don't." Their captor, who had not yet bothered to introduce himself, clearly liked to hear himself talk. Harlan had met lots of people like that over the course of his life.

He'd killed several of them for it.

"Of course, you could convince me you're useful," the scar-faced Aski Shantar said. "I'm not an unreasonable person." He moved his head from side to side, examining Skarst from multiple angles. "Under the right circumstances, I could even be considered . . . pleasant."

Skarst snarled at him and he backed away, gently clicking his tongue in amusement.

"We're no threat to you or whatever you're doing here," Doctor Tchkit said. "I know we're stranded and at your mercy, but certainly we can work off the expense of our rescue and passage back to civilization. I am a multispecies doctor, certified in Aski Shantar, Jemra, and Prodoni physiology." He flicked an ear at Harlan, perhaps a wink. "And I'm learning Human. Skarst is a skilled pilot and navigator. Harlan is an engineer."

Their host burst out laughing again, his tongue fully wagging from his mouth. "Work? Oh yes, I can most certainly promise you will work."

47

CHAPTER
FIVE

Over the next several local day-analogues, Harlan learned quite a bit more about certain industrial processes than he'd ever considered. Their host was named Prasek and he and his crew of thugs and heavies ran a facility manufacturing illegal weapons. They used slave laborers in place of robotic equipment that either couldn't function in the highly radioactive tunnels or couldn't be purchased and operated as cheaply. Harlan suspected the latter, as Prasek seemed the sort to pinch every penny he could get into his clawed hands.

The unnamed moon had rich underground deposits of radioactive ore that the laborers mined like termites burrowing into a thousand-year-old tree. They used energy drills, tractor beams not unlike the Hind technology Harlan had encountered, and various chemical and particle sprays. The process would have fascinated Earthly researchers, where the heavy radioactive metals were forced to degrade into rare isotopes with short half-lives, then compressed into stasis casings that kept them from degrading further. Those casings became the payload for warheads, the largest of which Harlan knew could decimate cities like the bomb the Hind had used to threaten New York.

By its very nature, the process was hazardous and the entire underground complex was suffused with radioactive particles. Doctor Tchkit was pressed into service working alongside a harried and exhausted Aski Shantar medical technician who was way over her head. Harlan and Skarst were dumped into the general population and assigned to the same work crew, which consisted of six more Aski Shantar, a Jemra, and a strange owl-like being Skarst identified as a Ri'Ar.

49

Harlan had spent time in prison—at least, he'd been a guest of a juvenile facility after he was first captured by Just Cause. That facility had been operated by the state of New York. Guidelines were established about what could and could not be done with and to the prisoners. No such guidelines seemed to be in place in the mining facility, and Harlan knew he was witnessing firsthand the far end of the road to prisons-for-profit.

"Who's buying these weapons?" Harlan asked Skarst as they loaded ore into a cart for processing. "Unless your navy runs on a slave labor economy, these aren't for them."

"No, they're not," Skarst said. Her scales were covered in a perpetual layer of grimy dust that clung to them with the tenacity of static electricity.

Harlan, too, was filthy and scratched where rock chips had cut him inside his suit. The mining residue was insidious and worked its way inside suits and equipment with an almost intelligent tenacity. The rocky tunnels were pressurized with atmosphere on the assumption that mining the radioactive material was dangerous enough without adding the risk of explosive decompression to the mix. Some crews shored up the digging by using some kind of fusion energy beam that hardened and strengthened sections of wall and ceiling, eliminating the need for timbers or other supports. By the end of every shift, Harlan found his strength flagging far more than it should. Like the other miners, he slept in a common room with uncomfortable plastic cots that seemed unsuited for any particular species. They were fed a tasteless gruel three times a day that didn't agree with him. He was slowly starving to death eating food that had no nutritive value for Humans. He was sick to his stomach all the time and if he didn't eat, he spent the following shift coughing up blood. Their food and water was heavily dosed with antiradiation medications. Every few shifts, a shuttle arrived bearing a new prisoner or two to replace those who died.

"The Hind," the owlish prisoner running the cart said, his strangely flexible tongue working to produce complicated sounds through his beak. "We supply our enemies." It was the first time the being had spoken since Harlan and Skarst were assigned to the crew.

Harlan lowered his beam cutter. It had been driving him crazy, knowing he could turn it into a weapon but doing so wouldn't get him to safety without a lot of help. "It makes sense now. No wonder they're hiding this facility from the Navy."

"Are you sure?" Skarst asked the other prisoner.

"You will see. A vessel should arrive soon to collect completed materials." The Ri'Ar slammed the hatch shut on their cart harder than necessary, using flexible wingtips to operate controls with surprising dexterity. Its featherless feet were scratched and the thick claws broken and blunted from the rough terrain. It was interesting to watch a creature that had no hands manipulating tools with wingtips, feet, and beak.

At their next meal break, Harlan pulled an empty shipping crate up to sit beside the Ri'Ar while they dined on the thin, bland gruel. The Ri'Ar had to lap it up like a dog drinking water, while Harlan sipped it from the bowl's lip, hoping his body might find some hint of sustenance in it. "Tell me about yourself," Harlan said. He wasn't especially interested in the Ri'Ar as a person, but very curious about the Hind. He knew from his hacking of Hind computers when he was their prisoner that they had conquered a species called the Ri'Ar. It was the first indication he might be able to narrow down if he'd been thrown through time as well as space.

The Ri'Ar was blunt, something Harlan appreciated. He also seemed driven by honor, almost as if he were a samurai of old, except in this case he was also a convicted terrorist. "My full name is Sonnactchekek Sharshaktitai Stertictiskekek. Everyone calls me Ekek. I will answer to that for convenience of the Flightless."

Harlan nodded in gratitude. "Why are you here, Ekek?"

"I fought for the freedom of my world, talon and beak, blade and wing." He snapped his beak with ferocity. "The occupying force chose to make an example of me instead of allowing me to die with a blade in hand. They will regret that decision. So long as I have feathers and draw breath, my hatred for them only grows."

Harlan could read between the lines and knew one man's rebel was another man's terrorist. "How long ago did the Hind conquer your world?"

The feathers around Ekek's throat bristled in an obvious threat display, but that threat didn't carry into his translated words. "They would say they defeated the Ri'Ar ten egg-seasons ago, but the Ri'Ar are not conquered. We fight to this day, and we will not cease until the last of us is sent to the Aerie of Heaven."

"You're not fighting now," Skarst pointed out, draining the last of her gruel and licking her eyes clean.

"There is no honor in a fool's death. That is the way of the Hind and will eventually be their downfall."

Harlan nodded. Hind culture was based upon honor as well, but theirs was more of an unquestioning, unthinking loyalty to the chain of command. "The Hind will get theirs. One way or another, I'll make sure of that." He paused. "When do you think the next vessel will arrive? I want to get a closer look at it and its crew."

* * *

The day the Hind vessel arrived, Harlan became acutely ill with radiation poisoning, requiring Skarst and Ekek to bring him to the infirmary and Doctor Tchkit. It had been several days since any of them had seen the Jemra, and he looked like he might not have slept during that time. His ears and whiskers drooped, and his eyes and lips were reddened. His fur was tangled and matted from the hours he had spent in a hazmat suit dealing with excessively irradiated patients.

"You look terrible," Skarst said in her tactless way.

"Shit happens," Tchkit retorted, then managed a small laugh. "This is a terrible place. Sapients shouldn't be on this moon or in this system." He looked critically at Harlan, who'd managed to vomit his breakfast sludge in order to get himself pulled off work detail. "I don't know enough about your species to have a sense of your well-being, but you look as if you've lost some weight and you're molting."

"I'm *what*?" Harlan blinked.

"Your fur. It's thinning. I presume that's a trait common to mammalian species when exposed to high levels of radiation. I've seen several balding Jemmar in the past six days."

"I'm . . . balding." This was something new. Harlan had never given much thought to his appearance and normally kept his hair short or shaved for ease of care and comfort inside his armor. Vanity was a stupid concept, well below someone of his intellect. Still, his first, unbidden thought had been that it would make him *look old*. Why should that matter? Surrounded by nonhumans in unfamiliar space, he had nobody to impress. Certainly not Penny, he told himself, and immediately hated himself.

She was long gone. He would probably never see her again—and why would he even want to? It's not like they were lovers, or even close. He'd entrusted her to the care of his Moonbase, to watch over his nephew, and given her the same nanotechnology he had carried in his own body. In short, he'd made her his successor. He'd saddled her with a duty, not given her a gift.

Still, the fact that she'd come to his mind so easily suggested his subconscious was far more interested in her than he was willing to admit. It would bear further investigation, he decided, when he wasn't so busy saving his own skin. To that end, he asked how the Hind loaded warheads onto their vessel.

"I presume they use laborers, not robots."

"That is correct," Ekek said. "How does that help us?"

"I know Hind technology," Harlan said, which was, at best, partly true. Much of the data he'd hacked on

Earth had been contained in his nanotech storage, which was now scattered across the surface of this irradiated moon in the wreckage of the *Yamar*. Still, the others didn't need to know that, and he was pretty sure his parahuman ability would help fill in the gaps once he was back aboard a Hind ship. Technopathy was like riding a bicycle—one didn't simply forget. "Can you get us onto the loading crew, Ekek?"

"No."

"Doctor, do you have any pull?"

"What do you think I am, a diplomat?" Doctor Tchkit stamped a foot in irritation.

In spite of himself, Harlan laughed.

"Is it dying?" Ekek asked as he peered owlishly at Harlan's amusement.

"No. I'm sorry." Harlan wiped his eyes. "On my homeworld, there was a rather famous doctor who spent an inordinate amount of time telling his fellows what he was not."

"Species inside joke," Skarst said. "Not funny."

"To you, maybe, but you clearly have no sense of humor," Harlan retorted.

Tchkit chittered at that. "It's like he's known you for years, Skarst."

"Look, you're a doctor," Harlan said. "You have access to things nobody else does. Narcotics. Painkillers. Better food, even."

"I . . . you . . . Are you suggesting I bribe someone with drugs? That is the most unethical—"

"Yes, I've heard all the arguments before. I've also been a dealer, and it's a surprisingly effective way to get things done. Get us onto a loading crew. No, wait." Harlan rubbed at his scalp, sending a small shower of fallen hair around him. "I've got a better idea."

Skarst made a snorting sound. "I can't wait."

* * *

The cart jostled, squeezing Harlan painfully against the interior of the case that he shared with a warhead. He tried not to think about how much radiation he was absorbing in the process. He had convinced Skarst, Ekek, and Doctor Tchkit to hide inside the irradiated shipping containers to smuggle themselves aboard the Hind vessel. The doctor gave them each six doses of his strongest antirad drugs with no promise they would be effective against the concentrated exposure. Then, at Harlan's direction, he released a full twenty percent of the facility's stock of narcotic painkillers and distributed them to the loading crew in return for their complicity.

As far as Harlan could tell from inside the shipping container, things were going to plan. He'd smuggled the smallest multifunction device he could carry with him from a mechanic's toolbox. It was like a combination Swiss Army Knife and wireless computer all bundled into a neat, handheld device. He wished he had a thousand like it, for he could have used them to create a suit of armor like no other. He switched it to a standby state. Once the Hind ship was safely away from the moon's surface and on its way out of the system, he would use that device to override the lock on the case and let himself out.

The thrumming of the cargo carrier's drive set Harlan's teeth on edge as he counted seconds by the hundreds. It was dull, repetitive counting, and threatened to lull him to sleep, but he'd committed himself to a twenty-minute delay after the engines started before he would take any action. He knew the Hind energy shields were exceptionally difficult to penetrate, and that defensive perimeter was likely proof against the hard radiation of the Tokras system. Combined with the apparent technology to allow non-skiplane faster-than-light travel, it was no wonder the Hind were warring against the coalition of species with such aggression. Trying to battle a foe who could appear anywhere at any time, who could shrug off the worst attacks before decimating their opponents, was a losing proposition.

Perhaps he could change that. Harlan was no slouch in the warfare department. In fact, he'd single-handedly destroyed a Hind cruiser before destroying the fleet with the aid of an antimatter bomb—which he had devised and built. He wasn't prepared to call himself an ally of the Aski Shantar and Jemmar species, or the Prodoni or Ri'Ar, or whatever other species he hadn't yet encountered. Alliances weren't really his style.

On the other hand, stealing and deciphering tech was very much his style, and he had already stolen quite a bit from the Hind. His parahuman power meant he understood tech and retained information about it without needing a digitally-stored catalog in his mind. He put that information to good use with the multitool.

Using the tool's wireless function, he connected to the case's digital lock and worked through the alien code until he found the trigger to unlock it. The lock released with a soft click and hydraulics hissed as the lid raised. Harlan rolled himself out of the case and a wave of dizziness overtook him. He sprawled on the cargo hold floor, his cheek resting upon cool metal, and tried to bully his body into functioning as designed.

It occurred to him he was still irradiating himself with the case open and managed to force it closed with his multitool. It might not have reduced the effect of radiation, but it *felt* like an improvement. He pulled himself to his feet and looked around for the cases that contained his partners by the identifying numbers upon them. A couple minutes later, Skarst, Doctor Tchkit, and Ekek were all out, struggling against the dual effects from radiation exposure and the heavy doses of antirad drugs the doctor had given them.

"I need a vacation," the Jemra complained. "Somewhere underground, with cool, clean water and a fat female companion."

"Open prairie for me," Skarst retorted. "Hot and dry with fleet-footed game to pursue."

"Craggy peaks and fog," Ekek said. "With freshly sharpened knives in my talons."

"The bridge of this ship," Harlan said. The others paused, considering. "Once we control this vessel, you can all get dropped off wherever you want."

"You make it sound simple," Skarst said. "The Hind are no joke when it comes to fighting."

Harlan smiled. "Neither am I."

Working quickly in case they tripped any sensors and a Hind came to investigate, the group scrounged around for weapons. If he'd had more time, Harlan would have rigged up a deadman switch for one of the smaller bombs in the cargo. Hind would be familiar enough with their destructive capability they might think twice about foolhardy actions.

Foolhardy actions.

This entire charade was one foolhardy action, Harlan thought. They had almost no resources, they were almost certainly poisoned and probably dying from the radiation, and they were aboard a vessel crewed with lion-sized centaurian beings with the kind of toughness that came from evolving on a heavy-gravity world.

"There's not a single gun in here," Skarst complained. "I'm no melee fighter. A Hind will cut me apart and use my skin for armor padding."

"The warriors carry their axes with them at all times," Harlan said, "but they may have an armory for their lasers. We'll raid it."

"What if shit happens?" asked the Doctor.

With one leg, Ekek raised a long, thin piece of sharpened steel he'd found in a corner of the bay that looked like the splintered blade of a Hind axe. He'd wrapped some rags around one end and his talons clenched it tight. "I will kill Hind with this. It is no sword, but a samurai adapts."

Harlan blinked. Surely the Ri'Ar hadn't used the term. His mind had translated it, meaning *samurai* was the term best matching the definition of the avian's language. "Another goddamn hero complex," he muttered. He thought he'd had enough of that with the Just Cause do-gooder superheroes, and then he'd found himself fighting alongside them against the Hind.

Well, if fighting the aliens who'd threatened his homeworld made him a hero, then he'd be a goddamn hero.

"How do we find the armory?" Skarst asked. "I've never been aboard a Hind ship before."

"I have," Harlan said. "I'll take point. Ekek, cover me."

They crossed the cargo bay to the exit hatch. Like most doors constructed for the Hind, it was as broad as it was tall. Harlan tried to remember everything he'd learned about Hind technology during the short period he'd been their prisoner. Much of the data had been stored in his nanotech memory, and was gone. But he knew technology, and he wasn't going to let something as simple as door controls defeat him.

Sweat trickled down his neck as he fought with the control panel, using the multitool's interface and then expediting the process by prying the panel back to expose the underlying circuitry. The Hind preferred a higher oxygen content than Earth-normal, and it made Harlan almost giddy as he struggled with the tech. He found the elusive circuit he needed and the door split into four parts, sliding diagonally into the corners.

Hind didn't like stairs, so the corridor beyond had a downward slope to it against the pull of the artificial gravity. The dim lighting had a redder tinge than that aboard the *Yamar* and was chilly like a fall morning. The musky scent of Hind filled the air, making Harlan's nose itch.

"How big is this ship?" he asked the others.

None of them knew. Nor did they have any idea how many Hind were aboard.

"Let's go," Harlan said. "Stay alert. We could get discovered at any time. We need to find a terminal so I can access the ship's systems."

"Wasn't that a terminal you just destroyed opening the door?" Doctor Tchkit asked.

"No, that was a dumb panel. I need something connected to the main computer." Harlan raised a hand to forestall additional questions. "From there I can find the armory, specs on the ship's size and complement, and—"

A Hind came around a corner at the far end of the hall and stopped dead in her tracks.

Ekek hurtled past Harlan's head, already nearly at full speed with a brief flurry of wing beats. He closed the gap in seconds. The Hind, clearly female from her lack of armor or armaments, made the smart choice to flee. She bellowed a word Harlan didn't recognize but the implication was clear. The alarm would be raised in a moment.

"Come, hurry," Skarst said. "We are out of time to sneak around." She tore down the corridor after Ekek, neck lowered to avoid braining herself on the ceiling. Her long legs ate the distance, leaving Harlan and Tchkit struggling to bring up the rear.

"I'm getting . . . too old for this," Harlan gasped as he felt pain shooting through his knees. His nanotech had alleviated many of the discomforts of aging and now it was gone, he was suffering old-man agonies.

By the time he and Tchkit caught up to Skarst and Ekek, the Hind was sprawled on the deck, orange blood pouring from a deep stab wound in one side of her neck. Ekek's feathers were raised like a cockatoo's crest and the Hind's blood was spattered on his legs. He still clutched the sharpened piece of metal and his head swiveled nearly one hundred eighty degrees as he watched in all directions.

"She raised an alarm," said the Ri'Ar. "More will come."

Doctor Tchkit's ears drooped. "She wasn't armed."

"She has four times Ekek's mass, a carnivore's teeth and claws, and evolved on a heavy gravity world," Skarst said as she rifled through the Hind's pouches. "Just because she doesn't have an axe or laser doesn't mean she wasn't dangerous."

Harlan noted the Hind's fur was ticked gray at the tips and tawny beneath. He spotted a small computer unit on the Hind's waist strap and lunged for it. "This is what I need. I just need a few seconds." He began frantically deciphering the Hind symbols, seeking the underlying meaning to find any kind of useful information.

A Hind male in full armor slid around a distant corner and crashed against the bulkhead with a tremendous clatter. Axe in hand, he scrabbled for traction and charged them, uttering an ululating battle cry.

"We don't have a few seconds," Skarst shouted. "Come on!"

Harlan didn't move, his fingers flying over the device's screen and controls. He could sense the alien tech trying to talk to him. He had once plugged into a Hind warship and stolen the secrets of its systems. His brain would remember. It only took time.

"Harlan!" Skarst cried, turning around and grabbing for him. "Run!"

He shook off her scaly grasp and, with a smile, touched a control on the unit he held.

An emergency bulkhead slammed across the corridor, catching the warrior in mid-stride. The axe clattered to the corridor floor at Harlan's feet, the warrior's severed hand still clutching the haft.

Harlan picked it up, letting the grisly remains slide off the handle. It was heavier than the one he'd taken on Earth, but a weapon was a weapon. The Hind kept the artificial gravity set to what was probably a refreshing, invigorating level to them, but to Harlan it felt like dragging his feet upon the Earth instead of the Lunar gravity he'd grown used to and the lighter gravity of the moon they'd just fled. Still, he wouldn't show weakness to his allies and he shouldered the heavy Hind axe even as his fingers dashed over the control unit he'd stolen.

"We're not far from the ship's arsenal, or the bridge," he reported upon deciphering the information displayed. As he touched spots on the screen, distant crashes echoed through the corridor. "I'm creating us a clear path to both."

"How?" Skarst lowered her head, the Aski Shantar equivalent of a human narrowing his eyes.

"Closing down bulkhead doors," Harlan replied. His ears popped as the Hind ship's interior pressure dropped. The others looked around, clearly noticing their own physiological effects. "And emergency venting."

"Wait . . . You're *spacing* them?" Doctor Tchkit's chittering was aghast.

"Do you think for a moment they would not hesitate to do the same to us?" Harlan asked. "We're stowaways on their weapon-smuggling vessel, and representatives of species they consider enemies."

Skarst's tail snapped on the floor. "He's right, Doctor. This is no time to be noble."

"Like when you shot the Captain?"

"He was *dying!*" the Aski Shantar argued. "Killing him was a kindness."

"And spacing the Hind is murder."

Harlan looked at Ekek, who ruffled his feathers and said nothing. If the Ri'Ar had any thoughts on the subject, he was keeping them to himself. "You may call it murder, Doctor, but I call it survival." He finished clearing the route to the arsenal. "Let's go take the bridge."

CHAPTER SIX

The Hind pilot on the bridge sold her life dearly, managing to shake off Harlan's first shot with the ungainly and inaccurate laser pistol he'd appropriated from the arsenal. She cuffed him aside with her first blow and raked her claws across Skarst's scaly face before Ekek shot her a second time through her skull. She collapsed against the bulkhead and Harlan stepped over her still-warm corpse to reach the flight controls.

Skarst hissed in pain as Doctor Tchkit examined the bleeding scratches. Aski Shantar blood was dark red and had a sharp, metallic scent.

"Hind don't treat injuries," the doctor said. "We won't find any medical supplies aboard this ship. I'll make do with what I can find, but these will probably scar and may become infected."

"At least she missed my eyes," Skarst said.

"Eye patches are appropriate for pirates," Harlan said as he worked his way into the Hind computer systems.

"Pirates?" Ekek asked.

"We've got a stolen ship full of illegal warheads. If that doesn't make us pirates, I don't know what does."

Ekek clacked his beak. "Piracy is honorable if used against oppressors. I approve of this role."

Harlan glanced back at Skarst, being tended to by Doctor Tchkit. "Will she survive?"

"Survive? Yes. Thrive? Probably. I'd like to get her to an actual medical center."

"Let's get out of this radioactive firepit of a star system and into deep interstellar space first. Then we can figure out our next move," Harlan said."

"Can you actually fly this thing?" Skarst said, voice muffled from the strips of cloth the doctor had tied over the wounds on her face.

Harlan slid aside a cover on the control panel and pushed a large button sized for a Hind's thumb. The flare star and nearby planet shimmered, vanished, and the stellar field changed as the ship flashed through hyperspace without the benefit of a skiplane to guide it. Hyperdrive was a far superior system than the *Yamar*'s skipdrive, for it allowed instantaneous travel between coordinates. "Apparently, yes."

* * *

In his selective sealing of corridors followed by emergency venting, Harlan had managed to eliminate the remaining crew members of the vessel, which he learned was called *Thrastharashothstross*, a nearly unpronounceable Hind word meaning *Firstborn Daughter of Hindmistress Thrasthar of Clan Ashoth*. He resolved to change it as soon as he thought of a suitable replacement. He took for granted that he had become the ship's *de facto* captain, as he was the most familiar with Hind technology and Skarst was in no shape to challenge him for leadership.

The vessel was fairly small as far as freighters went, the equivalent of a semi-truck in a world of supertankers. The cargo bay in which they'd first arrived was the only one aboard. The ship itself followed what Harlan figured was a typical Hindish design, blocky and linear without multiple decks. Also of typical Hindish design was the armored hull, the energy shield, and the heavy laser turrets on the highest point on the dorsal and lowest point on the ventral side. It would have seemed unusual for a ship that size to be so heavily armed, but the Hind viewed themselves as warriors and conquerors, and weakness was frowned upon.

For Harlan's purposes, he'd just acquired his own warship with a cargo capable of destroying multiple cities or fleets.

When he'd built his first Destroyer suit, he'd dreamed of wreaking destruction upon his hometown, punishing those who'd tormented him in his youth. He managed a lot of damage before Just Cause stopped him. Then later, he'd done more and far worse, even having a hand in the destruction of the World Trade Center, all over his hatred of the superheroes of Just Cause. Now he had the kind of power to sterilize hundreds of square miles of planetary surfaces, and instead of Just Cause, he was thinking about the Hind.

"Harlan, did you hear what I said?" Doctor Tchkit nudged him.

"No."

"I said, Skarst needs more medical attention than I can provide here. We need to fly to a safe port."

"I don't know your space," Harlan said. "Where should we go?"

"Lanovoss," Skarst said, her voice distorted by the swelling around the cuts in her face. "Frontier space. Less suspicious for us in a stolen ship."

"I have kin on Lanovoss," Ekek said. "They will aid us."

"Hey . . ." Doctor Tchkit looked up from a console. "This looks to me like life signs. There's no medical bay on this ship. Is there a brig, maybe?"

"Why would the Hind imprison one of their own?" Ekek asked.

"Dishonor worthy of public shaming or execution," Skarst said.

Harlan stood. "Sounds like our kind of people. Let's go find out."

Doctor Tchkit stood as well. "If it's a Hind, that doesn't automatically mean spacing them."

"It doesn't *not* mean that either."

* * *

The Hind had in fact imprisoned one of their own. Whereas many of the Hind Harlan had seen previously were varying shades of tawny yellow-gold, the Hind female behind the security field had black highlights in her fur that made her look like a tabby cat. The difference was distinctive enough to make him wonder if different clans tended toward similar fur patterns. She sat back on her haunches like a cat, resting on straight forelegs while her arms were crossed before her torso, fingers tapping on them with impatience. If she was shocked to see the motley party of hijackers on the other side of the field, she didn't show it.

"Are you going to let me out?" she asked without preamble.

Harlan was surprised he understood her. He didn't think Bubble the Prodoni had given him Hindish in its gift of psionic translation, but perhaps he hadn't had the opportunity to need it before now.

"I haven't decided," Harlan said, truthfully enough. "Who are you, and why are you imprisoned?"

"I could ask you who you are and why you are here," the Hind retorted. "You look like mine slaves."

"We're not mine slaves. We're the new owners of this vessel."

The Hind sneezed, which Harlan interpreted as a sarcastic snort. "Unlikely."

"And yet, here we are. I'm asking again. Who are you, and why are you imprisoned?"

The Hind stood, straightening up, her gray and black mane fluffing out with pride. "I am Submistress-Engineer Mrraurr of Clan Haurmash. I am imprisoned because I dared to speak ill of the ancestry of this ship's former captain."

"You were locked up for something you said?" Doctor Tchkit asked with interest. "What was it?"

"I don't answer to rodents. Or monkeys," said Mrraurr.

"This . . . *monkey* . . . has the power to release you or to space you," Harlan said. "And I don't particularly give a shit which. I've already spaced the rest of this crew. Are you so anxious to join them?"

Mrraurr burst out in Hindish laughter. "Good! Spoken like a warrior. I don't know what you are, monkey, but I like you." She dropped back to a seated position. "The *Thrastharashothstross* is a full half year behind in scheduled maintenance. We're transporting explosives in a highly radioactive and unstable environment. The shields are barely meeting minimum tolerances. Components and filters need to be scrubbed or replaced. I was promised that downtime before this voyage. Submistress-Captain Voshosa reneged on her word once more and I . . ." She stopped, face breaking into a toothy smile. "I suggested she was so irradiated that fucking her brothers would result in severely deformed cubs."

Harlan blinked, unsure he'd understood exactly what the Hind had said, but Doctor Tchkit fell onto the deck, laughing and pounding his heels onto the metal. Somehow, the Jemra's mirth was contagious, or perhaps Harlan simply needed an outlet for his stress, but he found himself laughing as well. For the first time in a very long time, his amusement spilled forth until tears leaked from his eyes.

"Blood and bone," swore Mrraurr. "Are you both diseased?"

Her words only made the two sapients laugh harder until Ekek and Skarst finally came down from the bridge to see what was causing all the fuss.

"What is going on?" Skarst asked, wincing at the pain from her wounds.

"Shit is happening," Doctor Tchkit said.

Harlan wiped his eyes. What was wrong with him? He was never so easily amused. "I'm sorry. I'm not myself right now." He cleared his throat and turned to the Hind prisoner, who stared in open-mouthed astonishment at the four non-Hind who seemed to have taken over the vessel. "Submistress Mrraurr, regardless of the circumstances of your imprisonment, I have need of your engineering expertise. If I release you, will you agree to return to your post and submit to my authority as your new captain?"

"What's in it for me?" Mrraurr asked immediately.

"If you stay aboard, I will ensure your required maintenance schedule is kept. I myself am an engineer and believe me, nothing makes me angrier than shoddy maintenance. If you choose not to stay, we will release you unharmed at our next port of call. You will have to make your own way, but you will be free."

Skarst's tail thudded on the deck but she said nothing. Harlan glanced at her, but had no experience understanding the nonhuman body language. She seemed to have already accepted her role as his second in command. It would be poor form for him to override her in front of the others, but it was clear they would have to discuss such things privately, and soon.

"What if I refuse?" the Hind prisoner asked.

Harlan went to the wall control panel and rested his hand on the bulkhead beside it. "Then you're consuming life support that would be better used for ourselves. I'll space you and manage the ship's systems without your help. It may take me a little while but believe me, I'll figure it out. I figured out the Sharassar systems and I'll figure out these."

Mrraurr's fur bristled. "Sharassar? What do you know of those fainthearted inbreeds?"

Hate was too strong a word for Harlan's feelings, which centered more on *active dislike*, but he thought the latter might not be suitable for a Hind's psychology. "I hate them. I have killed many and would do so again without hesitation."

"Those herbivore-fucking cowards. Release me, monkey, and you can tell me about your battles, and I will keep the *Thrastharashothstross* in working order for you.

"I accept your offer," Harlan said. "On one condition. We're changing the name of this ship."

"To what?" Skarst asked.

"*Regina*," Harlan said. "She is . . . *was* . . . my sister. She was very important to me."

Doctor Tchkit's sides still hitched from his laughter but he patted Harlan's leg. "To memorialize a sibling is a great honor. I don't know if I can pronounce your word, but I'll do my best."

* * *

Lanovoss was much closer to its star than the Earth was to the Sun, but the cooler red dwarf kept summertime temperatures around freezing while winters and polar weather trended much colder. It was a young planet, with sharper mountains and generally rough terrain overall, with far less water than land surface.

The *Regina* was directed to land upon a field of concrete surrounded by icy plains, in a spaceport with dozens of similar landing platforms to suit vessels from tiny one-being runabouts to bulk freighters. Skarst read off information from the ship's sensors and informed Harlan no military vessels were parked either in orbit or on Lanovoss' surface.

The hyperspace jump had been nearly instantaneous, but the journey from their egress point to Lanovoss had taken nearly two ship-days—which were something like twenty-five and a half hours long. During that time, Harlan had the others give him as much of a crash course as possible in the basics of political relationships between the species, cultural oddities that would be important to remember, and the economy.

With no real central government beyond the Aski Shantar homeworld, the planets of the unnamed multispecies collective were largely self-governing, with their own economies. The fractured system seemed to Harlan much like the Earth of the Nineteenth Century.

Lanovoss was a frontier world, with lots of rough edges and temporary construction slowly transforming into permanence. The population was a melange of Aski Shantar and Jemmar, along with a noticeable presence of the winged Ri'Ar and the Prodoni in their robotic exosuits. Harlan saw no Hind as they rode in a wheeled, open-air shuttle from the landing platform into the spaceport town. He'd left Mrraurr behind aboard the *Regina*, authorizing her to perform whatever repairs she could while they sought supplies and information.

Skarst was unhappy at Harlan's decision, and sulked on the other side of the shuttle, bundled against the cold in a thermal-electric suit. She'd argued, quite effectively in fact, that leaving the Hind alone aboard the ship was inviting a murderer into one's tribe and offering them a choice of weapons and throats.

Harlan wasn't a fool; he'd set up wards and blocks in the Hind ship's systems that should confound Mrraurr in the event she tried to access anything he'd deemed required securing, such as helm control, communications, weapons, armory, and the exits. She'd gone from a prison cell in the brig to being imprisoned with the run of the *Regina*. In Harlan's mind, that was a big step up and showed his willingness to give her a chance to prove herself. Should she give a good accounting of herself in his absence, he would entrust her with more. It was a technique he'd learned a lifetime ago when he ran a Philadelphia gang.

"I still think we're going to come back to a trap or an ambush or a stolen ship," Skarst said from behind the muffler over her face, her speech still roughened from the wounds on her face.

"Shit happens," Doctor Tchkit added.

Harlan ignored them to speak to Ekek. "Can you reach your people? We need supplies and Skarst needs medical treatment."

Over the course of the in-system journey to Lanovoss, he'd arrived at what he felt was the best course of action. He needed to find out if he'd been cast through time as well as through space. The only point of reference he had was the Hind attack on the Earth. He knew Clan Sharassar had been responsible for the invasion. Either the *Blood Afire* and its battle group had already departed for Earth and never returned, or that departure had not yet occurred. If the former was true, Harlan would know when and where he was in time and space. If the Hind had not yet departed for Earth—or possibly not yet discovered its existence—he would fight to ensure they did not ever learn of it.

Time travel was something Harlan had only considered peripherally. He knew it was possible, but the practice of it was well beyond his capabilities, so he'd ignored it. Now that he had practical experience with it, having created two different androids that were subsequently catapulted to different points in the past in the antimatter explosion, he had to accept the possibility that he himself had done the same. If he was in the past, what would happen if he stopped the Hind from sending their fleet to Earth? Would it create a paradoxical time loop or would he create an entirely new universe diverging from the original timeline? The thought of possessing the power to do so was dizzying.

The chill breeze ruffled Ekek's feathers. The Ri'Ar didn't appear to notice the cold and hadn't dressed in anything resembling warm clothes. "I have codes to contact them once we reach public terminals."

"How secure are the public terminals here?" Harlan asked.

"More so here than away from the frontier," Skarst said. "What is your plan, Captain? I presume you intend to trade the warheads away for supplies and trade commodities?" She winced. "And fix my face too, please."

Harlan noted that Skarst had called him *Captain* for the first time. Whether it was because his plan to attain their freedom had succeeded, or some other reason tied to Aski Shantar psychology, she'd thrown in her lot with him. He would endeavor not to let her down. "We will repair your face as soon as Ekek's people meet us. As for the warheads, I want to keep the bulk of them aboard. Possessing weapons of mass destruction makes us a force to be reckoned with."

"To do what?"

"Clan Sharassar attacked my homeworld. I warned them there would be consequences."

"You told me you destroyed their attacking fleet. What more consequences are there?"

"I don't know for certain I destroyed their fleet. It is a presumption based upon what I know of antimatter explosions."

"So now you want to continue the war with them? Seems a bit genocidal to me," Doctor Tchkit said. "Is that something your species does? Because we're not really like that here."

The doctor's mild tone belied the cutting words. Harlan frowned. He knew humans were war-like, and genocide had happened all too many times in their own history. Was he ready to be another despot? To have his name whispered in fear? Once, perhaps, the idea might have appealed to him, but he must have been getting soft in his old age. He suspected Penny, as bloodthirsty as she'd been in the short time he'd known her, would have balked at such an act of wanton destruction. Slaying civilians over the actions of what might have been a splinter faction of Clan Sharassar wasn't going to get him home any faster.

Home.

Did he really want to go home? He hadn't called Earth his home in a decade, preferring to live in isolation on the Moon in his secret base.

Penny's face appeared unbidden in his mind and he gritted his teeth. He was being ridiculous, crushing like he was thirteen years old again. It had been four decades since he'd had any kind of romantic thoughts and damn him, he was too old to start with that sort of nonsense.

No, he had other reasons to find his way back to Earth, he told himself. His nephew, March. His . . . well, he didn't know exactly *what* Mustang Sally was to him, but he was surprised to discover he wanted to see her again as well. He was growing soft. Sentimental. Weak.

"I hate them and I want to see them die," Harlan said aloud.

Ekek clacked his beak. "As do I, Captain."

"Well, I don't like it," Skarst said.

"You don't have to like it," Harlan said. "But first things first, let's resupply the *Regina* and keep our chief engineer happy so she doesn't try to kill us in our sleep."

"You think she would do that?" Doctor Tchkit asked.

"I don't know she wouldn't," Harlan said. "Not yet, anyway."

* * *

One of the peculiarities of the Lanovoss system was the huge gas giant occupying the closest orbital slot to the star. It wasn't so much a planet as a gray dwarf, a star that never quite ignited. It was large enough to regularly occlude ninety percent of the parent star in a ring eclipse the locals called *nearnight*. It so happened that the next nearnight was only hours away when the *Regina* landed, and Ekek's contacts wanted to meet at the darkest part of it. They gave Ekek a location, and shortly, Harlan and the others found themselves waiting on an unlit open lot between two long, low warehouses.

The temperature dropped quickly as nearnight began, and Harlan was glad for the extra layers of fur-insulated clothing, courtesy of the Hind preference for sleeping furs over blankets. The icy air crackled in his nose as he stared up at the dim ring of the gray dwarf's sunlit edges. "Where are your people Ekek?"

"They are here," the warrior said softly, and silent bodies dropped from the sky to surround Harlan and his crew.

Skarst swore at the Ri'Ars' sudden appearance. Like earthly owls, they made no sound as they swooped in to land. They were all armed with hip-mounted rifles, aimed by body position and fired by toe triggers. Harlan had been given to understand the Ri'Ar were generally primitive, but they seemed quite comfortable with their energy weapons. The warriors had bare scarred skin showing amid their feathers, and several had chipped beaks as well.

"Ekek, you're up," Harlan said.

The Ri'Ar warrior stepped forward. Hip-rifles tracked his every movement as he approached one of the other Ri'Ar and spread his wings wide. Feathers from the top of his head elevated like a cockatoo's crest. The other Ri'Ar matched his movements and the two of them began a complicated dance involving beak clacking and sudden lunges toward one another.

Harlan leaned down to speak to Doctor Tchkit. "Is that how they say hello? How do they get anything done?"

"I don't know. I'm unfamiliar with Ri'Ar customs. It's a combination of ritual greeting and threat display from what I can see," the doctor said. "I imagine they truncate it when there's no time."

"Wasteful," was Skarst's brusque comment.

The ritualized dance completed and Ekek and the other began speaking at length. The speed at which they conversed overwhelmed Harlan's psionic translation, and he was only able to pick out individual words here and there. "Are you following this?" he asked Doctor Tchkit.

"No."

"It's by design," Skarst said. "They are using a clipped language that obfuscates Prodoni translation. They developed it to mask their communication from the Hind." She shrugged, thumping her tail. "What? I read."

Ekek turned away from the other Ri'Ar. The others raised their hip-rifles to point skyward, but made a point of keeping their wingtips by them. "This is Kleketik. He and his samurai greet you as fellow warriors against the Hind. They can provide most of the items you have on your list." Ekek paused. "You may not like the price, and you may not like what they cannot supply."

"Okay, give me the bad news."

The list wasn't as bad as Harlan had feared. They had medicine for Skarst's wounds. Crew consumables and a recharged life support pack were available. The Ri'Ar could provide three replacement gravity grids, fuel crystals suitable for the Hind jumpdrive, and a short list of other supplies Mrraurr had requested. They did not have replacement emitters for the Hind laser turret, but knew where such things could be obtained. "But, they say, you won't like that either."

"Get me more information," Harlan said.

Ekek spoke with the others. Their voices and beak clacks rose and fell as their conversation grew more and more animated.

Harlan crossed his arms. He suspected he was about to receive bad news.

He wasn't disappointed.

CHAPTER SEVEN

The binoculars were recognizable as such, but made for Aski Shantar eyes. Harlan could only look through one lens at a time at the building at the far end of town. It was of newer construction than the original landing site. Something about the building didn't quite add up. The lines were wrong. Then he blinked and looked again. It wasn't a building, it was a huge spaceship—or at least, it had been.

"What is that?" he asked Skarst. "Bulk freighter? Passenger liner? Warship?"

Skarst took the binoculars from him. Doctor Tchkit had disinfected and sealed her wounds with a chemical spray. They stood out as brown lines across her otherwise green face. "Bulk freighter for sure. Looks like it's been here awhile."

Harlan took the binoculars back. "I suppose a downed freighter is as good a warehouse as anything if you don't intend to launch it again anytime soon."

"It was called the—" Ekek made a peculiar trilling sound punctuated by a beak clack that did not translate. "It belonged to a merchant house of my homeworld. They brought it here with supplies for the colonists. Unfortunately, upon landing, they found themselves overrun by a well-armed gang." He ruffled his wings. "My kin are the only survivors of the crew. They have twice tried to retake the vessel and lost members each time."

"This gang," Harlan said, the inkling of a plan starting to form. "Tell me about it."

"They are vile," Ekek said. "Thieves. Smugglers. All without honor. They steal from the wealthy and the poor alike, and only enrich themselves. They operate a storefront, with prices far higher than colonists can afford to pay. Yet, those who live here require those supplies to survive. Everyone is beholden to this gang."

"What can you tell me about the ship's interior?" Harlan asked without taking his eyes off the vessel.

The Ri'Ar conversed with his fellows for a couple minutes while Harlan examined a tall superstructure on the ship's dorsal side. He was certain it was a turret. Given its location, it couldn't have been effective against targets close by and at ground level. He smiled. It was a weak point.

"They've never managed to get inside," Ekek said. "That particle-beam turret is deadly."

"How large is this gang? How many soldiers can we expect within?" Harlan asked.

"Twelve, maybe sixteen sapients. All heavily armed. Mostly Aski Shantar. A couple Kglotan heavies."

"Who's in charge?"

Ekek spoke with the other owloids again. "An Aski Shantar named Quarest. She comes from the homeworld." He rattled his beak in a gesture of disdain. "Apparently she couldn't be more than a hatchling there, but here she can be a raptor."

Skarst muttered something profane and nearly inaudible behind him. Harlan looked back at the others, counting his own troops and estimating their strengths and weaknesses. "So she needs to feel powerful," Harlan said softly. "Well then, let's give her what she wants. Ekek, if we take that ship, I'm going to need to use it. Maybe for a long time. I promise your people will be part of its crew and when I no longer have need of it, I will give it to them freely."

"I will discuss this with them," Ekek said.

The conversation went on for a long time, and there was a lot of beak clacking and raising of crests. Harlan began to think that he might have bitten off more than he could chew, but then Ekek returned to him. "They are in agreement. Honor demands that if you succeed where they have failed, they are beholden to you."

"Good. I'll need a day in the *Regina's* shop to prepare. Then we go in."

"Just like that?" Skarst asked. "You're going to dance in on flutterbug wings and offer her the world?"

Harlan smiled. "Or something very much like it."

* * *

They returned to the *Regina*. Skarst was fully convinced it would be gone, or Mrraurr would have set up a trap for them. Harlan felt otherwise, figuring he'd spent enough time among the Hind during their attack of Earth to understand their base psychology. She was a blue-collar type, beholden to Hindmistresses to give her direction. She wasn't ambitious enough to try for command herself, given her propensity for speaking her mind when a more nuanced approach might be more successful. She believed he would give her the tools and materials to maintain her ship, because he'd spoken with brute honesty. That made her give him a chance to prove himself.

When the airlock door opened, they found her pacing back and forth, her fur smudged from grease and welding spots. She had a fresh scratch across one cheek with dried orange blood matting her whiskers. "Did you get my supplies?" she asked without preamble.

"We're working on it," Harlan said, appreciating her forthright communication. "I need to use your shop for a day, and I could use your help if you can set aside repairs to the ship."

Mrraurr snorted. "I can't repair my own ass if I don't have parts for it."

Doctor Tchkit chittered laughter. "No wonder she was in the brig. I can't imagine a Hindmistress who would tolerate such insubordination."

"What about the rest of us?" Skarst asked. "I assume we should prepare to die in battle for the sake of your parts?"

"Only if shit happens," Doctor Tchkit said.

"The idea isn't for us to die for the parts," Harlan said thoughtfully. "If anybody's going to die for the parts, it's going to be the other guys. I've run a gang before. There will be some loyal soldiers, sure, but most of them don't care who's running the show so long as they get their cut. We have to take down the leadership and loyalists and then ensure the remainder is well-paid."

"Wait, it sounds like you are intending to take over the gang yourself," Skarst said, licking one eyeball clean. Clearly it was an idea she hadn't considered.

"You were smuggling an Osi Fain egg when we first met. Then we stole this ship outright," Harlan said.

"And good job on that," Mrraurr added.

"You're not getting cold feet, are you, Skarst?" Harlan asked.

"No. And I'd like to remind you that egg is still on that moon, so long as Prasek's people haven't found it yet. Sooner or later the word's going to get back to Klorister that Krastins is dead and I'm not. His debt became mine the moment he died, because I was his second in command."

"That's a ridiculous bit of legal wrangling," Harlan said. "Can we buy off this Klorister?"

"I don't know. I don't think so. She's powerful and if she promised someone an egg that we were supposed to deliver, she's not going to be satisfied until we deliver an egg, or we're all dead and our ashes strewn across the galaxy."

"I'll work it into my plans. I promise."

"I suppose that's the best I can hope for," Skarst grumbled, having processed the consideration through to its logical conclusion. "What's your plan?"

"I will need you to fly the *Regina*, and Mrraurr will assist you. Doctor Tchkit will help me infiltrate the target."

"I'm no commando," the Jemra reminded him.

"Unless you can fly the Regina, I can't bring Skarst with me. Mrraurr is an enemy combatant given the current political environment. I will need Ekek and his squad on the target's exterior. Thus, you're it."

"Shit happens," Skarst supplied.

Harlan laid out the bare bones of his plan to take over the parked bulk freight. Skarst had a sharp tactical mind and offered both some useful suggestions and harsh criticisms. Unlike some gang leaders he'd known in his youth, Harlan had no problem taking criticism from someone with better understanding of a situation. Between the two of them, he felt like they came up with a plan likely enough to succeed.

Harlan left Skarst to coordinate prepping the Regina with Ekek's hard-bitten squadron and Doctor Tchkit. Mrraurr followed him to the ship's engineering deck. "What do you need me to do?" she asked.

"Those warheads we brought aboard? I need you to repack one into the smallest possible inert container that will release no more than ten percent of its total radiation."

Mrraurr's whiskers twitched. "You *want* it to leak?"

"Just a little," Harlan said. "I need the radiation to mask some other power signatures. Can you do it?"

"Yes, puny monkey. I'm not some pathetic Sharassar kitten with milk still dribbling off her lips."

"Then prove it." Harlan crossed his arms and then deliberately turned his back on her, showing he carried no weapon in hand and wasn't afraid of her.

Without another word, Mrraurr started working on the project he'd assigned her.

Harlan found enough of the technology and parts he needed for his own project, and got to work. It had been a long time since he'd had to build and fabricate with actual tools instead of directing nanotech. He found it simultaneously refreshing and aggravating. The tools were designed for Hind hands, which had two thumbs and four fingers. If he'd had more time, he'd have redesigned the tools. More than once, he had to interrupt Mrraurr to give him a literal hand.

"I haven't seen any indication of nanotechnology among the Hind or the other species," he observed as the two of them wrestled with some recalcitrant components. "Why is that? Your technology is sufficiently advanced for it."

Mrraurr set down the tool she was using, a nameless device that welded all kinds of metals and plastics without heat. "Clan Fashtras developed such technology, generations ago. They intended to use it to defeat the other Clans in the Accord of the Fist. You know of it?"

"I do," Harlan said. He'd learned about them briefly during his time as a prisoner of Clan Sharassar.

"The Fashtras Clanmistresses unleashed their nanotechnology upon their homeworld, intending to remake it as a planetary fortress and factory for warships."

Harlan winced. He foresaw what was coming in the story. "Gray goo."

"Oh, you're familiar with it," said Mrraurr. "Yes, the nanotech went uncontrollable. It devoured their entire planetary civilization in days. The Accord of the Fist shot down and destroyed every vessel leaving the surface to ensure the plague couldn't spread. The world is now uninhabitable. The nanites are constantly building things and destroying them within minutes as their programming conflicts."

"Safeguards can be built into nanites to prevent such things," Harlan said. "I did that with my own work. People may call me Destroyer, but I had no desire to wipe out my entire homeworld."

Mrraurr returned to her work. "Destroyer is a good name for a warrior, but you have an engineer's skill. It is very confusing, as if you are male and female at the same time."

Harlan knew Hind culture was stratified by its genders. Males were considered intellectually inferior—often rightly so—and their lot in life was to fight and die for their clans. Females were left to the actual running of society, making decisions, performing tasks that required a modicum of intelligence. "My species . . ." He stopped. He'd been about to say humans didn't identify jobs by gender, but that wasn't true. For that matter, human gender itself was such a broad spectrum that he couldn't classify it in a quick conversation with a fellow engineer. Nor was he interested in doing so. "I am both a warrior and an engineer. I mostly build weapons to use against my enemies. I used those weapons against Clan Sharassar when they attacked my homeworld."

"What is it called, your homeworld?" Mrraurr sealed up her project and set it aside. "This is done."

Harlan looked over it. "This is good work. The world of my birth is called Earth, but I haven't lived on it for many years. I live on my planet's moon instead."

"Earth, like ground, or dirt?" Mrraurr laughed in the peculiar, sneezing way that Hind did. "Destroyer of Earth. Like a digging drill. Good for making holes in the ground."

Harlan finished one of his own projects, a group of a dozen robotic insects, each the size of his hand. He snapped his fingers and they obediently trotted across the workbench to line up along its edge. "There is a scripture upon my world. Do the Hind have religious writings?"

"Yes. Beautiful, powerful epics that stir one's hearts. Far more than the simple Warrior's Catechism our males live by." Mrraurr bent her upper torso down to get a better look at Harlan's devices. "These are interesting. What are they for?"

"Destruction, of course." Harlan smiled. "It's what I do best. The scripture of my homeworld has a line, *Now I am become Death, the destroyer of worlds*. That's me. The Destroyer of worlds."

Mrraurr made a growling sound in the back of her throat. It wasn't a Hind indication of anger. Perhaps strong emotion? Harlan wondered. "I . . . like that," she said. "Perhaps it suits you. You certainly were the Destroyer of this ship's crew." She paused. "I hope you don't repeat it with this half-formed plan you've conceived."

"I haven't been alive this long just to throw away my life on a foolish decision," Harlan said, perhaps more sharply than he'd intended.

83

"It's not your life I'm worried about," Mrraurr retorted. "Monkey."

"Cat."

Mrraurr's face split in a toothy snarl of a grin.

Harlan returned with a smile of his own.

* * *

A chill wind blew across the plain as Harlan and Doctor Tchkit drove toward the bulk freighter-turned-warehouse in a hovercar Ekek's people had provided. Nearnight had been replaced by a grayish pre-dawn that was primarily due to reflected sunlight from the enormous gas giant overhead. The disassembled warhead in its portable case sat in the bed of the car, leaking just enough radiation by design that Harlan could almost feel his cells trying to turn precancerous.

Tchkit drove, despite protesting that he wasn't anybody's chauffeur. Harlan claimed he didn't know how to drive, even though the vehicle's controls were simple and intuitive. He wanted to give the entirety of his attention to the grounded vessel as they approached. He'd cobbled together some light-intensifying goggles from a spare set of Doctor Tchkit's pince-nez virtual displays. They gave him a clear image of it and he marked in his mind where the sentries were located. The turret, of course, was the biggest concern, and disabling it was his primary goal. Once it was inoperative, Skarst could bring in the *Regina* and put the freighter under her guns. Ekek and his rebels would flood out from the *Regina*'s locks and take down the sentries quickly and efficiently.

Harlan just had to take down that damn turret first.

An Aski Shantar sentry stepped out from a heated guard shack, a rifle clutched across its narrow chest. The tall lizard had a fur hat that looked incongruously like the folded paper hats Harlan and his younger sister had made when they were children. The sentry bent its head forward to peer through the windscreen at the hovercar's occupants.

"Good evening," Tchkit said pleasantly. "We're here to see, uh . . ."

"Quarest," Harlan said softly.

"Quarest," Tchkit repeated. He glanced nervously at the sentry's rifle and then sidelong at Harlan.

The sentry licked its eyes with a long, dark tongue, as if it couldn't quite believe what it was seeing. "What in the frozen hell are you?"

Harlan smiled. "A trader."

"You look like someone shaved the front half of a Hind," the sentry said.

Harlan patted the axe resting across his lap. "I took this from a Hind, and then I threw him out of an airlock."

The Aski Shantar blinked and canted his head to one side. "What do you want?"

"To see Quarest."

"She's not available."

"She will be for me. Tell her it's about the *Thrastharashothstross* payload." Harlan had written down the former name of the *Regina* and studied it until he could rattle it off without stuttering.

The sentry raised a communicator to his face and spoke into it, softly enough Harlan couldn't hear over the idling hovercar's repulsors. Whomever he spoke to gave the order and the sentry stepped aside. "That axe better stay in the car," he said. "Quarest won't tolerate weapons in her presence. Move it. Straight ahead, park beside the hull, and wait."

Harlan smiled mirthlessly at the guard as Tchkit engaged the drive. The expression wouldn't mean anything to the Aski Shantar but Harlan didn't care. Apparently the self-importance of bottom rung street soldiers transcended species.

"Well, that was pretty terrible," Tchkit said, barely loud enough to carry over the sound of the hovercar's repulsors. "Is this what doing crime is like?"

"You were doing crime when you picked me up," Harlan reminded him. "Smuggling is a crime."

"It's a clean crime," the doctor retorted. "You don't have to dig down through the sewer tunnels."

"You keep on believing that," Harlan said. "And maybe it'll help you sleep better the next time you're trading in sapients."

This last generated a wince from Tchkit.

"Park as close to the hull as you can. Easier to dispatch my tech that way." He tapped the microphone taped to his throat beneath the collar of his coat. "Skarst, Ekek, check in."

"I am here," the Ri'Ar said via the bone conduction speaker behind Harlan's ear. Ekek's voice was distorted by rushing air. "We are circling nearby."

"I'm here too," Skarst retorted. "Engines on hot standby. We can be there in six minutes. How do I know when you're ready?"

"When I say *Philadelphia*, you launch. Ekek, wait two minutes after I speak it and then take out the sentries."

"Understood," Ekek said.

"Yeah, this is going to go off like a bad fuel rod in a hot engine," Skarst said.

Two more Aski Shantar and one of the huge bear-like Kglotans awaited them by a broad docking ramp that had been lowered long enough to have dusty frost buildup upon its edges. The Aski Shantar carried rifles like the first sentry. The Kglotan held a Hind-style battle axe in one of its gigantic fists. The weapon seemed comically undersized, even though Harlan knew it was as big as the one he had with him.

"That's far enough," one of the Aski Shantar called. "Drop off your package and drive away."

"That's not how this works," Harlan called. "I deal with Quarest only."

"It speaks!" said the other Aski Shantar. "I thought it was some kind of weird monkey."

Harlan bit the inside of his cheek to keep from lashing out. This was part of the test. He knew how the game worked. If he lost his cool, Quarest would only send underlings while she remained safely ensconced within her freighter.

Doctor Tchkit gestured to Harlan. "He's the boss. I'm just the hired help."

The Aski Shantar laughed. "I hope you're being paid well."

"That's why we're here," Harlan said. "Now go fetch Quarest or I'll take this warhead to the next buyer."

The Aski Shantar glanced back at its fellows. "Warhead?"

Harlan smiled. "Your sentry clearly didn't pass along my information. This is a warhead from the *Thrastharashothstross* hijacking. Scan the case if you want. Or you can quit wasting my time and get Quarest out here to do it."

"Mosht," said the first Aski Shantar. "She says let them in. She wants to talk to them."

Mosht stepped aside and gestured toward an opening in the freighter's hull. "Park over there. I better not lose my tail for this."

Tchkit engaged the drive. "Shit happens," he said, and drove away.

Harlan said nothing. While they'd been sitting next to the freighter, his insectoid robots quietly dispersed themselves, climbing up the hull like spiders on a wall. They would send him telemetry messages and inform him when they were in their designated positions. One more piece in place.

Tchkit slid the hovercar sideways into the bay. It was still icy cold but at least the wind wasn't howling around them any longer. Harlan and the Jemra stepped out of the open-air cockpit and looked around. The bay was the size of a warehouse, and from the vessel's girth, it probably had six of them. The space within was largely wasted, with piles of supplies strewn haphazardly about, intermixed with broken shipping crates and packing debris. In Harlan's estimation, the *Regina* would fit cozily inside the bay with some careful piloting.

It gave him an idea.

A stocky Aski Shantar emerged from a hatch, flanked by taller specimens of the same species, cradling short and ugly rifles across their narrow chests. The shortest Aski Shantar wore a quilted parka of shimmering fabric and a knit cap that wouldn't have looked out of place on any human's head. The scales around its mouth were dyed, painted, or tattooed a bilious yellow and it regarded him with cool interest across its reptilian face.

"This will be Quarest," Tchkit whispered.

"What in the frozen arctic are you supposed to be?" Quarest said, drawing each word out like she was singing it.

Harlan crossed his arms. "I'm here representing a concordance of smugglers. Thieves." He smiled. "Lowlifes."

Tchkit's eyes widened but the Jemra, to his credit, said nothing to contradict Harlan.

"What do you want, lowlife?" Quarest asked, flinging the term back in Harlan's face.

He didn't mind; he'd dealt with people like her before. Whispers in the tiny mastoid speaker he wore told him his robotic insects were in place and ready to act upon his command. "We're taking over. Effective immediately. You can still run the day-to-day operation, but the organization's direction will change and you will report to me." Harlan stood still. He didn't expect his ploy to work on the aliens, and why would it? He was a stranger, of a species they'd never seen before, and he had no apparent weapons or soldiers to back his play. It would have been like a young man—still a boy, really—walking into the headquarters of the most powerful gang in Philadelphia and announcing his intent to take over.

He'd been laughed at then, too. By the time the gang leaders discovered he was not only serious but fully capable of backing up his threats, it was too late. Those that hadn't died were only too glad to pledge their support to him.

Quarest and her guards laughed long and loud, until he felt like tapping his foot in impatience. Instead, he made himself remain still until their amusement died away.

Quarest stepped toward him. "You're serious," she said after a moment. "You really think you can walk in here and take over my business?"

"I do," Harlan said. "And I already have. You just don't know it yet." He nodded toward the hovercar. "I'm not lying about that being a warhead from the *Thrastharashothstross* hijacking. I see you're familiar with it. Good. Then you know what this warhead can do if it is detonated, either by my hand or by the ending of my life." He held up the small detonation device he'd kept in his palm, attached to a ring over one finger.

Quarest snorted. "You'd die too, monkey."

Harlan felt a muscle jump in his cheek. "I'm getting a little tired of everyone calling me that. I didn't come all the way here from Philadelphia to be insulted by a bunch of scaly genetic dead-ends. You're nothing but a pair of fancy boots to me, Quarest."

At the code word *Philadelphia*, Skarst and Ekek were supposed to act. Harlan had to trust they would. At the same time, his robotic insects committed suicide in electrical flares, destroying carefully-identified circuits in strategic locations around the freighter. Chief among those targets was the controls for that turret which had so concerned Ekek. The lights of the bay in which Harlan and Tchkit had parked flickered for a moment, making Quarest and her escorts look around in alarm.

In that moment of distraction, Harlan flew into action. He didn't have time to build even a non-nanotech version of this battlesuit, but his parahuman affinity for technology had afforded him time for one simple invention. He triggered it with the device in his palm and raised his hands over his head. Instead of detonating the warhead packed in its case, a hatch opened and lobbed two objects toward Harlan. Aimed with precision, they slapped into Harlan's palms and he brought them back down: two laser pistols he'd redesigned to fit his hands. They'd been masked from detection by the warhead's radiation.

Doctor Tchkit threw himself to the deck as Harlan opened up with the paired lasers. Beams flashed out to drop both of Quarest's guards, leaving one with a smoking ruin where its chest had been and the other without a head. Additional beams took out emergency door controls, sealing the bay from the rest of the ship and closing the loading door.

The security cameras he left alone; anyone monitoring the situation would need to see what had happened.

Quarest smartly dropped to the deck when the shooting started. A moment later, when Harlan was finished with his tactical targets, he turned both smoking barrels toward the Aski Shantar. "So . . ." he said around a smirk of genuine amusement. He loved it when one of his technological plans went off without a hitch. "Do I have your attention now, Quarest?"

"Yes," she growled. She inched one slender hand toward the discarded weapon of one of her erstwhile companions. Harlan sent a laser beam sizzling into the deck beside her and she withdrew the hand.

"I wouldn't," he said. "Right now my troops have taken out your exterior sentries and my ship has a Hind missile ready to fire. A real one. You have one chance to survive this day. Surrender to my authority immediately and turn over control of this ship and its complement to me. There will be a few changes in your day-to-day operations and overall business plan, but the organization will remain in place and you'll even have a position in it." He raised his voice. "I trust the rest of your crew is listening, as I did not destroy any of the interior sensors in this bay. Every sapient who chooses to join me will have a lucrative position. Anyone who wants to leave can drop their weapons and walk away. You have my word you won't be fired upon."

Quarest snorted in contempt. "Submit to a monkey's rule? I'd rather die."

Harlan shot her.

* * *

Harlan's estimate of the gang's resiliency with a change in leadership was accurate. Of the twelve sapients who'd been part of Quarest's group, only one opted to leave. The Aski Shantar was divested of weapons and sent on his way. Harlan stood over Quarest's body and warned the lizard not to return under any circumstances or his life was forfeit. Aski Shantar were incapable of tucking their tails between their legs, but Harlan had the impression the fellow would have if he could while trotting away from the freighter.

"Now what?" Skarst asked. She'd landed the *Regina* beside the freighter. Mrraurr was already sorting through the equipment and supplies on the freighter to see what she could cannibalize for repairs.

"Skarst, we'll speak in a minute," Harlan said. "Ekek, take your people and form up new sentry positions. Let's make sure we don't get any unpleasant surprises from the locals."

The owl clacked his beak and raised his wings, spreading the flexible tips in a gesture that reminded Harlan of the way one of his lieutenants had directed street soldiers all those years ago in Philadelphia. The Ri'Ar marched back out of the bay, directing unblinking glares at everyone they passed before spreading their wings and flying off into the darkness.

"Let's find out what we have, and *who* we have," Harlan said. He pointed at a Prodoni in a mobile tank—unlike Bubble's, it had practical tank treads to get around. "You, sea-brother, what do I call you?"

The Prodoni said, via the expediency of a speaker, it went by Accountant and that was a stroke of good news for Harlan.

"I need a manifest of all the cargo in this vessel and a summary of the organization's financials. Doctor Tchkit, talk to the crew here. I want to know who I've got in this organization, what skills they bring to the table, and what they want to see happen."

"You want me to—to conduct *job interviews?*" Tchkit spluttered, his nose wrinkling like he'd inhaled an allergen. "I'm not a resource manager!"

"Yes, I know, you're a doctor. But you know people," Harlan said. "And I don't know enough about your species to form solid opinions yet."

"Oh, all right." Tchkit removed a multipurpose datapad from his belt and walked over to the nearest freighter crewmember. "You, what's your name?"

With the grounchy Jemra taking charge of his personnel, Harlan turned to the Prodoni. "Accountant, lead us to what used to be Quarest's office."

Accountant turned on its treads and its synthesized voice said, "Follow me, Boss."

"Skarst, with me," Harlan said, and followed Accountant.

The Prodoni led them through the bowels of the freighter, then up a lift to the command deck. Unlike the *Regina*, which seemed cramped even though it was made for Hind, the bulk freighter's command deck seemed more like an open floor-plan office. Workstations were clustered together in pods, presumably to focus on specific ship functions. A great semicircular dome covered the bridge, showing a clear view of the gas giant filling the sky beyond. It gave Harlan a mixed feeling of awe and discomfort. Awe because even a hardhearted bastard like himself couldn't fail to be moved by the beauty and wonder of the natural world. Discomfort because windows were, by their very nature of transparency, weak spots.

And Harlan was quickly building a list of people who would undoubtedly want him dead.

Still, there would be time enough to address the freighter's foibles and perceived flaws. Harlan followed Accountant into an office behind the bridge and looked around it with bemused interest.

Quarest clearly had enjoyed the finer things in life. Although Harlan knew next to nothing about preferences for interior design of the various species he'd met so far, he suspected the lavish furnishings were more indicative of decadence than cultural preference. A desk that appeared to have been carved from a single massive tree trunk dominated the center of the room. Behind it sat an overstuffed chair covered in a suede-like material, with a peculiar bifurcated back to allow an Aski Shantar tail to remain extended. Various trinkets and *objets d'arte* lined the edge of the desk. Real painted art and woven tapestries hung on the bulkheads, although Harlan couldn't identify most of the subject matter. Technology, too, was represented in quality devices and a terminal practically begging for Harlan's attention.

"Yes," he said after looking around. "This will do. Accountant, prepare those reports I requested and give me an hour before bringing them."

"Understood," said the Prodoni, and it rolled out of the office.

Harlan sat in Quarest's—in *his* chair—careful to lean to one side so as not to wedge himself uncomfortably in the gap, and kicked his boots up onto the desk. "Skarst, let's talk about the future."

CHAPTER EIGHT

Skarst went to a waist-level cabinet mounted upon one bulkhead and removed a container the size of Harlan's arm. She uncapped it and poured a fragrant, fruity-smelling liquid into a cup resembling a brass champagne flute. "This sounds like the sort of discussion I'm going to need to drink my way through," she said. "Do you consume nectar?"

"I would need Doctor Tchkit to check whether or not it would kill me," Harlan said. "But I don't drink alcohol, which is a thing humans do. I prefer to remain clear-headed."

Skarst thumped her tail in an Aski Shantar shrug. "Suit yourself. I'm having one." Instead of tipping the flute back to pour the nectar down her throat, she lowered her long tongue into it and quietly lapped at it. "Where do you want to begin, Captain?"

Harlan considered that. Where did he want to begin? Should he go all the way back to when he was thirteen, a precocious, angry child who built a giant robot to destroy his hometown? It wouldn't mean anything to Skarst. Perhaps a summary would work best. "I am what is called a parahuman," he said. "That means I have a genetic structure that manifests as abilities far beyond those of normal people of my species. My particular talent lies in a technological direction. I've been called a technopath and a technomancer, but I prefer the term electromechanokinesis. It means I can control higher technology—specifically things involving electric or mechanical functions—at a level beyond what should be possible."

"That's why you were able to reprogram the *Yamar*'s jumpdrive on the fly?"

"Yes. And why I could build those robots to take down this vessel's defensive systems in only a couple of hours. And how I destroyed a Hind fleet around my homeworld."

"Do other . . . parahumans . . . have different abilities?" Skarst asked.

Unbidden, an image of the other parahumans closest to Harlan came to mind. Mustang Sally, a super-speedster woman whose life path had intertwined with his for more than a quarter of a century. His older sister Irlene, who could shrink objects and herself to tiny size and had perished in the attack on the World Trade Center. His younger sister Reggie, who had created an entire Dreamworld for her subconscious mind to inhabit while she'd spent decades in a coma. His nephew March, who could enter his mother's Dreamworld. And . . . Penny. Why was he thinking of her? She was barely a parahuman at all. He'd connected enough with her to leave her in charge of his Moonbase. He'd given her his nanotechnology. His traitorous mind kept returning to thoughts of her at times he felt were thoroughly inappropriate.

"Yes," he said, feeling like the admission was strangling him.

"Such as what?"

Harlan shrugged. "Name it. The breadth of parahuman abilities is . . . staggering. Do you not have outliers with unusual abilities among your own species?"

"No." Skarst set her empty beverage flute down on the desktop. "To my knowledge, we are all quite mundane. What do you do with these abilities?"

"Some people use them for the greater good of humanity. Others . . . do not."

Skarst was putting both her brains to good use learning to comprehend Harlan's various nonverbal cues like body language and inflection. "Such as yourself."

"I ran a gang dealing in illegal narcotics, as I've already said."

"Is that your intent now?"

Harlan regarded Skarst with a cool, level gaze. "What would you think if it was?"

The tip of her tail twitched with vicious rhythm. "I'd think it was a step down for you. You seem far too intelligent for something as base as selling drugs. I believe you have set your target somewhat higher. If I were a gambler, I'd say you're looking to go into the full-scale piracy business."

"That's what I like about you, Skarst. You're smart and direct. Those are qualities I find admirable and unfortunately rare among my own people. Yes, I'm planning to use this facility as a jumping off point for a piracy campaign. From what I've seen, your society is capitalistic. That means I'll need funds for the next phase of my plan."

"Which, I presume, is to retrieve the Osi Fain egg and pay off my debts," Skarst said. "I would like the opportunity to not be murdered by a hunter. It's only a matter of time until a bounty on my scales is posted. I won't be much good to you if I'm turned into a cushion or set of luggage." She licked her drink for a moment. "Or, I believe *boots* was the threat you made to Quarest."

"I told you we're going to retrieve the egg, and I promise it will be soon. I've ordered Accountant to monitor intelligence and criminal networks for mentions of you, Krastins, or the *Yamar* in conjunction with an Osi Fain egg. It's also monitoring for any communications from Prasek trying to sell one. As long as things stay quiet, it means your former employer thinks you're dead and the egg is lost, and it means Prasek hasn't found it."

"That's the best plan you have? As long as nobody's talking, I'm safe?"

Harlan frowned. Skarst was calling him out without doing so blatantly. He respected her for it, and appreciated that she seemed well capable of thinking several steps ahead. "You're also not dealing in slaves. That's worth something to you, isn't it?"

"It's going to all catch up to me eventually. I've got to pay off the debt or my life is forfeit."

"Maybe we can trade something of equal value for the egg? Something to get you off the hook?"

Skarst snorted. "Unlikely. It would probably take a starship of some kind."

"Then we'll steal one. I'm planning to acquire more vessels anyway. We'll use one to buy your freedom from the contract."

"Why do you need more vessels?"

"I'm going to destroy Clan Sharassar."

Skarst picked up her discarded beverage flute and refilled it from the liquor cabinet. She spent a couple long, silent minutes drinking from it until it was empty. Then she refilled it a third time and returned to the desk. "I feel like you may have left a few steps out of your plan."

Harlan smiled. "That's where you come in. I need a second I can trust, who knows the system and how to get around it. Who knows the species we'll have to deal with. Who isn't afraid to get her hands dirty."

"So you're going to use this ship as your base and the *Regina* as your attack vessel? It seems a little small for fighting a war."

Harlan scratched his jaw. Stubble rasped beneath his fingers. When he'd had his nanotech, he'd used it to inhibit his beard growth because he hated shaving. Then the radiation from his stay in Prasek's mines had kept it from growing. Now that he was no longer irradiated thanks to a prophylactic treatment from Doctor Tchkit, it was finally coming in and it itched. "I've been giving this some thought. The most valuable commodity for me right now is starship technology. I think we'll turn this ship into a chop shop."

"My translation cannot adequately define that term," Skarst said.

"It's slang from my homeworld. A chop shop takes stolen vehicles and either disassembles them for parts or scrubs all identifiable marks and resells them. I want to do that, but with ships."

"That seems risky. Authorities will track stolen ships back to you."

"Not if we make proper use of our resources. Specifically, the citizens of Lanovoss Colony."

"Go on. I'm listening." Skarst dropped into another chair and curled her tail beneath it and around her feet.

"The word needs to go out to all colonists. Anyone who lives here, and needs supplies we can provide, will not pay for them. They'll be suspicious at first, but when they receive their goods for free, they'll change their minds. They will trust us."

"Giving away your inventory is not a good business model," Skarst said. "Citizens would be less suspicious at a rollback of prices to fair levels."

Harlan smiled. "This is why I need you, Skarst. Fine. We roll back prices to fair levels, and then roll them back a little further. I want people to be comfortable purchasing from us. Then when we tell them to spread the word that this port needs supplies and is not charging landing fees and tariffs—or perhaps, only charging minimal landing fees and tariffs—they will encourage freighters to come here. Freighter traffic will bring other traffic. Private vessels. Perhaps even warships. We turn Lanovoss into a destination port, and then we pick and choose which ships to hit."

"So you rebuild some ships, cut apart others, and then what? Build an attack fleet? Take on the Hind in open battle like some kind of renegade warlord?"

"If that's what it takes. They deserve the vengeance for attacking my homeworld." Harlan couldn't believe the words coming from his own mouth. He'd turned his back on the Earth in favor of the sterile silence of the Moon. And yet, when the Sharassar battle group had materialized in the Solar System, Harlan had leaped to defend the Earth. He, an avowed sociopath, had acted in service of his fellow man.

He was growing soft in his old age. Or maybe he was learning life wasn't quite as binary as he'd imagined it to be.

Skarst said something and he missed it, his mind engaged with the idea of becoming a warlord. "What?"

"I asked if you have friends and family back on your homeworld. Or a mate. I presume humans mate in some fashion. All species do." Skarst absently nibbled at one of her finger claws, the way a dog might have.

"I only have a nephew. The son of my youngest sister. All my family is dead. As far as friends or a mate . . ." A few faces came to mind immediately, one more so than the others. Mustang Sally and Minerva, who'd helped him to free his sister's spirit so she could escape to the Dream-world forever. Their faces were replaced by Penny's, who was not his friend. Not his mate, either. What was she to him, anyway? Not that it mattered. He would likely never know.

Skarst switched to nibbling on another finger. "Ah, your motivation becomes clear. You may think you're hard as battleship armor, but you want to return home."

Harlan snorted, but it felt hollow. "Unlikely."

"Clan Sharassar attacked your world. That means they know where it is. Somewhere, they may have a record of its location."

There it was. Skarst had put all the disparate pieces together and figured out what Harlan had hidden even from himself. He *wanted* to return to Earth. He wanted to stand on the surface of the Moon and look upon the beautiful blue and white surface of his homeworld. He wanted to feel the embrace of its gravity, the kiss of its winds. He wanted to see March again, and Mustang Sally, and Minerva. And . . . Penny.

Reality crashed upon him. "Even if I could find the location of my homeworld from Clan Sharassar, it doesn't help. I know for a fact the explosion that catapulted me through space sent other beings through time as well. Into the past. I ripped a hole in space-time and I went through it just as did the others. The attack upon the Earth might not have happened yet. For all I know, it might not happen for another hundred or a thousand years. Or it could have happened a thousand years ago. The odds of me only traveling through space and not time are low."

Skarst lowered her hand and leaned forward in her seat. "You will never know unless you try. That is why you must take on Clan Sharassar. To find out definitively *where* you are and *when* you are. You will need help, and I pledge you mine . . . Captain."

Harlan managed a wry grin. "I see you've figured it all out, Skarst."

She licked one of her eyes. "Well, I'm probably smarter than you."

The blunt admission startled Harlan into a laugh. "That's fine, then. Please enlighten me as to what is our next move."

Skarst drew her lips back in a passable imitation of a human smile. "I'll have the doctor try to identify a functional stimulant for you. We have a lot to discuss."

* * *

The first order of business was to get the townsfolk on their side. Lanovoss City was a grandiose name for the haphazard collection of prefabricated buildings, permanently grounded vessels, and new construction following the architectural designs of several wildly different species. The name was important. It meant the denizens were thinking ahead. Someday, Lanovoss City would be the most important settlement on the moon. Harlan and his new organization were working toward that goal.

Since it had a small-town, frontier vibe, Harlan had the news of the freighter's change of ownership delivered not to the local media, but to the spaceport taverns. That would be a far more efficient way to disseminate information far and wide.

Besides, the citizenry would need to see it for themselves. And see it they did, for many of them saddled up their hoverbikes and trucks to cross the pain to where the freighter sat. A steady stream of Aski Shantar, Jemmar, and Ri'Ar arrived with questions on their lips or beaks, and none left empty-handed. There were even a couple representatives of a species Harlan had only seen at a distance or never interacted with before: hulking bear-like Kglotans, a rank-smelling, bat-like homunculus called a Bris, and a tall, slender humanoid with magnificent antlers and a liquid-eyed herbivore's features called a Minan.

"How many species are there in your . . . What is your collective organization called?" Harlan asked after the Bris left and they had to step outside for some fresh air. The creature had a natural odor reminiscent of rotting meat and no amount of bathing or perfumes could disguise it, Skarst said. Briese—the plural of Bris—were repugnant to all oxygen breathers.

"The centralized government calls it the Confederation, such as it is. They control the Navy and they're trying to fight a war against the Hind, but they're not particularly effective."

"Sounds like every government back on my homeworld," Harlan mused. "Perhaps that's the mark of true civilization: ineffectual government."

"That's cynical," said Skarst. "And we number nine. The Aski Shantar, Jemmar, Prodoni, and Ri'Ar you know. Today you met Kglotans, a Bris, and a Minan. There are also the Indrans, which resemble you superficially but for six limbs instead of four and blue fur. The Valentians are the newest people to the Confederation, and as they are the most militaristic, they are often leading the battles against the Hind."

"Who make ten, and then there are Humans as well. Nearly a dozen sapient species. Amazing."

"I suppose some authorities also consider the Osi Fain to be sapient as well," Skarst admitted. "Although I suspect it's more likely they are sentient at best."

"And still you traffic in them," Harlan said.

Skarst's face twisted into a snarl. "It was not my choice to do so, and I have no choice but to fulfill Krastins' task. My life depends on it."

"I can protect you," Harlan said.

"I'll grant you are smart, but you haven't shown me much except an ability to plan, and any Aski Shantar worth her tail can do as much."

Harlan fought his rising ire. Arguing with Skarst wasn't going to get him back to Earth any faster. Neither would antagonizing her. He was going to have to do something about retrieving that egg or one like it soon. He hadn't lied when he said he intended to retrieve it. Harlan was many things, but he wasn't a liar, and he didn't break promises. He just hadn't figured out how to pull it off with the resources he had at the moment. Prasek was undoubtedly on a raised level of alert with the theft of his warheads. That would make approaching Tokras risky, and Harlan preferred to minimize his risks wherever possible.

Ekek stuck his beak into the room. "Forgive my interruption. The constable is here. How should we proceed?"

Harlan stood, straightening the front of his tunic. He was grateful for the interruption. It meant he could put the problem of the egg in the back of his mind and let his subconscious work on solving it. "Do nothing untoward. I expected the law to show up sooner or later. What species?"

"Jemmar."

Harlan frowned. He felt like he had a good handle on the Aski Shantar and their species' psychology, but he didn't know the Jemmar well at all. "Skarst, send Doctor Tchkit to meet me and take over for his interviews. I'll need his insights." He turned back to Ekek. "Make the constable comfortable. Offer refreshments without making it seem like a bribe. Do no harm."

Ekek snapped his beak in acquiescence and left the office.

Skarst stood to follow the Ri'Ar. She paused at the door. "I hope you know what you're doing, shouldering your way into the middle of a war."

"The war came to me," Harlan said. "I won the battle of my own homeworld. I'll win this one too."

"You're very confident."

"Stick with me and you'll see I can back it up."

"Have you ever been wrong?"

"I thought I was once," Harlan said with a smile. "But it turned out I was mistaken."

* * *

Constable Smitchy was so portly he made Doctor Tchkit look svelte and athletic. He didn't walk so much as hobble. Like the doctor, he didn't wear clothing— there was no need when Jemmar were wrapped in thick fur from head to toe. He did have a belt around his prodigious belly to which several implements, including a sidearm, were attached. A silver ring brooch was clipped to one tufted ear. Harlan immediately thought of it as a badge instead of a decoration, which Tchkit confirmed to him a moment later.

The Constable stared open-mouthed at Harlan until Harlan felt his ire rise. He quashed it; now was not the time to be reactive. He'd anticipated this situation would come sooner or later and needed to handle it appropriately. "What in the crags are you supposed to be, then?" the Constable asked without any of the polite preamble Harlan had come to expect from Doctor Tchkit.

"I'm from a distant world. I'm sure you've never heard of it," Harlan replied. This young Confederation was already a multispecies association. It stood to reason that not everyone would know about every other member race. "My name is Harlan Washington, and I've taken over the operation of this facility."

"Yes, I've heard about that. You're not very business-minded, giving away your inventory for a fraction of its worth to anyone who asks."

Harlan asked Doctor Tchkit if he would mind fetching the Constable some refreshments.

"I'm a doctor, not a waiter," Tchkit said, but disappeared in the direction of the freighter's galley.

"I'm willing to accept short-term losses," Harlan said to the Constable. "I've got long-term plans that will pay off handsomely."

"These long-term plans . . . they are against the law?"

Harlan shrugged, even though he knew the Jemra likely wouldn't understand the gesture. "That depends upon you, Constable."

"How so?"

"Aren't you the law here in Lanovoss City?"

"I and my department, yes." Without being asked, the Constable humped his considerable bulk over to a species-appropriate chair and flopped into it. His mouth hung open, and Harlan realized he was panting like a dog.

"How did you wind up in that position? Were you elected or appointed to it?"

"Appointed. I'm one of the original colonists. Lanovoss has been settled less than seven years."

"You must have seen a lot of changes," Harlan said. "What brought you here? My second in command tells me this is an out-of-the-way frontier system. Folks don't settle in remote locations unless they either want to stay away from cosmopolitan regions or they want to become one."

"This system is a gateway," Smitchy said. "Although there's only two skiplane nexuses in this system, the adjacent system has six, all leading to unexplored territory. We came here with the intent to become a jumping off point and trade center for frontier expansion. Unfortunately, with the advent of war with the Hind, funding for exploration dried up. That leaves us stuck aboveground without any nearby holes."

It took Harlan a moment to decipher the metaphor. Since they were not apex predators, being trapped aboveground was a death sentence. "So you are stuck keeping the law on a colony that has no growth prospects. I'm here to change that."

Doctor Tchkit returned with two shallow bowls of roasted, spiced seeds and wide-mouthed bottles of a commercial carbonated beverage. The doctor passed one bowl and bottle to Constable Smitchy and then sat to enjoy his own.

"I assume what you're going to do is break the law, which is why we're having this talk right now." Smitchy opened his bottle, releasing a surprisingly pungent aroma, and sipped at the foaming beverage.

"And I assume you're not fully opposed to it, which is why we're having a talk at all instead of you hauling me off to whatever passes for a jail here in Lanovoss," Harlan said. "Let me tell you where I stand first of all. I don't care much for the Hind but one Clan in particular has pissed me off, and my eventual goal is to cause them as much harm as possible. If I can eliminate them, so much the better."

"Xenocide?" the Constable asked. "I can't abide by that, no matter how noble your intentions are."

"Call it targeted vengeance, then. Clan Sharassar attacked my homeworld. They killed many of my people, and I am going to make them pay for their affrontery. You say you're at war with the Hind, but you're probably only in real conflict with one or two of the Clans. They war with each other and will align with whomever they see as the biggest benefit." Harlan leaned forward, holding the Constable with his gaze. "I give you my word I will not harm nor cause harm to come to the people of Lanovoss. If any of my own people do so, I will kill them. I have no patience for those who go back on their word or by their actions invalidate mine."

Constable Smitchy looked toward Doctor Tchkit. "Is it serious?"

"He is male," Doctor Tchkit said. "And yes, everything I've seen indicates he has no tolerance for those who step out of line."

The Constable ate a mouthful of seeds and regarded Harlan, crunching noisily. He wiped crumbs from his belly fur, then drank more of his frothy beverage. "What do you intend to do and what do you need?"

"I need freedom to operate here, in this system, without interference. In return, I will ensure that the citizens of Lanovoss have readily available supplies here at prices that are fair, and anyone who needs something and cannot afford it can have it for free. I need the port to be well-maintained and supplied, and to have low docking fees and tariffs to encourage traffic. I will ensure this colony is safe from threats both independent and organized, whether from within its own citizenry or from pass-through travelers or from external forces."

"You talk caverns, but Quarest did the same and she couldn't deliver on any of her promises," Constable Smitchy said.

Harlan smiled. Instead of immediately rejecting his offer, Smitchy had brought up other aspects of the conversation. That meant he was willing to be corrupted, as had his Earthly contemporaries when the opportunity arose. "I assure you, I can deliver. I destroyed a Hind battle group when it attacked my homeworld. I saved the Doctor here and his crew when their ship was disabled and crashing. I broke them out of indentured servitude on Tokras, and then took over the Hind ship that is parked in a hangar on this vessel. I also took over Quarest's organization." He indicated Doctor Tchkit. "Doctor Tchkit can verify everything I have told you from the time we met forward."

Smitchy glanced over to Tchkit and the Doctor made a one-handed motion like he was smoothing his whiskers. "Very well," the Constable said. "I accept that you have done those things."

"Good. I'm glad to know I'm dealing with a being of reasonable intelligence," Harlan said. "Now what do you require in return?"

* * *

Constable Smitchy had been thoroughly predictable and sadly unimaginative in his response. Like all small-minded people with a little bit of power, he'd craved more. More power, more perks, more adulation. Harlan was only too happy to give Smitchy what he needed. He allowed the Constable to put his own people in charge of the docks, providing security for the landing field and the cargo, and to collect and keep all docking fees. With Skarst's input, Harlan set an upper limit for docking fees and tariffs, and Smitchy kept all of them at that limit. If he could have gotten away with it, he'd have charged three or four times as much, but then Harlan would have put a particle beam through his face.

Like any project with an epic scope, things started small on Lanovoss. The crew began referring to the freighter as the *Vengeance*, as it was intended to become Harlan's instrument of vengeance against Clan Sharassar. Harlan liked the name. It carried connotations of fear and destruction, as did his own *nom-de-guerre* Destroyer. The Hind weren't the sort to cower in fear from a mere word, but Harlan intended the name *Vengeance* would eventually make them look over their shoulders, just in case.

At first, Harlan's organization hemorrhaged funds. The Confederation, still in its infancy, had no common currency, so most transactions took place using native coin. Money-changing was a big business and Harlan got his group deep into the middle of it, building their coffers full of Shantari *scalars*, Jemmar *kribt*, and Ri'Ar *ingots*. Money-changing could be profitable given time, but Harlan was spending it faster than they made it. Even with the amount they took from the docks and tariffs, and what they could scrape from transactions with the Lanovoss citizenry, the group still operated at a loss, much to Accountant's chagrin.

They bought tech to repair and fortify the *Regina* and *Vengeance*. Some of it, acquired on the gray and black market, was expensive. Mrraurr was a highly competent engineer and found value in tech that others might have cast away as junk. Slowly, the ships transformed from humble freighters and transports into vessels of war.

Skarst oversaw a crew who built an actual warehouse nearby the *Vengeance*, so there would be a place to store goods and transact business with the local populace when the bulk freighter was on the prowl. As goods were moved into it, the bays and holds of the *Vengeance* filled instead with specialized tools and dedicated facilities. The *Regina* fit neatly into the main auxiliary hold, with meters to spare. Harlan and Mrraurr redesigned the hold's doors to open and shut far faster than they'd originally been engineered. They cut the time to about one and a half seconds and Harlan decided that was plenty fast. It meant they would be able to hide or launch the *Regina* faster than the Navy could launch interceptors, according to Skarst.

The main hold was refit as a starship-stripping hangar, replete with multiple cranes and grapples to work either in zero-G or in a gravity well. Hovercars were outfitted as mobile tool carriers, some with smaller versions of the grapples and cutters mounted on the bulkheads, others as floating toolboxes. They held the wide variety of implements needed for disassembling—or occasionally re-assembling—captured vessels. One auxiliary hold became a barracks for the crew complement for the *Vengeance*. Another hold was reconfigured as a brig for captured prisoners, designed by none other than the good Doctor Tchkit.

"We're not spacing starship crews," he told Harlan in no uncertain terms as they ate in the *Vengeance*'s galley.

"Unless they're Hind," Harlan countered, spearing a piece of roasted meat on the spiked utensil Aski Shantar used, halfway between a knife and chopstick.

"Or sympathizers," Skarst added as she picked her teeth, something not considered impolite among her species.

"Or deserve it," Mrraurr said, who had a persistent greasy smudge behind one ear hole.

"Or dishonor themselves." Ekek tilted his head back and sucked down gibbets of raw flesh.

"If you kill crews, it will spread the wrong sort of reputation," Doctor Tchkit argued. "The Navy will take an interest in hunting us down."

"As far as the rest of the Confederation is concerned, we probably all died in the *Yamar*'s crash," Harlan said.

"Unless Prasek spread the word that we didn't," Skarst said. "He certainly seemed like the type to cash in on someone else's misfortune. That's why I don't believe I'm in the clear for Krastins' debt. After we embarrassed him and showed his mine isn't a safe site for illicit deals, he's probably had to spend a lot of capital in upgraded security and cleaning up his reputation. He'll want his revenge on us however he can get it. If that means spreading the word and hoping we get taken down by the Navy, or by bounty hunters, he wins by proxy."

"I think he'd prefer not to be noticed at all, since he's selling to the Hind," Tchkit pointed out. "We have a clean burrow," Tchkit said. "And we shouldn't shit in it."

"Shit happens," Harlan countered. "I'm willing to say we won't *intentionally* kill crews, but you can't be a space pirate without bloodying your sword on a few throats," Harlan said.

Ekek clacked his beak. "I approve of that phrase." He raised a flask and poured the dark liquid across his tongue.

Harlan nodded. "Thought you might." He drank some of the Jemmar tea that had a stimulant effect upon him, like strong coffee. It had a sweet, woody taste reminiscent of cinnamon and cedar. "Mrraurr, how ready are the ships?"

The Hind crossed her muscular arms across her upper torso and leaned back. "The *Regina* is full up on ammunition, power, and fuel. I've got her shield efficiency up to a hundred and fifteen percent. She'll shrug off anything short of a siege laser. And I installed that infernal device you gave me to modulate the shield frequencies. It seems to be working, but we won't know until we fire the weapons." She grimaced, showing all her pointed teeth. "I still think the beams will reflect back and blow us into shrapnel. Hind shields are not meant to be fired through. If we could do so, don't you think we would have developed the technology by now?"

Harlan finished his tea. "Sometimes these things take an outsider's perspective. How about the *Vengeance*?"

Mrraurr shrugged, a gesture similar enough to its human analogue. "She will fly. Her skipdrive is functioning. Her hull tests as spaceworthy. She needs a Hind jumpdrive to be truly effective. You should find me one."

"It's on the shopping list," Harlan said. "Skarst, what of our target?"

"The *Shostavari* is a medium freighter that blew through here three days ago. Refueled, two days of rest and recreation for the crew, and departed yesterday. Ship's manifest was plain enough. Sanitation components for another colony, or so they said. Her lift-mass ratio was way off and one of the Constable's techs managed to pull a sensor reading from it. They're smuggling high-energy power cores, which means military-grade tech. This far away from the front lines means they're probably moving stolen parts into the black market."

Harlan smiled. "Technically, that's us. Are we ready to get paid?"

Mrraurr slapped her torso. "Say the word, Captain."

Harlan looked around at his four officers: the Aski Shantar, the Jemra, the Ri'Ar, and the Hind. "Sapients, let's go hunting."

CHAPTER NINE

The *Vengeance* rose into the Lanovoss sky, her drive howling like a banshee. Skart's slender hands flew the ungainly vessel with confidence. A crew of two other Aski Shantar assisted her, and they would remain on station with the *Vengeance* when Harlan and the *Regina* departed. Doctor Tchkit was already aboard the *Regina*, preparing his sick bay for what he fully expected would be an upsetting number of casualties suffering from particle-beam burns, blade wounds, and the effects of explosive decompression. Mrraurr ran back and forth between the engine rooms of both vessels, alternately cursing out her incompetent crews or trying to make last-minute adjustments to the *Regina*'s power core to eke out every last erg of energy. Ekek and his marines, fully armed and armored, were ready to bring their wrath upon the hapless smugglers.

With the rest of his crew handling the details, Harlan was freed to work in his lab, but it was not going well. He'd spent every waking moment of the past weeks trying to recreate the nanotechnology he'd designed back on Earth, but it was a discipline that no race save the Hind had developed throughout the Confederation. From what Mrraurr had told him, the Hind had written it off as far too dangerous and unpredictable a technology to continue researching. That meant he was forced to reinvent nanotechnology from the ground up, designing the machines to design the machines to fabricate the machines to fabricate the nanites, and he couldn't get it to work. More than once, he'd thrown his inventions across the lab or smashed them with his Hind axe in sullen frustration.

His parahuman ability with technology didn't seem to work nearly well with the varying technologies of the Confederation. He could deal with it on a macro scale. Electricity and mechanical motion were universal constants, and he could work his power upon them. But when he got down to the microscopic robots of nanotechnology, his power was all but useless. Confederate computer programs operated on wide and variegated foundations, and he couldn't manage to make a synthesis to get them to work together on something they were not designed to do.

With Doctor Tchkit's help, he'd extracted a pint of his own blood and stored it in a device that kept it viable. He was using it as a testbed for the nanotech as he developed each new generation. The most recent version showed promise, but like all the others, it failed within minutes of its introduction to the blood. Even worse, it dissolved in the blood, introducing toxic elements that would have killed him had he injected it into himself.

He leaned back from the lab table and sighed, feeling the weight of his repeated failures. It had been years since he'd run across a really difficult technological problem. This one was repeatedly getting the better of him, and he was running out of ideas to pursue. On Earth, he'd developed his own nanotech based upon years of work done by others before him. Unfortunately, he had nothing to draw on here but his own knowledge, and it was incomplete.

What to do? He knew the answer; he just didn't want to admit it because it felt like such a huge step backward. He'd carried his armor within his own body. The knowledge of the internet and thousands of terabytes of accumulated data stored on the servers of the Preserve were ready for him at a moment's notice. He could fly through the skies and through space. He had defeated superheroes, invading aliens, and an entire battle group of warships, all on his own. Not anymore.

Fine. He'd go old school.

When he was a child, he'd built a mechanical suit of armor using wrecked vehicles in a junkyard. The Destroyer Mark I was a gigantic ungainly hulk, powered by internal combustion, hydraulics, and pneumatics. Mark II had basically still been a tank, albeit more svelte and functional. Mustang Sally herself had destroyed Mark III, which had been the pinnacle of his non-nanotech development. He could recreate that, he supposed, using Confederate technology.

No, he wouldn't accept that the Mark V would be a step backward. Confederate tech was far advanced over human tech in many ways, and he could utilize that advancement. He was Harlan Washington, the Destroyer, and he wouldn't let himself create substandard work just because he couldn't use nanotech. There would be another way. There was *always* another way.

He just had to figure it out.

In the meantime, he couldn't let his pirates do all the work of raiding and stealing without him. It was important for soldiers within a criminal organization to know their leadership was willing to do the same work. It strengthened team bonds, just like far more legitimate corporate enterprises had eventually discovered. More to the point, it showed street soldiers that the bosses were capable and dangerous, which tended to keep seditious behavior to a minimum. They respected strength and capability, and as a clear outsider, Harlan knew he needed to display those characteristics.

He spent time adapting materials and clothing already available within the *Vengeance*'s inventory. He started with a modified Hind skinsuit to protect him from vacuum exposure, either intended or accidental. He'd lopped off the back half of the suit and reconfigured the life support systems to function with his physiology. The helmet was the most frustrating, as no race in the Confederation had a head even remotely close to the size and shape of a human's. He wound up modifying a spherical storage container with interior padding, communication and light-intensifying technology. He was still working on developing a mobile heads-up display and knew that would take weeks.

The ship's stores didn't have any military-grade material from which he could fashion any suitable hard armor, but there was a supply of heavy ablative cloth that formed the basis for most soft body armor throughout the Confederation. Harlan was no tailor, but he'd managed to cobble together a serape-style poncho of ablative cloth treated to be resistant to particle beams and lasers. It would hurt if someone shot him—indeed, it could still kill him—but he had a far better chance of surviving such an attack. He'd added an underlayer of a cut-resistant mesh that would function like Kevlar. Kinetic weapons like bullets or edged weapons like blades would have their force redirected and spread out.

Doctor Tchkit, who was handy with such things, helped him fashion a pair of boots to which Harlan attached armored greaves, as he did with bracers for his forearms.

He pulled the serape over his head, then strapped his bracers over his arms. He pulled on his boots and buckled a holstered Aski Shantar-style particle beam to his hip. He'd drilled out the blade of his Hind axe, making it light enough for him to comfortably wield in hand-to-hand battle if that became a factor. He slung that over one shoulder. Other tools and implements he thought might be useful went into pouches around his waist. Finally, he set the helmet over his head and locked it to the skinsuit. With a couple finger taps, he activated the helmet's systems. It wasn't lost upon him that he was basically wearing a fancied-up version of a child's makeshift costume, complete with a pot for a helmet. He smiled at that. It wasn't quite the appearance of someone used to terrifying others with his presence, but it would be a start.

Outside of his immediate crew and the citizens of Lanovoss, nobody had seen a human before, and that gave him the advantage of being unknown. He would play that up as much as possible. He needed his reputation to spread outside of the system, carried upon fearful whispers and rumors. That reputation would in turn give him the cachet he needed when he took the war to Clan Sharassar. And who knew? He might even find a way back to Earth from them.

Back to Penny.

* * *

Harlan stepped onto the bridge of the *Vengeance* and looked out across the starfield. "How are we doing?"

Skarst didn't turn away from the controls. "All systems nominal, Captain."

"How long until we reach the skiplane terminus?"

"Six minutes," Skarst said. "If the *Shostaravi* is on course and on schedule, we'll hit the system two hours after her."

"And it's a transition system?"

Skarst spun her seat around to regard him. Her copilots continued their work, preparing the *Vengeance* for skiplane travel. "There's nothing of note in the Krewest system, but that doesn't mean it isn't the *Shostaravi*'s ultimate destination. Smuggling is risky enough work without inviting the scrutiny that comes from performing it in well-traveled systems. Krewest is an uninhabited system, with only a gray dwarf and few dozen planetoids. It has no significant resources worth exploiting." She turned back to her controls. "If it was me doing the smuggling, I'd want to transfer my cargo someplace like that."

"You and I see things similarly," Harlan said. "*Vengeance* has power to burn, and the *Regina* even more so. We'll run a sensor sweep as soon as we enter the system. Perhaps we'll get lucky and catch them napping."

Skarst's wordless snort made it plain she thought that unlikely.

One of Skarst's copilots triggered the shipwide intercom. "Skiplane transition in one minute. Captain, you should strap in."

Harlan knew he probably should do as suggested, but in all the work that had been done to make *Vengeance* spaceworthy, nobody had gotten around to fabricating a seat for his physiology. He took hold of the back of Skarst's seat with both hands. "I'll be fine like this."

He felt something wrap around his knees and glanced down to see Skarst's tail snaking around them like an organic safety belt. She said nothing and didn't even indicate she'd done anything, so he resolved not to mention it.

"Transition in six . . . five . . ." The copilot counted down, slightly faster than seconds as the Aski Shantar measured time in different intervals. At *one* the starfield seemed to shatter into a billion points of light, flying in all directions.

Harlan felt his own body torn apart at a quantum level as he experienced what Einstein had called *spooky action at a distance*. His subatomic particles entangled themselves with counterparts in the Krewest system, and as he ceased to exist in Lanovoss, so did he instantly become recreated many light years distant.

The violation of physics didn't bother Harlan—parahuman abilities had been doing that for as long as people had powers. His stomach didn't care for the transition across a skiplane, and he grimaced against the tide of bile threatening to escape. He'd have to talk to Doctor Tchkit about working out a chemical solution to his FTL-induced nausea.

"Transition successful," reported a copilot. "All systems nominal."

"Give me a full sensor scan," Harlan said.

Skarst turned her long neck to look back at him. "Is that wise? You'll be announcing our presence."

Harlan nodded absently before remembering that it was still a human expression. Then he shrugged it off; Skarst had been around him for several weeks. She was smart enough to start understanding his nonverbal communication.

"It's the most effective way to know if the *Shostoravi* is in the system or not. If they aren't, we'll know they moved on. If they're here . . ." He paused. "I want them to know we're coming."

* * *

Krewest being a small system, the sensor sweep was completed in a quick couple of minutes, and a copilot said, "Contact! One mark in polar orbit around the planet!"

"Is it the *Shostaravi*?" Harlan asked.

"No way to tell," Skarst said. "*Vengeance* only has basic sensors. It's still a freighter."

"What are the best sensors? Military?"

"I'd say first-in survey scouts," Skarst said. "Ships designed to enter a new system and fully map it within a few days, along with pertinent information on planetary subsystems. They can also be configured to locate specific energy emissions, which means technological sources."

One of the other copilots looked back over his shoulder. "Some researchers believe the Osi Fain can do the same thing with their natural senses."

"It would stand to reason that a natural spacefaring race would have senses attuned to it," Harlan mused. "I'll have to look into that. What's your name, pilot?"

"Miskabo, Captain."

"Give me your resume in less than a minute. I assume you're reasonably good or Skarst wouldn't have you sitting beside her."

Skarst clicked her teeth in agreement.

"I piloted a colony ship to Lanovoss. Fell in with Quarest and her outfit after I made some questionable choices in a card game. Haven't flown since then until now." He cleaned an eye with his tongue. "It's not very impressive, I'm afraid."

"I appreciate the honesty," Harlan said. "And your other copilot?"

"Triskewt," said the other. "I'm a skimmer pilot, and I'm only here because I can read a display better than someone who's never done it before."

Harlan sighed. "This is the best you could find?" He asked Skarst.

She turned to him. "Lanovoss isn't exactly a deep pool of talent."

"Any indication the other ship has spotted us?"

"Not yet. Or if she has, she hasn't responded. For all she knows, we're just another ship passing between skiplane termini. No reason to hail us if we haven't hailed her," Miskabo said.

"The ship's in a polar orbit around a gas giant in an uninhabited system," Harlan said. "There's no reason for it to be here at all. Let's get a closer look and see if it's the *Shostaravi* after all."

"Setting a course now." Skarst adjusted some controls and the *Vengeance*'s engines took on a sharper tone as more power fed into them. "Engaging skipdrive."

Seconds ticked by as *Vengeance* jumped a few thousand kilometers with each skip, racing in toward Krewest I and its silent satellite. Harlan felt a trickle of anticipatory sweat roll down his face. His stomach did barrel rolls from the repeated skips through alternate dimensions. "Can you pull up any more detailed information about that ship?"

"Negative," said Triskewt after adjusting the sensors. "We're still too far away and that gas giant has a powerful magnetosphere. It's scrambling the feed. Nothing but garbage is coming back."

"Let me see." Harlan reached past the Aski Shantar and pulled the sensor display toward him on its armature. The Aski Shantar leaned back to watch, content to let his captain do his job. Harlan caressed the sensors with his power, finding the settings deep within them to compensate for the planet's distortion. Of course they were using it, he reasoned. Natural camouflage was effective when someone didn't want observers to see what they were up to.

The recalibrated sensors began to pull more useful information, but Triskewt gnashed his teeth at the data.

"This makes no sense," he complained. "That can't be the *Shostaravi*. The profile is all wrong. The drive signature is detuned, like the damn thing is running a mismatched set of engines . . ." He trailed off as his brains put all the data together.

Skarst was ahead of her copilot. "It's two ships, docked together. They must be transferring cargo."

A bright indicator lit up on the board and Miskabo grunted something untranslatable. "Sensor ping."

The sensors finally resolved an image at extreme range to show two ships in proximity. One was unmistakably the *Shostaravi* from its hull profile and drive signature. The other had a wide, blocky appearance that Harlan found all too familiar. "That's a Hind ship."

"They're splitting," Triskewt said. "I don't know if they finished transferring cargo. I'm reading debris between them."

"Can we salvage it?" Harlan asked.

"No, it'll decay and fall into the gray dwarf before we can get to it," Skarst said.

"Leave it, then. Can *Vengeance* intercept the *Shostaravi* before it makes it to the skiplane terminus?"

"I don't know. Maybe?" Miskabo said. "It depends on how heavy a load they're still carrying."

"We're going to lighten *Vengeance* in a minute," Harlan said. "Do what you have to but do not let that ship escape the system. Shoot their engines out from under them if you have to. We're taking the *Regina* after the Hind target. Skarst, let's go."

Harlan and Skarst left the bridge, heading for the *Regina*.

"That other ship's a destroyer," Skarst said as she padded along beside Harlan. She wore a cloak of similar design to Harlan's poncho, deeply bifurcated in the lower back to give her tail plenty of freedom to move. The leather straps normally worn directly over her scales now rested atop the cloak for easy access. She had a particle beam pistol strapped across her narrow chest, but Aski Shantar had no need of knives with a mouth full of sharp teeth.

"So am I," Harlan said, rather amused by the pun. "The *Regina* can take her."

"You have no idea if that's true."

"No," Harlan admitted. "But I've never let that stop me before."

Ekek met them at the *Regina*'s hatch. His crest was raised in anticipation of battle. "My team is ready, Captain."

"Good. Tell everyone to strap in and hold on tight. We're heading out hot," Harlan said over his shoulder as he and Skarst hustled toward the bridge.

Mrraurr was just leaving the bridge as Skarst and Harlan squeezed past her. "I don't know if you will fit or not," she growled at Harlan. "You have an awkward and poorly-designed lower half."

Harlan looked and saw the Hind had made a seat that, although oddly-proportioned, he should be able to sit in comfortably enough. "Thank you," he said. "This is unexpected."

"Don't thank me yet," Mrraurr called as she pelted toward Engineering. "It was that or get the shields tuned. I didn't think we'd be departing so quickly." A pressure door slammed shut behind her.

"What does she mean, tuning the shields?" Skarst asked as she slipped into her own seat and began slapping controls, bringing the *Regina* to life like awakening a sleeping dragon. The *Vengeance*'s air pumps evacuated the hangar deck.

Harlan sat in his own seat, yanking straps across himself and tightening them. The seat was a little too wide with no lumbar support and lacking in padding, but it was better than nothing. "Hind weapons can't fire through their own shields. It's poor engineering. Back home, I developed an algorithm to modulate my laser frequencies to penetrate Hind shielding. Unfortunately, Hind weapons don't take well to that modification without losing efficacy, so I thought I could more effectively modulate the shielding—"

"By my tail, do you *ever* stop talking?" Skarst snarled. She tapped a button with one clawed thumb and the hangar doors wrenched themselves open, showing clear space beyond. The *Regina*'s lateral thrusters fired, sliding the ship out of its berth, and then Skarst opened up the main engines.

The *Regina* shrieked forward, leaving the *Vengeance* behind as if it were keeping station instead of burning flat-out.

An instinctive, ululating cry of pure joy echoed through the bridge and Harlan realized it was his. He hadn't felt such a thrill since the first time he'd fired up his experimental boot jets and catapulted his armor into the skies for the first time, some three decades earlier.

"Are you ill?" Skarst asked, her hands blurring across the controls. "I can call Doctor Tchkit."

"No. No, I'm fine." Harlan smiled. This was where he belonged. "Let's have a look at our prey."

He pulled the sensor display to him. It identified the Hind vessel as something called a *Lagash*-class destroyer. It was a small warship, barely larger than the *Regina*, with single laser turret and beam-resistant armor. Like all Hind vessels, it carried shields, and their shields were already engaged. The vessel was not broadcasting any type of transponder code, reinforcing to Harlan that they were engaged in the transport of illicit goods.

"They're more heavily armed than we are, and better armored," Skarst said. "But we're faster in normal space."

"How long will they need to activate their jumpdrive?" Harlan asked, knowing that if the Hind ship succeeded, they would escape.

"Three minutes to clear Krewest I's gravity well and then they're as good as gone."

"Can we intercept before then?"

"Depends."

"On what?"

"On whether you want any power to the shields."

"No," Harlan said. "Charge the cannon but put all other power reserves into the drive."

Skarst snarled at the controls. "Surviving is overrated."

Harlan reached out and patted her narrow shoulder. She turned to look at him, surprised at the contact. "We're not going to die today. Will they understand me with my Prodoni language ability?"

"Do you speak Hindish?" Skarst retorted.

Harlan opened the intercom to Engineering. The din over the small speaker was impressive as the engines drove the *Regina* forward, pushed to their limit. "Mrraurr, am I speaking Hindish to you now?"

"What kind of excremental idiocy is that?" The Hind yelled back. "Are you addled?"

Harlan shrugged. "Maybe. I need fractional control of the lasers."

"It won't work, Captain. I don't have the components installed yet!" Mrraurr yelled.

"Then I'll have to fake it." He looked at Skarst. "If the other captain can't understand me, I'll need you to translate for me."

"Of course. I don't have anything else to do right now."

"Just stay on an intercept course and be ready for evasive maneuvers." He wished he had the Aski Shantar gift for focusing on multiple tasks at once. His hands worked on the *Regina*'s weapons and defensive systems as he tried to use his parahuman power to force them to work as he needed them to. Ultimately, it would come down to trial and error, as so many of his inventions did. "Hail them."

Skarst tapped a button. "Unknown vessel, this is the *Regina*. Shut down your engines, depower your shields and weapons, and open your airlocks." She glanced at Harlan, who nodded.

"Good enough. Let's see what they have to say."

A growling Hindish voice emerged from the speaker. "This is Submistress Prokasher of *Rawarsh Dagger*. Who dares send empty threats to a proud vessel of Clan Rishkot?"

Harlan paused in his reprogramming of the laser system. "Rishkot. It's your lucky day, Captain Prokasher. If you'd said Sharassar, we'd have blown you to shrapnel without another word. I am . . ." He paused. His name would mean nothing out here. Honestly it meant nothing back on Earth either. There was only one name he'd ever used that left a lasting impression. People remembered it when they remembered nothing else about him. "Destroyer."

"Destroyer only of toilets, I suspect," Prokasher said with a laugh.

Harlan refused to be baited. "Surrender and prepare to be boarded, and you may yet get away with your hides intact."

Raucous laughter from multiple Hind throats echoed from the comm system. Harlan knew not only did Submistress Prokasher understand him, but so did her crew. "I'm going to take away the ship you've clearly stolen from its rightful owners and return it as my prize, and I will line my favorite pillow with your fur, thief."

"Good luck with that," Harlan retorted. He snapped off the comm.

"That went well," Skarst said.

"Give me fire control," Harlan said. Skarst complied. He was juggling settings on both the laser and the sensor readings of the *Rawarsh Dagger*'s shields. The Hind weapons system was temperamental, and each fractional adjustment he made seemed to have no bearing on the data the system reported back. His ears were growing hot and he wished he had functional nanotech so he could fly over to the *Rawarsh Dagger* and peel it open like a tin of sardines.

Then, without any fanfare, the laser quietly aligned itself within the frequency zone he needed to bypass the *Dagger*'s shields. He aimed at the Hind ship's drive section and depressed the firing stud.

Skarst whipped the *Regina* laterally as the *Rawarsh Dagger* dropped its shields and fired first.

Harlan cursed as his own shot went wide and the *Dagger*'s beam carved a white-hot groove across the *Regina*'s starboard armor.

"First blood," Skarst grumbled. "Still think this is a good idea?"

Harlan stabbed at the firing controls and was rewarded with a beam lancing across space to vaporize some of the radiation baffles around *Rawarsh Dagger*'s engines. His second shot struck the *Dagger*'s freshly renewed shields and dissipated without further harm. "Dammit!" He pounded his fist on the console. The *Regina*'s controls were so limited compared to the flexible technology his nanotech had provided. He had been a surgeon and was reduced to carving up his targets with a blunt axe.

Blunt axe.

"Skarst, give me helm control and take over the guns," Harlan said, an idea forming.

With a swipe of her claws, Skarst reconfigured the controls to switch them. "What are you going to do and is it going to get us killed?"

"Something unexpected, and I don't think so. *Regina* is a tough girl. She'll hold together." He opened the engines to full and the warship shot forward, closing the distance to the *Rawarsh Dagger* in seconds.

The other vessel fired again, burning all the way through the armor into one of the cargo bays. Alarms screamed for attention as pressure doors slammed shut to seal off the leak. Skarst wasn't sleeping on the job, and she stippled beams from dorsal and ventral turrets into the *Rawarsh Dagger*'s engines. Something flared and one of the drives dropped from a brilliant white-blue to a dull red before the shields went back up.

A moment later, Harlan brought the *Regina* alongside the *Dagger*. "All hands, brace for impact," he shouted.

"Wait, what are you doing?" Skarst shouted in disbelief.

Harlan wrenched the *Regina* over and sideswiped the other vessel like he was broadsiding a car off the road.

The *Dagger*'s shield generator was designed to repel high energy particle beams and lasers. It had no chance against several thousand tons of armored warship. The generator overloaded in a spectacular explosion amidships. Secondary explosions tore through the hull as additional systems failed from the energy feedback loops. The *Dagger*'s engines flared and died.

The *Regina* suffered in the impact too, although with her shields already down, the damage was primarily to her hull and those systems Harlan and Mrraurr had cobbled together from spare parts. The Hind typically overbuilt their ships and a collision was damaging but not necessarily fatal . . . unless one or both ships had their shields up at the moment of impact.

Skarst winced and her tongue lashed out to explore a cut along one cheek, oozing blood the color of canned beets. The collision had shaken her hard—and probably everyone else on the crew as well. If they hadn't been properly secured, well, Harlan and Mrraurr would probably be scraping their remains off the hull.

"Are you alive?" Harlan asked his copilot.

"I must be or I wouldn't be hurting this much. What in the icy frozen wastes were you thinking?"

Harlan bullied the controls until the *Regina*'s maneuvering thrusters grudgingly responded and put a few dozen meters of empty space between the vessels. Although most of the starboard side sensors hadn't survived the impact, Harlan managed to get a dorsal sensor realigned so he could take stock of the damage he'd done to the *Rawarsh Dagger*.

Extensive was the word that came to mind, and it did so with a wave of satisfaction in Harlan's spirit. The impact had been at an oblique angle that scraped and tore away hull plating along the *Dagger*'s port side. Her spine was twisted, with a definite cant that would undoubtedly cause major handling issues under acceleration or maneuvers. Atmosphere vented from several gashes along the impact site as well as from spots where explosions had caused additional trauma. Sparks spat from the turret mount as someone aboard the *Dagger* tried to turn it to target the *Regina*.

That wouldn't do.

"Since you're not dead, would you mind taking a few more shots at the *Dagger* so she can't shoot back or escape?" Harlan released his straps.

"Why, what are you going to do?" Skarst eyed him suspiciously.

Harlan returned her gaze. "Capture the ship. A prize is a prize."

"They'll never give it up without a fight."

Harlan smiled. "I'm counting on it."

CHAPTER TEN

One of Ekek's troopers had died in the collision when his harness snapped and catapulted him against a bulkhead, shattering his hollow bones. A few had broken bones and weren't in any condition to board the *Rawarsh Dagger*. Harlan sent them to see Doctor Tchkit. The rest were spoiling for a fight against the Hind and Harlan promised to deliver one. His only condition was none of them were to kill the ship's captain. Capture her if they could, wound her until she couldn't fight otherwise.

"The soldier who kills her will spend the next year on Lanovoss dock patrol under Constable Smitchy's close, personal supervision," Harlan said.

Nobody talked back to him. In the short time he'd been running the operation, it had become plain to everyone that he didn't make idle threats. He had neither the time nor patience to entertain fools who thought they could bluster their way through his resolve.

According to the *Regina*'s remaining sensors, the *Rawarsh Dagger* retained atmosphere in most of its sections, but the boarding party figured to make quite a few holes as they cleared the ship of defenders. Ekek's marines sealed their suits and helmets, as did Harlan. He kept his axe slung. The Hind would see it and although they wouldn't be afraid of him, they would be concerned how a mere monkey had obtained a true warrior's weapon. That overconfidence would be their downfall. The Ri'Ar couldn't fly with their wings encased in suit material, but they could still maneuver with their wings using small repulsor harnesses for

129

flight. With their hip-mounted energy beams and blades clutched in their talons, they would make a formidable fighting force.

They stepped into the *Regina*'s dorsal airlock, as the starboard side's portal was too damaged to open. The lock was built to accommodate Hind and fit all the Ri'Ar warriors easily. It cycled quickly and a moment later, fourteen Ri'Ar warriors and one Human emerged, all armed to the beaks. They jetted across the open space between vessels in tight formation, hip rifles at the ready. What they were doing went against conventional wisdom for boarding parties. The typical strategy would have been to disable the target's exterior defenses at a distance, followed by maneuvering the *Regina* close enough to connect a docking tube.

Harlan had eschewed that as too risky. Keeping the *Regina* at a distance and flying across a couple hundred meters of empty space ensured no enterprising Hind would slip behind them to attack Skarst, Doctor Tchkit, and a couple of reserve crew members. After everything Harlan had endured to obtain his first starship, he wasn't about to lose it in his first action of piracy. Attacking as individual soldiers gave them tremendous flexibility in where to strike. Ship defenses would be concentrated around the airlocks, leaving the rest of the ship much more vulnerable to what Harlan referred to as a *no-knock raid.*

The *Rawarsh Dagger* was a typical Hind vessel, long, flat, and ugly with one main deck and a superstructure jutting up from the front third. The bridge was on the higher deck, along with the Submistress's private quarters. The main deck would be awash with Hind warriors preparing to repel boarders and technicians and engineers trying to repair the damage Harlan had done in his sideswipe.

Harlan directed five of the Ri'Ar to move along the *Dagger*'s hull, setting limpet charges at vulnerable hull seams. The Hind most likely wouldn't send soldiers out to engage with the owl-warriors in open space. The powerfully-built centauroids would lose all their advantage in a zero-G situation against a foe evolved to fight in three dimensions. With the notorious inaccuracies in Hind targeting sensors and their general disdain for ranged weaponry, they might not even realize their hull was already crawling with attackers until it was too late.

"There, under the chin of the bridge section," Harlan said over his tightbeam communicator.

"Ri'Ar do not have chins," Ekek observed, "but I believe I understand your meaning."

"We'll blow into it from below. Anyone not in an emergency suit or belted down may get blown out through the hole."

"That may include the Submistress," Ekek said. "Have you reconsidered your intent to keep her alive?"

"I have, and if we lose her but gain the bridge, I call that a win for our side. There's a saying on my homeworld. *You can't make an omelet without breaking a few eggs.*"

"I find that remark in extremely poor taste," Ekek said. "Ri'Ar are an egg-laying species."

"What do you expect from a monkey?" another Ri'Ar said across the open channel.

Before Harlan could speak out, Ekek beat him to it. "Who said that?"

"I did. Kleketik," said the trooper from Lanovoss, bearing a long, *katana*-like sword.

"The Captain saved my life and won the *Vengeance* when you all failed to. Do you want to reconsider your words?" Ekek snarled.

"Jokes about eggs are rude," Kleketik retorted. "Captain or not, he shouldn't make jokes at our expense. Honor demands a response."

"Kleketik," Harlan said. "I am not given to apology as a rule, but I am also a stranger to your culture and I am still learning. Perhaps you can suggest a more suitable alternative to the phrase." It wasn't an apology, because as he said, Harlan didn't typically apologize for anything. It seemed to mollify Kleketik and the other troopers who had grumbled under their breaths.

"We have a saying as well. Perhaps you will agree with it, Captain," Ekek said. "*Before you fly, you must first fall from the nest.*"

"I see the truth in that," Harlan said. "And before we reap the spoils of this vessel, we must first take the bridge."

"Charges are set," Ekek reported. "On your order, Captain. I shall lead the charge aboard myself." He drew paired short swords and clutched them in his talons.

"That might be a death sentence," Harlan said. If the Hind were suited up and prepared for a boarding party on the bridge, the first two or three pirates through the breach were likely to die under the axes and lasers of the Hind crew.

"I will not send others in my stead. Honor demands I lead," Ekek said.

"Very well. All soldiers brace yourselves. Detonate the charges!"

The sound and fury of shaped charges carried into Harlan's suit through his grasp on a strut. He felt the vibrations from other detonations further down the hull. Something bulky flashed past him and he saw a vacc-suited Hind warrior floating away, twisting in vain to seal his helmet as his spinning axe gleamed in the sunlight.

From the pirates' perspective, they were standing above the hole they'd blown in the *Dagger*'s bridge, but compared to the alignment of the ship's artificial gravity, they were hanging below the floor like silver-clad bats. Ekek warbled a battle cry and jetted through the hole, his paired short swords flashing. Kleketik followed right after him.

Harlan drew his particle beam and dove head-first through the opening below him, meaning he'd rise up from the floor on the bridge. He emerged into a brutal but short-lived combat. Ekek was pinned against a bulkhead by a Hind axe buried in one wing. He spasmed as blood and air sprayed out in a bubbling mist. The Hind who'd struck him floated nearby, slowly spinning in the zero-G with one of Ekek's swords stuck hilt-deep in one eye.

Kleketik whirled through the bridge, his jets opened to full as a Hind tracked him with his laser. Harlan shot the Hind through the back of the head. A heavy body crashed into him as another Hind flew across the bridge toward him. The Hind was unarmed, which meant it was most likely a female as a male would die before letting go of his axe. Harlan twisted out of the centaurian's grasp and shoved himself down against the deck, using his legs to kick the heavy creature onward until she crashed awkwardly against a bulkhead. He shot her before she could gather herself for another charge.

The rest of the Ri'Ar troopers boiled through the breach, their jets venting clouds of propellant in all directions as they made short work of the remaining bridge defenders. Two of the Hind made the intelligent decision to surrender. They lowered their vacuum-suited heads and snarled as the Ri'Ar bound their fore and rear legs together. Their arms couldn't be bound behind them—Hind physiology didn't allow for it. Instead, their arms were bound tightly to their sides, drifting in the zero-G of the bridge.

Kleketik drew an emergency bubble made from transparent plastic around Ekek and took the wounded soldier back into open space, heading for the *Regina* and Doctor Tchkit. One team of marines headed down to the main deck to clear or capture any remaining defenders. The rest of the team erected an emergency force screen across the breach and repressurized it with breathable air.

Harlan removed his helmet to look upon his two captives.

The two Submistresses stared back at him in open-mouthed astonishment.

Their response to his appearance wasn't anywhere close to sufficient evidence that he'd arrived to the Confederation in a different time than he'd been in back home. It still felt like he was a man out of time as well as out of place, and he hated that feeling of not being in complete control of his surroundings. He quashed those feelings; they were unproductive and had no place in the psyche of a pirate captain. "Well . . ." he said as he regarded the Hind. "Which of you is Submistress Prokasher?"

"I am . . . *monkey*." The Hind's tone was challenging.

Harlan raised his particle-beam pistol and leveled it at her. "I'll thank you not to call me that again."

Prokasher spat, her globule dancing through the zero-G of the bridge like a wayward comet. "You are a filthy primate with bark beneath your nails and the stench of vegetables on your breath. You surround yourself with barbarians from an uncultured, undeveloped world with no more honor than insects. I wouldn't sully my claws and teeth with your stinking monkey flesh to kill you."

Harlan shot her, of course.

He turned his gun toward the other Hind. "It appears you've just been promoted, Submistress. Do you approve?"

She yawned to show her disinterest. "I'd have taken command sooner or later. Prokasher was . . . a poor strategist."

Harlan had learned much about the Machiavellian politicking that went on in Hind culture during his brief incarceration aboard one of their ships. The mix of aggression, drive, and bloodthirstiness formed a perfect storm of a society in constant conflict with itself. Harlan figured he could exploit that with a little consideration. "What is your name?"

"I am Submistress Tshalikah of Clan Rishkot. You clearly don't like being called a monkey, but I have no idea what you are. I have never seen your species before."

"I am called Destroyer, and that is all you need to know about me for the moment."

Tshalikah inclined her head in a small but gracious bow. "Then Destroyer is what I shall call you. What do you intend to do with me and my crew?"

"Your crew . . ." Harlan glanced toward one of the Ri'Ar troopers, who made a slashing motion with the blade clutched in one foot. ". . . Is dead. And the *Rawarsh Dagger* is now my ship."

Tshalikah said nothing. Harlan approved. She was adhering to the old Mafia philosophy of *let the man speak; when he is finished, let him speak some more*. He would have to be careful about falling into his old habit of monologuing. It had plagued him since he was a child, for he was always surrounded by people much stupider than him, and he felt like he constantly had to explain himself.

"You, however, present me with an opportunity. I'm going to let you live."

"I am grateful." Tshalikah watched him through narrowed eyes.

Harlan holstered his pistol. He wished he could pace but doing so in magnetic boots was awkward and would probably look foolish. "I'm going to let you depart aboard the *Shostaravi*. I have their cargo; I don't care about anything else."

"Why? Why release me? I'm your enemy, Destroyer. I will find my way back and decorate the bulkheads with your entrails. It may take me sixty turns of the seasons, but I will hunt you down. If I die before I find you, my spirit will carry on and you will never have a peaceful rest again."

"That's quite a threat. How about this in return?" Harlan narrowed his eyes. "I don't care about you. I'm not afraid of you. I don't care about your Clan. I care about exactly one thing in this universe, and that is the total destruction of Clan Sharassar. Go to their Clanmistress. You tell her . . . I'm coming for them."

* * *

Harlan had lied when he said he didn't care about anything except the destruction of Clan Sharassar. As he'd grown older, he'd been frankly *astonished* to discover there were things he cared about. He'd cared enough for his younger sister Reggie that he'd built an entire base upon Earth's Moon just to protect her. He cared about her son, his nephew March, whom had grown into a confident young man despite Harlan's awful parenting skills. He even cared about Mustang Sally, his former enemy, who'd given of herself freely to help him bring peace to his sister at last.

And then there was Penny. As he watched his crew stripping the useful components from the *Rawarsh Dagger*, Harlan found his thoughts straying back to the woman to whom he'd given everything he'd built upon the Moon. He wished she'd been around to see him drive the *Regina* into the *Dagger*'s side, to witness his ferocity as he fought alongside the Ri'Ar troopers. Would she approve? He hoped she would.

He'd probably never find out. Better he stopped thinking about her altogether. She might be a hundred years dead, or a thousand. Or she might not yet have even been born.

Submistress Tshalikah had gone quietly to the *Shostaravi*, disarmed and thoroughly humiliated at her defeat by what she saw as lesser beings. Miskabo and Triskewt had successfully intercepted the fleeing freighter with the *Vengeance* and escorted it back to rendezvous with the *Regina*. The *Vengeance* crew had imprisoned the *Shostaravi*'s skeleton crew in a hold while they unloaded her cargo and stowed it in one of their own holds for later inventorying. Now they were stripping the *Rawarsh Dagger* under Mrraurr's supervision. His Chief Engineer was giddy at all the components she found aboard that could rebuild and upgrade the *Regina*.

It took three ship-days of work, but the crew fully stripped the *Dagger* and set her remains on a degrading orbit toward Krewest I. All evidence of their activity would vanish beneath the clouds of the gray dwarf. *Vengeance* kept a sharp sensor watch for any vessels entering the system. Two did during the stretch, but neither deviated from the course between skiplane entry points and didn't even have active sensors running. Skarst inquired whether they should intercept either one, but Harlan didn't want to push his luck. They'd been lucky to deal with two vessels, one of which was a warship. His crew was tired from their ceaseless work on the *Dagger* and the *Regina* was in need of some dry dock time to fix the damage she'd suffered under Harlan's piloting.

Skarst had been quietly judgmental about the unorthodox tactics, but even she had to admit they had been effective. Such strategy was inspired and unfamiliar to her, which meant Harlan was bringing a unique perspective to the Confederation in general. He knew that advantage would eventually fade as word about him spread.

When the stripping was done and the last bits of debris tumbled into Krewest I's atmosphere, Skarst flew the Regina back into her berth aboard the Vengeance and they headed for Lanovoss.

Harlan took some time to visit Ekek in Doctor Tchkit's sickbay. "Come to see life in the neighbor's burrow?" Doctor Tchkit asked him.

"I've been busy," Harlan replied.

"Yes, I'm sure being a pirate captain is incredibly time-consuming," the Doctor said. "Well, I do have good news for you. Ekek here should make most of a full recovery."

"Most?" Harlan looked at the bandaged and immobilized wing. The Ri'Ar slept upright, talons locked around a floor-level rack designed for just such a purpose.

"Yes, most. He's going to have difficulty flying for the rest of his life. I can only do so much with the

137

trauma to the wing muscles and tendons. Plus I had to remove most of his feathers on that side to perform the surgery. He'll grow some new ones when he molts, but they may never be equivalent to those on his undamaged wing. At the very least, it will be an obvious flaw in his appearance and that may make him an unlikely candidate for breeding."

"Breeding?"

Doctor Tchkit checked information on his scanner without looking up at Harlan. "Ri'Ar mating rituals are complex and evolved through ritual displays. Does not appearance matter to Humans? It is common to all other species. Even the Prodoni select their mates partially based upon variations in physical appearance that most sapients cannot even detect."

Harlan considered this. "I would like to speak to him when he is conscious."

"I will notify you," said the Doctor. "Now, what about the dead?"

"The dead? You mean the crew of the *Rawarsh Dagger*? They died fighting, as is every Hind's wish."

"I mean your own dead. You lost three Ri'Ar crewmen in this incident. One from your ridiculous ram and two in the fighting." Tchkit opened a cabinet and withdrew a wide-mouthed plastic bottle. He unscrewed the lid and poured some fragrant, fruity alcohol down his throat. "By my count, that's fifteen percent of your boarding party. Twenty percent if you count Ekek here, who's unlikely to survive a future boarding action if he's idiotic enough to participate." Tchkit took another pull from his bottle before sealing it and tucking it away again.

"Piracy is dangerous work."

"Of course it is. If it were easy and safe, we'd all be pirates every day just for the swagger. But if you're going to keep losing people, you're going to find it harder and harder to keep your vessels crewed."

"You're saying I need to offer an incentive. A reason for sapients to *want* to join my crew."

"It would keep shit from happening." Doctor Tchkit chuckled at his own joke.

"The dead sapients will receive a full share of the spoils," Harlan said. "To be distributed to their surviving families if we can find them. In fact, I'll issue an order for all crew to designate their inheritors."

"What about those who are injured and can no longer serve in a useful capacity? Or those who choose to leave your organization?"

Harlan folded his arms. "You've been thinking about this quite a bit, I see."

Tchkit blew out his cheeks. "I'm a doctor. That's more than just applying salve to particle beam wounds and stitching up axe cuts. I have to think about the crew's well-being. And in this case, that tends toward financial reward." He chuckled again. "Nobody becomes a pirate out of the good of their hearts." He paused. "Except maybe for Skarst, because I'm not sure she has one."

"Has one what?" Skarst asked as she walked into sickbay.

"A reason for coming to sickbay," Doctor Tchkit said smoothly. "Are you wounded or ill?"

"No. I came to tell you that we're about to land, Captain."

"You couldn't have just mentioned it over the ship's intercom?"

The scales around Skarst's eyes darkened in an Aski Shantar blush. "Well, yes, I could have, but I also wanted to ask for a few days off." She held out a hand and Harlan saw the scales upon it had gone a translucent white.

Harlan looked sharply toward Doctor Tchkit, an unspoken question on his lips.

The Doctor tugged at his ears. "Ah. Of course. Captain, she's about to slough."

"Shedding her skin? Reptiles do that on my homeworld."

"It is more than that. It's a hormonal cycle as well. I don't know if the biological terminology will translate," Doctor Tchkit said. He rummaged through a drawer and found a tube that he handed to Skarst. "This will help with the itching." He looked back at Harlan. "It is called estrus."

Harlan blinked. "She's . . . in *heat*?"

Skarst's face scales darkened more. "It is a natural process of my species, and I'd be rid of it if I could. I hate the itching, the swelling, the stupid obsession with breeding." She thumped her tail in frustration. "All I can think about is those two fine copilots on the bridge and how badly I want to rut with them both." She rubbed her palms down her sides, shedding a few errant scales onto the sickbay deck. "It's tying up both my damn brains and I can't think straight."

"Take all the time you need," Harlan said. "We won't depart again until you're, uh, back to yourself." He paused. "Are you going to . . . lay an egg or something?"

Doctor Tchkit burst into laughter. "That's not how it works. I can provide you a treatise on the subject if you're really curious."

"I may kill you yet, Doctor," Skarst grumbled.

"Shit happens," Tchkit said with another laugh.

"I'm not curious," Harlan said. "I just want to know how long I'll be without my second-in-command."

"Four to six days for the biological processes to complete" the Doctor said. "You may notice lasting emotional effects for up to twice that period while her hormonal patterns return to normal."

"I'm right here," Skarst said.

Harlan turned to her. "I have no judgment against you, Skarst. Your biology is your own business. Take whatever time you need. The organization can function in your absence."

"Badly, I assume," the Aski Shantar retorted, and left sickbay.

CHAPTER
ELEVEN

Days stretched into weeks, although the Confederation didn't use an arbitrary number of days to measure the passage of time. With dozens of inhabited planets and asteroids and space stations all with different orbital and rotational cycles, *day* was a subjective term. The young central government of the Confederation had implemented the Universal Time Standard to facilitate in interstellar trade, politics, and military operations. Most planetary civilizations simply defaulted to their local schedule, and knowing what the UTS time was didn't matter to most sapients.

Harlan spent every waking moment that he was not being a space pirate in his lab, trying to reinvent nanotechnology that had never been developed except by Humanity and the Hind. Without a sufficient grounding in either civilization's precursors to nanotech, he wound up throwing away test after test. He was furious with himself. He was supposed to be a technological genius—at least, that was how he'd been described in Just Cause files. The problem was his ability grew less and less accurate as he reduced the size of his microscopic robots. Some fundamental flaw was not only preventing them from functioning as he'd designed them, but he couldn't even exert the least bit of control over them.

He'd even relented from his position of *I work alone* and managed to find a couple engineers and scientists willing to work with him on developing the proscribed technology. Both were Aski Shantar females and clutch-sisters. Their names were Lancas and Raskt, but

Harlan privately thought of them as Yellow and Green, from the coloring of their eyes. They cheerfully set all four of their brains to the task of developing a true Mark V suit, built from the ground up instead of repurposing scrap and cast-off tech. They never lost sight of the goal even though their work was largely defined by repeated failures.

His ability helped immensely with the design of macro-scale armor, utilizing the advanced electronics and flexible actuators that formed the backbone of Aski Shantar technology. Hind shield technology was powerful and could be miniaturized into a suit of armor. The generator for the shield they'd deployed over New York was small enough to fit in a shuttlecraft. He figured he could miniaturize it to backpack size, with a super-efficient Aski Shantar power cell driving it. The Mark V would retain cannons—primarily because there was something immensely satisfying to the thunderous roar of rapid-fire shells. They also formed a low-tech solution to the problem of Hind shielding, as it was far less efficient against kinetic weaponry than against energy.

Harlan didn't discount energy weapons, and chose to install lasers over particle beams as they scaled to a useful size better than the bulky particle beams. He could have gone with rifle-sized p-beams, but that wouldn't mesh with his chosen moniker of Destroyer. The Ri'Ar had given him the idea of hip-mounted auxiliary weaponry. The lasers could be used for surgical strikes and point defense when required, while the primary cannons could chew apart targets. If he could ever get his nanotech working again, he'd integrate the system he'd designed on Earth that allowed his armor to literally reload the cannons from the material on which he stood. He continued to experiment with nanotech using Confederation technology, and kept running into dead end after dead end.

As Harlan worked on his projects, his organization continued to grow and develop with little oversight from him. Constable Smitchy ran the docks so effectively and profitably that he decided to run for and was elected as the colony's First Selectman—essentially making him the Mayor of Lanovoss City. Unfortunately, that made him greedy, and Accountant reported to Harlan that there might be some profit-skimming happening to Smitchy's benefit. His waistline expanded at the same rate as his greed, and Harlan confronted him to rein him in before the Jemra overreached.

"We don't shit where we eat," Harlan told Smitchy, who blinked in surprise at the way the angry Human had interrupted his expensive midafternoon meal. "And you don't prey upon the citizens here. Ship crews are fair game, but if I hear one word about a protection racket, or price gouging the locals, I'm going to skin you and make you into a sleeping rug. Don't test me, Smitchy."

The threat was effective enough to make a roasted seed fall right out of the Jemra's mouth onto his plate. Having delivered his warning, Harlan returned to his work. He told Accountant to keep an ear out—metaphorically speaking, since Prodoni didn't have aural sensory organs—for any further evidence of Smitchy's cheating. He knew he would eventually have to kill the Selectman. Once someone like Smitchy got a taste of true power, they only wanted more and more.

Accountant gave him regular reports on the organization's profits, which were growing, and inventory, which was churning quickly thanks to the continued influx of stolen goods and distribution of said goods to the citizens of Lanovoss and to outbound freighters.

Skarst took the *Vengeance* out on a few raids of her own, returning twice with a hold full of stolen cargo. She also managed to capture three smuggling freighters and the chop shop crews took them apart with great efficiency. Taking a cue from Harlan, she was careful not to use her real name among the crews of vessels she captured or boarded. She'd chosen *Blizzard* as her name, which among her people suggested near-certain death.

Once, she came back empty-handed with several dead crew and limping in a badly-damaged *Vengeance*. They'd run afoul of a Naval cruiser she figured had been on the hunt for them. They were lucky to escape at all, and took a roundabout path returning to Lanovoss to avoid pursuit.

"I think we should lay low for a while," she said, scratching at a fresh scar across the scales of one arm that she'd earned when a console on the *Vengeance*'s bridge had overloaded and exploded.

"That's what I'm doing," Harlan pointed out.

"That's *all* you've been doing," Skarst said. "If you are trying to build a reputation, you're going to need to make an appearance now and then at your own piracy actions." She snorted derisively. "Right now, I rather think I'm more infamous than you as Blizzard."

"Is that so terrible?" Harlan asked. "It's more than you were before we met."

Skarst twitched her tail in growing irritation. "This is your war, Harlan, and you're not bothering to fight it. All you do is hide in this damn laboratory, working on your tiny little robots that don't work and your armor that doesn't seem to ever be close to finished. We have a saying among my people. Only a fool tries to outrun a river."

"What is that supposed to mean?"

"It means that you can run as hard and fast as you can until you drop dead from exhaustion, but the river remains and will flow over your body."

"Sounds kind of like the saying that insanity is repeating the same thing over and over again, expecting different results," Harlan mused.

"That's exactly what you're doing!" Skarst screeched at him.

Ekek took a step forward. The Ri'Ar had appointed himself Harlan's bodyguard since recovering from his wing injury enough to be upright and mobile. He could barely fly in a gravity well, and discovered that in zero-G he could do little more than spin in circles.

Determined to be of use, he shadowed Harlan as the man raced feverishly from one project to the next. He stood quietly out of the way, remaining as still as a statue for hours at a time until Harlan forgot he was there. At a perceived threat, the Ri'Ar was still quick to respond and his hip-rifle twitched at Skarst's effrontery.

She ignored the owloid and pointed at the jars of Harlan's failed nanotech experiments, mostly filled with inert, gritty slime. "Maybe it's time you gave up your nanotech dream and move on to more practical concerns, like the fact that the Navy is looking for us. Not just you. Us. Destroyer. Blizzard. Even the Doctor there," Skarst said as Doctor Tchkit entered the room.

"Sorry, what did I do?" Doctor Tchkit asked.

"Shit is happening," Harlan grumbled.

"Oh, right. Well, I just came to remind you to eat since you seem to have a tendency to forget when you're working in here. I'm pretty sure you've lost nearly five percent of your body mass since you sequestered yourself." He glared at the two Aski Shantar assistants Harlan had recruited. "And the two of you aren't doing a damn thing to help."

Lancas and Raskt had the temerity to look astonished. "But he's an alien," Lancas managed after a stunned silence. "We don't know what his metabolism is supposed to be."

Doctor Tchkit dragged his fingers down his jowls in exasperation. "Save me from engineers," he said to nobody in particular. He swept across the room with such ferocity that the Lancas and Raskt shrank back. The vision of the angry, portly rodent made Harlan giggle. He looked down at his hands and saw they were shaking with fatigue and his skin had gone an ashen gray.

"We've been talking," Doctor Tchkit said as he pulled Harlan away from his workbench. Harlan wanted to resist but the doctor would not be denied. "Skarst and I. You are doing more harm than good in this lab right now, to your fledgling organization and to your body. They both require more attention than you've given them for days. As your doctor and your friend, I prescribe a meal, a bath, a full night's rest and a full day away from your projects."

Harlan gaped at him, exhaustion and hunger having dulled his senses. "You . . . are my friend?"

"We both are," Skarst said, taking his elbow. "And we aren't going to stand aside and watch you kill yourself over a project you aren't going to solve today, or tomorrow, or maybe ever. Why are you so damned determined to make your tiny bugs work?"

Harlan opened his mouth to berate his first officer—his *friend*—for her words, but they cut him to his core as he realized he didn't really know. The Confederation had a much higher baseline level of technology than did the Earth. Why wasn't he working with their existing designs to make something new, building upon technology that already functioned? Why was he wrestling with tech that had no foundation in this society?

The Hind, of course. They'd made it work. Maybe they'd wrecked an entire planet doing it, but they'd created the proof of concept for the races of the Confederation. Harlan wasn't about to let a race of bullies upstage him. He said as much while Skarst and Doctor Tchkit squired him away from the lab. Ekek followed quietly, bare talons clicking upon the deck.

"I don't think it's that you hate the Hind," Doctor Tchkit said as he sat Harlan down at a table in the galley.

Mrraurr sat off to one side, all four legs folded beneath her as she stabbed a knife into pieces of raw meat in a bowl and ate them with gusto. "Although he does," she said.

"Not all Hind," Harlan mumbled. Skarst handed him a cup filled with the sweet, dark liquid that tasted to him like candied celery. It was a Jemmar tea that had both stimulant and calming properties. He drank it, even though it was a little too hot. "You're all right."

"You say that," Mrraurr said, chewing on some gristle, "but you haven't seen the state of the engine room."

"Why, what's—" Harlan began.

"No," Skarst said. "No project talk. Not right now. You eat and drink now. Then you bathe, because you smell like a clogged septic filter."

"That's lovely," Mrraurr snarled. "Let's talk about that more while we're eating."

Doctor Tchkit and Skarst both sat across the table from Harlan, far enough away for him not to feel like he was being grilled, even though he knew that was precisely what was coming. Tchkit nibbled on some of his favorite roasted seeds but Skarst ate nothing. She leaned back against the bracing of her tail and crossed her arms, resting fingertips on shoulders in the typical relaxation pose of her species. "So . . ." she began.

"This is an intervention. I'm not a fan," Harlan said immediately.

"A what?" Doctor Tchkit asked.

"An intervention. When your friends and family gather around you to have what my mother called a *come to Jesus* meeting about your behavior. I hated my mother." He paused. "I killed her."

Doctor Tchkit blinked. "Goodness!"

"Not really."

Skarst leaned across the table. "Why are you doing this? The piracy. The experiments. Everything has this overlying tone of dread and fear and desperation. You're terrified about something, Captain. What are you afraid of?"

Harlan snorted. "I'm not afraid of anything. I'm the Destroyer."

"Desperate, then."

"I want to destroy Clan Sharassar." Harlan picked up a piece of food and shoveled it into his mouth, chewing and swallowing automatically without tasting it. Food was fuel. That was all.

Mrraurr interlaced her twelve fingers. "No. It's more than that. You're talking about more than three billion Hind. You couldn't do that if you had a million ships and a hundred million soldiers. And even if you could somehow, don't you think the rest of the Hind race would take that rolling over to expose our bellies? My own Clan Haurmash would be pleased immediately, having had our competition reduced, but then cooler heads would prevail. The Hindmistresses would unite to meet the new threat under the Accord of the Fist."

"The only reason the Hind haven't done that to the Confederation is because of the infighting between the clans," Doctor Tchkit said. "And you'd give them a reason to do exactly that. They'd hunt you down and kill you. Hunt down your homeworld and reduce it to ashes. There would be no landing of troops to take over, no threats. They would just destroy it. And then, they might decide to take on the Confederation after all, and I don't know if we would win. Are you ready to consign billions upon billions of sapients to death just because of your little crusade?"

Harlan shrugged. "What? Are you going to lecture me now about the greater good and how I'm not seeing the big picture and every other trite homily you can think of?"

"What's her name?" the Aski Shantar asked, and those three words stopped Harlan's rant more effectively than the most dire threat could have.

"Who?"

"Your mate, I assume. Whomever you left behind. The one to whom you're desperate to return. The reason you're working yourself to death and not giving a moment's consideration to the consequences of your actions."

"She's not—I mean, we're not . . ." Harlan slumped in his seat. "Penny," he said at last. "And I'm an idiot for thinking I have any chance to get back to . . . home."

Skarst leaned back. "You said you weren't anxious to return to your homeworld. I think perhaps you weren't being fully honest with me."

"Maybe not." Harlan sighed.

"So now that we've identified the problem, we can help you solve it," Skarst said.

"Unlikely." Harlan yawned, suddenly struggling to keep his eyes open.

"You might be surprised what we can do," Skarst said, her voice sounding like it was coming from a great distance. "But for now, you're going to get some rest."

"D-did you . . . drug me?" Harlan's face felt thick and numb.

"Shit happens," Doctor Tchkit said, and it was the last thing Harlan heard for quite a while.

CHAPTER TWELVE

Harlan felt bright sunlight streaming upon his face even before he opened his eyes. He thought he should probably be angry at his crew. Clearly Skarst, Doctor Tchkit, and even Mrraurr and his avowed bodyguard Ekek had conspired against him. Drugged him.

They'd forced him to rest, damn them.

He opened his eyes and was nearly blinded by the bright blue sky overhead. He squinted, waiting for the floating pink and green spots to dissipate from his vision. He'd spent so long aboard his ships, darkened for the visual comfort of the other races, that he'd forgotten what truly bright light was like.

He was lying on a mat of woven grass, layered with some kind of cottony batting that made it soft and fragrant. The symphony of scents almost overwhelmed him—floral, sweet grass, and even dust. Birdsong and insect buzzing assailed his ears. The hot sunlight beat down upon him, making him feel like he ought to be sweating, but instead he was strangely dry. He sat up and raised his hand to shield his eyes so he could look around and froze as he saw his arm.

His skin was not his own; it was the right color, but had a peculiar grainy texture that seemed more like fine sand than flesh. He reached out to touch it and realized his other hand and arm appeared to be made from the same material. That led to further investigation by which he discovered he was naked, and his entire body appeared to have been transformed into sand. All the details were there from fingernails to nipples to his knobby knees, but they were all made from sand.

"This is a dream. I'm dreaming," he said aloud. He ran his grainy tongue across gritty lips and felt the roughness of his sandy teeth.

As a rule, Harlan never dreamed. If he did, the images and experiences created by his subconscious were fleeting, disappearing within a second or two of his awakening and only leaving behind a vague uneasiness, as if he'd been privy to something he had no right to see. If he was truly dreaming now—and he had no reason to believe otherwise given his peculiar bodily transformation—he wondered if he would forget it all when he woke. He was probably still aboard the *Vengeance*, lying in his berth with Doctor Tchkit's medical sensors keeping a watchful eye over him.

He stood and turned a slow circle, looking at the surrounding veldt, dotted with thick-trunked, wide-spreading trees that he tentatively identified as baobabs. That gave him pause. Baobabs. Veldt. Endless expanse of blue skies. It was central Africa, but not the Africa of his homeworld. No, this was the Africa described to him by Mustang Sally, Minerva, and his nephew March. It was the idealized Africa of the Dream-world created by his sister Reggie, a land of magic and wonder.

Why was he there?

His nephew March could enter the Dream-world thanks to the parapower he'd inherited from his mother, but Harlan had never experienced such a thing himself. He didn't know it was even possible. It made his scientific brain clench in white-hot fury. This went against *the rules*.

"Wake up, Harlan," he said aloud. "Wake up, damn you."

The land did not reply. Nor did the trees nor the birds nor the insects. Everything continued as it had, and would probably always continue whether or not he was present.

He might as well move. Sitting around feeling sorry for himself over his predicament would do nothing to improve his attitude. At least the act of putting one grainy foot in front of the other would give him something to do until he awakened.

His bare feet moved through the golden sward. He could feel the grass against his skin and the irregularities of the ground underfoot even though he was made of sand. He wondered if he was leaving bits of himself behind as he walked, and that was unnerving enough a thought that he turned to look. He only saw the bent grass as any mark of his passing. If he'd left sandy footprints behind, he couldn't see them.

The sun beat down upon him and he found himself wishing he could sweat. The air was thick and still, humming with the song of cicadas and the birds diving into the trees to pluck them free. Was this what it had been like for Sally when he'd sent her into the Dream-world to find Reggie? It seemed so real that his life aboard the *Vengeance* felt like it was the dream, fading into vague memories.

He reached the crest of a small hill and stopped. Below him, at the bottom of the gentle slope, was a river. Blue water swirled with mud from the hundreds of creatures interacting with it. He dropped into a crouch lest they see him and bolt or attack. He saw zebras and lions side by side, drinking the water and studiously ignoring each other. Waterfowl quacked and squawked at a crocodile as it drifted slowly through the water like a lumpy green log, content simply to exist within the cool liquid. A herd of deer of some kind nibbled delicately at the greenery along the water's edge, while a family of cheetahs lapped at the water nearby. Further downstream, he saw a pair of giraffes awkwardly bent over, their legs spread wide as they slaked their thirst. A mother rhinoceros stood belly-deep in the water while her calf frolicked in the mud, joyfully splattering through it as it chased after a pack of yipping hyenas.

Harlan didn't realize how long he'd been crouching, watching the creatures below, until a heavy footstep behind him shook the ground. He whirled to see a massive leathery gray pillar. His gaze traveled up until he was staring at the massive head of a gigantic elephant. He'd never been so close to one in his life, and he made a small, nonsensical bleat of terror.

"I will not hurt you." The elephant spoke in a rumbling whisper that reverberated around Harlan. "If you are thirsty, you may go down to drink at the river. It is a place of peace and safety."

"You . . . talk. Of course you talk. All Dream-world elephants talk, don't they?"

The elephant flapped its ears. "Why are you hiding here?"

"I—I don't know."

"Are you afraid of the beasts at the river? They will not harm you. They only come to drink, to bathe, and to enjoy the water. You can do that too."

Harlan looked down at his sandy flesh. "It's not that. I am hot, and thirsty, but I'm made of sand. If I get wet, I think I'll fall apart. That turns this dream into a nightmare."

The elephant regarded him. "You should not be made of sand. Sand is dead. It is of the earth. You are alive. You are of the stars."

Harlan laughed. "Life comes from the stars?"

"All life comes from the stars."

"So you want me to just . . . not be sand anymore? How does that even work?"

The elephant tore a swath of grass loose from the ground beside Harlan with its muscular trunk and tucked it into its mouth, chewing thoughtfully while regarding him with its unblinking eyes. "There are those who would invoke an ancient game when you want to ask questions. I, however, have no interest in playing that game."

"I don't know what that means."

"I would not expect you to." The elephant paused. "Come down to the river with me. Drink. Bathe. Enjoy it."

Harlan considered. "I'll come down with you, but I don't want to get in the water. I'm . . . afraid."

"You do not need to be afraid while I am with you," the elephant said. "You may ride upon me."

Before Harlan could say that he was just fine walking, the elephant curled its thick trunk about his waist and lifted him gently onto its massive back. He splayed out his limbs to keep from sliding off as the beast made its ponderous way down the gentle slope toward the river bank.

The other animals greeted the elephant as a friend, in voices ranging from the rhinoceros' gravelly roar to the hyenas' barking laugh to the high-pitched piping of the waterfowl. The elephant exchanged cordial greetings with all of them until the general goodwill and camaraderie made Harlan feel like diving into the river anyway just so he wouldn't have to hear it anymore.

The elephant waded out into the middle of the river until the water came up to its belly. It slapped its trunk against the water, splashing it everywhere, then flapped its spray into a fine mist with its ears. "Ah-h-h. That is so much better. You should try it, sandy-man."

Harlan shook his head. "I'll die."

"You won't die. Water is life."

"You just said life comes from the stars."

"Life comes from the stars, yes, but water nourishes that life. I will show you. Let me wash that dead sand off you that you may find your life."

"Wait!" Harlan cried, realizing he was trapped on the elephant's back in the middle of the river. The trunk came up and a jet blew him right off his perch. He felt his body come apart like a sand castle overrun by the tide. He tried to scream but his mouth was gone. His body was gone. His dream had become the worst nightmare.

He splashed into the river behind the elephant. How had he done that when his body had disintegrated? He had . . . limbs. His arms flailed and his legs kicked and his head sank beneath the surface. He struggled and managed to force his head above the water for a moment. "I can't . . . swim . . ."

The elephant splashed more water across its back. "Nonsense. Of course you can swim. Your body is a machine and you can speak to machines. All life forms are machines."

Harlan sank beneath the surface again. The water around him was filled with dark, swirling shapes. He kicked and found his way up to the surface long enough to gather one more lifesaving breath. "How can life be a machine?" he asked. Why was he continuing his conversation instead of screaming for help? It was a dream, of course, and logic had no bearing upon it.

"Life is the most complex machine ever devised, engineered through millions of years of trial and error, of innovation and discovery," the elephant said, sounding like an insufferable college professor. "And you can speak to machines."

Harlan slipped underwater again, and this time he felt his strength flagging. His lungs felt like they would burst against the water threatening to force its way inside his mouth and nose. If he died in the Dream-world, did that mean he would die in real life?

A shadow like a torpedo with legs and tail floated over him. It was the crocodile he had seen before. *All life forms are machines*, the elephant had told him.

Harlan reached for it—not with his hand, but with his power.

He nearly gasped with delight, which might have killed him since he was underwater. He truly *saw* the crocodile for the first time, through the filter of his ability to understand, communicate with, and control machines. It was more than just a submersion predator out for a lazy float down the river. It was an impossibly complex network of interconnected systems. Blood flowed through its veins, a hydraulic power system to feed the striations of its muscular actuators. An incredible reactor filled its torso, burning the fuel of its prey, of the very air it breathed, and converting it into the energy that powered the pump at its center. Even its tiny reptile brain, barely a few cubic centimeters of dense energy-rich matter, functioned like a high-end control system, delivering directives to the musculature, reporting on sensory inputs, and triggering specific responses throughout the creature's body. It was alive, but it was also a machine, and Harlan could speak to it like a machine.

The crocodile dove beneath him and rose, buoying him to the surface like a raft. They returned to the air and Harlan couldn't tell where he ended and where the crocodile began. They were connected at the most intimate level, their machinery interfacing and their control circuits aligned. He was the crocodile and it was him, and together they became an even more fantastic machine than the two by themselves. As Harlan looked down at himself in wonderment, the elephant spoke. "Now you understand."

"Life comes from the stars," Harlan breathed, feeling like a true living machine in a way he'd never before managed with his nanotech.

"And to the stars you shall return," said the elephant. "And thank you."

"For what?"

The elephant reached for him with its trunk. "You never stopped caring, even after half a lifetime."

The trunk touched him and the Dream-world flared into bright darkness.

* * *

Harlan's eyes flew open with a name on his lips. He sat up in his bunk, looking around the darkened chamber that was his kip aboard the *Regina.*

Regina.

The ship he had named for his sister, who had spent two decades in a coma after being assaulted as a teen. She'd died . . . or had she? Her spirit had gone out of her body, certainly, and the shell of her physical form had disappeared by a method Harlan couldn't understand. Sally said she'd gone into the Dream-world. She'd called Reggie the Elephant Queen. Had she survived beyond death? Physical laws didn't apply to dreams. Perhaps life and death had different meanings there as well.

Harlan felt an unfamiliar tightness in his chest. Someone else—a lesser, weaker person—might have called it sadness, but Harlan wasn't one to dwell upon emotions or their consequences.

Still, if Reggie's spirit was alive in the mysterious dimension of dreams, it wasn't something that should trigger sadness. It was good news. Maybe he would see her again there someday.

The dream fled his conscious mind as quickly as Mustang Sally running at the speed of sound. He didn't remember exactly where he'd been. He didn't remember what had been said to him, or what he'd said in return, but he remembered the elephant.

He ordered the room's lights up to a level where he could function comfortably, which would have seemed impossibly bright to the other crew members. He swung a workstation screen in front of him, activated a graphics application, and began to draw. He was nobody's artist, but he was an engineer, and if he thought of his work as a blueprint, it was easier for him to direct the display the way he wanted it to look. When it was finished, he regarded his work with a critical eye. It wasn't fantastic art. It might not even qualify as good. It certainly wouldn't strike fear into those who looked upon it—at least, not yet. On a black background sat a representation of an elephant's head done in white, with boldly defined sections representing ears, trunk, tusks, and eyes.

"Oh good, you're awake," said a voice, and Harlan turned to see Doctor Tchkit regarding him in the room's door. "I set the computer to alert me when you regained consciousness."

"You drugged me," Harlan said, accusingly.

"Yes. Yes I did. And I'll do it again if I see you doing such a poor job of taking care of yourself." The Jemra put his hands on his hips. "This is the part of my job that's, well, my job."

"How long was I out?"

"Most of two days. You were exhausted. Now I expect you to eat a meal, drink some fluids, and get some physical exercise before you return to your lab."

"I'm not returning to my lab," Harlan said. "At least, not yet."

"Good!" Doctor Tchkit squinted a smile at him, then grew suspicious. "Why not?"

"I've got a different idea and I'm going to run with it, see where it takes me."

"What's that?" Tchkit pointed at Harlan's art project.

"A pirate should have a flag. A logo. On my homeworld, the cliché logo is a human skull with two stylized bones crossed beneath it. It's supposed to strike fear into those who see it."

"That . . . doesn't look anything like a skull. At least, not for a Human like yourself. What is it?"

"It's an elephant head. They're the largest land animals on my homeworld. My sister had an elephant doll that she took with her everywhere she went."

"So this logo is to commemorate her? I approve of that."

"And to strike fear into the hearts of my enemies."

"If you say so." Tchkit tilted his head sideways as if to see how it changed his perspective of the image. "It doesn't seem particularly, uh, terrifying."

Harlan smiled. "Not yet. Can you have Mrraurr locate some paint for me?"

Doctor Tchkit sighed. "I'm a doctor, not a messenger."

"Then have Skarst prepare the *Vengeance* for departure."

"Still not a messenger. Where are we going?"

"Back to Tokras. I made Skarst a promise and it's time to fulfill it."

CHAPTER THIRTEEN

Harlan, following Doctor Tchkit's orders, had what was for him a large breakfast. He ate mechanically, not really tasting or even thinking about the food. It was a bun stuffed with a sweetish ground meat mixed into a binder reminiscent of sharp cheese. Bright, peppery herbs infused the bun, which had a crispy but bland coating brushed onto it. He supposed it was good. He finished it and washed it down with a large glass of the Jemmar stimulant tea. He was already anxious to begin the next phase of his project.

Ekek had waited patiently for Harlan to return to consciousness, and now that he was up and about, the owloid padded along behind him. The sound of talons clicking upon decking would have irritated Harlan, was it not so familiar that he didn't even think about it anymore.

He went to his lab and found his two Aski Shantar assistants cleaning up after their latest failure to make functional nanotech. "Boss," said one. "We tweaked your latest design to see if it would take, but we still can't get the processors to accept programming at that micro scale."

"Forget it, it's done," Harlan said. "We're going to approach this from a completely different direction. I can't make the designs from my world compatible with Confederate technology. Maybe given years to do it, I could make it happen, but I have a different idea."

"What's that?" asked the other.

"Make the Mark V ready for field deployment. I'm going to run with it for the foreseeable future."

"It's not ready!" Yellow raised her hands in protest.

"It will *never* be ready. There will always be something else I can add to it, something I can rebuild, something I can improve. That's the nature of technology. It never sits still for long. How soon can you have it running?"

The assistants conferred and decided they could have it operational in half a day.

"Good. Make it so." He called Accountant.

"Yes, Captain?" the Prodoni replied.

"I need all the information available on the Osi Fain species."

Harlan spent the next several hours reading and rereading as much as he could find about the peculiar spaceborne race. Little was known about them beyond their biology, which was as complex as could be expected for a species that had evolved in the ocean of space. Their name was Prodoni in origin, as they had been the first to positively identify and research the beings. The word was a bastardized version that could be pronounced verbally by the rest of the Confederate species, since Prodoni language was largely based upon color patterns and skin texture.

Osi Fain meant *Sky Crab*, which was an apt description.

The Osi Fain preferred to inhabit nebulae, especially in young star systems with lots of free minerals floating around for the taking. Their metabolism was partly photosynthetic and partly based upon complex organic chemistry. They clustered around gas giants the way undersea worms clustered around volcanic vents back on Earth.

They could jump from system to system on skiplanes, suggesting they could sense the points of entry and exit. They could accelerate and decelerate faster than the most powerful starships, and the only way to catch one was by repeatedly engaging a ship's skipdrive until it was close enough to use weaponry. Osi Fain were not without defenses, either. They could generate powerful plasma beams that tore through energy shields and turned ship armor and hull plating white hot. Their rocky shells were proof against lasers and projectiles.

Nobody knew how their senses worked, or anything about their unique form of telepathy. The consensus was they were sapient, but Confederate scientists continued to argue about how smart they actually were. Because of their ability to travel interstellar space without requiring huge reactors or fuel reserves, and their powerful offensive and defensive weaponry, Osi Fain were in great demand by the wealthy, who desired to control and display them, much like prize horses back on Earth. The military would have tried to use them as specialized scout and fast-attack vessels, but for the laws protecting them as sapients.

Skarst and her former captain must have been in a dire situation to have stooped to accept such a job.

Harlan had an idea about how he might make it right with the Osi Fain. His own take on the research suggested that they were definitely sapient and most likely intelligent enough to understand what he was going to attempt.

But first, he had some more work to do, and he returned to his lab fully against Doctor Tchkit's orders.

With Mrraurr's help, he installed a radiation shield on the Mark V. Together, they added layers of hardening protection to the systems of the *Regina* and the *Vengeance* so the radiation from Tokras Prime wouldn't destroy the vessels' operating systems. Using the knowledge he had about Hind explosives, Harlan added some enhancements of his own design to one of the warheads they'd acquired in their initial theft of the *Regina.* He figured the yield somewhat conservatively and asked Skarst to check his figures, since she was clearly better at it than he was. She came back with an amount that was higher than he'd hoped. When she said she thought it was stupid for anything that small to generate that much explosive force, he smiled.

"That's why people call me *Destroyer.*"

* * *

They hit Tokras immediately after the cessation of a flare from the parent star, using the Hind jump drives to bypass skiplane entry points to appear in between the gas giant and the moon upon which they'd crashed. Skarst thumped her tail in satisfaction as the *Regina* materialized out of jump drive exactly where she'd intended. *Regina* sported a fresh coat of paint across her bow, an uneven smear of black that looked as if someone had smeared the very depths of interstellar darkness upon it. Centered in the black was a brilliant white representation of the elephant head logo Harlan had designed, five meters tall and wide. The contrast in color also offered a contrast in sensor reflectivity, thanks to the lattice of energy-conducting microfibers. It could be masked when required, but the rest of the time, the elephant head would appear on sensor screens to announce the *Regina*'s presence to all and sundry.

Skarst had almost balked at the idea, but Harlan convinced her that spreading their reputation would be done most effectively by use of the logo, and since flags were impractical at the distances required for interstellar travel, this would be the most practical method. Harlan smiled to himself as he imagined Prasek's people activating their sensors after the flare's termination, only to see the *Regina* bearing down upon them from above. "Skarst, give me fire control," he said. "I'll do this myself." He disengaged the forearm cover of the Mark V and slipped his unencumbered arm through the gap so he could operate the *Regina*'s controls.

Skarst unlocked the weapons controls and Harlan set his targeting reticule upon the blocky ship Prasek's people had used when they'd salvaged the remains of the *Yamar*.

"Don't break the egg," Skarst warned. "Or this whole trip is for nothing."

"They'd be fools to keep it on a ship when it's safer from the flares underground," Harlan retorted, and fired the *Regina*'s laser cannons.

The beams slashed down into parked ship's hull, slicing into it and igniting its fuel core. A silent explosion tore from the ship's aft and the engines blew themselves apart. Debris careened across the moon's barren landscape, bounding in slow motion from the light gravity.

"Nicely done, Captain," Skarst said. She held her clawed hand over the communication controls. "Shall I hail them?"

Feeling giddy with success, Harlan changed the target of the ventral cannons. "No, I'm sure they're quite busy. We'll just let ourselves in."

Skarst's tongue dashed across one of her eyes. "All hands, brace for a hard landing. Marines, prepare to deploy."

Harlan fired upon the base's control tower. It was hardened against radiation to protect it from Tokras Prime's flares, but that hardening didn't extend toward defending against energy weapons. The tower shuddered and split at its base. Atmosphere burst outward in a cloud of icy particles as the tower toppled to crunch against the moon's surface. Harlan kept firing against the spot where the tower had been, sending heavy energy blasts against the floors below, cutting deep into the mine's administrative facilities. There might have been prisoners there, working as trustees or performing other menial tasks, but Harlan knew Prasek would have kept most if not all of them working in the mines below and left his own people up in their tower to lord over the prisoners. Unfortunately, any of the prisoners not in the lower levels would probably die from explosive decompression. It was better than dying slowly from radiation poisoning, which would be the likely fate of most survivors of the *Regina*'s assault.

"How are you going to find the egg down there in all that mess?" Skarst asked as she spun the *Regina* around to best strike the hole in the administrative building Harlan had made for her. "Assuming it's even still on this moon."

Harlan tightened his straps. "I whipped up a little something for that. I'll show you once we're down."

"Speaking of which . . ." Skarst dialed up the shields and inertial dampening field to full. "Contact in three . . . two . . . one!"

The *Regina* slammed into the wreckage of the administrative building, crashing through ceiling and three floors before coming to a rest. Even with the inertial dampening and the shields, the impact was terrific and Harlan felt like he'd been shot out of a cannon into a wall. Alarms hooted throughout the *Regina* as breakers tripped and reset or failed outright. Smoke poured into the bridge from the shield systems control panel, white hot and melting into slag from the massive power surge that backed up through it.

Harlan triggered the environmental systems purge to clear the air. "Mrraurr, dispatch your damage control team, prioritize for engines, shields, life support in that order."

Mrraurr's untranslatable growl was sufficient to tell Harlan she and her repair team were already hard at work.

"Ekek, is your team ready?"

"Aye, Captain. Kleketik will lead the assault."

"Secure the building and round up all survivors."

"What about the miners?" the Ri'Ar asked.

Harlan looked over at Skarst, who gave away no indication of her thoughts on her lizard face. He suspected this was potentially a turning point in their relationship as captain and first officer if he made what she perceived to be a wrong decision. "They're coming along. We'll have to pack the holds and corridors, but Reggie wouldn't want us to leave them behind. She's got enough life support capacity to keep everyone breathing for the couple hours we'll need. Doctor Tchkit?"

"Yes?"

"Break out your antirad injectors and prepare to receive patients. Maybe . . . a lot of them."

"I don't have enough on hand for that, and the miners are going to be dangerously irradiated," Doctor Tchkit chittered. "We'll have to keep them in the hold as far away as we can from critical systems and crew."

"Do what you can. I don't know how many we'll have." Harlan turned to Skarst. "You got this?"

She looked around the bridge, assessing the damage from their hard landing. "Yes, Captain. We'll be ready to leave on your order."

He held up a small unit he'd cobbled together as they were making final preparations to depart. "This little gizmo will detect Osi Fain electrochemical signatures, even amid all the hard radiation in this damn crypt."

Skarst blinked. "You just . . . *invented* that? Scientists have been trying to do that for years."

Harlan clipped it to his belt. "I didn't have years." He pulled his arm back inside the Mark V, sealed his helmet, and left the bridge behind.

Unfortunately, despite Harlan's faith that his device was assembled and functioning correctly, he couldn't track down the Osi Fain egg with it. Either the ambient radiation caused greater interference than he'd anticipated, or it was no longer on the moon. Frustrated with that discovery, he pocketed the device and went to dirty his hands himself.

Ekek's marines used life-detecting sensor sweeps and portable emergency airlocks to track down sapients trapped in chambers and sealed corridors. Most of the mine's administrative staffers did not survive the overhead bombardment, but to Harlan's great pleasure, Prasek turned up in the third group of survivors.

"He was hiding in a closet, Captain," Kleketik said, shoving the Aski Shantar forward with his hip-mounted rifle. "Like the coward he is."

"Now look," Prasek began. "We can work something out here. I'm connected. I'm very well connected. You need me." He blinked and squinted his one good eye under the brilliance of Harlan's suit lights.

"Do I." Harlan said it without making it a question.

"Oh yes, most definitely. I'm in touch with most of the smugglers in this region of space. You're that pirate, the Destroyer. You want rich prizes? I can deliver you rich prizes."

"Can you."

Prasek stammered as he realized his negotiation wasn't having quite the effect he'd hoped. "Y-yes. Rich cargoes."

"Name them."

"Well, there's, uh . . . I mean, I don't know specifically what any of them have on board right this second, but I've got sensor logs. Drive signatures. Last known courses."

"In your command center?" Harlan asked, motioning to the destruction around them.

"I've got backups!" Prasek screeched. "Secured and only I have the access."

"Hmmm," Harlan said. "Let's recap. You promise rich cargoes but you can't tell me what any of them are. You have course information for vessels within the system on the way to and from skiplane points, of which there are only two in this system. You have information stored in a mysterious backup that only you can access that will give me drive signatures of vessels. That information is useful to me how?"

"Well, I mean, it's drive signatures. You know, drive signatures? They, uh, they help you identify a ship."

"Which I couldn't possibly do any other way." Harlan raised his visor to let the scarred Aski Shantar look upon his face. "I'll tell you what, Prasek. You can buy your freedom with exactly one piece of information."

"What is it? Because I'm, uh, eager to help."

"Where is the Osi Fain egg you took from our wrecked vessel?"

"The what?" Prasek's eyes bulged out as he struggled to make himself as useful as possible.

"The Osi Fain egg," Harlan repeated patiently. "That you took. From our wrecked vessel."

"I d-don't know what you're talking about," Prasek said. "An egg?"

Harlan laughed. "You really don't, do you? You idiot. You left it on the wreck. You probably took the easy-to-reach components that you could salvage but you didn't bother to really search or you'd have found a prize worth more than all the components you took from the *Yamar.*"

"So . . . so are you going to let me go?" Prasek asked hopefully.

"Let you go. Yes, I suppose I will. You're no use to me. Go back to your closet," Harlan said, and turned his back upon the erstwhile mine director. Behind him, the fearful Prasek ran away.

"Captain," Ekek said softly. "Don't be a fool. Kill him."

Harlan shook his head even though the Ri'Ar might not understand the gesture. "No, don't waste your effort on him. We'll deal with him soon enough. I want to find that egg first. Have the troops salvage any medical gear and drugs you can, then get the surviving miners aboard the *Regina.* Doctor Tchkit has final say on where they go and if any of them are not worth saving."

"That's harsh," muttered one of the Aski Shantar marines.

Harlan ignored the lizard. "Find me a functioning surface transport. The Mark V doesn't have operational flight systems yet. I don't want to have to launch and land the *Regina* again."

"Aye, sir." The marines jumped to obey.

Harlan smiled. It was nice to be respected and feared again. It made him feel like a young man.

* * *

In Harlan's estimation, Prasek's people had done at best a slipshod job of stripping the *Yamar.* He might even have gone so far as to call it shitty. Dozens if not hundreds of useful components remained in the vessel, patiently awaiting someone with sufficient motivation to take them. It galled Harlan to leave them, but he'd come for only one thing, and he needed to find it and get away from the Tokras system before another flare erupted and stranded them—perhaps permanently. If a flare struck the *Regina* at the wrong moment, she'd wind up spiraling down to crash alongside the *Yamar*, or perhaps simply disappear into the clouds of the gas giant. Either way, it would mean the end of Harlan's war against the Hind and no chance of him ever returning to Earth.

There, he'd finally admitted it to himself.

He wanted to go home. Although he'd never been the least bit social or gregarious throughout his life, he wanted to see another human face. And if he closed his eyes, it would always be Penny's. Yes, all right, he was . . . attracted to her. This was a foolish notion, he knew, because the odds were great that he was in a completely different time than he'd left. He was pining after someone he'd probably never again encounter.

Penny being unattainable made it easier for him to allow his mind to wander, to fantasize about the reunion that would never take place.

He found the hold in which the egg had been stored. The hatch was jammed shut. He used a laser torch to slice through it. The severed door fell back into the corridor with a crash Harlan felt rather than heard. He stepped through the hole he'd made, careful not to touch the dully glowing edges. His suit lights lit the hold, showing where one side had completely crumpled against the side of the slope where the *Yamar* had come to her final resting place. Crates of whatever additional supplies they'd been hauling were crammed into one corner, overturned and battered.

The egg was still there. The spiny protrusions had an oily sheen from the complex chemical reactions they sustained to keep the hatchling within alive.

. . . Or *was* it alive? A jagged crack ran down the rocky surface, marked by a glittering white crystalline material. Was it like the albumin of an egg, and its leakage indicated the creature inside might have already perished? Or was it a natural sealing response to damage sustained before a living Osi Fain was ready to emerge?

Harlan reached out to touch the egg, careful to move his hand between the spines so he didn't slice open his suit. Despite their pliant and soft appearance, each one was as sharp as volcanic glass. His fingers brushed against the egg's surface and he shut his eyes, concentrating upon his parahuman power—something normally unconscious for him. If the Osi Fain's physiology truly resembled machinery more than biological life, he might sense something.

It spoke to him.

CHAPTER
FOURTEEN

The Osi Fain didn't use words any more than did a machine, but it definitely registered his presence. He could sense its entire self within the egg. It was like the most complex computer system he'd ever encountered, with its silicon-based physiology having far more in common with circuit boards and complex mechanical systems than their biological equivalents. He understood that he could have controlled it as easily as he could control any machine, but that felt . . . wrong.

Harlan had no desire to be a slaver, and whatever else the Osi Fain might have been, it was a sapient being. Controlling it without consent would have made him no better than the white men who'd dragged his ancestors across the ocean in chains. Once, when he was younger and angrier, he might have thought differently, but his hate had been tempered under the fire of decades. He understood tools for what they were and people for what they were, and the two were not always interchangeable.

The Osi Fain wriggled inside its egg, sensing his contact, reaching for him with something that wasn't quite telepathic, wasn't quite radio, wasn't even words, but it was definitely communication. He felt the creature's discomfort with its surroundings. Harlan knew the species thrived upon solar radiation, spaceborne minerals, and the complex chemicals of gas giant atmospheres, but here in the Tokras system, it was suffering.

The radiation infusing everything was too strong, too toxic for the Osi Fain's youthful metabolism to process.

The moon's gravity, light as it was, crushed the creature indelicately within its eggshell. It was . . . afraid. It cried out without words, begging for safety, for succor, for survival. Harlan felt something he didn't understand, because he had such a limited vocabulary when it came to feelings. Spending decades suppressing them wasn't conducive to learning to understand a new life form, especially one who was just a baby and terrified to boot.

Compassion!

The realization hit him like a laser beam. He felt compassion for the unhatched child. What was a baby Osi Fain called, anyway? The best thing he could do would be to remove it from this dangerous, toxic environment. Using his power, Harlan tried the unfamiliar task of sending telepathic waves of comfort at the baby. He felt foolish doing so, like he was trying to comfort a toaster.

Whatever he did had a soothing effect upon the child. Its unreasoning fear lessened underneath Harlan's mental touch. "All right," he said aloud. "Let's get you out of here."

Harlan's decision was far easier spoken than acted upon, for the egg was too large for him to pick up. Although it was roughly spherical, it was covered in the oily spines that would make rolling it difficult, for they would catch on everything and could easily pierce his suit if he wasn't careful. On Earth, he suspected it would have probably weighed as much as a piano. If he could figure out a way to roll, drag, or carry the egg without harming himself, he knew he could move it on the moon's low gravity.

Harlan smiled to himself. This was an engineering problem, and he knew how to solve those better than anything. He began scrounging around the wreckage for things he could repurpose into a useful conglomeration. At first, he'd been harshly judgmental of Prasek and his people's lax salvaging of the *Yamar*, but now he was glad for it. They'd left behind much he could use.

The baby Osi Fain's feelings ebbed and flowed as Harlan worked around it. His very nearness seemed to offer comfort even when he wasn't actively concentrating upon it. It grew more anxious as he moved away to retrieve tools, parts, and components. At least its cries were not so disturbing that he couldn't work. His improvised hoversled began to take shape. It wouldn't be easy, but it would be the safest way to move the egg back to the surface transport he'd left parked outside the wreck.

He flipped the switch he'd wired into the units that would raise the sled off the deck and a humming vibration transmitted through his boots. The sled shook and lifted off the ground a few inches, canting awkwardly as the repulsors he'd salvaged were functioning at different power levels. Without a master control panel to adjust them, he was forced to tune them manually, a process that was awkward, slow, and fussy.

A surge of alarm and terror from the infant hit him hard enough to make him drop a tool and knock a repulsor hopelessly out of alignment. He'd damn near have to start over. He turned to look back at the egg and gaped at it. The seam lined by the white crystals had split open, showing beneath a pulsing bluish material with faint pink and red lines swirling beneath its surface, like barely visible veins.

"What are you *doing*?" Harlan was aghast as the seam split further apart.

It was a stupid question, of course. The egg was hatching, and no wonder the baby was terrified. Being birthed was most likely a traumatic experience for any creature aware it was happening. Osi Fain were supposed to inhabit outside gravity wells, and Harlan had no idea what it would do to the baby, emerging from the safety of its cocoon into gravity and hard radiation.

The Osi Fain flowed out of its shell and Harlan gasped in spite of himself. It was a *fluid*. As it slid outward, Harlan was reminded of the Silly Putty Reggie

IAN THOMAS HEALY

had liked to play with—a cheap, rubbery toy made from an interesting chemical compound. It was something Harlan had later learned was called a non-Newtonian fluid, which was a fancy way to say sometimes it was soft and flexible and sometimes it was hard and resistant to impacts.

Harlan sensed the fear coming off the infant and he reached out with his mind, trying to contact the alien's own mind and offer what little comfort he could. He might have been a cruel and heartless bastard, but he had an ulterior motive that depended upon keeping this little bugger alive. He was going to trade it to the other Osi Fain in return for information. They were telepathic and he was perhaps the only sapient alive who might be able to speak with them, thanks to his parahuman power. As a spacefaring race, they might recognize what he knew about the Solar System. They might be able to tell where he was from, and show him the way to return. It was too much to hope that he was in the same time he'd left, but maybe he hadn't been thrown through time very far.

The two androids he'd built had helped him destroy the Hind fleet that attacked the Earth. They'd helped place the antimatter bombs and were, like him, trapped within the focus of the detonation. The Steel Soldier had been catapulted into the early '70s. Carousel had arrived more than two decades later. It wasn't unreasonable for Harlan to consider that he might have been thrown into his own past, but during his lifetime, or possibly into his own future.

The Osi Fain made a peculiar chirping sound in Harlan's mind and he wondered if it was crying, the way babies did. He didn't know what to do to soothe it, but it was probably hungry and miserable, stuck in an irradiated gravity well. An idea occurred to him and he reached toward the bluish putty. "Come," he said to it. "Let me help you. I know you can fly in deep space but maybe not here. Or maybe not without help. I can't lift you when you're just a puddle of slime, but I can be a crutch."

It was a complicated concept to convey, and Harlan was still learning how to use his powers in this new way. The Osi Fain infant spread out onto the deck in a perfectly circular puddle. Small bits on its surface jumped up, shaped like wave forms and even more complex structures that held only for a second or two before falling back into itself. Like Harlan, the Osi Fain was still learning about its environment and the being in communication with it. How intelligent were they? Was it like a human infant, basically a blank slate awaiting environmental stimuli and the instruction of a loving, nurturing parent? Or was it a fully-formed sapience, capable of higher thought and learning from the moment it left its shell?

Harlan knelt beside the puddle and extended a hand toward it. A column of the Osi Fain's body rose to meet it, separating into five finger analogues. It could count. It could mimic. It understood the gesture. It *had* to be sapient. Harlan wished he could touch it without the barrier of his gloves. Would that boost the level of communication? Would it be dangerous to the Osi Fain, or to him? He had so many questions and no way to gain answers short of his own experience.

The Osi Fain's pseudolimb wrapped around his hand, grasping it like a handshake. He felt its curiosity along with the underlying fear and . . . *pain*. It was hurting. Whether from the gravity, the radiation, or something else, the infant was suffering. Maybe it was dying, and it didn't want to be alone.

"Let me help you," Harlan whispered. Years ago, Mustang Sally had helped his sister. Her selfless act had changed Harlan. After decades of surviving on hatred and anger, he didn't need to be furious any more. Giving aid to another was a powerful feeling, even more so than destroying them.

The Osi Fain flowed up his arm, moving in a jerky, hesitant way. It squeezed too tightly and Harlan winced, making the creature freeze for a moment. It had understood his pain and when it moved again, it was more careful. "That's more like it," Harlan said. He knew he probably didn't need to speak out loud, but he was an inexperienced psi, and it made more sense for him to communicate verbally. His mind would echo his words and ensure there was no miscommunication.

The feeling of the Osi Fain flowing over his body was akin to being wrapped in thick mud. It was heavy even in the low gravity of the moon, and Harlan didn't think he'd be able to carry it in normal gravity without powered assistance from the Mark V. His mind started to work on the problem of adding high-powered artificial musculature to the armor, but he forced himself to set that aside so he could face the problem at hand. Osi Fain could fly, though. Perhaps it could fly with him inside it, like his suits of armor.

"Careful of my life support," Harlan said. "I need it to breathe. And don't cover my face unless you can make yourself transparent. I need to see where I'm going. I . . ." He stopped, then laughed. "I have eyes. No idea what *you* have."

The Osi Fain wrapped itself around him. He couldn't see himself, but if he could, he probably would have looked something like the Michelin Man, like a buffoon. Certainly nothing to strike fear and terror into those who looked upon it. Well, he would have to work on that. It closed over his helmet and face plate and for a moment claustrophobia took hold. He was used to being inside suits of armor, but not when he couldn't see at all. Then light began to show through as the Osi Fain did, in fact, make part of itself transparent. "More . . . More . . ." Harlan said, guiding it. "There." He could see through it as clearly as if he had nothing over his head at all; only a few pinkish veins around the edges gave any indication that the Osi Fain was still encapsulating him.

He tried to move and couldn't at all. He took a deep breath. He was going to have to teach the infant about joints and rotational points that he had but it did not. It had understood his need for a transparent face plate, and that he needed his life support. It would understand his need for movement too.

"I can only move in certain ways. Not like you," he said. "If you try to move me where I have no joint, or move a joint the wrong direction, I will break. It will be extremely painful or possibly fatal to me. Listen to my thoughts. Feel the pressure of my body as I move. Don't anticipate. Move with me. Don't resist my movements. Flow with me, like you are my own skin."

The Osi Fain understood him. At first, when he moved, Harlan felt like he was pushing through the water of a swimming pool. As he moved fingers, hands, head—every way he could bend, flex, or twist himself within the Mark V—the Osi Fain learned. It hardened itself along sections that didn't move, and retained maximum flexibility around the joints. It was like wearing a completely responsive suit of armor, something Harlan had never experienced before. His previous suit, the nanotech model he'd been struggling to recreate, came close. But it had been a part of him at a fundamental level. When it wasn't engaged, it sat within his body, just below the surface, ready to emerge at a moment's notice.

He wondered what it would be like to wear the Osi Fain without the Mark V between them. Would it still be flexible and move with him? He thought it probably would. Having intelligent, sapient armor would be incredible. It would make his nanotech-based Mark IV seem like a cheap copy.

"Good," he said. "You're using me as a framework, but you're supporting and augmenting my muscles and bones as well with your own body. It's a good start to a symbiotic relationship. Let's see if we can get out of here and back to my ship so we can get off this planet and out of this system."

The Osi Fain's flesh shivered around him and he received a strong emotion of anticipation mixed with fear.

"Don't be afraid. I'm taking you somewhere safe." As he said it, he realized it truly *was* his intent. The old Harlan might have simply used the Osi Fain as a tool, a vehicle for his personal transport. Now, he was thinking about its well-being and how he could ensure its survival. He snorted in amusement at himself. Any day now, he'd find himself sitting in a rocking chair on the deck of the *Vengeance*, drinking whatever was the nearest Jemmar equivalent to lemonade, reminiscing about the good old days and complaining that the youngsters today *just didn't understand.*

Walking carefully to give the Osi Fain time to learn more about the way his body moved, Harlan picked his way back out of the wreck of the *Yamar*. In the back of his mind, he complained about leaving behind useful and valuable tech, which went against every instinct. He made himself ignore that internal complaint; he'd found an even richer treasure than he could have imagined.

The Osi Fain was a fast learner. By the time Harlan reached the surface of the moon, the Osi Fain was moving with him as fluidly as if it were part of him. It added support to his limbs against its own mass by strategically hardening itself. When loose stones shifted beneath his feet, the Osi Fain shot out tentacles that stiffened against the ground and kept Harlan from a tumble. "Good," he said. "You're doing great."

A vaguely questioning sensation came from the Osi Fain. Harlan wasn't sure what it was asking him. It was like a computer running a language he didn't know. He could learn it, given enough time and exposure to it. Until then, there would be a great many things he didn't understand. He only hoped the Osi Fain would be equally curious and eager to learn as he was.

He couldn't keep calling it *the Osi Fain*. It wasn't just a tool or a suit. It was alive. He didn't know if Osi Fain even *had* names. But Humans gave names to things, to their pets, to their children. The Osi Fain was none of these things, but as Harlan felt more or less responsible for it, he would give it a name.

"I'm going to call you Crocodile. Croc, for short," he announced.

Reggie would have approved.

CHAPTER FIFTEEN

"If I wasn't seeing it with my own eyes, I wouldn't believe it," Skarst said as Harlan walked aboard the *Regina*, fully wrapped within the Osi Fain's embrace.

"Skarst, say hello to Crocodile. My . . ." What *was* the Osi Fain to Harlan exactly? "My charge," he said at last. "Is the mine cleared?"

"Yes, Captain," Skarst said. "Prasek and his people remained behind, unharmed as per your order." She crossed her arms in a familiar expression of disdain. "I don't like that you're leaving them there."

"You let me worry about that."

Harlan took Crocodile to a small auxiliary hold and disabled the artificial gravity grid in the deck. He still spoke aloud to it, but it had yet to speak anything aloud or telepathically back to him. He had to figure out a way to break through the language barrier. Communication would be the key to understanding and the basis for the alliance he was hoping to forge.

"This is a safe place for you. It will protect you from the dangerous radiation in this system. It is not a prison. If you wish to leave, you can," Harlan said to Crocodile. "I . . . I hope you will stay." He felt his cheeks grow hot. He wasn't used to asking others for things.

Crocodile hesitated, then slid off Harlan. It floated into the hold, reshaping itself into a flattened spheroid with sensory tentacles emerging to gently wave like cilia in a current. Flickers of energy traced across its surface, miniature lightning storms of sensory data. Harlan felt the creature extending its senses to the fullest as it examined its surroundings.

::STAY::

The word bubbled through Harlan's consciousness like a faint musical melody heard at extreme distance, distorted by range and echoes. His heart jumped with the thrill of success. It was only one word, but it was the sapient's word, not his own. "I'm going to leave the hatch open so you don't feel like a prisoner. There's gravity in the corridor beyond, because my people find zero-G uncomfortable for long periods of time. If you want to explore, please tell me so I can warn the other people aboard this ship. I don't want anyone to be startled by seeing you."

::STAY:: the creature repeated. It spun slowly as it floated untethered in the hold's center.

Harlan stepped back and moved several paces up the corridor, feeling awkward and naked without the Osi Fain's body armoring him inside it. He stopped at a pressure hatch and spoke softly. "Can you still hear me?"

::HEAR::

Harlan smiled. "Keep listening. There's a lot to learn, and you're still . . . new."

He returned to the bridge and took his customary spot, standing behind Skarst.

She looked back at him, twisting her head all the way around on her flexible neck. "Another mouth to feed?"

"They live on solar radiation and minerals."

"So do we all. Ours is just has to be more processed first."

"I suppose you're right. Take us up to a high geostationary orbit over the mine, please."

"Aye, Captain." Skarst worked the controls with her deft, slender fingers and the *Regina* rose clear from the base, barely jarring Harlan with the smooth takeoff.

Harlan touched the intercom. "All hands, this is the Captain." He paused for a moment, exulting in the power of that simple phrase. "Besides the mine refugees, we've also taken aboard an Osi Fain. It is currently resting in Hold Number Three. Please do not disturb it as it is young and doesn't know us yet. I'd be extremely put out if someone were to startle it and have it put a hole in my ship. Stand by for jumpdrive transit." He shifted to a different intercom channel. "Doctor, how are your patients?"

"Dying, mostly." Doctor Tchkit sounded inexplicably cheerful for someone delivering grave news of that sort. "But I think most, if not all, will survive to reach Lanovoss. Once we're there, I should be able to salvage most of them. It may be a backwards frontier dirtball, but they've got top notch medical facilities, thanks to your, er, creative interpretations of the law."

"Good." Harlan switched channels again. "Mrraurr, how's the ship? Any damage?" He recalled the shield control panel had melted.

"Nothing of note," the engineer replied. The fact that she hadn't mentioned the shields told Harlan she'd already repaired or replaced the damaged components. "Hind build ships to take a beating. It'll take more than a rough landing to ground *Rrresheena*." That was the closest the Hind could manage to pronouncing the name Harlan had given his ship. He didn't mind; at least she made the effort. She was also a damn good engineer and although she wasn't psychologically the type to be happy about anything, at least he could try not to antagonize her by correcting mispronunciation.

"Orbit achieved, Captain," Skarst said.

Harlan checked the stellar emissions and determined it would be awhile yet before they were at risk of experiencing a flare. He activated the *Regina*'s recording software, including an active hololens within the bridge itself.

"What are you doing?" Skarst hissed, and scooted herself out of the holo's field of view, being naturally camera-shy.

Harlan frowned. He'd have to edit this part later. He tapped some more controls to unlock the *Regina*'s weapon systems. "At some point, I won't be able to just be an independent warlord. I'll have to ally myself with the Confederation against the Hind if I want to continue my war against Clan Sharassar. That means becoming a privateer."

"What's that?" Skarst asked. "It's not translated."

"It's a pirate operating under permission of a government. I would basically agree not to attack Confederate vessels and worlds in return for being given free rein to fight the enemies of the Confederation however I see fit."

"That sounds exactly like being an independent warlord," Skarst retorted. "With a sneaky endorsement."

Harlan smiled. "More or less." He returned his attention to the holo. "It will help my case with the Confederation with some evidence of my intentions. You have the sensor logs of our approach to the moon?"

Skarst thumped her tail. "I do."

"I also have the holos recorded by Ekek's marines as they attacked Prasek's people and liberated the imprisoned miners. And Doctor Tchkit is kindly logging all the medical care the survivors require. By any stretch of interpretation, it will be clear to any independent third party observer that we freed sapients from a prison camp."

"That *is* what we did," Skarst pointed out.

"But now we have proof," Harlan said. He faced the holo and spoke to it. "My name is Harlan Washington, the Destroyer. The facility below my vessel, the *Regina*, has been covertly supplying smugglers with high-radiation warheads for Hind warships to use against Confederate ships. That ends now."

Harlan turned and deliberately touched the firing stud on the weapons console.

Skarst made a surprised squawk as a missile roared from its tube. It lanced to the surface, driven by a bright blue jet from its powerful engine. Harlan watched as the spark shrank to a pinpoint and then burst into a flash upon the moon's surface. A bubble of fiery energy expanded from point of impact with a shock wave flowing outward in all directions. Harlan smiled at it, then looked back toward the holo. "That's what happens to anyone aiding and abetting my enemies. If you are smuggling for the Hind, or in any way assisting them in the war, I will hunt you down, and—"

"Captain!" Skarst hissed.

Annoyed, Harlan spun around. "What?"

And then he saw what Skarst had seen, and the words backed up like a logjam in his throat.

The moon had been an excellent place to mine the high-radiation material for warheads, because it had been suffused with heavy particles and ionizing radiation for millions or even billions of years. A lot of material was concentrated in and around the mine, and when the *Regina*'s missile struck, it started a chain reaction in the processed ore stored in the facility. That reaction spread into the unprocessed ore, exposed by mining, and somewhere along the way it hit a critical mass.

The moon was breaking apart, driven by massive explosions. Surface features blew themselves into space, riding columns of vaporized rock and metal. Instead of winding itself down, the explosive energy drove deeper into the core where a white-hot core of degrading heavy radioactives found release at last.

Both Harlan and Skarst lunged for the controls. The Aski Shantar was faster and she slammed the *Regina*'s engines to full. Barely three seconds later, the moon exploded.

"Skarst, get us out of here!" Harlan shouted.

Skarst engaged the skipdrive and sent the *Regina* skating across the system, bouncing across the surface of an adjacent dimension and putting distance between them and the rapidly expanding debris field that had been a small moon. Harlan wondered if it would eventually coalesce back into a new moon of white hot magma, cooling over thousands of years, or if the debris would fall into Tokras I's cloudy atmosphere, or if it would instead spread outward and form a ring around the gas giant.

Whatever happened, the destruction had Harlan's name upon it, and that pleased him.

* * *

"Blew up a damn planetoid!" Skarst shouted with laughter and banged her drinking flute upon the table in the *Vengeance*'s mess hall. Other pirates roared their approval and likewise expressed their admiration for their captain by whatever methods were most species-appropriate. The Aski Shantar cheered boisterously. Mrraurr and another Hind technician whom she'd recruited uttered deep-voiced howls. A smattering of Jemmar whistled through their front teeth. The Ri'Ar made no extraneous noise as was their wont, but they raised their wings straight over their head like feathered flags of approval. Even the lone bear-like Kglotan punched the bulkhead beside him as he had no fellows handy to brawl with—and no other species was foolish enough to fight him in single combat.

Harlan acknowledged the celebration with a nod from his place on a dais at one end of the mess hall. He knew it was basically a throne for a king, but he tried not to think of it that way. He was the captain and fleet commander and that warranted a certain amount of respect.

He caught motion in the corner of his eye and looked over to see Accountant floating in its treaded tank. It was waving a tentacle in his direction. That meant there was news. "Skarst," he said over the throng of celebration.

Skarst looked his direction. Harlan motioned with his head toward the Prodoni in its tank. Skarst understood the meaning if not the specifics of the gesture and drained her flute. "Miskabo, Triskewt, try to keep them from starting any fights," she ordered the *Vengeance* copilots and ostensibly third in command behind her and Harlan.

"Aye, Commander," they said together, and turned their attention back to the pirates.

Harlan and Skarst followed Accountant from the mess hall into the corridor beyond where Doctor Tchkit intercepted them.

"Doctor, how are your patients?" Harlan asked.

"Well, surprisingly, I think they're going to pull through," said the Jemra. "In fact, a little more than half have asked to join your crew, which tells me they're probably suffering from severe brain damage."

Skarst snorted in amusement. Harlan cracked half a smile. "Then, Doctor, I'll need you to handle their induction and duty assignments, to each according to their abilities and physical readiness."

Doctor Tchkit grabbed at his cheeks and dragged them down, making his face a distorted Halloween mask. "I'm a doctor, not a resources administrator!"

"Then appoint someone to the task. Either way, you're in charge of it," Harlan said. "I've got a special project I'm working on."

"Of course you do," Tchkit grumbled. He spotted an Aski Shantar, clearly intoxicated, stagger out of the mess hall and sway toward the latrines. "You! Yes, you!" he shouted as the Aski Shantar looked around guiltily. "What's your name?"

"Uh . . . Jollechi."

"Congratulations, Jollechi. I'm promoting you. Back to sick bay with you so I can sober you up and tell you about your new duties."

"Looks like you have this well in hand, Doctor," Harlan said. "We'll take our leave now."

"This isn't over," Doctor Tchkit called after them. "I still want to examine you after your extended exposure to that Osi Fain."

"It'll be fine. It's on our side."

Harlan and Skarst followed Accountant back to the chamber Harlan had decreed his office. He sat in the chair fabricated for his physiology while Skarst chose to remain upright, leaning back against her tail as if it were a stool.

"Report," Harlan said.

A synthesized voice emerged from the speaker on Accountant's treaded transport. "The holos from your actions in Tokras have been distributed to the Confederate media and governing body as per your orders."

"Any responses yet?"

"Nothing of note. The media has not yet reported upon it. They are probably seeking independent corroboration and have sent a ship to the system to verify your actions."

"What about the government?" Skarst asked. "Or the Navy?"

Accountant's tank bubbled quietly for a few seconds. "You destroyed an entire moon with sapients upon it. They're seeking you. Your presence on Lanovoss is not as secure as it should be. You should expect Confederate Security Forces to arrive soon."

"I'll be long gone by then," Harlan said. "And they're going to find it very hard to arrest someone who is winning their war for them." He rubbed his face thoughtfully. He'd taken the time prior to planetfall to have a discussion with Crocodile. The Osi Fain had agreed to remain in orbit for the time being, as it was still very curious about Harlan and his ability to communicate with it. He was pretty sure it could hear him all the time, regardless of range. Telepathy wasn't governed by such things. His power didn't have the range. He had to trust that the bond he'd forged with the sapient was enough for it to stay instead of fleeing to richer pastures than the Lanovoss system.

Of course, richer pastures were what he had in mind as well.

"Skarst, I'll leave it up to you to select our next base of operations. Work with Accountant here to make sure it is better secured than this one is. Send out the orders that we're pulling up stakes. I want all ships above atmosphere in three hours. Anyone who chooses to stay gets their full share. Nobody new joins the crew effective immediately. That's a security thing. Any questions?"

"Yes," Skarst said. "How do you feel about deserts?"

"I . . . like deserts?" Harlan hazarded.

"Good, because I'm damn tired of being cold all the time on this planet."

CHAPTER SIXTEEN

It turned out they had quite a bit less time than three hours to get off-planet. Barely an hour after Harlan had given the order to evacuate, the Navy came blazing through the skiplane, and they were loaded for bear. Or maybe *loaded for Kglotans* would be a more accurate term, Harlan thought as he read the information on the *Regina*'s tactical screen. He'd planned ahead enough to have one of their stolen ships parked on an innocuous asteroid near the skiplane, sensors open wide in all bands. When the Naval battle group arrived, that ship sent out a tightbeam transmission, barely strong enough to carry over the solar wind. Harlan had calibrated a receiver in polar orbit to pick out that exact frequency, and it relayed that information down to the *Vengeance* and *Regina*.

"They certainly seem like they're spoiling for a fight," Doctor Tchkit observed as he counted the pips of the battle group. Two cruisers approached Lanovoss from the skiplane egress, flanked above and below, port and starboard by four frigates.

"I blew up a moon," Harlan said. "They're rightfully concerned about what else I might do."

"What *are* we going to do?" Tchkit retorted. "I mean, shit has happened and I presume you have a plan? You usually have a plan."

"I do," Harlan said. "Skarst, tell your copilot pals I want to be airborne in ten minutes. You'll stay with me aboard the *Regina*. I need your knowledge and skills more here anyway. Doctor, call Constable Smitchy and tell him to clear as many people as he can from the south end of the port."

"Why?" Tchkit asked.

"Because the only way he gets out of this clean is if it looks like we shot our way out," Harlan said.

"So we're shooting our way out?"

"Indeed," Harlan said. The *Vengeance* began to hum as her engines warmed up to full power. "Skarst, I want one strafing run. Tell the boys to try not to blow up any occupied vessels or ground crew."

"Aye, Captain."

Harlan watched the timer on the tactical screen, and the decreasing distance from the approaching fleet. Part of him very much wanted to fight them. He'd always relished in battles where he faced overwhelming odds. He felt they presented the most worthy challenges. To fight the Navy would be a losing proposition. Even though he'd dressed up the *Vengeance* as a warship, she was still essentially a freighter and would be punching well above her weight class trying to take on a single cruiser, let alone an entire battle group. The *Regina* was more a warship than her larger sister vessel, but she'd struggled against the *Rawarsh Dagger*, and that vessel had barely qualified as warship.

No, this was a time to flee, not a time to fight. "Doctor?"

"I passed along the message, Captain."

"It'll have to be enough." Harlan touched the intercom to transmit to the *Vengeance*. "*Vengeance*, this is Captain Washington. Launch and strike."

"Affirmative, Captain," said one of the Aski Shantar copilots whose names Harlan still couldn't remember.

Vengeance spun around on her repulsors and peppered the southern landing field with blasts from her ventral cannons, doing superficial damage to the facilities but actually blowing up one parked vessel.

"I hope there wasn't anybody on board that one," Tchkit said.

"Have Smitchy identify the ship and her captain to you. We'll see about reparations once we're safe," Harlan said. He returned to the comm board. "*Vengeance*, we're dusting off as soon as you clear the atmosphere."

"Aye, Captain," said one of the *Vengeance* pilots. "What's our destination?"

Harlan nodded at Skarst. "Not over a non-secure frequency," Skarst said. "Check the most recent log entry. Make sure you hit at least six different skiplanes to throw off pursuit. Boys, I'm trusting you to be better pilots than those Navy hacks."

"Tails and heels, Skarst. Stand by to launch in twelve seconds."

Harlan hit the shipwide intercom button. "All hands, prepare for evasive maneuvers." Then he shut his eyes, concentrating on reaching Crocodile. "I know you're out there," he said. "I can feel you listening. Come back to the *Regina*. I'm going to . . . take you home."

Harlan felt Skarst's eyes on him but she said nothing as the *Vengeance*'s bay doors slammed open to reveal light years of the black ocean beyond. With one deft hand she worked the repulsors, casting the *Regina* clear of the bay even as *Vengeance* poured on her own speed. The moment the *Regina* fully emerged from the metallic cocoon of her parent's hull, Skarst lit off the engines and sent her looping across space.

::*I COME*:: cried the voice in Harlan's head, launching him from his seat like he'd been catapulted.

"Where in the frozen hell are you going?" Skarst shouted over the din of the *Regina*'s engines.

"I'll be back. Don't engage the jumpdrive until I give the order." Harlan sealed the seams of his body suit, knowing he might have to expose himself to vacuum before they could jump clear of the Lanovoss system. The flexible fabric gave him as much range of motion as if he were wearing nothing, and an integral life support pack rode high on his back.

"The Navy's still out here," Skarst called after him as he left the bridge. "What about that?"

"Fly better than them," Harlan called back, and pulled his helmet over his face. The rest of the Mark V was in his lab, partially disassembled for a power systems upgrade. He felt horribly naked and exposed without a suit of armor around him when a potential combat situation was bearing down upon him.

He ran through the *Regina*'s corridors as best he could, considering his age. It had been so long since he'd felt the effects of it because of the nanotech supporting his physiology. Now that he was without it, he was reminded every day that he was closer to sixty than he was to fifty. "Old man," he grunted at himself. "Too old for this shit."

Regina jostled suddenly, throwing him against a bulkhead. "We're taking fire, Captain," Skarst said over his suit radio.

"Don't leave yet," he ordered. "Not until Crocodile is aboard."

"Aye aye."

Harlan slammed his hand against the control panel for the auxiliary hold and slipped inside. He sealed the internal door and then staggered across the deck as *Regina* twisted through space to avoid fire from the Navy. "Where are you?" Harlan shouted in his mind.

::AFRAID::

"Don't be. Daddy's here," Harlan grumbled. He clipped a safety line to his suit and another to a stanchion beside the external doors, then cycled air from the hold. Once the lights on the panel indicated the hold was depressurized, he opened the external doors. They yawned open to reveal a gyrating star field as Skarst put the *Regina* through defensive maneuvering.

"Cruisers have launched interceptors," Skarst reported. "I don't think they're intending to take us alive."

"Return fire if you judge it's required," Harlan said as he braced himself against the edge of the door frame. "If we lose shields, jump us away." Lanovoss flashed across his field of view, a brilliant white and brown disc against the black ocean, leaving green afterimages in Harlan's eyes.

He saw the flare of the dorsal turret firing, a red reflection against the hull metal. More flares and flashes appeared and disappeared as quickly as lightning as the pursuing interceptors closed the distance, gauging their range with regular laser volleys.

"Captain, shields are down a third. We're being ordered to cut engines and heave to."

A gleaming, spiky sphere appeared behind the *Regina* as Crocodile raced in toward her, glowing with its internal energy. The Osi Fain approached like a missile, energy crackling around the tips of its spikes. *::AFRAID. AFRAID::*

"I'm here!" Harlan shouted. He held his hand out toward Crocodile. Surely it could see him, could sense his presence. "Skarst, tell them to kiss your ass,."

"Eat my shedding," Skarst retorted. A moment later, she said, "Torpedoes inbound. Evading!" The star field whirled crazily as she spun the *Regina* to avoid the Naval torpedoes, throwing Harlan across and out of the doorway. He arced around and smashed against the hull, damaging his suit. Warning lights filled the corners of his visor display. His safety strap stretched across the edge of the frame and snapped, sending Harlan flying out into empty space.

"Skarst!" he cried, flailing uselessly as the *Regina* blasted away from him.

Stars swirled around. The twin spotlights of Lanovoss' sun and the planet itself flashed past as Harlan spun and spun. Panic filled his lungs and he gasped, trying to find his breath. The suit had its own life support, but it had been damaged when he smashed against the bulkhead and his air wouldn't last more than a few minutes.

Skarst would find him. She was a good pilot. No, she was a *great* pilot, but she was fleeing the Navy and Harlan would be dead before she lost them and came back to find him. He only had one chance to survive. The tightness in his chest was growing and he wondered if on top of everything else, he was having a heart attack. The irony wasn't lost on him: he'd survived decades of superhero battles, an antimatter bomb explosion, being marooned in deep space, and being irradiated on an alien penal colony, only to be felled by his own traitorous heart. "Crocodile," he cried. "I need you!"

A moment later, something solid collided with him, driving the air from his lungs. He gasped and winced, straining against the invisible fist squeezing the life out of him. Pink-veined blue flowed over him, obscuring his vision and freezing his limbs in place.

::AFRAID::

Harlan's vision cleared as Crocodile reoriented itself around him. He found himself able to take a shuddering breath and winced at the pain in his ribs. "You got me. I'm here. Little more gentle on the grab next time. I'm old and fragile."

The starfield no longer wheeled before him. The Osi Fain had halted his tumble. With no point of reference, he had no idea if he was floating motionless or flying along at top speed. "Okay, buddy. You and me are going to work this out. There's a lot for you to learn and I don't have much time. You're going to have to keep me alive and I'm going to get us back to the *Regina* in one piece. You with me?"

::WITH YOU::

"Good. I need you to turn your fancy senses upon me. I'm organic. My body is built from carbon the way yours is from silicon. You have chemical processes that keep you alive, and I do too, but mine are different. I can't live in vacuum like you. I have to breathe. Look at the gas flowing into my body. Look at the pressure and the concentration of chemicals within it. See how it changes in my lungs. That air is keeping me alive. Without it, I'll die." Harlan paused. "Can you make it?"

::AIR::

"Yes, air. Mostly nitrogen, and the rest is mostly oxygen. That ratio is important. Too little oxygen and I die. Too much and I die. It has to be just right. Can you do it?"

::*YES AIR*::

Harlan shivered. He was trusting his life to this infant. If it made a mistake, he'd die. The Osi Fain's bodily material reshaped itself around his head, forming a vent within the helmet. He felt a breeze play across his face, cooling the panic sweat that had built up upon his skin. He steeled himself and inhaled. The air was warm and moist, and smelled like a swamp, but it didn't hurt his lungs. It didn't make him faint from lack of oxygen or break up into panicky paroxysms from too much of it.

"Yes, air," Harlan repeated. "Okay, we're getting somewhere. Long as I can breathe, I can keep us alive. Now, we need to find the *Regina*. You know, the ship, right?"

::*REGINA SHIP*:: The Osi Fain flew into motion, or at least Harlan thought it did. Without any points of reference, he had no sense at all of their speed. He couldn't feel the acceleration, either because it was so gradual or because the Osi Fain had some sort of innate inertial dampening. He picked out engine flares against the star-speckled black, and then spotted the flashes of beams as the Naval interceptors pursued the *Regina*. One cruiser was off to the left, gradually falling behind as the other vessels poured on the speed.

Crocodile was closing in on them all, accelerating fast enough to give the stars ahead a noticeable bluish tinge. Harlan wondered how fast he was going. He wished he had a data feed like the one his nanotech had provided. Maybe he could create a synthesis using Crocodile's senses fed into a simple helmet display. The Osi Fain's body was flexible and configurable. Maybe its senses could be made compatible with Harlan's technology.

On the heels of that thought came a surprising realization. It was surprising in the sense that Harlan hadn't typically put the needs and wants of others ahead of his own. Now he was thinking of this infant he'd adopted with uncharacteristic charity, and even though its natural abilities were augmenting his own, he still intended to see it back to its own people. It would be a detriment to Harlan, a step backward in his life. No . . . it was a step forward for him—maybe not technologically, but emotionally. It was a baby step. He smiled wryly even though there was nobody to see it. If Penny knew how sappy he was being, she might have punched him. Or maybe not.

The drive flares of the interceptors glowed bright ahead of him as Crocodile drove forward, already having passed the cruiser several seconds earlier. It gave Harlan an idea.

"Hey, Croc," he said. "You've got a laser. Let's give the *Regina* some support. Can you fire it from anywhere? Anywhere on your body?"

::YES LASER::

"Okay, here's what I want you to do . . ." Harlan considered how to best explain something that would have been second nature to himself. Then he realized he didn't have to explain it; he could interact with Crocodile like it was a machine he'd built. Without forgetting that it was a sapient creature, Harlan started thinking about directing it the way he'd done so with his nanotech—using his power to encourage it to do what he needed.

The Osi Fain reconfigured itself into less of a generic lumpy shape and into something more like a battlesuit, with a shape that Harlan found both pleasing and utilitarian. He discovered a method by which Crocodile could share its sensory information with him in a way he could comprehend, using an organ that translated and shared data directly into his ocular and auditory nerves, which his brain interpreted as visuals and sounds. It was like he couldn't tell where he ended and the Osi Fain began. They were a single organism . . .

. . . with a powerful laser.

Harlan flew between the two interceptors, clearly Aski Shantar in their design from the graceful curves and gently sweeping arches. They were beautiful vessels. Harlan had never been one for incorporating beauty into his work. He always preferred function over form, but a feeling struck him that destroying the interceptors would be like defacing works of art. The pilots within bore no hatred for him or his crew. They were only doing the job they'd been assigned to complete. That didn't rate death, heroic or otherwise.

Harlan cut his speed to match that of the interceptors. Crocodile's sensory data fed into him and he could tell there were three sapients aboard each ship. Their power systems glowed bright in Harlan's vision, and when he sought a weak point, he found one that he could reach with his laser. He spread his arms out to his sides, aiming at two separate targets without needing to clearly see either. He felt a powerful release that shook his entire body. It wasn't orgasmic, but more like a really good summertime sneeze, satisfying and powerful.

Lasers flashed out from each arm, flaring pink as they blasted through shield and hull and put a neat hole through each interceptor's plenum reaction chamber. The exotic matter that fueled their plasma thrusters spilled out and immediately transformed into a solid state. It was as if a jagged, rocky tumor suddenly sprouted from the aft of each interceptor. Sparks shot as the ships' systems collapsed, leaving them adrift.

Harlan could still read the life signs aboard each vessel and smiled. He hadn't hurt so much as a scale on anyone's tail. He reduced the power of his laser and used it to burn his elephant-head logo into the hull of each craft before reconfiguring his body for rapid flight. Leaving the disabled interceptors behind, he charged after the *Regina*.

"Skarst, come in," he transmitted, using the Osi Fain's innate ability to broadcast.

"Harlan? I thought you were dead!"

"The rumors of my death were . . . greatly exaggerated."

Skarst snorted. "Where are you? How'd you survive getting tossed out?"

Harlan reached over and tapped his hand against the transparent material of the *Regina*'s lateral cabin windows. Inside, Skarst turned to look, shock plain upon her reptilian face. "Knock, knock. May I come in?"

CHAPTER
SEVENTEEN

Skarst took the *Regina* through jump after jump, nearly burning out her drive until Mrraurr threatened to skin her alive. They passed through a half dozen systems in as many minutes, only staying in each one long enough to reorient the ship for the next jump. Even if the Navy had their own Hind jumpdrives, they'd have gradually fallen further and further behind the *Regina* until Skarst's course would have lost them.

At last, Skarst leaned back from the controls. She looked exhausted. Her tail hung limp and her tongue lolled out as she panted like a dog. "We're safe," she announced. "At least, for the moment."

Harlan patted her narrow shoulder. "Take a break. You've earned it."

The Aski Shantar twisted her neck around to look at him. "I'm not sure about leaving you alone with that thing."

"*That thing*, as you call it, has a name, and it is Crocodile." Harlan looked over at the Osi Fain with real fondness. "It is my friend, as are you, Skarst." Crocodile had reverted to what Harlan thought of as its natural state, an oblate blue spheroid with pink-tipped spikes emerging from it like a chestnut husk. "And I'm a little surprised that you waited for me. You could have taken the *Regina* and followed your escape vector. You had no way of knowing I'd return."

"No, I didn't," Skarst admitted. "And I considered that fleeing might be the best option for survival."

"But you didn't. You stayed. Why?"

Skarst stretched out her arms, fingers clasped in a gesture that was almost Human in its familiarity. "I've seen you accomplish a lot of wondrous things in the short time I've known you, Captain. When they told me you couldn't be found aboard, I suspected you might have had a backup plan. You seem like the type that has contingencies upon contingencies."

"You could have had your own ship, Skarst."

"Yes, but I kind of like this one," the Aski Shantar retorted. "And it's not mine. It's yours, until I see your dead body with my own eyes." She paused, her nictitating membranes flashing across her eyes. "And in that event, I will do my best to continue your war myself."

Harlan smiled at that. "You are a good friend, Skarst. If you want your own ship, I'll give you one. Even if it's the *Regina*. I can always steal another. Or build one." He leaned forward to look over her shoulder. "Where are we?"

Skarst waved toward the display. "This is the Sto Shantu system. The second system the Aski Shantar colonized. We can be a lot more anonymous here than we could along the frontier. I told the *Vengeance* to rendezvous with us here above the system's orbital plane."

"Above it?"

She thumped her tail on the deck. "No reason for anyone to be out here except for quiet meetings. *Vengeance* will ping us when she arrives in system." She stood, twisting her spine and rolling her tail. "I need some sleep."

"Go take it," Harlan said. "I have my own work to do."

"Somehow I figured that would be the case."

* * *

While awaiting the *Vengeance*'s arrival in-system, Harlan figured out how to use the *Regina*'s engines to generate the kind of radiation the Osi Fain needed, and set them to a slow bake while the creature fed. While it did so, he tinkered with a display interface that would feed him the kind of information he needed in a format he could easily understand. Mrraurr stopped into his engineering lab to ask why the engines were running and the ship wasn't moving. She wasn't impressed when he explained that they were feeding the newborn.

"You're treating it like a pet," she said. "Keeping pets is something Hindmistresses do, because they don't work for a living."

"No, I'm treating it like an equal," Harlan retorted. "It's sapient."

"Barely," she growled.

"It's as intelligent as you or I," Harlan said. "I just happen to be able to speak with it more easily because of my parapower."

"You're using words that make no sense. I don't like it." Mrraurr glanced down at Harlan's project, then looked again more closely. "What's that? It looks interesting."

Harlan showed her the display interface he was building and she offered a couple of suggestions he found useful. In turn, he made a suggestion on a way to route energy through the drives that would increase power output while reducing visible light emissions.

"Running dark," Mrraurr said. "I like it. I'll try it out." She paused at the door to the lab. "That thing . . . what do you intend to do with it? If it's as sapient as you say, you can't treat it like a tool, Captain. That makes you a slaver, and I'm not willing to work for a slaver. It's bad enough when they exist among my own people. I'm not going to let an alien do it on my watch."

"We're going to return it to its own people," Harlan said. "Skarst is going to take us to the person who gave them the egg in the first place. We'll follow the trail back to where it came from."

"You swear on your blood?"

"I do," Harlan said.

Mrraurr wrinkled her nose in approval and padded down the corridor.

Harlan booted up his display. He'd gone with quick and dirty coding, using a hybrid mixture of Aski Shantarese, Hind, and what he recalled from his time spent researching nanotechnology on Earth. If he could ever get back home, he'd have super-hacker Vanitha Bhat fix it. "One more reason," he murmured. The display worked well enough for the moment, he decided. It was a work in progress, and he suspected he'd be working on it for many weeks. He felt himself wanting to fold up and pull inward, to single-mindedly focus on a single tech task until he solved it, but that wouldn't solve the bigger problem. This wasn't a time for micromanaging; he needed to step back so he could see the whole picture.

He needed to speak with Skarst, but she needed rest. He smiled. As long as she was sleeping, he could permit himself to work. He called Doctor Tchkit.

"Yes, Captain?"

"I'm going to be engineering in here for awhile. Please check on me at regular intervals to make sure I'm staying hydrated and getting enough calories. I promise not to yell at you. Much."

Doctor Tchkit's snort was untranslatable.

* * *

By the time the *Regina* docked aboard the *Vengeance*, Harlan had already run the first and second generation of his display and was teaching Crocodile to interface with it. The Osi Fain, as with everything else, was a fast learner. The two of them made a few jaunts around the exterior of the *Vengeance*, checking their targeting and information displays. Satisfied that his and Crocodile's communication was better than ever, Harlan considered his next move as they flew back into the open cargo bay.

"Gravity," he said aloud. "Can you function in a gravity field?"

::*YES*::

"Does it . . . hurt you?"

::*NO. TIRING*::

That was interesting. It implied that Osi Fain could function down a gravity well, but chose not to because it strained them. Perhaps that could be rectified through training to build stamina and resistance to gravity. Or more likely, Harlan thought he could devise a method to provide concentrated sustenance to the Osi Fain, keeping its energy reserves peaked even while functioning within gravity. In the end, he supposed, it would probably require a combination of the two. He would requisition Mrraurr's assistance and they would build a portable feeder. He explained his plan to Crocodile, who seemed amenable to the proposition.

After Harlan closed the bay and cycled atmosphere back into it, Crocodile flowed off him to form a broad, lumpy pancake shape across the bay floor. It told Harlan it was holding onto the deck with thousands of microscopic feet braced against seams and irregularities in the decking so it wouldn't fall when he engaged the gravity.

Harlan did so slowly, bringing up the grids in the bay to only ten percent of normal. Crocodile shivered as its material settled and redistributed against the new sensation. "Can you handle this?"

::YES::

"I'm going to make you something to keep your strength up. I'm keeping this display active. Transmit to me if you need anything."

::YES::

Harlan yawned. He'd had a busy couple of days and, as was usual when he was involved in heavy tinkering, he'd gone short on both food and sleep. "Skarst?" he asked into the intercom.

"Yes, Captain?"

"I'm going to catch some rest. Take us into Sto Shantu. Make sure you engage the drive harmonics and use the secondary transponder."

"Yes, Captain."

Harlan went to his bunk but tossed and turned fitfully, unable to sleep as the *Vengeance* drew closer to Sto Shantu. He had ideas upon ideas churning around inside his brain. A portable feeding source for Crocodile. An upgrade to the helmet display. A direct cerebral communication interface. At last, he gave up on sleep and wandered back to the bridge where he could watch the landing.

Although the *Regina* was easily identifiable by the elephant-head sigil painted across her bow, the

Vengeance looked more or less like any number of bulk freighters. Harlan and Mrraurr had developed and installed a device that introduced random variations into the ship's engines. It reduced the vessel's flight speed by almost twenty percent, but bulk freighters weren't known for their fleetness. On the other hand, it would make identifying the vessel by her drive signature nearly impossible. Thus disguised, the *Vengeance* entered Sto Shantu's traffic pattern and was directed to a landing pad in a city called Miskonen.

Harlan regarded the city as the *Vengeance* made her approach, identifying herself as the *Plains Roamer*. Unlike Humans, Aski Shantar didn't build their cities *up*. Although he saw many structures of three or four stories, most of the city consisted of large sprawling compounds, divided by wide grassy boulevards. Hovercars and trucks traversed some lanes, while others were dedicated solely to pedestrians. Aski Shantar raced along these, kicking up clouds of dust with their clawed feet as they moved about their errands.

Some sections of the city showed off variations in architecture, perhaps identifying enclaves of different races. The hillside to the south was honeycombed with maintained cave entrances that might have been for Jemmar like Doctor Tchkit, probably leading to a complex and massive underground warren.

Miskonen City sprawled along the edge of an ocean, traversed by surface and subsurface traffic. Tentacled shadows flitted back and forth beneath the surface, suggesting perhaps a large Prodoni population as well. *Vengeance* set down on a pad jutting into the harbor at the end of a long causeway, giving plenty of room for the large bulk freighter.

"Ah, civilization," Doctor Tchkit said beside Harlan. "It's good to be home. I grew up here, right over there in Jongi District." He pointed toward the large hill. "If we're going to be here any amount of time, I know some excellent restaurants there."

"We're not going to be here long," Harlan said. "We're just here to follow the trail of the Osi Fain egg until we can get Crocodile back to its point of origin."

"Very noble of you," Doctor Tchkit said. "And that's going to accomplish what, exactly? I mean, piracy is about profit and this seems like the opposite."

"I'm hoping to make a deal with the Osi Fain. To see if they can point me toward my own homeworld," Harlan said, glad to finally make that admission aloud. "If they can direct me there, I'll at least check to see *when* I am in relation to when I left. It'll be good to know where home is, even if I can't go back again."

"If we can find it," Doctor Tchkit said, "we can take you there. The question is, if we did, would you stay?"

Penny's face crossed Harlan's mind, clouding his judgment. "I don't know," he said.

CHAPTER EIGHTEEN

Miskonen was as cosmopolitan as any large Human city, Harlan decided, and in that bustle his crew found easy anonymity. He wore the portable energy source for Crocodile like a backpack. Doctor Tchkit had immediately named it the *feed bag*. It was an innocuous name for what amounted to a portable nuclear reactor, but Harlan wasn't going to go into the technical details and put off his shipmates. Crocodile had sampled the energy, pronounced it *::GOOD::*, and proceeded to form itself around Harlan once more. Its structure was sturdier, better suited for carrying its own weight as well as the weight of Harlan's devices around. Without the Mark V armor worn beneath it, he could almost move normally as Crocodile moved itself around his joints. When he examined his appearance on a large display that functioned as a mirror, he looked like he was wearing antique full plate armor, albeit made from the organic flexible silicate that formed Crocodile's flesh. It was a dark, rich blue with faint pink traceries that moved throughout its flesh, rising toward the surface and sinking to the depths without a discernable pattern or purpose.

Disguising him was a separate problem altogether. Even on a world populated by a half-dozen different species, an obviously new one would be cause for notice. He was too short and broad to pass for an Aski Shantar, even if Crocodile formed a pseudo tail. He was too tall for a Jemra. Passing for a Prodoni would be impossible, and although he and Crocodile probably could have managed a Hind through careful morphing, they were not welcome deep within the Confederation.

At last, after several minutes of brainstorming, Harlan took a blanket, fashioned it into a large, hooded cloak, and said if anyone asked, he would be a Kglotan. One of the large ursinoids nearly shat herself laughing at that declaration, but eventually sobered enough to offer a few useful suggestions. "You can be young, perhaps," she said in her guttural growl. "Foolish. Full of bad decisions."

Harlan shrugged. "That's an apt description of my life to this point."

There were plenty of taxis available along the docking slips to ferry passengers and crew back and forth between their vessels and the mainland. The cabbies, representing a broad cross-section of Confederation species, zipped around slower cargo vessels with little regard for their safety or the safety of their passengers At least, that was Harlan's impression as they nearly died a half dozen times between the *Vengeance* and the mainland. The driver, an older Jemra with piebald patterning on his fur, kept up a steady chatter about local politics and sporting events, one hand on the steering lever and the other gesticulating at pedestrians who didn't clear the way fast enough. Cabbies, it seemed, were the same on every world, Harlan thought. Perhaps it was a universal career.

The cab skittered to a halt, poorly-tuned repulsors strobing against the absorbent material of the loading zone. Skarst gave the cabbie a handful of Confederation scrip—in Harlan's estimation far more than the ride had probably been worth—and said, "You never saw us. You were watching sports."

The cabbie blew out his cheeks. "Yeah, sports. Real interesting stuff there, sports." He looked past Skarst. "Hey! Hey buddy, you with the kinked tail. You need a cab?"

Skarst led Harlan and Ekek away from the waterfront. Harlan kept his head bowed and his hood pulled low to avoid any other pedestrians getting a good look at him. Ground-effect hovercars and trucks flowed past on the street while air-skimmers followed their own lanes, several dozen meters above the rooftops. The smell of the alien world was immediately as familiar and strange as New York could be. Hovercars didn't run on internal combustion, but they left a sharp ozone tang in their wake. Scents of cooking and baking emerged from restaurants and food stalls, ranging from the appetizing to the nauseating. Street performers played musical instruments, or danced, or simply stood and orated. Harlan saw citizens whose apparent wealth ran the gamut from homeless to one-percenter.

He was immediately intrigued and disgusted by it all. He'd fled to the Moon to avoid these kinds of crowds, the press and stink of Humanity on all sides. But he'd also spent many years on the streets of New York and Philadelphia, and he understood city life, alien or not. "Where are we going?" he asked Skarst.

"We need to rent or buy a skimmer," she said. "We don't want a cabbie involved for this next part. Doctor Tchkit said he has a niece who can hook us up. We're going to meet her."

Doctor Tchkit's niece was slender for a Jemra, and had her fur trimmed in a pattern of horizontal bands that Skarst told him was all the rage among young Jemmar. She had a chirpy voice that grated on Harlan's last nerve, but he kept his head down and let Skarst handle the business transaction. When they were finished, the cousin skipped away, tucking her payment into a pouch and retrieving the local equivalent of a cell phone to call a friend.

Skarst regarded the transport they'd acquired with some dismay. "It's . . . not great," she said at last.

"Why, what's wrong with it?"

"It's a young person's vehicle." Skarst gestured to the intake vents, both of which were rusty and one missing its grille. "It's been poorly maintained." She raised the hatch and swept out a handful of chewed-upon nut shells. "It's not very clean, either."

"Are we going to a good part of town?" Harlan asked.

"Well, no."

"Then this should be fine. We don't want to stand out. A good quality vehicle says *money* to a potential thief, and in the wrong part of town it might as well be like setting off a warning flare."

"I suppose you're right," Skarst said with grudging acceptance. "I wish I'd brought gloves, though."

* * *

They wound up in the oldest part of Miskonen, in the shadow of Jongi District, where the buildings were more run-down and a hodgepodge of competing architectural styles. The streets were far less crowded and pedestrians tended to either move openly in small groups or furtively by themselves. Most of the businesses Harlan saw had extra security measures around their entrances and display windows, from armor plating to poorly-concealed weapon turrets to armed bouncers. Many of these last were Kglotans, who despite being from a more primitive culture, had found gainful employment where they could bring their primitive brutality to bear on a moment's notice. Aski Shantar watched from shadowed doorways, keeping their faces hooded and their hands near their openly-worn weapons.

Skarst parked in front of a broad, single-floor building with a stylized holographic display in a script Harlan couldn't read. "What's this?" he asked.

"A wagering parlor," Skarst said.

"Is it illegal?"

"Depends upon what contest they are wagering."

"Captain, I do not like this place," Ekek said, leaning forward from the rear seating compartment. "A building this size with only one entrance? It is a choke point, like trying to attack a vessel through its airlock. We go inside, we may not easily be able to get out."

Harlan smiled back at his bodyguard, enjoying the feel of Crocodile moving itself to facilitate the action. "Getting out in a hurry will not be a problem. Just keep your eyes open and your guard up."

"First problem," Skarst said, indicating the Aski Shantar guards at the door. Unlike many of the other people they'd seen in the neighborhood, they looked clean and professional, their scales gleaming under the garish lightning of the casino. "We'll have to check weapons at the door. Employees within are certainly armed."

"Anybody bring anything they can't do without?" Harlan asked, glancing toward Ekek.

"My talons and beak are sharp," Ekek replied. "I need no blade to kill."

Skarst looked down at her laser pistol. "I suppose not."

"Leave it in the car," Harlan said. "Maybe it'll still be here when we come out."

"And what are you going to do?" Skarst asked him. "You might look like a dumpy Kglotan to a casual glance, but anyone paying attention to you is going to see that face of yours, Human."

"I've been thinking about that." Harlan concentrated on an image in his mind, picturing one of the Kglotans on the *Vengeance*'s crew. He directed Crocodile to reshape itself around his head, changing his profile to match the hairy, ursine face of a Kglotan. "How's this?"

"Creepy," Skarst said. "But reasonably accurate. Keep your hood up and if they don't look too close, you'd pass for a Kglotan. Just don't try to talk, because your voice is definitely the wrong pitch and timbre."

"I'm content to let you do all the talking," Harlan said. "I'm just here to make sure we get the right information so we don't have to come back later."

They locked the car and headed for the casino entrance.

The two security guards only gave them a passing glance once they divulged they had no weapons. Harlan was surprised that a search or scan hadn't been involved. The former would have been difficult to pass, but he could fool the latter by having Crocodile emit the proper kind of electromagnetic radiation to interfere with scanners. They gave no more than a cursory look at any of them, showing such massive disinterest that it transcended species barriers.

Inside the casino, Harlan saw dozens of different games of chance and devices facilitating the separation of funds from marks. Some games involved dice, or items recognizable as cards or tokens. Others used implements that seemed to have no comparison to Earthly games. He found himself staring in curious horror at a game that involved competitors squeezing some kind of organic bulbs until they burst and then having the splatters measured.

Where some players challenged opponents, others played alone on machines—certainly the equivalent of slot machines, although they ran the gamut from purely mechanical to hologram-based. Groups of sapients gathered around displays, arguing about competitive sporting events shown upon them. Harlan smiled. No matter the event, someone would find a way to bet upon the outcome. He'd never worked in the illegal gambling rackets when he ran his gang, but he'd known others who made a very comfortable living with it.

Skarst led the others through the casino, pushing past the crowd at the bar and pressing herself against the wall in a narrow corridor to let a pair of Prodoni pass, riding in a double-wide walking tank. Harlan was grateful for the light intensification he'd built into his display. He'd been in clubs that were better lit back home. The only thing he liked about the Hind was their preferred level of artificial lighting was close to what Humans chose as well. A thumping soundtrack played over the casino's speakers, loud enough to be heard but quiet enough not to disturb the players. The music involved a dissonant rhythm in a repeating six-beat pattern with whistles laid over it. It seemed to be entirely bass and treble with no mid-range at all. Harlan hadn't spent any time studying the different cultural music of the Confederation, considering it a waste of his time. He wondered idly whose culture provided the background sound, but not enough to bother Skarst with it.

They reached the end of the corridor and found another guarded door, this time by a pair of Kglotan heavies wearing laser-resistant vests over their massive chests. Each ursinoid held a sword as tall as it was, point resting against the floor, arms draped upon the cross braces. Each blade was as wide as Harlan's torso and he imagined they must weigh a few hundred pounds each.

He knew he'd never pass for a Kglotan with them and had Crocodile pull itself away from his face, subtly redistributing that mass down Harlan's sides and legs. If they were going to speak to the Big Boss, whomever that might be, he'd do so as the pirate warlord Destroyer of Earth. Hopefully his reputation had reached this far into the Confederation.

"What . . . is that?" one of the guards asked, looking down his snout at Harlan.

Skarst turned and from the twitching of her lips, she hadn't expected to see him unmasked. "That is . . . uh . . ."

"Tell them who I am, Skarst," Harlan said softly. "Who I *really* am."

Skarst was quick to understand his plan immediately and jumped upon it. "Tell Klorister that the Destroyer of Earth has come to speak with her."

"Who?" asked the other guard.

"Just tell her. She will want to hear us out."

One of the guards turned and went through the door behind him.

"I hope you're prepared to spend a lot here," Skarst said. "Klorister isn't a pushover like Quarest was. Her organization spans multiple worlds."

Harlan shrugged. "I'm not trying to take over all organized crime in the Confederation. I have a different goal in mind."

The Kglotan guard returned. "She will see you." He stepped aside to allow Skarst, Harlan, and Ekek pass through. He didn't ask about weapons or issue any warnings. Harlan presumed it was because they'd been scanned at the entrance and a certain amount of organizational overconfidence was common to all large organized crime rackets.

Klorister's office was the size of a gymnasium, with a floor of natural prairie grass blowing in the breeze that emerged from hidden vents. A single overhead grow lamp burned with a dim light Harlan assumed was equal to the sunlight of the Aski Shantar homeworld. Skarst sniffed the air as they entered and gave a kind of funny sigh. "It's like coming home every time I'm here," she said quietly.

"Been here a lot?" Harlan asked.

"Twice before."

Harlan requested Crocodile to uncover his head. The Osi Fain obliged.

An Aski Shantar trotted over to them through the waist-high grass. She wore a holoprojector on a harness but no weapons. She lowered her head, twisted it to one side, and bared her teeth in a snarl. Skarst raised her own head, presenting her defenseless throat in a display of submission that made Harlan seethe. How *dare* this Aski Shantar presume herself to be *that* superior to his own second in command? He expanded his awareness through Crocodile's senses. With the Osi Fain's help, he located three concealed laser turrets, two antechambers filled with heavily-armed sapient guards, and a Hind-built force field projector that could provide instant defense against any threat.

Klorister turned her attention to Ekek. "You . . . are nothing. But you . . ." She looked at Harlan. "You are a new species to me. Interesting."

"I won't show you my throat," Harlan said.

"A talking monkey. How quaint."

"I killed Quarest for calling me that. You know her?"

"I know *of* her. I presume you are the outsider who came into Lanovoss and took over her operation. It was small business at best. Barely worth the time and resources spent collecting my cut." A holo flickered into life beside Klorister. "I'd been meaning to send someone to collect back pay, but . . ." She licked her eyes. "I have much larger investments to devote attention to."

"Were any of those tied up in Tokras?" Harlan challenged.

"No," Klorister said. "But I'm impressed that you managed to destroy an entire moon nonetheless. The Confederation has taken quite an interest in you over that. I could turn you over to them for a large reward."

"But you won't do that," Harlan said. "Because you have enough to hide yourself that you don't want to pick up any additional official attention."

Klorister chuckled, her teeth clacking together. "You're right. What should I call you? *Destroyer* seems rather fanciful, and *Captain* isn't appropriate for someone not on your crew."

"Harlan. Now that we all know each other, let's get right to the point."

"Of course, Harlan." Klorister knitted her fingers together. "But first, I'm afraid your friend Skarst owes me quite a bit of money. I hired the crew of the *Yamar* to deliver an Osi Fain egg to a well-paying client, and to date, said client has not yet received his property."

"It's not our fault," Skarst said immediately. "We got caught in a flare from Tokras Prime and crashed on the moon. The egg was . . ."

"Lost in the crash," Harlan said. "I was a prisoner in the mines. Skarst and her surviving crew joined forces with me and we escaped."

"How very fortunate for you," Klorister said. "That, however, changes nothing. You owe me for the commission you were paid. I'll take that now, please, or you won't leave this office alive."

"How much?" Harlan asked.

Klorister named a figure that was, in Harlan's estimation, well beyond excessive. It would wipe out all the gains he'd made in his fledgling piracy ventures. He would probably have to sell the *Vengeance* just to cover the fine, which would make recouping any additional income much harder. He grimaced. Klorister probably had numerous forensic accountants and investigators available to her to provide accurate information about the state of Harlan's finances. His initial inclination was to lash out, to destroy her with Crocodile's lasers and then to lay waste to her casino, her whole fucking empire.

But then another solution presented itself, one not borne of destruction, and he decided to follow that path for once and see where it might lead.

CHAPTER NINETEEN

"I have a counter-offer," Harlan said.

Klorister blinked. "I'm listening."

"You have a customer who requires an Osi Fain egg. I have the capability to retrieve another one for you. I just need to know where you got the last one and I will bring you a replacement."

Klorister's teeth clacked with laughter. "That's your counter-offer? I'm supposed to just let you go with a promise that you'll deliver? I'd be a fool to accept that."

"You might well think that at first, but put those brains of yours to work on the problem," Harlan said.

"What are you doing?" Skarst hissed.

"I'm *working*," Harlan retorted.

"Go on," Klorister said. "Please, enlighten me as to why your idea is better for me."

"Reputation is everything in this business. You know that as well as I do," Harlan said. "You made a promise and right now you have a customer who thinks you can't deliver on it. You're going to have to refund the customer's payment, which is probably a sizable amount. Sure, you've got a large organization. You can probably absorb the financial hit, but the damage to your reputation can't be absorbed so easily. People talk. Word gets around. *Klorister's a failure. She can't follow through on a job. Maybe we should take our business to someone else.*" He smiled. "Don't lie to me and say you're not already considering that."

Klorister spun around, whipping her tail through the tall grass. "Of course I'm considering it. The only reason I'm even listening to you right now is that I'm

217

considering it. You've got very little tail to balance with right now. You failed in a contracted job."

"Your contract was with Captain Krastins, who's dead now," Harlan said.

"And Skarst was part of that agreement, which means it's still in full effect," Klorister said. "I'm owed a refund of my investment."

"Or one Osi Fain egg," Harlan pointed out. "Which I can deliver. I assume time is of the essence here. You want an egg quickly, so you don't have to tell your customer you failed. That means you keep your reputation intact."

"And what makes you think I haven't already sent someone to get another egg?"

"Because we're having this conversation. Either you can't get one yourself, or you're not convinced you can do so quietly. Either way, I can succeed where you won't."

"And why is that?"

"Captain . . ." Skarst said. "Don't."

Harlan ignored her. "Because I can talk to them."

Klorister narrowed her eyes at him, the tip of her tongue flicking in and out of her mouth rapidly. "I don't believe you."

"I'm a member of a species new to you," Harlan said. "You have no idea what I can or can't do." He asked Crocodile to flow off him. The Osi Fain sloughed off him like a second skin. It reformed into a spiky sphere the size of a yoga ball, hovering a foot off the ground before Harlan.

Klorister sprang back, clearing impressive distance in her surprise. "That's—that's—"

"An Osi Fain," Harlan said. "My partner. Come back to me," he said to Crocodile. The Osi Fain returned to surround him in its embrace. "Now, do you believe me?"

"I don't want to . . . but that's a demonstration I can't deny. If it's some kind of trickery, it's using technology I've never even heard of."

"Why haven't you procured a replacement egg yourself, Klorister?" Harlan asked.

"The Navy, of course. The damned Navy found the source system twelve days ago and have restricted it. Protecting a sapient species' home," she spat. "They have the skiplanes interdicted. Any ship emerging from a lane is going to get blasted or impounded, or probably both. Until we find another source system, Osi Fain are off the market."

"I don't need a skiplane to enter a system. I can jump in from anywhere in the *Regina*."

Klorister crossed her arms. "That sounds like you're using illegal Hind technology."

"I have it available. I presume you do not."

"No." Klorister paced back and forth, her tail making angry sweeps through the grass. "I'll buy it from you."

"It's not for sale."

"Everything is for sale," she countered.

"So now you're offering me money. Five minutes ago you were ready to charge me for Captain Krastins' contract." Harlan smiled, even though Klorister wouldn't understand the expression. "The system. Tell me where it is and I'll bring you an Osi Fain egg."

He waited. He could tell both her brains were working hard, thinking and calculating. She had every reason to suspect a trick, but Harlan had played the best card he had. He'd told her the truth. The only things that were inaccurate couldn't be proven.

"What assurances do I have you won't just go on the run?" Klorister asked at last. "Or take an egg and sell it yourself instead of bringing it to me?"

"Keep the *Vengeance* as security against our return."

"What?! Are you addled?" Skarst burst out.

Klorister laughed. "I detect some dissension in your crew, Captain Harlan. You should see to that misbehavior."

Harlan looked at Skarst and felt proud of her for standing up to him. "I would fire her on the spot if I thought she was not being the best officer in my command. She's right to question me here, and I commend her for it." He smiled. "She's also extremely bright, and she knows two things. I have nothing else I'm willing to put up as collateral, and because the *Vengeance* is important to me, she knows I'll fulfill the mission so I can retrieve it."

"Supposing I choose to keep it and have you put to death instead?"

Harlan's smile turned feral. "You can try. I've already destroyed a moon in the course of my business. How much harder can it be to break apart an entire planet? It's just a question of scale."

Klorister laughed again. "You're not shy about that. Still, it would be very easy for me to make this problem of you simply . . . go away."

Harlan heard Ekek's feathers raise in an unconscious threat display. He raised a hand, indicating the Ri'Ar should relax.

"You won't do that. It would harm your reputation far more than you would gain from it. Besides, my quarrel is not with you, nor with the Confederation. I've only got one enemy in mind, and all my actions are perpetrated toward defeating them. Clan Sharassar of the Hind."

Klorister knitted her fingers together. "I would not want to be a member of that Clan, I think, knowing you're hunting them. You are certainly an interesting person, Captain Harlan, and one of considerable intelligence. You've presented a well-played position and I am going to accept your offer. I feel like letting you live free to continue your war will be much more interesting and entertaining than it would be to kill you and squash your petty criminal enterprise."

Harlan let the slight go. As much as killing Klorister would improve his afternoon, it wouldn't benefit his overall plan. "Skarst, order the *Vengeance* crew to retrieve their personal effects and berth aboard the *Regina*. Pay the docking fee ahead for thirty days. We'll lock down the ship when we depart."

"Yes, Captain," Skarst said through clenched teeth.

Harlan turned his attention back to Klorister. "On the thirty-first day, if I haven't returned with an Osi Fain egg, the ship will unlock itself and list you as its owner of record. Now, where did the egg come from originally?"

"The Gabelko system. As I said, it's interdicted by the Navy."

"You let me worry about that," Harlan said. "One egg, as agreed upon, in return for the name you've provided and the cancellation of debts owed by Captain Krastins."

"Agreed," Klorister said. "It's a pleasure doing business with you, Captain Harlan. I can't wait to board my new ship."

"And I can't wait to make you eat those words." Harlan said with one last smile.

* * *

The crew took the consolidation onto one vessel rather well, all things considered. There were a few hurt feelings, and much general grumbling and complaining, but in the end only one Aski Shantar opted to leave the company. Harlan paid the fellow his shares, gave him a bonus to keep an eye on the *Vengeance* while it was berthed, and offered to hire him back with no questions asked if he was still around when the *Regina* returned.

Mrraurr was angry about the extra bodies creating such a strain on the *Regina*'s life support system. Harlan asked if she'd failed to maintain it to proper standards. That was, of course, equivalent to waving a red flag in front of a bull. He let her rant and scream and yowl for two minutes before reminding her that the *Regina*'s systems should be able to handle the additional life support requirements, and if it couldn't, it meant Mrraurr had been slacking off in her duties. If she didn't want to be replaced by someone more qualified, Harlan suggested she run the numbers again and make sure everything was in tip top condition.

"You handled that well," Skarst said after Mrraurr had loudly banged her way down the corridors back toward Engineering. "I probably would have fired her on the spot."

"I'm just a bit more familiar with the Hind than I am with other species," Harlan said. "I understand their psychology. Mrraurr is an excellent engineer, and she knows it, and she knows I know it. She'll keep the *Regina* in better shape than anyone else I could hire. She loves this ship. It's in her bones."

Skarst received clearance from Miskonen Control to depart and sent the *Regina* hurtling skyward, making for orbit under the assumed registration of a stock light freighter called the *Dreamcatcher*. With the elephant's head logo splashed so boldly across the ship's prow, it would be best to get the *Regina* away from observing eyes as soon as possible.

Harlan pulled up information about the Gabelko system on his terminal. It was a young system on the galactic time scale. Its star burned bright and hot amid a disc of particles that were ever so slowly accreting into planetary bodies. With so much available solar energy and so many complex molecules floating free, it would have been a paradise for Osi Fain. No wonder they'd made it their home.

Skarst looked over his shoulder at the display. "With all that loose matter, we're going to make a wave wherever we arrive. There's no way the Navy will miss it."

"Well, wouldn't want it to be *too* easy, would we?" Harlan shrank the system image, trying to get a better sense of the surrounding spacescape. He pointed to the largest protoplanet, a slightly denser cloud of gas coalescing around a rocky core. "This is where we need to go. We'll find the Osi Fain colony here. I'm sure of it."

"What makes you so sure?" Skarst asked.

"It's the biggest planet. That means more gravity to pull more material in from the surrounding area. It's an all-you-can-eat buffet for the Osi Fain."

"That checks out. How do you want to approach?"

"Since we're going to make ripples when we arrive, subtlety is out. I guess we go for fast and bold." Harlan shut the terminal down and leaned back in his seat, kicking his feet up onto a locker that held emergency supplies.

"Also, try not to get killed."

"That goes without saying."

"And yet, here I am saying it."

* * *

In the end, they decided the safest thing would be to blink into the system and drop Harlan out of the airlock, wrapped in his Osi Fain armor, then to jump out again. The *Regina* would remain safely hidden in deep space far above the ecliptic plane where the Navy wouldn't find them. Harlan and Crocodile would seek out the Osi Fain themselves. The spaceborne species might find Harlan much less of a threat when approaching with one of their own instead of in a starship.

"Those lasers of theirs go right through shields," Skarst pointed out. "If they choose to take a shot at us, there's not much we can do to defend against it."

"I remember," Harlan said, recalling how easily Crocodile's lasers had holed the Navy interceptors as they fled Lanovoss. "But they'll also go through Navy shields. Just because the Navy has interdicted the system doesn't mean they're interfering with the Osi Fain. They're just trying to keep others from doing what we're about to do."

"Are you going to steal an egg?" Doctor Tchkit asked. "Because—no offense meant to you, sir Captain sir—but I'm pretty much the opposite of suicidal."

"No, I'm not going to steal an egg." Harlan said.

"Oh, that's a relief," Doctor Tchkit said, chittering with laughter.

"I'm going to borrow one."

Ekek had to take the good doctor down to the galley to have a drink for his nerves.

"You're going to send him to an early mulching," Skarst said, watching the doctor leave the bridge.

"Jemmar mulch their dead?" Harlan asked.

"They're an underground race. It makes more sense than burning or burying their dead."

"I suppose," Harlan said.

"You really think you're going to pull this off?"

"I think I have a pretty good chance."

"What if the Osi Fain don't want to listen to you?"

Harlan smiled. "I can be very persuasive." He stood. "I'm going to go suit up. Get the ship ready to jump into Gabelko." He paused by the bridge hatch. "If I do die, the *Regina* and *Vengeance* are yours, Skarst. Do with them whatever you wish."

Not for a moment did Harlan worry that he'd signed his own death warrant by granting that potential inheritance to Skarst. She had proven herself trustworthy, reminding him of a friend from many decades earlier, when he was still finding his way in the world after escaping juvie hall.

"Hmmm . . ." Skarst interlaced her fingers together beneath her chin in the pose Harlan identified as being deep in thought.

"What's on your mind?"

"Just imagining how I'm going to enjoy captaining my two new ships . . ."

CHAPTER TWENTY

The *Regina* flashed into the Gabelko system, appearing a mere half-million kilometers from the largest protoplanet. Her sudden arrival, as predicted, sent a shockwave throughout the dust clouds, driven by electromagnetic energy. The ripples looked as if Harlan had thrown a rock into a shallow pond.

Skarst couldn't have jumped any closer to the protoplanet because the density of the gases would have been too great. They had a lengthy distance to cover before they could drop Harlan out of the airlock, so she ratcheted up the throttle to full power.

The Navy flagged them almost immediately and began issuing dire threats and warnings. Two destroyer-class ships fired up their engines and angled inward on intercept courses, their skipdrives sending wave after wave of through the system congestion. "They'll be in range in six minutes," Skarst warned.

"I'll be out in three," Harlan replied, and left the bridge wearing his skinsuit and a stripped-down version of the Mark V helmet that replaced the bulky armor plate with a lightweight framework to hold the display and communications gear. He'd supplanted it with a short-duration life-support system and boot jets, because he was fairly sure he'd be returning under his own power, without Crocodile.

Ekek was waiting for him in the corridor. The Ri'Ar had his spacesuit on with the helmet dangling over his chest, ready to be locked in place. "Captain, I would join you."

"Sorry, no. Not this time." Harlan moved past the owloid.

225

"Captain . . . I'm sworn to protect you."

"I understand that, Ekek, but this is not the time for you to get all noble on me. I need to be out there alone except for Crocodile. I don't know how the wild Osi Fain will react to me, and I won't let my lack of knowledge result in your death."

"You . . . what?"

"I appreciate you, Ekek. I really do. You're a loyal soldier and those are in precious short supply in this universe. You keep watch out here. I promise there will be plenty of opportunities in the future for you to bodyguard me to your heart's content."

Ekek made a peculiar salute with his wings and Harlan nodded, then ran for the airlock.

Crocodile awaited him at the airlock hatch and flowed over Harlan between steps. By the time he was shutting the hatch behind him, he was completely enclosed in the Osi Fain and ready for space travel. Excitement radiated off the spaceborne alien for both a return to the void in an idyllic environment and the opportunity to reconnect with its people. Harlan wondered if Osi Fain had parental relationships with those who'd laid their eggs, or if *laying* was even the correct mechanism to describe the process. There was so much he didn't know about the silicon-based life forms, and it would take him years he didn't have to research them further.

::HOME::

"Yes, we're going back to your home," Harlan said as he cycled the airlock. "I hope this works. I couldn't tell Skarst, but I have no idea what I'm doing right now."

::SAFE::

"I hope you're right," Harlan said. "Or this is going to be the shortest negotiation of all time." He switched to his external communications frequency. "I'll see you in twelve hours, Skarst. Go on a three count."

"Aye, Captain," Skarst replied. "One . . . two . . ."

Harlan shot out of the airlock, using the Osi Fain's biological spacedrive to accelerate from the *Regina*.

Behind him, the vessel winked out of existence as Skarst jumped away, leaving the Navy destroyers chasing dust. Harlan knew their sensors would flag him; even with only visual reckoning he was leaving a swirl of dust in his wake. Wrapped in an Osi Fain body, he should read as Osi Fain to the Navy. True to his prediction, the destroyers peeled off to return to their station-keeping coordinates. "Nice when things go right," he muttered. "Call your people, Croc. Get their attention."

Crocodile issued a call, a signal mixing telepathy and long-form electromagnetic bandwidth. It wasn't anything Harlan could translate but he understood it essentially meant *here I am! Where are you?*

They flew on through the dust, which gave all the stars and distant sun halos like streetlights in fog. The nearby protoplanet glowed with its own internal heat, and Harlan aimed for it. Crocodile kept calling out to its fellows and suddenly a half dozen apparitions came out of the dust, pacing alongside them.

The smallest was the size of a van. The largest was as big as a house. The rest roughly split between the two sizes. Their skin coloration varied across the spectrum from red-tinged to bluish violet with all hues in between represented. Like Crocodile's native form, they were generally spheroid with spikes of all lengths. Energies crackled along the spikes and traced back and forth across their rocky skins. Harlan marveled that he could sense them, even though he couldn't completely understand their communication.

The newcomers exuded a mixture of relief, curiosity, and wariness. Harlan made the most of the communication interface he'd developed for Crocodile to try to understand what was going on in the minds of the Osi Fain.

They were relieved at the infant's arrival. The theft of an egg was a worrisome, frightening event and although they were no cowards, they feared battle with what they called *The Soft*. They were loath to leave the safety of this system, so rich in nutrients and energy, especially when some of The Soft had set up a perimeter guard to keep others from sneaking in to steal away the unborn.

Their curiosity was strong about how the infant had found its way back, and how it had come to arrive within a vessel of The Soft. More than anything, they were curious about the Soft creature wrapped within the infant's embrace. It was a strange, symbiotic relationship that they had not encountered before, through millions of years of racial memories.

Millions of years, Harlan thought in astonishment. A race as old as theirs *must* have explored the galaxy. Surely they'd been to Earth—or at least, to the Solar System. He longed to ask them, but had to wait impatiently for the awkward and barely effective translation he'd built into his display.

The wariness expressed itself in the way the group formed an effective cage around Harlan and Crocodile, with the largest directly before them, two more flanking left and right, one each above and below, and one behind. He didn't know if their own bodies were proof against the lasers they generated, but if size was any indication of laser power, he figured he wouldn't have the chance to find out because if they fired, he would probably just be atomized.

"The other Osi Fain . . . can I speak to them? Can they understand me?"

::YES:: Crocodile replied

A new voice filled Harlan's head, a richer, more refined version of the voice he heard from Crocodile. This one spoke more fluidly, with the experience and knowledge that came with age. *::I HEAR YOU, SOFT ONE::*

For the first time in a great many years, Harlan felt fear. No, that wasn't quite right. He wasn't afraid of the Osi Fain confronting him. He was . . . in awe. These were beings that had traveled the cosmos for perhaps thousands of years and they were speaking to him, a lowly Human from a backwater planet at the fringe of the galaxy. He licked his lips with a tongue that had gone suddenly dry. "Someone stole an egg from you. It hatched. I have brought it back to you."

The Osi Fain were silent.

Harlan felt like he needed to say more. "I can't pronounce this Osi Fain's name. So I call it Crocodile. That's a creature from my homeworld, called Earth. But I imagine that name doesn't mean anything to you. I came here, hoping you might help me find it."

More silence filled his ears, a roaring void of nothing. Seconds ticked by, marked by a maddening trickle of sweat down Harlan's temple that he couldn't wipe away.

"Can you help me? Hey, are you even listening?"

::*SHE LIKES YOU*:: said the new voice.

"She? Crocodile is a female?"

::*ALL HARD ONES ARE MOTHERS*::

So they called themselves Hard Ones. It was less poetic than the Prodoni translation of *Osi Fain* as *Sky Crab*, but the Osi Fain had probably never seen a crab. They were a single-sex species, and since they all reproduced, they identified as female. Or perhaps that was just how Harlan's display was interpreting the words as they passed through Crocodile. "Well, I like her too. She saved my life."

::*YOU SAVED HER LIFE. SHE LIKES YOU*::

It was a definitive statement that Harlan didn't know how to respond to. The Osi Fain had a directness about them that he appreciated, but their bluntness was hard to deal with when he'd spent decades learning how to talk to Humans that spent uncounted minutes getting to the point.

"I was hoping that by bringing Crocodile back here to her people that you might help me get back to mine," Harlan said.

::*NO*::

That was Crocodile's voice, and the forceful negative startled him. What was she disagreeing with?

::SHE DOES NOT WANT TO LEAVE YOU. SHE LIKES YOU::

Harlan felt like slapping his face. Crocodile had *imprinted* upon him, like a lonely duckling connecting with the first being she saw. She'd been his bargaining chip, and now it looked like trading her for information wouldn't be an option. On the other hand, he realized, she had performed admirably as a replacement suit. Between her native sapience and her similarity to a machine, Harlan could communicate with her better than he ever had with his nanotech. If she wanted to stay with him, he would be better off both in the short and long term.

::TELL US OF YOUR HOME:: said a new voice.

Harlan felt the words back up in his throat as he tried to figure out how to describe the entire Solar System to these beings. "It's a . . . a yellow star. Do you know what that is? Of course you do," he said quickly. "You probably have words for colors that I can't even see. It has eight—or nine planets, depending upon who you talk to and how old you are. Four or five terrestrial worlds. Four gas giants. An asteroid belt—"

::STOP. STOP USING WORDS. WORDS ARE WEAK. SHOW US::

Harlan stopped babbling. He happened to agree with the Osi Fain on the subject of words. He'd always communicated better without the crutch of language, by speaking in the tongues of machinery. How would a machine describe the Solar System? No, how would he describe it to a machine? He shut his eyes and imagined the blue curve of the Earth seen from the surface of his adopted homeworld of the Moon, with its spiraling cyclones and sparkling thunderstorms. The brilliant golden-white light of the Sun. Saturn's silent beauty. Jupiter's roiling fury. The rusty austerity of Mars compared to the scintillating pearl of Venus. Harlan standing atop a rooftop as a teenager in a powerless city, staring up at the starry sky he'd never see with his own eyes before. The arc of the Milky Way as it stretched across the night sky over the Guatemalan jungles. Even the pattern of craters on the Moon and how they'd sparked the imaginations of skywatchers for an uncounted thousands of years.

That was the Solar System. His home.

::WE DO NOT KNOW DIRECTLY OF THIS SYSTEM::
The one whom Harlan thought of as the elder Osi Fain spoke with definitive authority.

"Oh," Harlan said, feeling a wave of crushing disappointment.

::BUT WE KNOW OF ANOTHER FAMILY THAT LIKELY DOES::

Harlan's disappointment immediately transformed into hope, and he hated himself for daring to think he might get some good news. "More Osi Fain? Are they here, in this system?" He realized if they were not, he had no frame of reference to find them, any more than he could tell Skarst he'd grown up in Harlem and have it mean anything to her.

::THEY ARE PRISONERS OF THE SOFT::

"There are many different species among the Soft," Harlan said softly. "Show me."

An image formed in his mind of a Hind. Of course it was the Hind—or more specifically, Clan Sharassar—he thought. Everything was tracking with what he knew. They must have captured several Osi Fain and figured out some way of communicating with them, either through voluntary conversation or some method more diabolical. One of them had given up the location of the Solar System and subsequently sent their axeships to Earth under the command of one Clanmistress Rhaorhir. That Clanmistress had died by Mustang Sally's hand, but not before hundreds of New Yorkers had been harmed or killed by the expeditionary force. It was why Harlan intended to take his vengeance upon them—to punish them for their transgressions against his world.

"I know this particular breed of the Soft," Harlan growled. "They are my enemies. If I free your people, will you share with me the location of my homeworld so that I may return?"

::WE AGREE TO THIS::

"Can you give me the location of the system where they are being held? It will mean I can act against their captors right away."

A complex map with hundreds of layers, locating objects not just in space but in time, appeared in Harlan's mind. It struck with such force that his eyes began watering at the massive amount of data. It would have taken him years to decipher it all if he had to do so alone, but he had Crocodile to help him. He was beginning to understand that although she was still basically a newborn, Osi Fain infants were not the helpless squabs that Humans were. She was intelligent —and even more importantly, she liked him. Still, he wished he could wipe his running nose. He sniffled and grimaced in disgust.

"I . . . have another question. Well, several, actually," Harlan said.

::PROCEED::

Harlan scanned what he could about the protoplanet near them, noting its orbital velocity. "Do you always . . . lay eggs that are viable?"

::THAT IS A CURIOUS QUESTION TO ASK. WHY?::

"I had to make a deal to get the location of this system. I put up my ship for collateral. Do you know what that means?"

::A SECURITY AGAINST FAILURE::

"That's close enough. I had to promise to return with one of your eggs, but I never specified it would be that could hatch."

::AN INFERTILE EGG::

"Yes, precisely. Can you provide me with something like that? I can return it to the, er, Soft holding my ship, which I'll need to free your people."

::ATTEND::

The command was given in a tone that brooked no argument, so Harlan figuratively settled himself in to watch, even though he, Crocodile, and the other Osi Fain were hurtling through the dust clouds circling the protoplanet. They kicked up patterned swirls in their wake, like Mustang Sally's long braids before she'd cut her hair.

One of the Osi Fain, the one with the distinctive greenish cast to its skin, flipped itself over to display a swollen lump pushing outward. Its spikes moved aside as the swelling grew. The way the creature's flesh moved was familiar; he'd seen Crocodile's do the same thing when she morphed herself. The green Osi Fain flexed and jerked herself and ejected a misshapen lump of herself the size of a large pillow. It spun in the dust surrounding them all, smoothing itself out until it attained the characteristic spiky sphere of an Osi Fain egg.

"Is it . . . alive?"

::NO. IT IS TOO SOON FOR THE BUD TO GROW::

By using the term *bud*, Harlan immediately understood something that was as yet unknown to Confederation researchers. Osi Fain eggs weren't actually eggs; they were growths that separated from the parent. That was what the Osi Fain meant when she said all of them were mothers. Buds probably retained the Osi Fain equivalent of genetic information, and probably a chain of memories of some form stretching back across the mists of time.

"This bud will never grow into a Hard One? I don't want to take away something that could live."

::NO::

Harlan raised a hand toward the green Osi Fain. "Thank you. I will bring back your lost family to you. You have my word."

::TRUTH:: That was Crocodile, adding her voice to the conversation. Harlan silently thanked her. He hoped her endorsement of his abilities would convince the Osi Fain

to help him. He checked his chronometer. By prior arrangement, Skarst would bring the *Regina* back to coordinates several hundred kilometers away from the drop-off point. It would ensure any Naval vessels nosing around the drop-off point would be too far away to intercept the *Regina* before Harlan got aboard.

Until that moment, he had some time to kill. "Can I just fly with you for awhile? Give Crocodile some time to be around her own kind?"

::YES::

Well, Harlan thought. That was easy.

Probably the easiest thing he'd do for the next several days.

CHAPTER TWENTY-ONE

"It certainly seems like a real egg," Doctor Tchkit said, straightening his glasses as he looked up from the scanner. "The scan reports it's Osi Fain biology. You're sure this isn't going to hatch?"

"The Osi Fain assured me it wouldn't," Harlan said. "I think it's probably akin to a tumor."

Skarst stepped back, making a slight growl in the back of her lengthy throat.

"That's probably an accurate assessment," Doctor Tchkit said. "Tumors will resemble the biology of their host organisms, because they're made from that host's biological material. We just don't know enough about Osi Fain biology to say definitively that this is or is not an egg. I'm going to assume it is."

The *Regina* had dropped into the Gabelko system at the coordinates Harlan and Skarst had previously agreed upon, and Harlan got aboard before the Navy could do more than issue a couple of angry threats. "You know they will probably increase their presence in this system," Skarst said as Harlan returned to the bridge.

Harlan shrugged. "That's not really my problem. We got what we needed. Let's go get the *Vengeance* out of hock. I've got another mission for us."

The *Regina* sat far above Sto Shantu's orbital path, waiting for a window to approach without getting tagged by local law enforcement. One of the Aski Shantar on board had hacked into the local database and snooped around, looking for information on Harlan, his crew, and the *Regina*. They'd been lucky to get out of port without being stopped, but departures were always easier to pull off than approaches.

Doctor Tchkit went to a cabinet, removed a wide-mouthed ceramic bottle, and took a hefty swig from it. "Well, let's see. We've taken over a small sector crime syndicate, trafficked in illegal sapients, smuggled contraband, and performed numerous acts of piracy. When will the fun ever end?"

"What's the mission?" Skarst asked, ignoring the doctor's sarcasm.

"We need to free a group of Osi Fain prisoners from the Hind."

"Do all Humans have a desire to die in the pursuit of futile goals or are you six scales off the tip of the tail?" Skarst asked.

"I don't know that idiom, but I believe I get the gist," Harlan said. "I don't have a death wish. Quite the opposite, in fact. The bottom line is that I need information the Osi Fain have to find my homeworld, and they will share it with me if I rescue their prisoners."

"Raising your head above the grass like that, you're just begging to have it cut off," Skarst said.

"There's more to it than my own selfish desires," Harlan retorted.

"I'm grateful to know that." Doctor Tchkit took another drink from his bottle. A trickle of liquor leaked around the corner of his mouth and soaked into his fur. "I'm a big supporter of altruistic deeds. It's why I'm a doctor."

"The Hind have figured out how to get information from the Osi Fain. I don't know if their solution is technological or psionic, but they're grilling their prisoners for information on inhabited systems. I'm positive that is how they found the Earth. Or will find it." Harlan slapped the scanner in frustration. "I hate being unstuck in time like this!"

Doctor Tchkit solicitously offered his bottle to Harlan. Harlan shook his head, so the Jemra tipped it back again and drained it.

"If what you say is true, they could find other races to conquer," Skarst mused. "And with their jumpdrive technology, they're not bound to skiplanes like the Confederation is. They'll be able to expand their empire a hundred times, and we won't be able to stop them." She went to retrieve a long flute of the extremely sour juice that was her preferred alcohol-equivalent. She canted her head toward the doctor. "You're right about this being altruistic, Doctor. We have to rescue those Osi Fain—"

"To save the galaxy," Harlan finished. "Now, I'm going to need some time with Crocodile to translate the maps the Osi Fain gave me. Between the two of us, we should be able to figure out where the prisoners are being held."

"What should we do?" Skarst asked.

"First, we deliver this egg to Klorister and get her to release the *Vengeance*."

"What if she won't?"

Harlan smiled. "Take Ekek and a handful of Ri'Ar marines with us and convince her."

* * *

While the *Regina* burned toward Sto Shantu under Skarst's steady hand, juking back and forth to avoid sensor sweeps, Harlan sequestered himself in an auxiliary hold. He'd turned off the gravity grids but kept the inertial dampening field operational to keep any of Skarst's sudden maneuvers from splattering him against a bulkhead. Crocodile seemed to enjoy the sensation of the inertial dampening, and she slowly rolled in place, occasionally extruding tentacles to brush against the deck or bulkheads to nudge herself this way and that.

Harlan plugged his display into a large holoprojector and turned to his aide, the Prodoni known as Accountant. "Ready?" he asked the telepathic squid.

The Prodoni rolled forward a few centimeters on its treads, which Harlan had discovered were magnetized. "I am not a xenobiologist or xenopsychologist. I am an accountant. Perhaps there is a mistranslation occurring? I work with figures."

"So you do math. That's great, because everything in the universe is math. I need someone wired for that, because there are going to be a lot of numbers to crunch here." He indicated the holodisplay, containing a map of known Confederation and Hind space. The Confederation systems were connected by glowing threads representing skiplanes. Some systems had only one lane in or out. Others had many. Harlan wondered if skiplanes could be created through technological means. Then he shook his head. That was a question for another time.

The Hind systems were much less detailed. Much of that data had to be inferred either through the reports of first-in scouts who hadn't been summarily executed by the Hind, or through direct observation by extreme-range sensors. The important information would be available, and that was where Harlan was hoping to find his mystery system.

The Osi Fain used skiplanes to travel between systems. The system where the Osi Fain prisoners were being held did not apparently have a skiplane ingress/egress. That meant the Hind were capturing Osi Fain elsewhere and transporting them to the mystery system by use of jumpdrives. Harlan would have to get them out the same way, and only the *Regina* could enter a system like that. He considered the problem for a minute and then called Mrraurr.

"Question for you."

"Hello, Captain. I'm doing well. Thank you for asking." Mrraurr's voice snarled across the intercom.

"Social niceties aside, can you increase the breadth of the jumpdrive field to pull additional mass along?"

"How much mass, and what shape? Jumpdrive fields are roughly cylindrical, tapering to a point fore and aft. It's why Hind vessels are shaped the way they are. Obnoxious wings and superstructures and the like require drives way outside of the required size. It's inefficient. Like that monstrosity you call the *Vengeance*. I'd have to put a system massing sixty times the size of the one in this vessel just to give it the same performance."

Harlan knew the *Regina* massed somewhere around three thousand tons, roughly equivalent to a frigate-sized oceangoing vessel back on Earth. Crocodile didn't mass very much by herself, but there could be prisoners the size of the large Osi Fain he'd encountered in Gabelko. "Let's assume they can form-fit around the exterior hull, so they won't add significant girth. If you allow for, say, an increased field draft of two meters, how much additional mass can you carry with our existing drive?"

"Maybe an additional thousand tons, but I don't like the risk. If the extra mass overloads the generator, that would end our trip real quick."

"If that happened, could you fix it?"

Mrraurr snorted. "If that happens, I'll be too busy disintegrating into my component atoms to turn a damned spanner, Captain."

"Understood. We'll try to keep the additional mass below the margin of error."

"You truly have the hearts of a warrior, Captain."

Harlan didn't miss the dig. Hind warriors were male, and generally not good for anything except hitting people with axes. "There's no need to be rude, Mrraurr."

"There is *always* need to be rude," she countered, and broke the connection.

Harlan turned back to Accountant, who was interlacing its tentacles nervously. "All right, we're looking for a system without skiplane access points. It will be in or near Hind space. The Osi Fain do not know its exact location, but they can infer it from the systems around it. Jumpdrives require a certain level of physical proximity, unlike skiplanes that can bypass dozens of systems." Harlan used his hands to direct the holoprojector, zooming it in on the region of territory claimed by the Hind.

"This would appear to be like finding one dark lightshrimp in a mass migration of thousands," Accountant said.

"We call it a needle in a haystack, but you're right. Let's see if we can narrow down the field of candidates." Harlan closed his eyes, imagining the data the Osi Fain had given him. "Crocodile, help me to overlay the Osi Fain map over the holo."

Crocodile swirled her tentacles through the holoprojection, at first tentatively and then with more conviction as she learned how the energy responded to her touch. She drew a series of lines, tracing between some stars and avoiding others.

Harlan looked at her marks, trying to interpret them. He had a sense of the past from Crocodile. "These relationships . . . are they routes between systems? Routes Osi Fain use?"

::*YES*::

"Okay, now we're getting somewhere." Harlan drew in the net further, keeping the routes visible but cutting down to a fringe of systems around them. "The Hind are taking Osi Fain from these paths. Where are the known Clan Sharassar systems?"

Accountant marked them on the map, a small cluster that was reasonably close to three Osi Fain paths.

"All right, now start digging into data on all star systems within, say, three jumps of the Clan Sharassar systems. Discount any that are within another Clan's territory, or within what would be considered Confederation space. How many targets are we looking at now?"

"Two hundred seventeen," Accountant said immediately.

"I'm liking those odds better already. Now eliminate any that are two systems or closer to Hind shipping routes. Sharassar will not want to risk an accidental discovery."

"One hundred fifty-three." Accountant marked them on the map.

Harlan scratched his jaw. "They're transporting the Osi Fain on ships. They have to hold them and keep them secure. Osi Fain plasma beams can cut through Hind shields, but that takes energy. They've got to be starving the Osi Fain, giving them just enough energy to keep them alive without allowing them to generate their beam weapons. That means a low-energy star with a low concentration of nutrient minerals." He crossed his arms. "How many of the remaining systems are white dwarfs?"

"Seven," Accountant reported. The way the Prodoni's tentacles were flapping around made Harlan think it was growing excited as well.

"Now we're talking. Here's where we have to be clever. How many of those systems either have no planets or we have incomplete information on them?"

"Five," Accountant said.

"Better, but still not good enough. What we really need is a way to track traffic into and out of those systems, but with Hind using jumpdrives, they could come in from anywhere." And then he had it, and snapped his fingers. "Can you track traffic in all the adjacent systems? Somewhere in one of those systems is a ship that leaves one and doesn't reappear where expected. Trace them further back if you have to, from the Osi Fain routes."

"This will take some time," Accountant admitted. "Data on Hind shipping is monitored by Confederate Intelligence."

"Can you get it?"

"Yes. There are Prodoni in the Intelligence division who will share it with me if I ask."

Harlan smiled. "In this business, it's all about who you know."

The *Regina* touched down on a landing pad and Harlan cracked his knuckles. "Let's go get the *Vengeance* back and get off this rock before somebody takes it in their head to cause problems for us."

* * *

Klorister was suspicious, of course, but her scanner tech thumped his tail and said it looked like an Osi Fain egg to him.

"How many have you actually seen?" she asked pointedly.

The other Aski Shantar licked his eyes clean. "Including this one? Two."

"So how do you know?"

Behind him, Harlan could feel Ekek itching for a fight. The Ri'Ar was still peeved at Klorister calling him *nothing* during their previous visit. He'd made no secret of the joy he would feel at opening her throat with his talons. He hoped the Ri'Ar kept himself under control. Negotiations were hard enough without incipient violence.

The technician's tail twitched. "Look, allowing for the fact that it was probably laid by a different mother and it's at a different stage of development, the biology is right. It matches Osi Fain across the board. If it's a forgery or a hoax, it's a better one than I can see."

"Is there an Osi Fain inside it?" Klorister asked.

The tech shrugged again. "There's something in there, but what it is, I can't say." He looked over at Harlan and Skarst. "How'd you say you got this again?"

"I didn't," Harlan said. "But it's freshly-laid, if that's what you need to know. We . . . happened upon a laying mother."

"And she just let you take her egg? Without a fight?" Klorister's suspicion crossed species barriers.

"We're pirates. Stealing is our specialty," Harlan said. "I've held up my end of the bargain. I'll take my ship back now." He paused. "Unless you intend to renege on our agreement. I would highly recommend against it." He patted his forearm. "My Osi Fain has quite a potent laser, and she's very well fed."

Klorister may have been a lot of things, but she wasn't a fool. Although her personal distaste at Harlan's species might have inclined her otherwise, her business savvy won out in the end. When one ran a large criminal syndicate on a single world, having a space pirate with no ties to any world in particular could turn out to be advantageous, especially when said pirate had connections both to the Hind, the Osi Fain, and his own mysterious race of aggressive hominids.

Although there were no actual keys to the *Vengeance*, Klorister herself contacted the dock supervisor and ordered the embargo on the vessel lifted on her authority. She turned her attention back to Harlan. "I still don't trust you, Human."

Harlan smiled. "The feeling is mutual, Klorister. See that it doesn't get you into trouble."

"Steer clear of Sto Shantu," said the Aski Shantar. "Next time, I won't be so charitable."

"Next time," Harlan said evenly, "neither will I."

CHAPTER
TWENTY-TWO

By the time Harlan and the others returned to the *Regina*, the crew was already dividing itself, some members staying aboard the smaller frigate while others returned to their berths aboard the bulk freighter. Frankly, Harlan was glad to see them go. He'd never liked crowds, and with two ships'-worth of crew crammed aboard the *Regina*, he'd felt like he could never get a moment's peace.

While the *Vengeance* crew prepared the ship for liftoff, Skarst deftly maneuvered the *Regina* back into her bay aboard the freighter. They'd been lucky not to be tagged by law enforcement or curious onlookers during their brief time on Sto Shantu, and the sooner they returned to anonymity, the better.

The *Vengeance* was heading into space by the time Harlan finished the various administrative tasks required of a ship's commander. He left the bridge in the capable hands of Skarst's team of pilots and returned to the hold on the *Regina* where he and Accountant had been working on narrowing down their target.

The Prodoni had managed to reach its contacts in Confederate Intelligence and when Harlan returned, it had eliminated one of the five systems entirely. Of the remaining four, Accountant had calculated percentages of how likely each one was to house the Clan Sharassar facility. One had a greater than fifty percent likelihood and Harlan pointed at it. "Why here?"

"There are two possible ways the Hind have been communicating with Osi Fain," the Prodoni said, lecturing like a professor. Or an accountant, Harlan thought wryly.

"Either they are using technology, or they are using telepathy. As telepathy does not exist among any other sapient races—barring your own, I'm given to understand —that would mean they are using one or more Prodoni to translate between the Hind and Osi Fain. I checked into distribution of required nutrients and other life support items traveling from Prodoni sources into Hind space and found indications that a small but statistically significant percentage are being shipped into the systems adjacent to this one." He highlighted the one in question. "If the Hind are keeping Prodoni in an otherwise empty system, they will need to import foodstuffs."

Harlan considered, and Accountant's logic tracked. "If they were using technological methods, we might not be able to identify it. You approached it from a different direction and I think you're right. Would a Prodoni agree to work for the enemy? Possibly in the equivalent of a concentration camp?"

A stream of bubbles rose from the tips of Accountant's tentacles. "Prodoni are each their own people, Captain. They can be as good or as evil as anyone else. They can be bought or be so focused upon the science of their work that they do not see the detriment."

Harlan snorted. "I understand that last better than you think." He reached out to the holo and expanded the display again, taking a closer look at what was still just a featureless white dot. "We've got our target. It's time to figure out a strategy. Take some time off, Accountant. You've earned it."

The Prodoni bubbled again. "On this ship? Is there a new zero-g lake in one of the holds of which I am unaware?"

"No. I'll look into it, though." Harlan paused by the hold exit to tap the intercom. "Skarst, Doctor Tchkit, Ekek, meet me in my office."

A few minutes later, Skarst and Doctor Tchkit arrived at Harlan's office with Ekek in tow. Ekek took up his usual station off to one side.

Skarst stepped over the back of a bifurcated chair in a peculiar display of dexterity that wound her up seated, her tail twitching like a cat's. Doctor Tchkit made a beeline for the sidebar where Harlan kept a small stash of snacks for when his blood sugar got too low for him to think.

"Everybody comfortable?" Harlan asked. He received a general noncommittal response that he felt was probably the best he would get. When he'd run the Philadelphia gang, he'd had to have occasional meetings of his lieutenants. They were invariably boisterous affairs that accomplished little except to convince him he'd be better off on his own. He'd been young then; now he knew he needed help with the upcoming mission.

He laid out what he and Accountant had derived from their research. "What this leaves us with is a target," he said in conclusion. "But what we don't know is vast."

Doctor Tchkit snorted. "We don't even know what we don't know."

"Clan Sharassar is holding at least one and most likely several Osi Fain prisoner. They're certainly starving them to keep them weak, and they must be using Prodoni to communicate with their prisoners. We can't risk jumping into the system and scanning. In a low-energy system like that, it would be like setting off a flare on a dark night."

"We can get a lot of information in less than a minute," Skarst pointed out. "And they'd have to have sensor buoys blanketing the system to mark us before we jumped back out."

"They're operating a clandestine prison and research facility. Why *wouldn't* they have sensor buoys everywhere?" Harlan asked. "It's what I'd do. No, we can't risk giving them any warning that we're onto them. That gives them time to prepare. I'd like to think we're a hell of a good crew in a hell of a good ship, but if they have any proper warships in that system, we're going to be a hell of a good cloud of radioactive ash."

"What if we jumped into the system fringes? The cometary cloud?" Doctor Tchkit asked. "Then we could fly in slow and quiet-like."

It was Skarst's turn to snort. "You should stick to doctoring, Tchkit. It would take us a year to close in from that far out, and we'd likely be detected from our drive signature before we covered a fraction of the required distance."

Tchkit blew his cheeks in a shrug. "We're brainstorming. There are no bad ideas until someone can laser them apart."

"Well, that's a bad idea," Skarst said.

"A frontal assault is out of the question?" Ekek asked. "We come in fast and hard from the darkness, strike from above while they're unprepared. We've had success with that tactic before."

"Maybe if we had good intelligence about what we're likely to face, that might work," Harlan admitted. The idea held a lot of appeal thanks to his destructive nature, but his common sense overrode it. "We could find ourselves facing an entire battle group or worse. I'm sure someday I'll go out in a blaze of glory, but I'd rather this not be my last stand." He sat at the end of the table, suddenly feeling like the old man he was fast becoming. "I . . . I want to see my home again. The only way I can see for that to happen is to free the Osi Fain prisoners."

"So here's how I see it," Skarst said, ticking off the points on her fingers. "We don't know what kind of facility is there. We don't know what kind of security it has. We don't know how many prisoners there are or how they're being held. We can't get any advance intel."

"That would seem to summarize things nicely," Doctor Tchkit said. "Maybe we just go up and knock politely on their front door and ask to see the pretty sky crabs."

Silence settled through the room.

"Why can't we do just that?" Skarst asked suddenly into the quiet. "We're in a Hind ship. If we just show up like we're supposed to be there, maybe they don't immediately blow us apart."

The germination of a plan began to form in Harlan's mind—not an assault, but a trick. A scam to take the Hind and leave them holding nothing while he and his crew got away with the Osi Fain. He touched the intercom. "Mrraurr, come to my office."

The engineer arrived a minute later, her fur blackened and smudged and stinking of an electrical fire. "What?"

"Something I should be concerned about?"

"No. What do you want?"

Harlan rubbed his chin. "You're doing good work here aboard the *Regina*."

"Yes, I know. What of it?"

"I think you're due for a promotion."

Mrraurr narrowed her eyes and bared her teeth in what was for her a subtle sneer. "To what?"

"Captain."

* * *

Work proceeded apace to transform the *Regina* back to something resembling her factory appearance. To Harlan's chagrin, part of that required painting over the elephant-head logo on the ship's bow. He knew this was temporary, but it was still disappointing to see it returned to its bland coloration. Using spare parts available on board the *Vengeance*, another crew worked feverishly to alter the *Regina*'s sensor profile and drive signature, using data provided from Harlan's memory and Mrraurr's knowledge of Clan Sharassar vessels. Their ultimate end game was to disguise the *Regina* as a Sharassar vessel, albeit one not on any registry. The implication was for her to be from a covert organization within the Clan, one devoted to dirty tricks and espionage. It would make their appearance easier to swallow for whomever was operating the Osi Fain prison facility.

Harlan wasn't about to allow the ship to be renamed the unpronounceable garbage she'd borne when he and his team first took command, even though Mrraurr was in favor of it. Clan Sharassar had battleships with poetic names like *Blood Afire.* Harlan decided *Midnight Blade* conveyed suitably mysterious origins while giving credence to their fictional origin story.

While Mrraurr and the rest of the pirate crew worked on the *Regina's* hull and engines, Harlan had his own project to complete. He still had most of the warheads he and his team had stolen from the Tokras system. He worked on installing a valve in each warhead's radiation shielding. His intent was to allow a controlled amount of energy to escape through a filter of his own design, that converted the hard radiation into something softer, resembling sunlight. He estimated the valves would function as designed for several hours before they failed. In the interim, they would suffice to provide safe, consumable energy to the Osi Fain prisoners and perhaps give them the strength they would need to fight or flee.

He bound each warhead to a canister of compressed gases and aerosolized minerals. Between that and the radiation, he felt like he'd built a suitably nutritious portable snack for Osi Fain. Crocodile examined his work and agreed that although it might not be what they got in a natural setting, it would provide them sustenance.

"Sustenance," Harlan said aloud. "That's not the same as food. *Sustenance* keeps you alive. Food is supposed to be enjoyable." He himself had never given much thought about food. It was fuel for his body and mind, and a necessary distraction from his work. If he could sustain himself without the hassle of eating and eliminating waste, he might take that step.

::*NOT ENJOYABLE*:: Crocodile said, a distinct peevish tone to her mental words.

Harlan snorted. "I'm nobody's chef. This is just supposed to keep them alive. You agree that will work?"

::*YES*::

"Then don't be rude."

Mrraurr padded into Harlan's workshop, her fur matted with sweat from several hours spent in a vacc suit crawling across the *Regina*'s hull. Harlan didn't hassle her about her stink, her appearance, or her unannounced entrance. She wasn't given to niceties of polite, civil behavior, and he appreciated that she didn't try to hide who she was. On the other hand, he was about to ask her to do exactly that, so at the very least she was going to have to clean herself up to be presentable to other Hind.

"How goes the redecoration?" he asked her.

"We'll be done in two hours," she said. "But there's a problem that you haven't addressed yet, Captain."

"What's that . . . *Captain*?" He emphasized the last, reminding her that it would be her title when they arrived at their destination.

"No other Hind aboard the *Regina*," Mrraurr said. "Unless you're planning to simulate that somehow too, it'll take one cursory scan to see this ship is full of non-Hind life signs. I don't care who's running that mysterious installation. They see a ship full of Aski Shantar and Ri'Ar, they're going to blow us into dust first and ask questions later."

Harlan reached under his workbench and withdrew an innocuous-looking component. "I'm glad you brought that up, Mrraurr. It means you're thinking along the right lines. I did consider that and this is my solution." He handed the component to her.

"What is it?" she asked, turning it around in her powerful hands where it seemed even smaller and less impressive.

"I don't know what else to call it, so I'm calling it scramble projector." Harlan was quite proud of the little device he'd created by synthesizing his knowledge of Earth technology with that of the Hind and the Confederation. "Plug it into our own sensors, right at the receiver array."

"What will it do?"

"When it detects a sensor query, it will use the ship's hull as a canvas and overlay Hindish life signs upon our crew, but it will also scramble the data. Anyone scanning us will get heavy interference, which would make sense if we're from a covert organization. They will get enough data to suggest the ship is populated with Hind, or mostly Hind. It will depend upon how curious a sensor operator gets. If they work at it, they'll be able to unscramble the data, but it will take some time."

"How much time?" Mrraurr asked.

Harlan shrugged. "Hopefully longer than we need it to."

"That's a shit answer."

"It's a shit problem. I'm improvising here and we don't have a lot of time or resources."

"Why the hurry?" Mrraurr asked. "What is six more hours? Or six days? Or a sixth of a year?"

Harlan turned away from her. "The sooner we free the Osi Fain, the sooner I can find out where my home system is and go there."

"Are you expecting it to be gone?"

Harlan sighed. "I hope not. I could be an accidental time traveler, maybe by hundreds of years or worse. I need to know."

Mrraurr put a heavy hand upon his shoulder. "Your mate. I understand."

"She's not my mate," Harlan swiped the hand away.

"But you want her to be." Mrraurr chuckled. "You're like a moon-sick cub in estrus for the first time, pining for a warrior who's away at battle." She turned and loped back to the door. "See that you have your hearts focused for this mission, Captain. We can't afford for you to be thinking with your gonads."

CHAPTER
TWENTY-THREE

The white dwarf star didn't have a name, only an eight digit survey number on Confederate star charts. No planets orbited the tiny stellar remnant. It was significantly cooler than any other white dwarf that had been surveyed or scanned by astronomers, making it one of the oldest stars in or near the Confederation.

A sensor mark posted on the holo display, orbiting the star at a distance of several hundred million kilometers. It would have taken the *Regina* many days of travel to close the distance under conventional thrust, but between Skarst and Mrraurr, they figured a micro-jump could get them to within less than a hundred thousand kilometers.

"Incoming message from the sensor mark," Skarst said over her shoulder.

"Here we go," said Doctor Tchkit.

"Play it," Harlan ordered, and folded his arms.

"Unidentified vessel . . ." the Hind voice growled. "This system is forbidden to travel. Leave now or be destroyed."

"I'm overcome with emotion at such a warm reception," the Doctor said. "I might actually cry a little."

Harlan turned to Skarst, whose dexterous fingers flew across multiple keyboards as she tried to decrypt the bare bones of the transmission. "Anything? Any kind of identifier at all?"

"No, damn them!" Skarst slapped her tail on the deck in frustration. "It's all . . . wait! Found it in the carrier wave. *Icecloud!*"

Harlan opened the communication circuit. He'd built an analog filter into it that converted his voice into that of a female Hind. "Icecloud Station, this is the *Midnight Blade*. We are here by order of Clanmistress Shmirash of the Black Claw." According to Mrraurr, Black Claw was the covert intelligence division of Clan Sharassar. Harlan understood it to be roughly analogous to the black ops side of the American Central Intelligence Agency. It would make sense for the Black Claw to take an interest in an Osi Fain prison compound. Harlan was gambling with his life and those of his crew, but no plan was without risk.

There was a lengthy pause before anyone from Icecloud Station responded. Harlan hoped it was because their arrival in system and subsequent identification had raised a panic among the station personnel. It was the equivalent of unmarked black SUVs rolling up outside of a business and disgorging a couple dozen faceless agents with mirrorshades and earbud radios.

The Hind who'd initially threatened them was much more subdued in her next communication. "What is your mission here, *Midnight Blade*?"

"Our mission is not to be transmitted over an open channel," Harlan retorted "We will discuss it after we dock. Prepare a suitable receiving platform. Any hostile actions will result in destruction of your facility, and I don't give a damn about your prisoners."

"Confirmed, *Midnight Blade*. Dock on Three Starboard."

Harlan switched off the comm and looked at Skarst. "Are you ready?"

"Yes." The Aski Shantar adjusted some controls. "I've got a scan of the station. There's a large spherical chamber one end, made of radiation-absorbing material and then wrapped up in an energy shield, directly opposite the reactor. It's probably where your Osi Fain prisoners are being held. They won't get the slightest bit of stray solar energy through that shield. It's not going to be easy to get inside."

Harlan nodded. "Fortunately, we're not the ones who need to do that. Ekek, are your soldiers ready?"

"Affirmative," said the Ri'Ar over his suit radio. He and a half dozen of his best soldiers were waiting patiently outside the *Regina*, their talons locked around perches mounted just ahead of the drive shielding. They'd be impossible to see on sensors and difficult to spot with the naked eye. They had the radiation canisters held inside a protected pod, their weapons and gear, and a device Harlan had built that would create a hole within a Hind shield. He'd used one to breach the Hind field encapsulating New York City. Getting through this shield would be child's play.

"Stand by for microjump," Skarst warned as her hand hovered over the engagement button. "Four . . . three . . . two . . . mark." She touched the button. Within the bowels of the ship, the massive bank of capacitors spat their accumulated energy into the interdimensional black box that formed the heart of the ship's jumpdrive. It twisted itself inside out, shuffling through spacetime on its predetermined course and dragging the ship along with it. A moment later, the *Regina* was drifting less than a hundred thousand kilometers from Icecloud Station.

"Nicely done," Harlan told Skarst. "Bring us in."

"Aye, Captain."

* * *

Harlan wasn't surprised to see a half dozen armed warriors arranged in a semicircle outside the airlock when he and Mrraurr emerged. It was a sensible precaution when a strange vessel suddenly appeared in what should have been a system devoid of traffic. The warriors kept their small laser sidearms holstered as it was a poor choice to fire weapons of that sort in a boarding corridor to prevent sudden and irreversible explosive decompression. All of them had their axes out and at the ready. Grumblings and murmurs ran through them at the sight of the peculiar bipedal alien that was Harlan, but they'd been well-trained and none of them leaped to attack despite their obvious desire to do so.

Humans

"I am Hindmistress Mrraurr of the *Black Claw*," Mrraurr announced in her most haughty voice. "Bring me the Mistress in charge of this facility immediately."

Two of the warriors moved aside to let a female through. Her mane was tied up into twin poms that reminded Harlan of a poodle. He smiled at the thought. "I am Hindmistress Vashaktes. What is the meaning of this intrusion?"

Mrraurr folded her arms over her massive torso. "The Clan is disappointed in your lack of progress with the prisoners. I am here to fix that."

Vashaktes eyed Harlan in his plain skinsuit but did nothing else to acknowledge his presence. To do so prior to an introduction would have been a violation of the complex rules of Hind social interactions. "Our Prodoni are working as hard as they can, but it is an arduous process. Translating their language is a difficult and imprecise science. In many ways, the confounding creatures are more like machines than living beings, and as useful as Prodoni telepathy is, it does not work on machines. The Clan asks me to do the impossible and then complains that I don't provide sufficient results."

Mrraurr glanced at Harlan. The conversation was already going in a direction they hadn't expected. He knew his ship's engineer was imaginative when it came to solutions to technical problems, but he had no idea how she would respond in a situation requiring layer upon layer of falsehoods. He silently implored her to step up and bluster, the way a government stooge would with the weight of powerful, shadowy agencies behind him.

"We are the Black Claw. We don't allow impossibilities to stop progress," Mrraurr said with all the conviction of a zealot. "Take us to see your captives."

A warrior raised his axe a few centimeters—not an overt threat, but a subtle reminder that Mrraurr and Harlan were outnumbered. Vashaktes made a quick lateral gesture with one hand and the axes dropped once more. "Not without an explanation of this . . . *primate*." The Hindmistress made the term sound even filthier than the much more offensive *monkey*. Still, Harlan kept his temper in check. It was imperative that he was seen as the tool, not as the one wielding it.

Mrraurr looked down her broad nose at him. "This creature is of a race who can communicate with Osi Fain."

"Bullshit."

Harlan had to cough to cover his snort of laughter. The telepathic linguistic ability he'd received from Bubble the Prodoni sometimes provided unexpectedly accurate translations.

The warriors raised their axes. "What is wrong with it? Is it about to attack?" one of them shouted.

"Stand down, idiot," Mrraurr ordered. "It is but four-sixths of an Indran, by the Accord of the Fist. Are you such a coward that you fear a tiny being as this? It couldn't threaten a Jemra."

Doctor Tchkit would have been so offended at that, Harlan thought. Absolutely as angry as a giant prairie dog could get.

The warrior, cowed by Mrraurr's call-out, stepped back in chagrin.

"I have myself seen this creature speak to Osi Fain. It will succeed where your Prodoni have been failing repeatedly. Now, are you going to take me to see your prisoners or are you going to keep me here in the corridor to gossip like a pair of Submistresses?" Mrraurr drew herself up to her most imperious height.

"Of course," Vashaktes said through clenched teeth. "Fall in," she ordered, and the warriors moved aside to allow Mrraurr and Harlan passage. Vashaktes turned and led the two of them through the ranks of males, who then moved into marching formation behind them. Harlan's nerves sang like violin strings drawn too tight. He had no weapons, no armor. Crocodile had her own mission and it was imperative she wasn't seen until the moment Harlan called for her.

Like most Hind-built construction, Icecloud Station was a single deck with ramps and spirals leading to super- or substructures, as the centaurian beings disliked stairs. The interior was spartan, without so much as a single splash of color to break up the monotonous gray metal walls and decking. If it wasn't for the warriors' armor, the entire facility might as well have been monochrome. Hind warriors decorated their armor with martial patterns representing their clans, their family lines, their exploits, and those heroic deeds of their ancestors. Each warrior's armor was different in its intricate detail. From what Harlan knew, any damage to their armor would be repaired and then the graphics painstakingly recreated.

They arrived at a broad control deck with a wide window overseeing the interior of the force field sphere. A clump of Osi Fain clustered together across the central ring, huddling together for warmth, for companionship, and to stay as far away as possible from their captors. Where Crocodile's silicon flesh had a healthy blue cast with pinkish streaks crisscrossing it, the prisoners were a dark indigo and their skin had taken on a rocky appearance. It was as if they were transforming themselves into asteroids. Or more likely, Harlan thought, it was the indication of a slow death by starvation. It made him uncomfortable, like someone was digging a needle into the space between his eyes.

Still, he had a job to do. He stepped forward as if to get a better look at the prisoners and leaned casually against a console. It would have been easier if he still had his nanotech. He could have slipped a slender thread of microscopic machines into the hardware and taken command of it from within. Without that tool, he had to rely more heavily upon his natural parahuman ability to control machinery and devices.

He'd encountered Hind systems before. Using his parahuman ability, he dug into the system and disabled the sensors pointing into the spherical pen, while freezing the displays so they would continue to show all systems functioning correctly. Once he'd completed that task, he searched Icecloud Station's database for something he could use.

And there it was: a place labeled *Monkeyworld*. It was what the Hind called Earth. They knew where it was. Harlan felt himself starting to tremble with anticipation as he dug deeper into the data.

It was fourteen jumps away. It had been a period of time equivalent to ten years since station personnel had first pried that information out of an Osi Fain, and nine years since the Sharassar battle group had departed for their failed invasion of Earth. They'd had no choice but to win or die, Harlan thought. The ships would have had no fuel left for their return trip and synthesizing enough from the outer planets would have taken decades.

The Hindmistresses of Sharassar had judged Clanmistress Rhaorhir's mission a failure. Monkeyworld was too far to reach with current jumpdrive technology, and they had never sent a follow-up mission. That, at least, put Harlan's mind at ease. They'd ordered *Icecloud Station* to find a closer civilization to conquer, and save Monkeyworld for a future war. The timeline meant that Harlan had indeed been catapulted through time as well as space, but not nearly as far as he'd feared. It had been 2013 when he left. It was probably 2021 or 2022 now. It was likely then that his nephew was still alive, and Mustang Sally and Minerva as well.

And . . . Penny.

He knew where he was. He knew *when* he was. He could make some excuse, return to the *Regina*, and flee this system, never looking back. He could go home.

His eye fell on the captive Osi Fain. Technicians used tractor beams to separate the cluster of spaceborne beings. As the inexorable beams pulled apart the weakened creatures, they exuded tendrils of their flesh, reaching toward one another in a futile attempt to retain physical contact. At last, the techs successfully separated one completely from the others and used their beams to hold the rest of the group back. The separated Osi Fain's flesh grew hard and rocky once more as she was tugged across the empty space within the force field.

No, Harlan decided. He wouldn't turn his back on them. He reached out mentally for Crocodile, knowing she was close by and awaiting his signal. A tiny flicker of recognition tickled at his mind at the extreme edge of his range. He sent her the simple one-word command she'd been awaiting.

Go.

* * *

The captive Osi Fain was dragged into an airlock that would be pressurized for the convenience of the interrogators. Harlan and Mrraurr were escorted from the command center. A Prodoni in a mobile tank joined them outside the airlock. Vashaktes motioned to the squid in its quadropedic tank. "This is Linguist. It will monitor you and your attempt to communicate with the prisoner."

The Prodoni said nothing as it regarded Mrraurr and Harlan through the dark eyes in its arrow-shaped body. Its mottled flesh cycled through subtle color changes. Harlan knew he couldn't let it dig deep into his psyche. Whether or not it could actually understand his communication with the prisoner, it could certainly comprehend his plan if it caught a stray thought. He decided more direct action was required.

He reached out with his power for the environmental controls in the mobile tank. They were simple and easy for him to alter. A nudge to the filtration system and several trace elements began to leach into the water at several hundred times their normal levels. An equally subtle nudge to the internal display and Linguist would never discover it was sitting in a toxic solution until it was too late.

While they were in the airlock with the Osi Fain, Harlan hoped things were going smoothly for Ekek and Crocodile. The Ri'Ar marines were supposed to crawl across the outer surface of the ring bisecting the force field. When they reached the edge, they would activate the device Harlan provided, which would create a gap in the field large enough for Crocodile to slip inside. She would configure her shape to carry all the warhead capsules with her, delivering an immediate dose of nutrients to the prisoners. By calling to them, the group of Osi Fain could drift across the pen to where Crocodile awaited, and she could mix with them so the Hind couldn't tell another had joined the prisoners.

Once they delivered the payload of warheads and Crocodile into the field, Ekek and his soldiers would spread out across Icecloud Station, targeting communications and sensor arrays, weapons turrets, and docking tubes with shaped charges. At the prearranged signal, they would detonate and then make for the *Regina*. Between the pandemonium of an attack from all sides and a suddenly powered Osi Fain population, Harlan hoped that they would be able to escape the station with minimal casualties.

But first, he needed to give Crocodile enough time to fulfill her task.

"Well?" Vashaktes growled. "We're waiting, primate. Show us you can do better than Linguist, here."

Harlan took a deep breath. He had committed to this rescue. It was time to see it through.

CHAPTER
TWENTY-FOUR

Hello? Can you hear me?

:: . . . ::

Harlan tried to reach out telepathically, and had no idea if it was working. When he'd first communicated with Crocodile, he'd had better luck using simple, non-lingual concepts. Then later, he was most comfortable speaking aloud. It was only most recently, when he and she had truly built their own form of communication, that he could think to her and she to him. This prisoner before him was terribly weak, with sluggish thoughts barely traversing the creature's organic circuitry.

"She's starving," he said aloud.

"This prisoner is starving," Mrraurr repeated. "I do not approve of this mistreatment. Holding prisoners is unnatural for the Hind."

"They are lesser beings," Vashaktes said. "Star-travelers or not. Our destiny is to conquer them and theirs is to submit. Accord of the Fist!" She raised her fist.

"Accord of the Fist!" the two warriors in the room echoed.

"Don't spit your foolish catechism at me," Mrraurr snarled. "The Black Claw has no time for fanatics. We want results. Now feed it so it can speak."

Vashaktes snorted. "We're not about to give it anything above bare subsistence. They're still prisoners and they still have biological weapons." She pointed to a discolored scar in the metal of the bulkhead, which Harlan identified as an inexpertly completed repair job. "There was a prisoner who had an idea about trying to escape. The others gave up their own nutrients to give

263

everything to that one. It fired a laser in here and killed two technicians and a warrior before we killed it."

Harlan wasn't paying any attention to Vashaktes. His attention was on the Osi Fain. *Hello? Can you hear me?*

:: . . . ::

I'm trying to save you and your kin, but you have to help me.

::HELP::

That was progress. Harlan reached out to place his bare hands upon the Osi Fain. Her skin was cold to the touch, almost unpleasantly so. It was like handling a piece of ice without gloves. Still, Harlan wanted the creature to feel his familiarity with another of its race. *I can help you, but you must not fire your laser.*

::NO::

The interior door slid open and a technician entered with a device that looked like a syringe the size of Harlan's arm. At Vashaktes' order, the technician activated the device. The airlock filled with acrid smoke as a laser burned a hole in the Osi Fain's flesh. Her psychic scream of pain nearly made Harlan dash his head into a bulkhead. The tech jammed the syringe into the open wound she'd just created and injected the solution within into the Osi Fain.

::PAIN::

I know it hurts, Harlan thought. *Be strong.* "What is that you gave her?" he asked.

"A cesium suspension in a mineral slurry. Just enough to wake it up a bit," Vashaktes said. A turret lowered from the airlock's ceiling to point directly at the Osi Fain. "If it so much as twitches, I'm putting it down, and I'm not going to be too careful about who's in the way. Make it talk, primate."

Harlan glanced at Linguist, floating in its watery chamber. He had no idea what kind of physiological response to expect from the Prodoni as its environment slowly grew toxic. As far as he could tell, it was still paying attention to him. He turned his full attention to the Osi Fain before him.

"Do you hear me? Move your flesh if you do." Harlan asked aloud. *Respond to me. Ripple your flesh.*

::PAIN::

Please. The pain will end soon and you will be free to travel the stars once more. I promise.

A ripple traveled down the Osi Fain's flesh, slow and deliberate.

Harlan wanted to look back at Vashaktes in triumph, but knew he needed to at least give the appearance of subservience to Mrraurr.

"You see?" Mrraurr crowed. "It responds to him."

Vashaktes wasn't impressed. "That's the best he can do? Ask it something of consequence. Give me the location of a race the Hind can conquer."

Harlan glanced at the Prodoni once again. It was drifting listlessly in its tank, tentacles brushing against the bottom surface. A quick check of the mobile tank's environmental monitoring system showed that the creature's life signs had dropped to a dangerously low level. The conflict Harlan had set up in the system's programming was keeping it from responding with corrective or emergency notification measures. He smiled. Now it didn't matter what he said to the Osi Fain; he was safe from telepathic monitoring.

He conversed with the Osi Fain for a few minutes, sensing how tired and hurt she was. He promised her once again he would free her, and it would be a short time coming. *We have brought you nutrients. Your family in the pen is hiding it for you. My partner is one of you. She will tell you the details of the plan. Be ready to act when it is time.*

::COMPREHENSION::

Satisfied, Harlan turned to Mrraurr. "Tell her I need to see her star charts."

* * *

Soon, Harlan thought. Crocodile reported she had successfully smuggled the nutrient canisters into the pen and quietly distributed them to all the Osi Fain prisoners. Each canister was snuggled deep inside the flesh of the beings, leaching its controlled radiation and nutrient blend into them, giving them strength and hope. She herself was anxious about Harlan's safety, and to a lesser extent to that of his ship and crew. She understood that even though they were *Soft Ones*, it didn't mean they were lesser beings. They were important to Harlan, and that made them important to her too.

Harlan poked through the Hindish star charts until he found the Solar System among them. He took his time to locate it, extending the drama. He pointed to it on the holographic display. "This system," he said. "A small yellow star, many jumps away from here. Notable for a gas giant with a spectacular ring system, another with an extreme axial tilt, and a planet harboring a native species of sapient primates." He smiled, showing his teeth. "*Monkeys*, if you wish."

Vashaktes' eyes narrowed. "Wait . . . This seems familiar."

Ready, Crocodile, Harlan thought.

::YES::

"It should seem familiar," Harlan said. "Because your Clan sent a battle group of axeships there. I know, because I was there. I and my people destroyed them all, Vashaktes." He drew himself up to his full height. Out of the corner of his eye, Mrraurr yanked her emergency hood over her head and slapped it against the collar of her suit. "I am Harlan Washington of Earth!"

Brilliant pink laser light flashed across the broad viewing portal of the command center, splitting it from edge to edge.

The portal blew outward into the pen, sending screaming and flailing Hind into vacuum. Harlan tumbled afterward, blinking furiously to keep his eyes from freezing over. Although his instinct was to hold his breath, Harlan knew to do so would cause his lungs to rupture and instead he exhaled as forcefully as he could. A shadow blotted out the stars and a moment later Crocodile enveloped him in her warm and loving embrace. He felt fresh oxygenated air flow into his lungs, manufactured by her complex internal chemistry. His exposed skin stung with the tingling pain of ruptured capillaries and tingled as if he'd just had a bucket of ice water thrown on him.

"Hi," he said.

::HI:: she responded.

His lightweight Mark V helmet flowed from her body material to fit itself over his head. Something collided with him. He saw Vashaktes floating beside him, clutching feebly at him as the last of her life leaked away. She'd held her breath and her sides were torn open, orange ice forming along the edges of the wounds as her blood froze. He kicked her away, a piece of useless, frozen space debris.

"Mrraurr?" he called.

"Here, Captain." A centaurian figure amid the others floating across the pen waved and set off her emergency beacon.

"I'm calling you an Uber," Harlan said. "Don't go anywhere."

Mrraurr's retort was untranslatable.

At Harlan's behest, Crocodile sent one of the other Osi Fain to collect Mrraurr. As it did so, brilliant emergency lights filled the pen as Icecloud Station began to respond to the sudden and unexpected attack. Even though the command center was a total loss, Hind elsewhere in the station had the wherewithal to seal sections and use auxiliary controls to take charge of the station's functions. Laser turrets activated and swung around to point inward toward the Osi Fain in the pen.

"Ekek, now!" Harlan called.

With a series of brilliant flashes, it seemed like the entire surface of Icecloud Station exploded outward. The coordinated charges blew apart laser turrets and communications arrays. A globular debris cloud expanded away from the station. Atmosphere burst out from several more sections and electricity arced between damaged conduits. The force field encapsulating the Osi Fain pen flickered and died, leaving the creatures free to escape. Then, from one top corner, a turret that Ekek's soldiers missed opened up, firing a steady stream of crimson beams toward the Osi Fain with little regard for any collateral damage that might be sustained elsewhere on the station.

Harlan approved of the mindset, even though it would ultimately be for naught. Hind lasers were notoriously inaccurate, a fault more of the designers than the machinery. "Scatter and regroup at the *Regina*," Harlan called over his radio. "Skarst, go!"

"Already in the sky, Captain," the Aski Shantar said even as the *Regina* rose past the curve of the station's hull, her own lasers far more accurate. The last turret exploded in a spectacular blossom of released fusion energy and debris.

A flock of Ri'Ar emerged from the far end of the station's ring, hip lasers at the ready, tiny jets mounted upon their wingtips giving them the same mobility as if they were aloft in atmosphere. They swooped along the ring, picking targets of opportunity as they made for the *Regina*'s yawning cargo hatches.

"Crocodile, get the others to follow us and spread themselves across the *Regina*'s hull. I know they're still exhausted and we can get them out of the system safely."

An Osi Fain flew past them, faint energies dancing across her flesh as she sucked more of Harlan's nutrient cocktail into her system. Mrraurr was perched upon the Osi Fain's dorsal surface, her four feet splayed wide for balance and her hands wrapped around protruding spikes. She looked like a high-tech cowgirl riding a bucking bronco. He paced her in toward the *Regina* and when they got close and the Osi Fain slowed, he reached out a hand. She hesitated, then took it, jumping clear of the Osi Fain.

Crocodile braked hard and set Harlan and Mrraurr upon the cargo bay deck with barely a bump. "Nice job," Harlan said to her. "Mrraurr, are you all right?"

Mrraurr sneezed with laughter. "That was fun, monkey."

"That's *Captain* Monkey."

Mrraurr laughed harder. "Let's do it again."

The hull around them thudded as Osi Fain struck it, spreading themselves out like a layer of rocky armor.

"Get to the Engine Room," Harlan said. "We've got a lot of extra mass to transport."

"I'll do my best, Captain."

"Mrraurr . . ."

The Hind twisted her upper torso around to look over her shoulder at him. The death of dozens of her fellow species didn't seem to have discomforted her in the least. "Yes?"

"Nobody gets left behind, understand? Every living Osi Fain leaves this system with us."

"Aye, sir."

Crocodile, make sure your people leave the forward missile tubes uncovered. Three holes at the prow. You know where they are. I showed you once.

::YES::

"Make yourself comfortable. We'll be jumping out of this system in a few minutes."

::YES::

Harlan headed for the bridge. He ran across Kleketik and his troopers exiting another cargo bay. The Ri'Ar were jubilant, shouting boisterously about the destruction they'd wrought upon Icecloud Station. Harlan didn't mind the celebration. They'd done good work, and he told Kleketik so.

The Ri'Ar inclined his head, his feathers sticking up wildly from being cooped up in a helmet for hours. "It was a genuine pleasure to punish the Hind. We hope to do so again soon."

"I'll make sure you have the opportunity. Where's—" He looked around and started in surprise as he saw Ekek standing silently behind him, just off his shoulder. "Damn it, Ekek, stop being so unobtrusive."

"It is my job, Captain. You should never notice me until such a time as my presence is required."

"I suppose that's fair. Sorry you missed all the excitement."

Ekek snapped his beak. "Commander Skarst allowed me to fire the *Regina*'s lasers. I feel my participation wasn't lacking."

"Nice shooting, then."

"Thank you, Captain."

They entered the bridge. Skarst thumped her tail at him while Doctor Tchkit jumped up and down in chubby excitement. "That was very exciting!" the oversized rodent crowed. "Next time, I'll make sure I have enough snacks to really enjoy it."

Harlan dropped into his seat, grateful to finally have a moment's rest. "Skarst, how are we looking?"

"She's very heavy, Captain. The *Regina* might once have been a cargo vessel, but those Osi Fain are *massively* dense. We've got almost double our rated mass spread across the hull right now."

"What's our worst case scenario?"

"The generators fail explosively and we get to do our best impression of a supernova."

"What's slightly better than that?"

"We can't exceed our mass limit. Part of the ship jumps and part of it doesn't. I wouldn't want to be in either portion."

"Understood. Let's get rid of a little bit of mass we can spare. Fire missiles from tubes two and three at Icecloud Station. I want it gone."

Skarst tweaked some controls and looked back at him. "Do you want to do the honors, Captain?"

Harlan made a conciliatory gesture. "No, go ahead."

A brief shudder and roar of the missiles' drives firing passed through the *Regina*'s frame. On the holo, the bridge crew watched as the twin points of light drove out and downward toward Icecloud Station. The concentration camp vanished in a flare of brilliant energy, to be replaced by an expanding cloud of irradiated particles.

"Beautiful," Doctor Tchkit said. "What a pity nobody will ever know."

Harlan smiled. "Well, I could hardly not leave a calling card." He touched a button. A thump below their feet indicated he'd dropped a repeater buoy from the ventral socket.

Skarst adjusted the controls, then adjusted them again. She turned to Harlan. "I know you dropped a buoy. The inventory's right, and I heard it leave, but I can't find it. What did you do?"

"Just a little stealth technology. It won't be impossible to find, but it'll be very difficult without some fairly sophisticated sensors. Better than what we have."

"I'm getting a signal," Skarst said.

"Put it on the speakers," Harlan advised.

Skarst did so and Harlan heard a recording of his own voice played back to him. "*I am Harlan Washington the Destroyer, and I have eliminated this facility.*" A few seconds of silence passed, and then the recording began again.

"Well, technically it was me who did it," Skarst pointed out. "But you can claim the credit, Captain."

"Thanks, I will," Harlan said.

"You ready to risk departing?" asked Doctor Tchkit. "We could always make two or even three trips to get everybody."

"No, every time we leave Osi Fain behind, it would increase the chances the Hind come here and recapture them. We all go at once." Harlan patted the arm of his seat. "*Regina* is a good, strong ship, with the best crew in the Confederation. She won't let us down." He leaned back, crossed his legs and said to Skarst, "Go."

They went.

CHAPTER
TWENTY-FIVE

The journey back to the Gabelko system took longer than it would have without nearly two dozen Osi Fain in tow. First the *Regina* had to successfully escape from Hind space, evading military patrols and civilian vessels alike. Fortunately, Skarst's piloting managed to keep them at safe distances from deep sensor scans while the overstressed jumpdrive recovered from the tremendous mass it was being asked to transport.

They took a three-day rest in a system off the main trade routes in Confederate space, giving the former Osi Fain prisoners time to soak up solar energy and harvest chemicals from the upper clouds of a dark and stormy gas giant, marked with a sparkling halo ring of ice crystals and near constant lightning dancing between cloud summits. During that time, Harlan repainted the elephant logo on the *Regina*'s prow. Like any good pirate, he felt it was important to have a symbol by which others would associate him.

When he wasn't space-walking with a high-tech paintbrush in hand, Harlan spent his spare time in Engineering with Mrraurr, working to keep the jumpdrive generators in top-notch condition. The Osi Fain could travel via skiplanes, but that would have required them to travel through some high-traffic areas. Protected species or not, the Navy would take a special interest in an entire colony of them being escorted by a known space pirate. It was best for them to move between systems with the aid of the *Regina*'s jumpdrive and avoid traffic altogether.

"You're playing with a high explosive with a short fuse," Mrraurr complained after the portside generator burned through its insulation for the third consecutive trial. "These generators were never meant to support so much mass. We need generators from Axeships to do this, and we're making do with middling civilian models."

"Replace the insulation," Harlan said. "We'll manage. Four more jumps and we're in Gabelko."

"Why not just go? They're spaceborne. They've been existing for millions of years. I'm sure they'll manage." Mrraurr used her powerful arms and claws to rip away the burnt insulation instead of a more appropriate tool. Her frustration was evident in every motion.

"Three of them are still too weak to travel on their own," Harlan said. "And I made a promise. I've done a lot of unflattering things, but I have never reneged on a promise. I don't intend to start that now."

"So much honor," Mrraurr grumbled. "You sound like a stupid Hind warrior."

"There's no need to be insulting."

"You'd rather me call you *monkey*?"

Harlan smiled. "I believe you are the sole member of your species to have earned that right."

* * *

At last, they jumped into the Gabelko system, appearing only a dozen planetary diameters above the protoplanet where they'd first found the Osi Fain colony. The former prisoners wasted no time tumbling off the *Regina*'s hull to rejoin with the others. The spaceborne danced back and forth, intertwining their spines and spinning around each other in the species-equivalent of joyful hugs.

"Navy's still two hours out," Skarst said with satisfaction. "If they're this worried about people like us, they should have a larger contingent in-system."

"Plenty of time," Harlan said, watching the Osi Fain cavort through the dust clouds. *Are you sure you don't want to join them?* he asked Crocodile through the telepathic link they shared. She was in her cargo bay, the door open so she could enjoy the taste of space dust and hot sunlight.

::*STAY*:: Crocodile was as verbose as ever, leaving Harlan to fill in the blanks himself. He'd given her every opportunity to leave, to rejoin her kin, and she had chosen to stay time and time again. As the elder Osi Fain had said, she had imprinted upon him and didn't want to leave.

Maybe we just go fly with them for a little while then?
::*YES*::

Harlan turned away from the viewport. "I'm taking Crocodile out for a spin with her friends and family."

"Don't be long," Skarst said. "There *is* a cruiser inbound."

Harlan snorted. "If they want to fire on us, I suspect they'll have almost fifty angry Osi Fain to contend with. I wouldn't put odds on any vessel surviving that kind of rage." He nodded toward the protoplanet outside. "Especially when the natives are so well fed."

"You know, Captain, I'm a little concerned about what kind of lasting effects you may suffer from your repeated physical contact with the Osi Fain," Doctor Tchkit said. "There's so much we don't know about them, and it's entirely possible your physiology may suffer deleterious effects. Or hers, for that matter."

"Chronologically, I'm well past the halfway point of my lifespan," Harlan said. "And with the kind of life I've led, I'm already living the bonus years. Whether I die from space cancer or a space heart attack, one day I will die." He nodded toward the Osi Fain playing outside. "This makes it worth it."

Doctor Tchkit took a drink from his bottle. "Shit happens to all of us eventually."

Harlan joined Crocodile in the bay that he thought of as her nest. She was spinning slowly in midair as he entered through the hatch. As soon as she sensed him, she flew over to encapsulate him. His own sensors came on line instantly as she interfaced with the display in his helmet.

"Hi, Croc," he said, surprising himself with the cheerful note in his voice.

::HI::

The bay depressurized and opened to space. Harlan flew out and came to a sudden stop as he realized what looked like the entire Osi Fain colony was arrayed before him, spread out in a lattice formation with thin tendrils stretching between them and linking them together. "What's going on?" he whispered to Crocodile.

::SINGING::

One of the larger Osi Fain moved several meters closer. Her mental intonations seemed familiar and Harlan thought she was most likely the one who had spoken with him before. "Hello?"

::YOU KEPT YOUR WORD, SOFT ONE. WE WILL SING OF YOU. YOUR STORY WILL BECOME PART OF OURS FROM NOW UNTIL THE END OF THE UNIVERSE::

With that, the Osi Fain moved herself back into formation and they began to glow. A beautiful, yet discordant sound emerged from the speakers in Harlan's helmet, and at the same time it played directly into his brain via his power. As the sound rose in volume and complexity, the Osi Fain brightened until they were blazing like miniature incandescent suns. Harlan realized the spaceborne were using the song to write new data into their brains, like saving a file onto a hard drive. They were encoding Harlan's story into their own story. From what he knew about their physiology, the data would remain intact until the Osi Fain died, and would be passed along the genetic code of their offspring.

When they said until the end of the universe, they weren't being poetic or metaphorical.

The song came to an end several minutes later, and Harlan wondered how many terabytes of data they had shared between them. There could be data in that song passed along from Osi Fain that had existed thousands, or even millions of years previously. The sheer amount of potential knowledge captured within that song was enough to make Harlan's breath catch in his throat.

At last, the lattice of Osi Fain broke apart. A few of them—the weakest of the rescued prisoners, Harlan supposed—returned to the protoplanet to heal. The rest lit out in several directions, flashing away so fast that Harlan could only track them using Crocodile's senses. "They're leaving," he said.

::*SHARE*::

Of course, he thought. They were spreading out to travel to other systems, to find others of their species so they could share their song. Other Osi Fain would have different songs. He supposed that upon meeting, they would sing for each other, and so would the song of their species continue. It was a symphony of space and time, and Harlan found himself blinking away an unexpected burning in his eyes. The Prodoni naming them *Sky Crabs* was wholly inaccurate and lacking in every way. Whatever else they might be, Harlan would think of them for the rest of his days as the *Singers*.

* * *

Skarst jumped the *Regina* out of the Gabelko system mere minutes before the inbound cruiser was in missile range. The vessel's Jemra commander was so mad he was actually hopping up and down on the viewscreen as he issued impotent threats and warnings. The crew of the *Regina* had a good laugh at his expense as they jumped through two systems in quick succession and then reoriented themselves to rendezvous with the *Vengeance*.

"So what happens now?" Doctor Tchkit asked. "You got the location of your home system. When are we going?"

"*We?*" Harlan rubbed his jaw.

"Well, of course. We're not going to let you go traipsing off across the galaxy alone. Besides . . ." Tchkit waved at Ekek, who stood silent in the corner. "I don't think he'd let you."

"It's a long voyage," Harlan said. "And it may be a one-way voyage. I don't think we can carry enough fuel in the *Regina* for the return trip. The Hind battle group couldn't have left my system even if they'd wanted to."

"I'm sure you'll think of something," the Doctor said airily. "You're kind of clever like that."

"Tell Mrraurr you don't think she can double fuel efficiency," Skarst said, leaning back against her tail. "She'll have the ship skating on sips instead of guzzling in no time. Besides, what is jumpdrive fuel anyway but hydrocarbons compressed into unstable crystalline matrices? Didn't you tell me there's a moon in your outer planets swimming in the stuff?"

"Titan," Harlan said. "So we could make our own fuel?"

Skarst's tongue lashed out to clean one of her eyes. "All we need to do is steal some harvesting gear, a processing unit, and enough shielded storage from one of the cartels. They're so corrupt, we could probably pull it off in a couple of hours with some bribes. Probably wouldn't even have to heat up the lasers."

Harlan smiled. "Well, we *are* pirates. Take the *Vengeance* and get the gear we need. I'll work with Mrraurr to turn the *Regina* into a long-hauler."

"Captain," Skarst said. "When we get to your home system, are you planning to stay behind?"

"Honestly, I don't know yet."

* * *

Once again, Harlan nearly worked himself to death getting the *Regina* ready for her voyage to Earth. Skarst and her crew aboard the *Vengeance* bribed and threatened their way through a fuel cartel to acquire production equipment small enough to be installed on the *Regina.* Harlan and Mrraurr stripped out as much mass as they could safely remove and left it on the desert sands of the nameless world where they'd set up shop one jump closer to Earth than the fourteen required from Icecloud Station. When Harlan awakened after realizing Doctor Tchkit had sedated him again, he took a meal seated on the ship's dorsal hull, letting the sunlight bake away his weariness as he ate and drank. They'd removed so many components from the ship there was practically enough leftover to build another ship.

Harlan and Mrraurr had argued back and forth over what constituted *necessary equipment*. Harlan was willing to remove weapons, shielding, even armor plating. Mrraurr wouldn't hear of it. "We might as well slit our own throats and be done with it!" she'd said.

In the end, they'd compromised and removed about thirty percent of the *Regina*'s mass, and that was going to have to suffice because they would add that back in and more with the fuel harvesting and processing equipment and as much additional fuel as they could cram inside. They'd have to run a skeleton crew: Skarst, Doctor Tchkit, Ekek, and Mrraurr would be the only ones to join Harlan and Crocodile in their bid to reach the Solar System.

While one work crew installed the new equipment into the cargo bays and ran fuel lines through corridors in the *Regina*, another loaded all the stripped out components into the *Vengeance*. "I'll want all that back," Harlan said. "Or Mrraurr will turn me into a leather tail braid."

Mrraurr, overhearing this, raised one hand toward him and extended one of her middle fingers in the gesture Harlan had taught her. It lost a little of its weight since Hind had six-fingered hands so it looked off-balance, but he got the gist.

At last, there was no reason to delay their departure any longer. Harlan placed the *Vengeance* under Kleketik's command, telling him to raise whatever ruckus he felt was appropriate. If the *Regina* didn't return, he could do whatever he wished with his new command. Kleketik and the rest of the Ri'Ar marines gave him a feathery, martial salute. Harlan squeezed through the congested corridors and made his way to the bridge where his skeleton crew awaited him—save for Mrraurr, who was crouching in Engineering and probably already cursing out the engines.

"Ready, Captain?" Skarst asked from her seat.

"No time like the present, Skarst."

Doctor Tchkit raised a flagon. "Here's to shit not happening."

"Are you drinking on my bridge, Doctor?"

Tchkit tipped the flagon to his lips. "Yes, I am, Captain. Don't worry, though. It's strictly medicinal, and I'm a doctor."

CHAPTER
TWENTY-SIX

Thirteen jumps and thirty-one grueling hours later, the *Regina* burst out of jumpspace to appear a couple million kilometers above Earth's orbital plane. Harlan opened all the sensors and communications receivers and listened, his heart in his throat, as he heard the collected babble of human voices on radio signals crisscrossing the globe below his feet. "We made it," he said softly.

"I wasn't worried," Doctor Tchkit said.

"We're down to thirty-five percent of our fuel reserves," Skarst reported, checking the display. "Good thing we brought that processing equipment."

Doctor Tchkit brought up a holo of the Earth and examined it. "Pretty planet. Lots of mountains, lots of water."

"Lots of people," Harlan said. "They're ruining it." He frowned. "I was once of a mind that most humans don't deserve to live. They take more than they give and leave behind blighted air, poisoned water, and ruined land."

"Charming," Skarst said. "You sure you want to go back?"

"I didn't live on the Earth for many years. I had a place on the Moon. That's where I'd like to go."

"Aye, sir." Skarst opened up the sublight engines and pointed the *Regina* toward the gray disc circling over the dark side of North America. An alarm buzzed and a warning indicator on her console lit up. She tapped the screen with a clawed finger for more information and grimaced at what she saw.

"What is it?" Harlan asked.

"Something like a missile or a tiny spacecraft on an intercept course. It wasn't there a moment ago and now it's inbound. It's like it just appeared." Another indicator illuminated. "It's . . . hailing us." She touched a control so they could hear the message.

"Attention, unidentified vessel. Power down your engines and weapons and identify yourself or be destroyed."

Harlan froze. He knew that voice. It was the last human voice he'd heard before being catapulted through time and space. "Penny," he whispered.

"You know the language?" Skarst asked. "Oh, good. It would be really great if you'd say something to keep us from getting killed, because with that last jump, I'm showing a cascading systems failure. We've got life support and sublight drive, but I believe our shield generator is sitting in a hold on the *Vengeance*."

Doctor Tchkit waved a furry hand in front of Harlan's face. "Captain? Hello?"

"Say something!" The normally reserved Ekek fluttered his wings and scratched his talons on the deck.

Harlan lunged for the transmitter and words backed up in his throat like they were choking him.

"Unidentified vessel, this is your last warning. Power down or be destroyed."

Harlan shook his head, trying to clear it. "Skarst . . . kill the engines. No maneuvering. Don't arm any weapons."

"Captain, they're *also* in the *Vengeance*," she said, but she disengaged the engines and sat back from the controls. "Now will you please convince them not to blow us up? These are your people, aren't they?"

"This one is." He took a deep breath and pressed the transmit button. "Penny . . . it's me. It's Harlan. Stand down. We're not a threat."

"It's still on an intercept course," Skarst said. "I don't think it worked."

"Harlan? Harlan Washington?" Penny asked, incredulity carrying across thousands of kilometers.

"The same. I'm back. Penny, what's the date?"

"Oh hell, I don't know. Um, it's January eighteenth. Twenty twenty-two. You've been gone almost nine years. Assuming it's you."

"I promise, it's me."

"Yeah, well, the Hind are sneaky bastards, and that looks like the same architecture of those ships that attacked us back in the day. Forgive my distrust, but I'm going to need some proof or I'm going to have to get rowdy with you." A blue and red armored figure flashed across the front viewport, glowing with incandescent energy.

Harlan dry-scrubbed his face, feeling the stubble of many days. "What would convince you?"

"You gave me something before you blew yourself to hell and gone. What was it?"

"Captain, whatever you're doing, you better figure it out quick," Skarst said quietly. "We are completely vulnerable right now."

"I gave you a lot of things," Harlan said quickly. "I gave you your armor. I gave you the Preserve. I gave you the entire Sentinel Protocol. I swear it's me. Please. I came all this way to—to . . ." He stopped, unable to finish his sentence.

Penny paused before replying. "Son of a bitch. It *is* you. Where the hell have you been for the past decade, you bastard?"

Harlan stood. "Stay there. I'm coming out, so you can see it's me."

* * *

Harlan wanted nothing more than to throw his arms around Penny, but that would have been awkward when both were wearing armor and they were floating in space in front of the *Regina*. Instead, he reached out to touch her suited hand with his own. She'd made what he considered improvements to the nanotech armor he'd given her. That was to be expected. It would have upgraded itself over the years with or without her guidance. She made her visor transparent so he could see her face, and he'd asked Crocodile to do the same.

"You don't look a day older," Penny said.

Harlan had to admit that Penny did. She had a gray streak in the front of her hair now, wrinkles at the corners of her eyes, and scowl lines. If anything, they only made her look better in his eyes. She'd been almost a quarter of a century younger when they'd first met. Now she'd closed that gap by almost a decade, and like fine wine, she had definitely improved with age. "Neither do you," he said, knowing what was expected.

"Liar," she said. "Not all of us get to shortcut nine years like you did. How does that even work?"

"I have no idea," he said truthfully.

"And you lost your nanotech somewhere along the way, I see. Cain can't detect a trace of it in you." Cain was the name she'd given the AI that controlled her nanotech and the entire Preserve. "So what kind of funky alien shit are you wearing now?"

"This is Crocodile," Harlan said. "She's a member of a species that some call the Osi Fain, which means Sky Crab in the Prodoni tongue. I don't think that's an accurate descriptor, though. I call them the Singers."

"Who are the Prodoni? Another Hind clan?"

"No. They're, uh, telepathic squid. And they're not the only species out there. I've got an Aski Shantar, a Jemra, a Ri'Ar, and even a Hind on my crew."

"You have a Hind?" Penny's eyes narrowed in suspicion.

"She's the ship's engineer. She's very competent and I trust her."

"Well, I have a Hind back home too. Nice fellow named Garragh. He's become quite the scholar of comparative religions. I think he might be writing his own holy book."

"A holy . . ." Harlan realized he was at a loss for words. "I guess I've been gone a long time. I have a lot of catching up to do."

"I'll fill you in on the way back to the Preserve. I hope you like what I've done with the place."

"What *have* you done with the place?"

"It's . . . complicated. But first, what is that?" Penny pointed to the elephant logo painted across the *Regina*'s prow. "It looks intentional."

"It's an elephant," Harlan said stiffly. "My logo. I'm a space pirate."

Penny burst out laughing. "That is the most ridiculous goddamn thing I've ever heard. It's probably true." She tempered her mirth. "Is your ship spaceworthy? I'm reading all kinds of power fluctuations from it."

"The *Regina* could use some repairs. She beat herself up pretty hard getting us here in one piece."

"We can take care of her at the Preserve. I'll have my people ready to get to work with your people, assuming Juliet and Garragh can figure out how to translate."

"Juliet?"

"Like you said, you've been gone a long time, Harlan."

"Not from my perspective. It's only been a few months."

Penny's voice softened and her volume dropped to almost a whisper. "I'd given up hope. I'm glad you didn't."

* * *

January, 2022
The Preserve, Luna

Harlan was amazed to discover just how much Penny had changed . . . and *improved* upon his original idea for the Preserve. It was more than just a retreat from the Earth where he could do science undisturbed. She had transformed it into a fully functional security base, with a small but dedicated team of former and retired superheroes assisting her in the arduous task of monitoring and protecting the entire Solar System. "The various Just Cause and national superteams have a pretty good handle on terrestrial problems," Penny said as she led Harlan through his own base, expanded so greatly that he almost didn't recognize it. "That leaves the few of us to watch the stars. Nobody's come calling since the Hind back then, but we're ready in case they do. I've flooded the system with silent RF buoys. Just little dumb radios that don't do anything unless they get a signal. They pinged you as soon as you materialized in the system and triangulated your location. Then Benjie transmitted me there."

"Circuit Breaker. I remember him sending us to Deep Six for the antimatter we used in the bombs to destroy the Hind fleet."

"Well, he's gotten a lot better at what he does now. Long as I have a self-contained life support system, I can survive in transit for hours. Want to go see Saturn? That's the furthest out I've got buoys. It's only a ninety minute flight. That's taking the train from New York to Philly."

Harlan laughed. "Maybe later. I'm still wrapping my mind around the concept of what you've done with my Preserve."

"Well, it's mine now. You gave it to me, you unselfish bastard." Penny had taken the idea of the Preserve literally. She had a team combing the world for genetic samples to salvage and store in a secure vault deep inside the Moon. In the event of a worldwide catastrophe, she had enough species in storage to recreate a few limited ecosystems, and was acquiring more every month. Another team, spearheaded by the parahuman über-hacker Vanitha Bhat, was retrieving and archiving the sum total of human digital creations. Everything from books to photos to Tweets was being uploaded and stored in the Preserve's massive server storage space.

"It's like a giant secret museum," Harlan said. "It . . . *is* a secret, isn't it? I don't think people would appreciate you acquiring all their personal data and business information and such."

"Yes, it's a secret. And I realize there are certain ethical concerns about what I'm doing," Penny said. "But then, I've always had a certain amount of flexibility when it came to things like that. It's not like I'm sitting down in the server room, reading everybody's private Facebook messages. Ain't nobody got time for that shit. It's secure. Vanitha built an AI named *Sonata* to protect the internet from rogue AIs, and she uploaded a copy to manage and maintain the Archives."

"And you trust it? Science fiction is rife with stories of AIs deciding humanity isn't worth the trouble."

"My, aren't we cynical? Yes, I trust it. The same way I trust a defected enemy combatant. The same way I trust a former supervillain. That's you, you bastard." She smiled at him and it made his heart skip a beat. He still didn't know how to tell her how he felt. He was as inexperienced in emotional dialogue as a newly-hatched Osi Fain. "I presume you trust your alien buddies, right? You do it because you have to. If you don't, you're stuck on your own and can't ever get ahead."

"I understand."

Penny had taken the meeting of Harlan's crew in stride. Her psionic assistant Juliet, the former Lucky Seven member, had tried to recreate the Prodoni telepathic translation with some limited success. In the end, it was Mrraurr and the defector Garragh who had to do most of the translating. Penny had snickered quietly to Harlan that he was traveling with Fat Gopher, Samurai Owl, Angry Kitty, and the Geico Lizard.

"How did you keep our arrival a secret?" Harlan asked. "I assume that even years later, there are people on the Earth watching for the arrival of more aliens."

"Someone would have to see you through a plain telescope without any kind of digital assistance," Penny said. "Vanitha's already scrubbed your digital footprint. Which means if anyone actually saw you, it was probably a crackpot in the backwoods, living in a cabin and writing manifestos."

They reached the end of a corridor, where Harlan had kept his quarters. The door slid aside to reveal his room unchanged as the day he'd left. It was clean, thanks to the Preserve's nanotech, but it was strangely bland and without character. It was the room of the ascetic he'd been before, instead of the dashing space pirate he'd become. The space pirate would never stand for such blandness, whether in personal environment . . . or demeanor.

He turned to Penny. "Penny . . . It's hard for me to say this. I'm not good at it. I didn't have to come back. I found a life out there. Allies. Friends, even. I came back . . . because I wanted to see you. I wanted to know what had happened to you. If you were still alive or hadn't yet been born or were long gone. I—"

Penny placed a finger over his lips, shutting him up instantly. "Kiss me, you asshole."

He kissed her.

* * *

"You really should stick around and meet your great-niece and nephew," Penny said, leaning on one elbow amid the mussed sheets of Harlan's bed. "They're great kids. Four years old and probably going to be as fast as their mother."

Harlan still couldn't quite believe that his nephew had wound up with his longtime rival Mustang Sally, or that they had twins named Jason and Regina. "No, it's not fair to them for me to drop back into their lives just for me to leave again."

"So you *are* leaving again," Penny said. "You think that's fair to me?"

"No. And it's not fair to me either, but I started a job back in Confederation space, and I need to see it through to the end."

"That's a diplomatic way of saying you're taking revenge on the Hind."

"Not all the Hind. Just Clan Sharassar. They need to be shown the error of their ways. The other Clans will step aside and let them fall. And they'll learn from the experience."

Penny kissed him on the tip of his nose. "You better be careful, old man. People are going to start looking up to you and thinking you're all heroic and shit."

"And you know better?"

She moved underneath the sheets, letting them fall away without the least bit of shyness, and straddled him. Then she bent forward to kiss him. "Yes, I know better. You either die a villain or you live long enough to see yourself become the hero, Harlan Washington. You can pretend the contrary all you want but in the end, you are a hero." She began to move her hips back and forth.

"You're making it tough for me to leave," he admitted, feeling his pulse quickening.

"No," she breathed in his ear. "I'm making it tough for you to stay away."

* * *

The *Regina*, repaired and fueled, departed from the Preserve under Skarst's confident guidance. Harlan sat back and watched from his command seat, dressed only in his skinsuit. He'd considered long and hard whether he wanted to reintroduce nanotech to his body, to the point where he'd even discussed it with Crocodile. In the end, he'd decided to only take a little. Where he'd once had a hundred kilos of nanotech suffusing his system, now he only had a few grams. It was enough to keep his body repaired and healthy, and to replace the need for the Mark V helmet for interfacing data with Crocodile. His brief dalliance with the Mark V was over and done. Crocodile had superseded it at a higher level than he could have imagined. She was the Mark VI and he couldn't imagine anything that could improve upon her.

Harlan had accepted an unabashed kiss from Penny at the hatch before they departed, and he promised her he would return when he could. The memory of her lips lingered upon his own, and he smiled at it.

"So, she seems nice," Doctor Tchkit said cheerfully. "And bald. I always thought primates were supposed to be covered in fur." He tweaked his own pelt. "Like this."

Skarst snorted in mock disgust. "Mammals."

"Reptiles," was Ekek's response from behind Harlan.

"Where to, Captain?" Skarst asked.

"Back to Confederate space to start," Harlan said. "We started a war. I think it's time we got serious about building an army to fight it."

"What do you have in mind?"

"Klorister has built herself an impressive organization, but it's only the limb of a larger organization. We start small, and work our way up the food chain."

"You want to take over all organized crime syndicates in the Confederation?" Doctor Tchkit chittered a laugh. "I was just getting used to the idea that I wasn't going to die young."

"Shit happens," Harlan said, and Doctor Tchkit laughed even harder. He tapped the intercom. "Mrraurr, are we ready to jump?"

"Yes, Captain," she said, sounding subdued. She'd spent some time with the defector Garragh on the Preserve and he'd given her a copy of his writings.

Harlan wondered if he was inadvertently carrying the prophetess of a new religion in his engine room.

"Very good. Skarst?"

"On your mark, Captain," said the Aski Shantar.

Harlan leaned back in his seat. "Let's go win a war."

COMPONENTS
A *Just Cause Universe* short story

December, 1984
New York City, NY

Some men might have returned to their hometown to great fanfare, like a victorious warrior celebrating an overthrown tyrant. There would be ticker tape falling from the high rises, brass bands, and soldiers kissing nurses in the streets. When Harlan Washington returned to New York City from Philadelphia, he did so under the cover of darkness, with his collar turned up and his hat pulled down, and that was good enough for him. In his mind, he was the victorious warrior, but the tyrants hadn't yet been overthrown. They were still there in the World Trade Center, looking down upon all the little people supposedly under their protection.

Harlan knew better.

Just Cause was full of assholes, like Javelin and Pony Girl. Even Harlan's older sister Irlene was part of that team who thought they were so much better than everyone else. She had played just as much a role as the others in taking him down, ruining his Destroyer suit, and sending him off to juvie hall because of all the damage he'd caused and the lives he'd taken.

It wasn't like Harlem hadn't been about to burn down anyway from all the firetrap tenements. He'd just helped them with a little urban renewal. And as for all the jerks who'd been in the wrong place at the wrong time? *You can't make an omelet without breaking a few eggs*, as Harlan was wont to say, and there had been plenty of bad eggs in his neighborhood that he hadn't minded breaking; not even the bitch who'd once called herself his mother.

The next suit was going to be incredible. Much stronger. Much faster. And it would be able to fly. The machinery sang to Harlan in his sleep, telling him its secrets, and when he awoke it was with plans and schematics dancing in his eyes.

"Yo, man, we're here," said Bay, the giant man with a baritone voice that could frighten Darth Vader. Harlan looked up from where he was doodling a circuit design for the Destroyer Mark II. The U-Haul's headlights made two bright spots against the rolling vertical door of a Manhattan warehouse. Bay was Harlan's go-to guy, who solved problems and dealt with people so Harlan didn't have to.

Bay had been a guest of the New York Juvenile Corrections System, like Harlan, who had been almost fourteen when he was remanded into custody of the state. Bay was three years older and serving time for burglary and arson, and based upon his behavior in the clink, wouldn't be an adult long before graduating to assault and murder. Harlan had shared a cell with Bay. At first, Bay had been disinterested in the slight, smelly thirteen-year-old, but then Harlan had put together an electric shock stick out of some parts he scrounged up and used it to stop the heart of a much larger boy who'd been amusing himself by fucking younger boys in their asses in the middle of the night. He'd come for Harlan and left in a body bag, and after that Bay showed him great respect, even stepping up to protect Harlan when someone started hassling him. Harlan learned a very important lesson during his time in juvie: respect wasn't only about who had the biggest muscles. Intelligence was a clenched fist or a shiv in the dark, and Harlan had brains to spare.

When he made his escape on the eve of his fifteenth birthday, he brought Bay with him. The two boys lugged Harlan's steam-knife, built from parts he cannibalized from laundry and kitchen machinery, through the sublevels of the juvenile facility, cutting through wall after wall until they found freedom. A few carefully-timed gas grenades in their wake prevented pursuit from the hapless assholes tasked with guarding children, and the boys had a few moments to savor their freedom.

"We go to Philadelphia," said Harlan. "Just Cause is still here. They're going to be looking for me."

"But I don't know nobody in Philly," said Bay.

"All the better. Gives us a place to start fresh."

"What we gonna do?"

Harlan smiled at the bigger boy. "Whatever we want."

What they had done, in fact, was to get connected with an up-and-coming organization in Philadelphia known as the Black Mafia. They were looking for good street soldiers, people who could follow orders, like Bay, and people who could give them, like Harlan. The two of them took charge first of a block, then a street, and eventually an entire neighborhood. Between the drugs and skin trade, the protection racket and the smuggling, Harlan and his group were taking in the money hand over fist.

But then the nightmares started. Bullies and rapists who looked like the superheroes of Just Cause ran rampant through them, chasing him through darkened alleys where he had no escape, no suit to protect him from their fists and worse. He found only tinkering could alleviate them, so he left Bay to run the business and Harlan became the threat in the background, the person in the shadows no one wanted to piss off.

The sound of another engine shook Harlan from his own thoughts back to the present. He looked out the window to see the one-eyed monster of a Pontiac that belonged to Barry, one of the young toughs Bay had recruited to Harlan's New York crew. The other three dark heads in the car's interior would be Darrell, James, and Troy. His time in the Black Mafia had taught him the usefulness of having local talent handy when one needed to hit the ground running, and he was determined to get his big project underway.

Just Cause had peeled him out of his first suit like someone picking a scab off his knee. They would find that a lot more difficult in the Mark II, and someday he would use it to get back at them for the humiliation he suffered the night of the Blackout, the night he'd cut his whore of a mother's throat as she slept in her chair and escaped into the riotous darkness with only his little sister Reggie to keep him company. If there was one person in the world Harlan could say he cared about, it would be Reggie. She had always respected him when they were growing up together in that roach-infested rathole of a Harlem apartment. She gave him space when he needed it, she kept secrets for him, and she had a sense about when he truly needed help.

Being a fugitive meant he couldn't risk getting caught for a few minutes of face time with Reggie, so instead he had to monitor her from afar. Coming back to New York made him feel strangely moody about her. She was thirteen now, in middle school, and living with Irlene and Irlene's boyfriend, that Puerto Rican scumbag Javelin. In a moment of weakness, Harlan had picked out a postcard from a service station at the edge of Pennsylvania. It was an African veldt, with a herd of gray elephants basking in the bright sunlight. Harlan's strongest memory of Reggie was her dragging around that stupid, filthy stuffed elephant. He didn't even remember what she'd named it, but she'd loved that toy. He mailed the postcard to her blank, unsigned, nothing to show it had come from him. Maybe she would know he was thinking of her, and that made him almost feel something, although he didn't have the vocabulary to put it into words.

He stepped out of the truck and looked up at the building. It was a run-down, nondescript warehouse like so many in New York. The windows were caked over with dust, the paint peeling from the wood after years of coastal weather and neglect. It wasn't nearly as nice as the place he and Bay had left behind in Philly, but appearances weren't everything. Like Yoda had said, "Judge me by my size, do you?" Harlan wasn't imposing to look at, but people feared him just the same, and that was exactly how he liked it. "Pay the boys," he told Bay.

Bay handed each of the young men a bundle of singles. It was only a hundred dollars for each of them, and they knew that was all they were getting, but a stack of dollars felt like a lot of money, and it was easy to spend, unlike trying to unload a c-note at the nearest bodega. "Get the truck unloaded," said Bay. "We'll get settled in and then you can help us with the setup."

Over the next few hours, Harlan's workspace took shape. He and Bay set up the security system while the other four fellows unloaded crates full of tools, equipment, and components for the next Destroyer suit. They didn't ask about what they were moving; they'd been paid not to ask questions. When Harlan snapped at them because they weren't being careful enough in his eyes, or were putting things down in the wrong spot, they shined him off and let Bay smooth things over.

The Eggbreaker railguns Harlan set up to guard the warehouse entrances were his fifth iteration. They used motion sensors calibrated for human-sized targets and fired machined steel needles. His speakers and warning lights were less lethal, but had proven their effectiveness time and time again when vagrants and other undesirables found their way in, usually looking for something they could steal and sell. And if the warnings didn't drive them away, well, that was what the Eggbreakers were for, and Harlan's incinerator had seen plenty of use in eliminating bodies.

At last, the lab was set up the way he wanted it. The half-completed Destroyer Mark II suit hung from its frame, lurking like the skeleton of some monster from an engineer's nightmare. The basic design was smaller than the first Destroyer suit, and unlike that one, this was being built with all new, state-of-the-art technology.

Harlan could barely wait for the first time he could try it on.

He looked around the workshop, fingers itching to hold tools, to weld and solder, to wrench and create. "Bay, pay them the bonus."

Bay handed each of the young men another bundle of fifty singles. "Thanks for your help tonight, guys."

The young man named Barry tucked away his money. "Hey man, you gonna need any help again tomorrow?"

"Yeah, we ain't doin' nothin'," said Troy.

"'Cept shakin' down old ladies in the subway for their Social Security checks," said Darrell, and the others laughed.

"Yes," said Harlan. "I've got some work for you. Guy who knows electrical components named Goetz. He should be taking a train into Manhattan to get some items I need. If he won't do it . . ." Harlan managed a smile. "Convince him." He turned away from them to start rummaging through his tools. He had an idea screaming in the back of his mind and it wouldn't let him sleep until he acted upon it. "Torque converter," he mumbled.

"You gonna need anything else tonight?" asked Bay. "There's an all-night diner a mile up the road. Bring back some coffee and a sammich?"

Harlan didn't answer. He was already deeply engrossed in his tinkering. Bay knew to leave well enough alone, and he departed after the other young men.

Harlan worked.

* * *

It must have been many hours later when Bay burst into the workshop, his face pale and his eyes bulging with fear. Harlan jumped at the sudden intrusion, hands automatically reaching for the nearest lethal device before he recognized Bay. "What is it?"

"They got shot up. All of them," said Bay, sounding like he was holding down his gorge. "Cops everywhere. I was gonna meet them before they talked to Goetz. Kinda smooth things over. But somebody done shot 'em all up and he run. I saw them on the stretchers."

"Who got shot, Bay? What are you talking about?"

"The boys, man. Barry, Darrell, James and Troy. They been shot up. All of them by some dude in the subway."

"Did they get the components from Goetz?" Harlan felt irritated. He didn't need this kind of delay.

"Did they . . . Man, are you even hearin' me? Naw, they didn't get no components. They got shot!" Bay stomped his foot in frustration.

"Who shot them?" Harlan had been trying to work on redirecting his exasperation at Bay's suggestion, so he got up from his work and went over to investigate the sandwich and coffee that had been fresh hours ago.

"I dunno," said Bay. "I been askin' around. Don't nobody know. They said the dude ran into the subway tunnel."

"So they didn't get him." Harlan bit through the stale bread to the congealed filling beneath, not really tasting it. He didn't much care about eating, found it a waste of effort, and rarely bothered to taste anything. Food was fuel, like the electricity that powered his Mark II. "Anyone see him?"

Bay nodded. "A couple of passengers. The conductor even talked to him before he ran. Asked if he was a cop. Dude said no, of course. Just a white man with a piece, lookin' to shoot hisself some niggers. We seen plenty of those types in Philly."

Harlan drank the coffee. "What did he look like?"

"Skinny ass cracker. Goofy hair. Big square glasses."

Harlan looked up. "Square?" He went to the mishmash stack of papers that served as his files and dug through it until he found a ragged-edge newsprint clipping. "Like this guy?"

Bay looked at the picture Harlan was waving at him. "Mebbe. I didn't see him. I'm just sayin' what I heard."

Harlan looked at the paper himself. It was an advertisement for a store that dealt in custom electrical components. The picture was of the owner, Bernie Goetz. "It was you, wasn't it? You son of a bitch," whispered Harlan. "I'm gonna find you."

Bay stepped up beside him, always the faithful soldier. "What you need me to do, Harlan?"

"Charge up the suit batteries," said Harlan. "Then we're gonna go find Goetz ourselves."

"Doin' the cops' jobs for 'em?" asked Bay.

"No. I don't care about cops. But he threw off my whole schedule. I was going to use those components in the new targeting array and missile lock system. Now I'm going to have to go get them from him myself. And he's going to be sorry he messed with me and mine." He paused, and then lowered his voice to a dangerous growl. "I'm Destroyer, and this is my town now."

* * *

The suit wasn't ready to fly. It wasn't even armored, and not quite weatherproof, as evidenced by the persistent leak of icy air playing across the back of his neck as he stepped out of the truck. He and Bay had driven past Goetz's house and seen the car with plainclothes officers parked out front. Harlan needed to get into the house where he could run a full sensor sweep with the advanced equipment he'd installed right before they left Philly. If Goetz had left any evidence behind of where he might have gone, Harlan would find it.

"Okay, give me a five minute head start to draw 'em off and then go," said Bay out the truck's window, revving the engine as if it were a high-performance racing car.

"I could just chew them into kibble," said Harlan over the hiss of the suit's hydraulics. He hadn't put in the voice modulator yet so he had to shout to be heard. "Guns are full up."

"There's a time and a place for shootin' cops," said Bay. "This ain't it. Go find what you need and then we'll hunt down the man."

"You gonna need someone to peel you out of a squad car?"

"Maybe. You don't see me come back around the block in ten, come get me." Bay hammered down the accelerator and popped the clutch. The truck lurched into motion, swaying as Bay pulled away from the alley onto the street.

Harlan stood in his suit, patient and monitoring his systems as he counted down the seconds. Five minutes later, Destroyer burst from the alley, running up the road as fast as a car in the evening darkness. He knew people saw him. Some folks were coming home from their Christmas shopping, or from work, and they stared in disbelief at the eight-foot monstrosity that was the Mark II as it charged down the road like some monster from a summer tentpole movie.

His cameras enhanced building numbers until he spotted the apartment where Bernard Goetz lived. He switched the Mark II into its stealthy mode, making it quiet enough not to wake a sleeping dog. It couldn't stay stealthy for long because of overheating, but it would be fine for the few minutes Harlan would need in Goetz's apartment. He stood the suit in a shadow, shutting down all nonessential systems, and slipped out of the canopy. "Door," he whispered into the mic at his throat.

The onboard processor identified the target and fired a single round from the starboard cannon. The supersonic steel needle cracked into the doorknob of Goetz's back door, shattering it. "Protect," said Harlan, and he slipped into the building, knowing that Destroyer would keep him safe from prying eyes while he worked.

There was no sign of Goetz in the tiny apartment. A quick search told Harlan that the man had come back and packed in a rush, leaving dresser drawers gaping open and the closet light still on. Harlan helped himself to some components he figured would be useful in his projects and then turned his consideration to where

Goetz might be. The man didn't have a car, and would most likely be avoiding public transportation. Harlan doubted the man would be much of a car thief. He'd probably rent a car.

The Mark II had a projection screen that stored computerized maps with details pulled from the phonebook. A little research turned up a likely car rental place. Harlan grinned as he sealed himself back into Destroyer's loving embrace once more. He'd find Goetz soon enough, and the man would pay for his temerity.

* * *

The Hertz car rental company closest to Goetz's apartment was closed by the time Harlan and Bay—who had managed to avoid getting arrested by the cops purporting to watch over Goetz's place—rolled up to the lot. The gate was padlocked shut and Harlan spotted a couple rangy dogs wandering through the lot in search of something edible. "Whatchoo wanna do?" asked Bay. "Them dogs look like trouble. What if there's a guard listening for them to bark?"

Harlan hopped out of the cab. "They won't bark with holes through their heads."

Bay looked dismayed. "Aw, come on, man. They's dogs. I can't watch you kill a dog. I love dogs."

"Then don't watch me." Harlan rolled up the back door of the truck and climbed back into the Mark II once again. The servos played their sweet music for him as he stepped down from the truck. Bay grimaced and turned away as Harlan locked in on the dogs and fired. The second one might have whimpered a little before the second needle silenced it permanently.

"Goddamn," muttered Bay.

Harlan ignored him and lowered the pincers on the left medial arm to cut the lock. He grasped the gate and pulled it aside, mechanical muscles flexing as the steel bent. "Go into the office. Check records. Even if he paid cash, there has to be some record of him renting."

Bay spat onto the ground, his face twisted up as he tried not to look at the dead dogs. "What if he didn't use his real name? I wouldn't."

"Then I'll think of something." Harlan wasn't given to extraneous motion, especially when cramped inside Destroyer. Where someone else might have paced back and forth outside the rental office, Harlan was content to stand quietly and think about how he would track a rented car that could have been driven in any direction.

His motionless silence probably saved Bay's life, for a security guard with a pistol came around the side of the building and hollered at Bay to freeze. Bay raised his hands and the guard grinned. "Boy, you in the wrong place at the wrong time. I can shoot you right now and the law's on my side."

Harlan turned on his exterior speakers. "Not if I shoot you first." He pulled the trigger on an Eggbreaker and watched dispassionately as the guard fell, twitching out his final throes on the cement. "Bay, hurry up."

Bay hurried inside the office, saying "Good shot, man," over his shoulder.

Harlan knew there was no way he could track a rental car short of putting a beacon on it, and if he could put a beacon or some other kind of marker in it, he wouldn't need to. There needed to be some kind of audio and video surveillance system, covering everywhere that he could access. He used cameras in his own security. Perhaps he might use some of his ill-gotten gains to develop surveillance devices that governments and private companies might be attracted to, devices which he could access at any time. With that kind of unfettered data within his reach, he would be able to find anyone or anything he needed to help with his projects. He could already see how computers could assist in such a task, and ideas were already firing off fast and furious in his mind as Bay came back out of the office again. "I got it," he said, waving a piece of paper. "Blue '81 Dodge, rented by a Bernard Hugo. Paid in cash. That's gotta be him, right?"

"Yes," said Harlan. "We're not going to find him ourselves. He's been gone for hours. He could be anywhere by now." He marched the Mark II back to the truck.

"So what we gonna do?"

"Get the word out on the street. Description of the car and of Goetz. Tell them I will personally pay a reward for good information."

"And what are you gonna do?"

Harlan raised the canopy and smiled down from the darkness in the back of the truck. "I'm going to make Destroyer fly."

* * *

Harlan retreated to his lab in a fever of creation and fabrication. While the word spread up and down the East Coast about the search for Bernard Goetz and his rented car, Harlan cut sheet metal, bent piping, mixed fuel, and wired igniters. Bay brought him food and drink regularly, and hours later, when it had gone cold and flies were crawling over it, threw it away. By the third consecutive day, Harlan's skin was covered with grease and metal dust, solder residue, welding burns, and he was hallucinating images of his dead mother. Dehydration sores covered his mouth and he stank of days-old sweat and burned materials. When Bay found him screaming in frothy-mouthed laughter while staring at nothing in particular, he busted Harlan across the jaw.

When Harlan awoke, a day and a half later, he was hungry and thirsty for the first time in days, and somehow during his brief coma, he'd solved a fuel-mix ratio problem that had confounded him for some time. Bay looked at him with apprehension as he set a tray of silky grits and crispy bacon on Harlan's lap. "Hey, man, you all right?"

Harlan wiggled his jaw. It was definitely sore. He couldn't quite remember what had happened while he was in his fugue state of creation. Whatever it was, though, Bay had looked after him, like he always did, and Harlan respected that if nothing else. "Yes, I think so." He took a piece of bacon and dipped it into the grits. It was rare for him to have an appetite and he figured he'd make the most of it. "Any word on our missing quarry?"

"Not yet, but we got eyes all over the region. He sticks his head up anywhere, somebody's gonna spot it." Bay snagged a piece of bacon for himself. "How 'bout you?"

Harlan opened the paper carton of milk that sat on the corner of the tray and drained it. "I need six hours and sixty gallons of kerosene, and then we're ready to be airborne." He burped and Bay grinned.

"I'll go find your kerosene. Get that sumbitch up in the air."

Harlan smiled. "Oh yes."

* * *

The boot jets worked, of course. Harlan's inventions always did. He just had the juju for technology. All the same, though, he was already considering improvements during his maiden voyage into the skies. He'd designed the jets after he had the opportunity to dig through the guts of the robotic superhero Steel Soldier during his first outing as Destroyer. He could already tell he needed better and more control surfaces for stabilization, better vibration and cavitation control, better armament, and of course, better soundproofing, as his ears were ringing within seconds.

Still, flying was amazing, and Harlan figured once he perfected the technology, he might never walk anywhere ever again. He buzzed the George Washington Bridge once, amusing himself by targeting the cars crawling over it, and thought seriously about pulling a helicopter out of the sky, but he knew that despite the power of his jets, he wasn't faster than a police radio, and as an early-morning unidentified flying object, it would be better initially for him to be more discreet.

There would be time enough in the future for further destruction.

The same afternoon after Harlan's test flight, Bay informed him that they got a hit on Goetz. "He's in Jersey," said Bay. "A brother seen his car and followed him. He gone from one motel to another."

"He's hiding," said Harlan.

"Looks like it," said Bay. "Brother's waitin' by a pay phone for orders. You want him to take out Goetz?"

"No, I want to talk to him," said Harlan. He looked around. "There's no phone in here, is there?"

"Naw, but that deli has a pay phone."

Harlan set down his welding gun and pulled his goggles off. "Got any dimes?"

"Yeah, man, but you need to wipe off your face. You look like you done fell into a trash heap. Kind of smell like it, too."

Harlan sniffed at himself, but all he caught was welding smoke and rocket fuel, neither of which he found unpleasant. "I'm all right. Let's go make that call."

A few minutes later, Bay stood by the corner of the deli, his collar turned up against the cold, getting the motel address from the guy who'd found Goetz. Harlan paced back and forth. He had no patience for the telephone and left that unpleasant task to Bay. At last, Bay hung up and checked the coin slot just in case the quarter hadn't yet dropped. "Got it," he said with a triumphant grin. "You want to take the truck?"

"You can," said Harlan. "I've got a faster way to get there."

* * *

The Mark II dropped out of the sky like a missile. Harlan was half-frozen from the cockpit leak, had a developing migraine from the combination of noise and fumes, and was happier than he could ever remember being. He felt powerful, like a force of nature. Massive shock absorbers in the suit's legs softened the landing, even though Harlan's teeth clacked together so hard he thought he might have bitten off the tip of his tongue.

His sensors had spotted Goetz's car turning out of the lot of a seedy motel and Harlan wasn't going to lose him again. He grabbed hold of the car's bumper with the Mark II's primary arms and lifted it right off the ground. The memory of the look of sheer terror on Goetz's face as he looked behind him would keep Harlan warm for many cold nights in the future. The car's engine howled as the rear wheels spun in midair to no avail. "Goetz," said Harlan through the external speakers. "Don't move."

Goetz tumbled out of the door, slipped on the ice, and wound up face down in gray Jersey snow. Harlan threw the car aside and smiled as it crashed into a parked truck and caught flame. Destruction was singing that familiar refrain, a song Harlan knew by heart. He lunged down with a pincer claw and grabbed Goetz by the shoulder, hauling the frightened man to his feet.

"I'm sorry! I didn't do anything! I'm sorry! P-please ..."

Listening to Goetz grovel and blubber was sorely tempting Harlan to say to hell with the components and pinch the man's head from his shoulders. Instead, he lifted Goetz off the ground altogether. "Shut up," said Harlan. "You're Bernard Goetz. You shot my employees, and you inconvenienced me."

"I ... I ..."

"I'm going to give you the chance to make it up to me." Harlan pulled Goetz in close to the Mark II's head unit. "I'm going to give you five thousand dollars, and you're going to give me the following items from your inventory." Harlan ran down a list of high-tech electrical components using the newest microprocessors that Harlan had yet to take the time to understand.

"How ... How do you know about th-that?" Goetz stammered like a pathetic cartoon character.

"It doesn't matter." Harlan smiled beneath the layers of metal and plastic separating him from his prey. He didn't enjoy dealing with people for the most part, which was why he had Bay. Scaring them, though, that felt powerful. The truth was he'd seen some of Goetz's work elsewhere and was able to derive some of the man's other developments using his sense of technology. "You can agree to the deal and walk away, or you can refuse, and then I keep my five thousand and take your components . . . and your head."

Goetz took the money, and Harlan got what he came for.

He dropped Goetz, who stumbled and fell as he tried to run away. Harlan looked down at the components in Destroyer's medial claw. They were so small, and yet they would unlock the secrets to his targeting systems and make him powerful enough to take on a fighter jet, or a military helicopter, or a Just Cause asshole. And yet, now that he had them in his possession, he could see how they worked. He could extrapolate new, better designs from them. It wouldn't be hard.

It wouldn't be hard at all.

He tapped his microphone with his chin, activating his external speakers again. "Goetz," he hissed.

Goetz shrieked, like a scared little girl. Harlan wanted to laugh at him, but kept himself sounding scary and mean.

"Here I've been thinking these would be difficult designs. Something I'd need someone who had your specialized knowledge to acquire, design, and repair. But you know what? They're not, and I don't need you."

Goetz let out one final terrified scream, urine staining the front of his trousers just before a dozen finely-machined steel needles turned his chest cavity into ground meat, making it look like someone had splattered an industrial-sized can of chili across the snow.

"Guess you'll miss your trial date." Harlan had found his components, salvaged his wasted time, and wrought destruction.

It had been a good day.

Harlan fired up his boot jets. The Mark II shot into the darkening sky like a missile. Harlan swung around in a semicircle, orienting himself toward Manhattan. "New York, what a town," he whispered to himself with glee. "Destroyer is back."

ABOUT THE AUTHOR

Ian Thomas Healy dabbles in many different genres. He's a multiple participant and winner of National Novel Writing Month. He created the popular ongoing superhero series, the *Just Cause Universe*, and is also the creator of the *Writing Better Action Through Cinematic Techniques* workshop, which helps writers to improve their action scenes.

When not writing, which is rare, he enjoys watching hockey, reading comic books (and serious books, too), and living in the great state of Colorado, which he shares with his wife, children, house-pets, and approximately five million other people.

Visit *www.ianthealy.com* for more information.